RACHEL HOBBS

Soul-Strung

Copyright © 2021 by Rachel Hobbs

All rights reserved. No part of this publication may be reproduced, stored or transmitted in any form or by any means, electronic, mechanical, photocopying, recording, scanning, or otherwise without written permission from the publisher. It is illegal to copy this book, post it to a website, or distribute it by any other means without permission.

This novel is entirely a work of fiction. The names, characters and incidents portrayed in it are the work of the author's imagination. Any resemblance to actual persons, living or dead, events or localities is entirely coincidental.

First edition

ISBN: 978-1-9168939-1-7

This book was professionally typeset on Reedsy. Find out more at reedsy.com

For my close friends and their undying support. I couldn't have done it without you.

Chapter 1

The dream was always the same. Standing just a few feet away, Drayvex had his back to her. He was exactly how she remembered, and yet, it was all wrong.

Ruby breathed in, ignoring the prickling tension gripping her shoulders and back. "Drayvex. What're you …?"

She trailed off as he turned to face her with a slow and lazy grace. As their eyes met across the space, her entire body tingled in memory-induced anticipation. Dishevelled hair, dark and unruly, with a strong jawline framing the arrogant slope of that perfect mouth. Those piercing eyes, the colour of bright, fresh blood, snared her from across the space. That was when she saw it.

Ruby sucked in a breath as she took in the limp form held loosely in his arms. The familiarity of that shape smacked her in the gut.

Drayvex held Sandra in the same way that Ruby would carry her dirty laundry to the bathroom, parts of her trailing down in careless streams. Her throat had been torn open, almost every part of her splattered with garish stains, a shocking contrast to the bloodless complexion beneath. Her waxen skin shined under the sticky layers that coated both her and the demon who gripped her.

Ruby swallowed back the bile that crept up her throat. Sandra was dead.

This wasn't possible. She was dead again.

"Ruby."

She looked up in dismay and found him, his familiar tone commanding her attention in an almost knee-jerk compulsion. He grinned at her, and his playful smirk peeled back into a sinister smile. His fangs were red.

"Want a bite?"

As Drayvex held the ravaged Sandra out towards her in offering, Ruby's stomach heaved. No, no, no. This wasn't happening. She stumbled backwards, holding her arms out in front of her as if she could sweep them both away with a wave of her hands.

"Drayvex," Ruby begged him, dropping her gaze to the floor in a last-ditch attempt to keep her stomach from coming undone. "I can't… I don't under—" There was something on her hands.

Ruby flipped her shaking hands and failed to stifle the scream that ripped from her throat. There was blood on her hands; caked into the grooves of her knuckles, under her nails.

Sandra's blood was on them both.

The sound of raw terror followed her out of the nightmare.

Ruby sat bolt upright as her dim room snapped into focus. Panting hard, she ran a shaking hand over her face. Damn, that was getting old.

As her brain wheezed through its start-up sequence like an old computer, her heart began to settle. She looked down and blinked. She was on the sofa. She'd never made it to the bedroom.

Heaving herself to her feet, Ruby rubbed the sleep from her eyes and shuffled through her modest flat towards the window. It wasn't much. It comprised a small open-plan kitchen that merged into a lounge space, a bedroom just large enough to fit one single bed and one wardrobe, and a shower room that made the entire room wet. It wasn't much by anyone's standards, but it was hers.

Pulling up the blinds, she squinted out into the day. Living in Callien again was a dream. She was in the city's heart, surrounded by concrete and glass and the many variations of life that buzzed around her night and day.

Chapter 1

She cracked open the window and embraced the tumble of sounds that entered on the morning breeze.

As fresh air tickled her clammy face, Ruby's thoughts drifted against her will, lingering on the broken, bloodied form in her nightmare. She squeezed the handle in her grip, rendered motionless for a moment of painful recall. It had been two months since that day. And not one had gone by since that Ruby hadn't thought of her best friend. Ruby never forgot.

The media were very quick to forget about the demonic showdown at Crichton village. Within days, the terrified speculation had turned into humorous headlines of 'FOOLED YOU! THE FILM SET HOAX THAT CONVINCED THE NATION'. There were those persistent few that had dug beneath the surface, but their voices were a drop in a loud ocean of noise. And just like that, they swept the countless deaths under the media carpet, never to be disturbed again. Because some big shot wiping a tiny village off the face of the Earth for entertainment value was easier to swallow than the bitter truth.

The truth was tragic and painful. Terrifying. But Ruby clung to it all the same. *She* would never forget.

Her grandma's diary lay open on the small desk next to the blinds. Still gripping the window's cool handle, she lingered on its crinkled pages, the fancy pen that lay in the inner groove, remembering the many sleepless nights she'd had that first month she arrived. The studying of its pages, trying to decipher her grandma's strange code. Ruby's results had been mixed, and her headaches many.

She shuffled from room to room, collecting her thoughts as she collected her clothes. She hadn't seen the real Drayvex since then, and he hadn't tried to reach out to her. Most of the time, Ruby found this an immense relief, but in quieter moments, she caught herself asking *why?* If she didn't know better, she'd swear that the demon had been a figment of her imagination. Except, the scars she'd collected—the crescent-shaped bump on her neck and the indentation on her palm—were very real.

Dressed for the day, Ruby grabbed a jacket and headed for the door, swiping for the keys in the dish. Well, whatever he was doing, she wished him the best. Drayvex had given her a fresh start. And she had no intention of wasting it.

The sound of knocking stopped her in her tracks. She glanced towards the noise, lips pressing together. There was someone at the door. Dropping her coat on the back of a chair, she slipped towards it and, without pause, yanked at the handle.

Her keys slipped through her limp fingers as the door swung wide, landing on the carpet at her feet. The figure at the door was tall and thin, with lean muscle clinging to a feminine frame. The way she held herself reminded Ruby of carefree days long past, and yet she was almost as a stranger to her. Coiled and on edge, burdened.

A tidal wave of emotion gripped Ruby as Sandra bore into her from across the threshold, her wary gaze holding Ruby in place. "Rube. It's ... good to see you." As she spoke, Ruby's eyes were drawn to the pink, puckered scarring on the right side of her face.

They'd both been wounded that day at The Golden Spoke. Sandra substantially more, having knocked Ruby clear and taken a face full for her trouble. But Ruby's injuries had been healed by Drayvex, the demon who'd abandoned humanity to its fate, shortly after she'd abandoned Sandra to hers.

Ruby fought the urge to squirm in her own skin. "S-Sandra?" She swallowed, a lump sticking in her throat. She hardly dared to breathe as she edged towards the ghost in the doorway. Was this another nightmare?

Sandra's gaze fell to the floor. "I, uh. I'm sorry it's taken me so long to get here. God, I'm a horrible friend." She looked up, and the corner of her mouth lifted the smallest amount. "Can I come in?"

A single tear slid down Ruby's cheek. Then, as the realisation finally hit her with full force, she crossed the remaining space between them and threw herself around her best friend.

Sandra was a solid thing beneath her. It was almost too much to take, too much for her poor brain to process. Ruby had grieved for Sandra, was still grieving, had phoned her parents and begged for their forgiveness. Neither had corrected her on their daughter's life status. She'd spent the past two months thinking she'd left Sandra, alone and scared, to die a violent death. And yet, here she was.

Ruby pulled back, pushing Sandra out at arm's length. "I don't understand." She had a hundred questions spinning in her head, and none of them were easy. But right now, crippled by her relief, she knew she would forgive Sandra anything.

Sandra's gaze was a silent plea. "I brought cake?" She rustled a bag behind her back.

Ruby blinked. Cake. She took a step back, a humourless laugh drifting out under her breath as she let her arms fall. "Well played," she mumbled, sidestepping to let Sandra through, closing the door behind her. Ruby watched her glide into the flat, unable to shake the odd sensation of being stuck in a dream—or a nightmare. Was this really her oldest friend?

Sandra stood just inside the lounge-kitchen, taking in the room. "This is nice," she said. "You live alone?"

Ruby leant against the closed door, her heart pounding, unwilling to be pacified. "Where were you?"

It was barely more than a mumble, but at those words, Sandra tensed. For a moment, she didn't move or speak, and Ruby stewed in a soup of emotion while staring at her back. But after a pause, Sandra turned around to face her. "I thought about you every day, you know. You were my constant."

Had Sandra been this built when they'd last seen each other? Had Ruby been so absorbed in her own problems, in Drayvex and the stone, that she just hadn't noticed? She hadn't meant to linger on such an insignificant detail, but she couldn't help it.

"I wanted to find you. I really did. But Dad wanted me to focus on myself first." She sniffed and looked down at the bag in her hand. "These past couple of months have been Hell, Rube."

Ruby's lungs squeezed as she watched her friend struggle. She dug her nails into the door. All this time.

"The pain was so bad, I wanted to die. I questioned why I was still alive, why that beast didn't finish me when it had the chance. Nothing in the world made any sense." She reached up to touch the pink ridges on the side of her face but pulled away sharply. "I still feel it sometimes."

A silent horror washed through Ruby, Sandra's words cutting into her like a knife. All this time, Ruby had been oblivious to Sandra's pain, to her very existence. She should have been there. She swallowed and pushed off from the door. But how could she have been, if she wasn't considered 'need to know'?

Ruby walked over to where Sandra stood and put a hand on her arm. "I'm sorry, Sand." She squeezed, and after a moment, Sandra looked up. "I'll stick the kettle on. And you can tell me everything."

Sandra stared at her, motionless for a lengthy pause. Then she smiled." That's actually why I'm here." The smile didn't touch her eyes.

Ruby made herself smile in return. She took the bag from Sandra's hand. "Need a hand with anything?"

Ruby shook her head. "Nope. Go make yourself comfortable."

"Yes, ma'am." Sandra slipped her a smile with genuine warmth and then wandered off to find a seat. As Ruby watched her take in her surroundings, she struggled to break the surface for air. The only way out of this was through. It was time to go back to Crichton.

The sound of the kettle boiling was a soothing balm. Ruby bustled about in the open kitchen, listening to its steady rumble fill the immediate space. Her head was spinning, but there were now some things that she could say with absolute certainty. One, Sandra was alive and well, but not unscathed. Two, her demon-hunting dad was the reason she hadn't got in touch to say 'I'm alive and in good hands' these the past couple of months. And three, soon, she and Ruby would finally be on the same page.

Ruby pulled two small plates from a cupboard and placed a wedge of chocolate cake on each one. She wasn't unhappy to see her dead best friend arrive on her doorstep out of the blue. Ruby was ecstatic. If she had a faith, she'd be thanking her God right about now for sending a miracle her way. But it took seconds to make a phone call or send a quick text. Was Sandra really so scared of letting her dad down that she'd leave Ruby in the dark, grieving and guilt-ridden, for months on end at his say so?

Hearing the kettle click, she poured boiling water straight into the tea-

Chapter 1

bagged cups and went for the milk. It didn't matter. Right now, Sandra needed her to understand. Ruby would do her best.

Ruby navigated the laden tray around the counter and over to the sofa, where Sandra had placed a small table she'd found just in front. She stood up to help as Ruby approached, and Ruby supported the tray as it got steadily lighter.

"I've missed this," Sandra sighed, retaking her place on the sofa.

Ruby gripped the empty tray, her mind dredging up unwanted memories of using one as a shield at the Spoke, glass shards pelting them both as a demon screamed in fury. She squeezed her eyes shut and shoved the memory away. "My amazing tea making skills?" She put the tray on the floor and kicked it under the sofa.

Sandra's lip twitched. "Yes, your tea skills. That's what I've missed." She reached for a cup and cradled it against her, half-smile slipping. "How's your mum, Rube? I heard she was in a coma."

Ruby's heart lurched at the mention of her mother. She'd heard? Then her parents must have told her. Lowering herself onto the sofa, Ruby angled herself towards her guest. "The same. No changes."

"I'm ... sorry."

It was a medical mystery. She was in a coma, but no one knew why. Ruby had her suspicions. It was possible that a certain demon had tried to resurrect her—for reasons she didn't dare think about—and had failed. Because of this, her mum was now alive but missing her most vital element. Her soul.

It was farfetched, she had to admit. But it was far easier to think this way than to allow herself to hope, to believe that one day, her mum might wake up and say her name again. Ruby had *watched* her die. Had looked on helplessly as her mother was torn open in front of her.

Ruby couldn't help but feel that, as usual, she was giving him too much credit. But who else but Drayvex would have such a power, could even consider raising a person from the dead? Ruby herself had been on the brink of death. And he'd found a way to save her.

Could she really allow herself to believe that everything would be okay?

Ruby sucked in a breath, remembering Sandra. "Yeah. It's tough, but at least I get to see her every day."

Sandra looked away, her features hardening in a way that was a hundred miles from the bubbly, cheerful person Ruby knew and loved.

Unnerved, Ruby looked down at the little table. Her own tea was untouched, little wisps of steam rising from its surface.

"Those creatures that wreaked havoc that day in Crichton have a name."

Ruby held her breath. She made herself look around to her left, to where Sandra sat with her tea. Demons.

"They're called demons. And my dad hunts them for a living."

Ruby's skin prickled. This was her cue to say, "I know more than you think, Sand." But her tongue was dry, stuck to the roof of her mouth. She reached for her tea and took a gulp.

"It was my dad that saved me. He found me and killed the demon."

Ruby felt tea burn down her throat. Sandra's dad had come for her, like a badass knight in dark armour. No wonder he'd been distant on the phone. Ruby was the best friend who'd left his daughter to die. "About that. Sand, I can't—"

"Rube, whatever you're about to say, save it. I *told* you to run." Sandra's gaze was fierce as she held Ruby's." Okay?"

Ruby took a breath. "O-okay." How much had Ruby missed him by? Minutes? Seconds?

Sandra put her half-empty cup back on the table. "I wanted to tell you everything; that my dad was a monster hunter, that I was training under him at his base. But they swore me to secrecy, and Rube, these people take themselves *very* seriously."

Ruby sat and stared at Sandra, trying to process everything. Ruby had suspected that Sandra was being trained. But to hear her say 'his base' in such a casual way tweaked at the back of her mind. "Is your dad a big shot, then?"

Sandra froze in the motion of reaching for cake. Chocolate fudge, the Serling signature peace offering. She smiled, and for a moment, she looked like *her* Sandra. "So you did get my hints."

Chapter 1

Ruby felt her cheeks grow warm. "Yeah, well, I was looking out for you, wasn't I? You'd have done the same." If only Sandra knew how *much* Ruby knew. Could she finally come clean about her relationship with Drayvex?

Taking a plate off the table, Sandra sat back and ran a finger through the sauce on her plate. "Dad is the leader of his base. Which leads me to my next confession."

Ruby's jaw dropped. Well, holy Hell. "That's … amazing."

"Being my dad's apprentice, I'm privy to a certain level of information that I wasn't before. Like how, of course, they want to take out the small fry demons that cause trouble for regular people, but also that their prime target is the demons' ungodly leader. The Lord of *all* Demons." Sandra fingered her cake, her jabs into the soft sponge becoming more and more forceful. "He's the tyrant king of an entire race of demon scum and a piece of work."

Ruby had forgotten how to breathe. "Oh?" she croaked, squeezing her cup and burning her hands.

Sandra paused, hesitating. "They recently discovered his other face, the one he uses to blend in around us. And Rube, I'm so sorry." Sandra dropped her plate back onto the table and swivelled around in her seat. Meeting Ruby's gaze head-on, she reached out and put a hand on Ruby's arm, just like Ruby herself had earlier to comfort Sandra.

Ruby fought the urge to recoil in alarm. There was no way out of this. No way to stop their two lives from colliding in a catastrophic way. She had thought her and Sandra being on the same page would be like a weight lifted off them both. But the weight of Ruby's secrets would crush them both.

"When they showed me his face, I felt sick. Because Rube, I pushed you right into his claws." She stopped and took a breath. "It's tavern guy. His other face is tavern guy."

Ruby could do nothing but stare. How would Sandra react to the truth? What *was* the truth?

"Please, tell me you've left him far, far behind you. Tell me you haven't seen him since that day when you rang me and told me he'd stood you up?"

Ruby looked into the fearful eyes of her best friend and found clarity. She'd been wrong. She could never tell Sandra about Drayvex. Not ever. Licking her lips, she cringed inside as her response left her lips. "I, uh—jeez. No, I've not seen that guy in a good while. It didn't work out. Now I know why!"

She was an idiot.

Sandra's body visibly relaxed, and as she dropped her arm from Ruby's, she sank back into the sofa. "My God, Rube. That's good. I couldn't live with myself knowing that I'd encouraged you to date the devil himself."

For every ounce of guilt that left Sandra's drooping form, Ruby's tripled. This was the right thing to do. This was the right thing to do. This was—

"Don't worry. We'll get him. And when we do, we'll make sure the evil bastard pays for every single one of his crimes on this Earth before he dies."

Ruby stared at the little scar on her palm, her heart pulling in strange ways. "Great." And the only person in existence that would give a damn would be her.

Chapter 2

Drayvex narrowed his eyes at the vainglorious creature across from him. His curved claws drummed softly against the crudely carved throne where he sat. "Is there a problem, Your Highness? Have we lost our way?" He allowed a slow smile to creep across his face. "The pieces won't move themselves, you know."

As always, he had the attention of every lowlife body in the vicinity. Drayvex basked in their contempt, dismissed them all. There was only one creature in this sad rabble that had *his* attention: the Goblin King.

His green foe was throned opposite at the head of the long, narrow table. It was a face that would out-ugly the arse end of his most 'exotic' minions. Multiply that by the twelve surrounding goblin henchmen, and the levels of tension in the Cavern of Woes had soared to ludicrous levels.

The demons that surrounded Drayvex rumbled at the provocation, the bulk of the throng on a knife-edge.

The Goblin King's enormous face contorted into a snarl. "My Lord's concern is touching. But Mortimus does not throw himself into the fire for kicks like a screwball demon." He leered, and as his lips rolled back, his tusks doubled in size. He gripped the armrests with beefy hands as he eyeballed Drayvex down the table, his grubby yellow globes piercing the darkness that melded with his foe's flesh. After a pause, they dropped back to the board.

The map of claw marks on the expanse of table between them served as well as any real Jurok board. The pieces were spelled and bound in blood. This Drayvex had found to be a necessary incentive, especially when gambling with goblins. There was no backing out of this bet. Not unless he enjoyed the feeling of his blood boiling to nothing in his veins.

The Goblin King leant in, heaving his massive bulk forward. Then, he brought his fist up and in one swift move, slammed it down on the table. "Six square twelve," he blasted in triumph, causing the goblins closest to him to jump. The disc-like counters sprang to life, several sliding along the gouges in the wood and stopping near the centre. As more pieces reached the middle and collided, they flipped and landed on each other, starting a pile-up.

As his oafish host threw back his head and barked out an echoing laugh, Drayvex held himself in check. The tips of his already enlarged fangs inched down inside his mouth, dripping with venom. Game over, scumsack.

The Goblin King rose to his feet, throne scraping against the cavern floor. His henchmen crowed, converging around their exalted king in a rising rabble.

"Nine mark one."

The echoes of the goblins' cheers bounced around the cavern walls long after the source fell silent. The expression of every goblin face was the same, a collective sheer, dumbfounded horror; all but one.

As the remaining scattered pieces twitched to life, Drayvex leant back and planted his feet on the table, one after the other. His tail snaked up, coiling around the arm of the wooden throne in a black reckoning. And as he fixed on his seething victim, he took wicked pleasure in the slivers of fear he saw there.

The counters were sliding towards the middle, one by one launching themselves at the growing mountain and adding to the heap. A clean sweep.

"Oh dear. Things are looking bleak for your highness." Drayvex flashed him a vicious grin, counting down in his head to the inevitable backsliding. A bet was a bet. A bet made in blood was a bitch of a deal to lose.

Chapter 2

The heaving green wall of muscle at the far end of the table let out a rumbling snarl. "I don't think so." The Goblin King smashed his fist through the table, sending pieces flying in all directions. Chaos erupted on both sides.

As demon and goblin clashed with each other left and right, Drayvex remained motionless, chaos dancing around him as he became glacial. "Give me what is mine, you pathetic sack of puke," he hissed.

The Goblin King grabbed a demon from the fray and squeezed it in his massive fist. The demon writhed within his grip. "Come and take it, demon. I *dare* you."

Drayvex laughed, black magic skittering from his tongue, the sound sending demon and goblin cringing in pain, and knew that it had been a mother of a week. "You really are a special kind of stupid."

The Goblin King froze, stilling in a full body lock that only deal-breaking magic could cause. A distant smash sounded from the back of the cavern, the sound of victory. His prize would come to him.

"Well, this is my stop." Drayvex stood, addressing the snarling, quivering beast with a dismissive glance. "I'd stick around for the show, but, well, I have a life." He raised his arm and reached out, the power in his blood extending out to brush against the cloaked portal behind him.

The demons that sensed its emergence dropped their opponents and bolted for the exit, knowing all too well what would happen if he beat them to it.

Drayvex held up his open palm, waiting for the object that was hurling towards him on its own power. He could outsmart every one of these miserly fuckers at once. And yet, somehow, Saydor continued to evade him, time after time.

The portal's blood-red hue flickered, reacting to the interference of his blackening mood. His spherical prize landed in his open hand, almost punching through it with its cannonball speed, and he closed his fist around it. He couldn't put it off any longer. Ruby had to know what they were dealing with.

Turning his back on the writhing Goblin King, he strode towards the portal, adjusting its destination. Nothing stayed hidden forever.

Leaving this godforsaken world behind him, Drayvex stepped from one straight through to another. As he entered the somewhat familiar terrain, the portal dissipated and, with it, his demon form.

His lungs and senses protested as he forced them to adapt, briefly flooded by city overwhelm, before settling to his new surroundings. Callien City, Earth.

Drayvex looked down at the object he had gambled with his ancestors' mojo to possess. The luxlor was small enough to fit in his palm, but it had been its sheer crippling weight that had caught him off guard. It glowed with a hazy gleam, its edges blurring and distorting as it sat dormant in his grip.

It was cold to his touch. But Drayvex knew it would sizzle under hers. Like Ruby, it was a perfect amalgamation of darkness and light, a rarity, even among his kind. Like called to like, after all.

Slipping out onto the street, he tucked the object out of sight and merged into the oblivious multitude of the city.

It wasn't long before he located Ruby's place. Drayvex had been here before, just not in person. He skirted around the high-rise block, ignoring the filthy bundle of rags propped against one side of its base, and let himself inside.

The painfully slow ascent of the lift gave his mind too much freedom, and soon, it had regressed into Saydor territory. Drayvex glared at the empty mirror, at the space where a human would see a reflection of themselves. He felt his eyes change, and knew that pupil and iris would be swallowed in a flood of darkness that was never-ending and all-consuming. He indulged for a moment before beating it back and attempting to manipulate their colour.

Drayvex sneered and quickly gave up. Ruby wouldn't give a damn what colour they were. The lift pinged. The doors slid open.

* * *

Chapter 2

The cheap metal of the serving tray distorted beneath her grip. She could hardly believe the morning she'd had. Still in a daze, she picked her tray up from the floor and began clearing the empty cups and plates from the table.

A knock sounded at the door, three strong raps. Ruby's mind flipped.

Abandoning the tray, she rose to her feet and padded towards the door. Deja vu, much? She grabbed for the handle and yanked at it. Sandra would forget her head if it wasn't—

Ruby's breath was snatched from her lungs. It wasn't Sandra.

It was like being punched in the face. The demon on her doorstep was just the way she remembered, except her nightmares couldn't possibly have done him justice. She stared for a moment from the entryway, her mind stuck.

Drayvex idled as she collected her scattered thoughts. Dark and magnificent in her doorway, he held her hostage with an ashen gaze that gave nothing away. "I concede," he said, tilting his head to study her through hooded eyes." You do belong in this incorrigible place."

Ruby flailed. Sandra had *just* left. They could have passed each other in the stairwell for the time that had passed.

When she failed to respond, the corners of his mouth twitched. "Me? Oh, fine. Just peachy." He folded his arms and looked her over, not bothering to be subtle.

Ruby felt her face grow warm. "Drayvex. I, uh…" Damn it all. She threw the door open wide on its hinges. "I wasn't expecting you." Ever, if she was honest. But seeing him standing there stirred up all kinds of maddening, terrible things. Things that were best left buried.

"No shit."

Her body was yet to get the memo.

Drayvex folded his arms, and her gaze snagged on those curved black hooks at his fingertips. Small, but wicked sharp.

Ruby tore her eyes away, narrowing them at him. "Don't tell me—the world is ending." She was only half-serious. But when those infinite eyes flickered at her jibe, she hastened to add, "I'm kidding. Please say no." Where Drayvex went, chaos and mayhem trailed in his wake. This was a fact that neither of them could deny.

A moment longer, and the slick persona was back. "The world is as screwed up as ever. But you knew that already." And with that, Drayvex slid past her, taking a touch too long as they met in the middle.

Ruby matched his nonchalant gaze as that fierce heat briefly hit her and withdrew. And even though she knew it was pointless, that her heart would betray her racing body, she refused to give him space as he let himself into her flat.

Another pattern that Ruby had learnt all too well from experience was that Drayvex always had an agenda. It was never *her*, but rather, what he needed from her. And she didn't see why that would be any different now. "Come in, why don't you?" she muttered. "Door's open." Closing the door behind him, she gathered her thoughts and spun to face the music.

Drayvex's gaze flicked around the flat, just as Sandra's had not too long ago. As they fell upon the glass dish on the side, his mouth pulled in disapproval. The lingering traces of good humour dropped from his face, to be replaced by an unnerving darkness that Ruby could only assume had nothing to do with the innocent object he'd snagged on.

She hesitated, taken aback. This wasn't the sharp, tightly guarded demon she was used to dealing with. Mental baggage? Oddly enough, she knew the feeling.

"So if nothing is on fire," she probed, vying for his attention, "why are you here?"

Drayvex looked up and slid those two pools of liquid ash towards her. They lingered for a moment on hers, and in those brief seconds, she felt something click deep inside her. Like a static calm landing on a radio station.

Ruby blinked. She was losing her mind.

Drayvex turned away, giving her a narrowed side-eye. "Don't worry. Next time, I'll make an appointment."

Trying to ignore the heat once again creeping up her neck, she watched the demon navigate her flat, distracted by the effortless way he moved through the surrounding space, and considered his response. Why could

Chapter 2

he never just be straight with her? "Were you always this annoying?"

He reached the sofa, running a black tip along the fabric as he passed. "Were you always this cynical? You've gone from docile to volatile in the space of a good, interspecies scrap."

Ruby blinked, his words poking at a wound that had barely scabbed over. "I met a psychopath that thought he could screw an entire world, then save it in time for dinner and call himself lord and saviour. Blame *him*."

In the silence that followed her knee-jerk jab, her flash of annoyance trickled away and was replaced with a heavy sense of dread. Why did she let him push her buttons?

From across the room, Ruby saw a flash of fangs for the first time. "Ouch. My heart." The sarcasm that bled into his words sent goosebumps skittering down her arms. "Oh, wait," he murmured, placing a clawed hand over his chest. "I don't have one."

Heaven help me, Ruby prayed, biting down on her cheek as she crossed the lounge towards him. He'd been back in her life for five minutes, and she was all ready to implode. She navigated around the sofa and stood toe to toe with the demon who, according to Sandra, was public enemy number one, her heart beating up a storm. Locking gazes, she folded her arms. "That's old news."

This was too close for comfort. She knew this more than ever as she glowed from the heat that radiated off his body, as she noticed the small wisps of blue that bled into the edges of that stony gaze, the tiniest of details on the beautiful monster before her; details that she should never be close enough to a killer to see. But despite her overstepping in her eagerness to prove that she was Ruby Mark Two, and therefore wiser and stronger, Ruby held her ground.

Drayvex looked down on her, also giving no ground. The way he was looking at her made her feel like a mouse with the illusion of freedom, one that the cat could wipe out whenever it wanted a change of pace. His lip twitched as she chewed on hers.

Suddenly, he broke into what, to Ruby, felt like the first genuine smile she'd seen since he'd arrived. "I hope you don't flirt this way with every demon you meet." And just like that, all the ground she'd gained crumbled under her feet. "Because, you know," he purred, flashing a dozen razor fangs without care or consequence, "I'd have to kill them."

Hit by a dual twinge of disgust and twisting desire, Ruby stumbled backwards. "Please," she shot out, too fast, as annoyed with herself as she was with him. "Don't flatter yourself." *How about my fist flirts with that perfect mouth of yours?* she thought, surprising herself with the ferocity of it. It was true: some people really did bring out the worst in you.

Drayvex lingered on her for a moment longer before stepping back. His eyes were no longer that neutral grey but almost the same pale blue as when they'd first met.

She blinked, getting distracted. "Not doing yourself any favours on the psychopath front."

He shrugged, a nonchalant gesture. "It's an acquired taste." His gaze fell as he spoke, landing on the half-cleared table beside them.

Ruby froze. Sandra's cup and plate were next to Ruby's on the table and the tray under it. She tried to uncoil, forcing her muscles to comply. "I have friends," she blurted, feeling the need to explain the debris.

He narrowed his eyes, piercing her to the spot, and she immediately regretted it. Probably wondering why she was being a weirdo over a couple of cups and plates.

The silence stretched for a moment longer before Drayvex relaxed his death stare. "Mmm. If you say so."

Ruby was grateful he'd decided not to push her. But as she took a breath to pull herself together, she noticed that the mingling grey was back in his eyes. It had swallowed the blue like storm clouds, and with an odd twinge, she realised she was what had killed it.

"So, um," she began, using the strange lull to say what she'd wanted to say ever since she'd woken up in Callien in one piece. Taking the coward's route, she put Drayvex behind her and wandered over to the window. "You saved my life. I guess that means I owe you a lot more than thanks."

Ruby watched the cars below, crawling along in rows. She watched the people, barely listening to the distant ting-ting of building work carrying on the breeze.

"As exquisite as the thought of you *owing* me anything is—"

Ruby held her breath.

"I'd rather draw a line."

She puffed out, all at once, clouding the glass. That wasn't what she'd expected. She spun around and stared at the empty space where Drayvex had just been.

"Right now."

His voice came from her left. Ruby started and twisted towards him. Dear god, she hadn't missed that. Drayvex was leaning against the wall by the desk, turning something he'd found over and over in one hand. Ruby's heart calmed as she processed his words. A clean slate?

Ruby swallowed back the mixture of emotions that rose up her throat. Drayvex was never what she expected him to be. Was he implying that he wanted them to be even?

She shook her head, losing her thread. And she'd just worked up the nerve to ask him about her mum. But not every stain could be wiped away. Could it?

Ruby studied him. Devil may care demeanour, perfect still, every unnatural upper hand imaginable. Maybe it was enough, the *want* to start again. Enough to try. "I … suppose that would be the decent thing to do."

Drayvex stopped spinning the pen in his hand. "I'll take your word for it."

Despite herself, she smiled. Yes, decent was definitely more her forte than his.

Chapter 3

It was as though the atmosphere was catering to his preference. The grey, soulless sky seemed to almost suck the life out of the human population of Callien city centre, and one would be forgiven for thinking he had a direct line to the mass dirge that ran straight to him.

Drayvex was sure he could navigate these crowds in brazen, semi-demon get-up, and none of the automatons that flowed around him would notice. Still, he preferred to be thorough. And so, as he made his way through this urban labyrinth, he blended in with the natives as well as any demon with shape-shifting prowess. He would be one of many. Demons gravitated towards Earth's cities like maggots to a wound, and as such, there were large numbers in every city on this overcrowded rock.

And any one of them here could be reporting back to Saydor, drawled a voice in his head that was his own, but wasn't.

Drayvex felt a flare of annoyance. And the award for *most useless commentary* goes to …

His true form flexed beneath the tenuous surface of this skin, teeth filling the confines of his mouth. He knew this. He was all too aware of how precarious this situation was. He didn't need the reminder.

He breathed out in a jet, cool air warping with the heat as he burnt. He'd had every intention of telling Ruby yesterday. Of looking her in the eyes

Chapter 3

and shattering that shiny new bubble she'd made for herself in his absence. He'd never got that far.

Drayvex manoeuvred through the sprawling streets, blocking out its traffic, its faceless crowds, tightening his control as those bodies in his way parted around him in a magnetic repel. The humans knew, deep in their subconscious. The primal parts of them that screamed to live at all costs sensed his unconstrained aura and knew to avoid him. This, of course, was a two-way deal. They wouldn't get close enough to irritate the living piss out of him, trigger a primal instinct that knew no bounds or make him hungry, and he in turn wouldn't make himself late by eating them. You're welcome, humanity.

Drayvex never dragged his feet. He willed a thing and then made it so. But this girl had a history of making him look *weak*. Him, Lord of the entire demon scourge, first-born pure blood spawn of the late Cannibal King. An arsenal of ancient power in his possession and a dozen hard-won titles to his own name. And he had failed her the moment he let Saydor slip away with his life. Little had Drayvex known then, this was the first in a long line of toppling dominoes.

As he turned onto the street labelled Grover Avenue, he slowed. This recent self-pity that had taken to growing inside his mind like a plague often met its end with one effective method. Rage was not an option when face to face with the human in his life. Filling her full of nasty holes would really kill the mood.

Drayvex stopped outside a suave coffee shop that clearly fancied itself as the place for *somebodies*. This, in direct competition with the place across the road, where the *nobodies* bought their coffee. Ruby stopped at this particular spot for her superior coffee every morning after visiting mother dearest. She bought two grande lattes, one for herself and one for the vagrant that had settled outside her flat, and then holed up for the afternoon doing Satan knew what, before slipping out into the night to make a living. Sleep was clearly low on her list of priorities.

He leant under the black canopy, the indulgent aroma of fresh coffee teasing at his senses. If he was anything other than a demon, and so carrying that colossal weight around the neck otherwise known as a conscience, he would think twice about the value of using this dead woman's face as a tracker. Ruby spoke to her mother every day. Gave her little pieces of her week, left herself open in ways that Ruby could never, ever afford to be around the likes of him. Little pieces of light that he both did his best not to witness and couldn't bring himself to turn from.

Lucky for him, demons didn't have a conscience. Monsters didn't bleed in that way. Lucky for her, on his watch was the safest place that any human could be. Her ignorance was the price for that safety; and his sanity.

Drayvex sensed Ruby before he saw her. Even part of a crowd, her scent rose to brush against his senses above all, oil on the basic pool that was humanity. He didn't know whether it was feckless familiarity or a part of the creeping madness that she'd infected him with some time ago. He no longer cared either way. What once would have made him hold pause no longer warranted his attention.

Trying not to think about his deteriorating standards, he closed his eyes and picked his timing, ignoring the physical response her scent always provoked. "I see some things never change." He spoke into the general vicinity, staring dead ahead at two human males attempting to take chunks out of each other, disappearing and reappearing behind traffic across the road. "For example, the quantity of caffeine in your bloodstream."

Seconds passed as she rooted herself against the flow, an immovable object in the rush. Drayvex could almost hear the cogs of her mind turning.

"Are you following me?" The voice to his immediate right was sprinkled with humour.

Drayvex smirked, the reference to their last cafe meet tickling him despite his grim resolution. "Yes. I have nothing better to do with my time, and your life is *so* much more interesting than mine. Why not?"

The pause between beats was a little too long. "Goodbye," she said, dismissing him with an admirable drawl.

He closed his eyes and counted to three before turning to grab for her. "Wait." He snagged on her arm and gave it a tug. "We need to talk."

Ruby emerged from the crowd, coming to an abrupt stop in front of him

Chapter 3

as she caught her breath. Giving him a look that could freeze, at the very least, a small puddle, she tugged herself free and folded her arms. "We did. Yesterday."

"Humour me?" Drayvex kept his voice light, attempting to keep the tension that dragged through his veins from bleeding into his tone. She didn't need his problems. She would soon have plenty of her own.

Her eyes changed as she watched him, her blatant suspicion morphing as she worried at her bottom lip with her teeth. "I ... yeah, fine. Okay."

Always suspicious, and yet so willing to trust. It both irked him and triggered a burning need to protect those ridiculous, innocent qualities in her. Of course, he was undeserving of that trust.

"Walk with me?" Ruby gestured towards the coffee shop with a nod of her head. "I just need to grab some coffee."

Drayvex met her gaze. He took her trust anyway. Because there were two types of beings in every world; takers and givers. And he was a taker. "Go ahead."

Her green eyes briefly filled with warmth, and a slight smile curved her lips. "You want one?"

He returned it, considering her offer. A hundred times yes. "Pass." The potent effects of demon plus caffeine were not something she would ever be ready for.

"Suit yourself."

As Ruby disappeared into the coffee shop to the sound of a bell, Drayvex held back, lingering for a moment more as a shadowed undercurrent crept over him, making his blood boil, and a thing of rage and darkness took hold.

He will pay for his crimes. Have no fear.

It was the one thing they both agreed on, himself and the detached self in his mind that had so many unfiltered, unwelcome opinions. But Drayvex was not about to make the same mistake twice. And so, when he finally got his claws on that piece of living garbage, it would be quick and painful. And Saydor would get his wish in death. Drayvex would make sure that Saydor was elevated, on display for all to see *forever*.

Ruby had already ordered when he entered. She glanced towards the door as the bell signalled his presence before glancing away.

The small coffee house was full of bodies that didn't want to be near each other. All human. He looked back at Ruby, and his mind wandered as he watched her, hair sprawling down her back in a merlot cascade that enhanced her pale-as-death complexion. When he'd left her in the care of her kind, she'd been freshly reanimated, barely a poke from a permanent slumber. And she'd looked it.

As he relaxed against the wall at his back, Drayvex found himself scanning her critically for the first time. Of course, he'd known Ruby would be just fine. Within forty-eight Earth hours, the sliver of himself inside her would have embedded completely. He narrowed his eyes, probing with illogical intent, as though the piece would reveal itself to him if he looked at her in a certain way.

"Here we go, hun. Is this okay?"

"Thanks. That's fine."

Ruby looked more than fine. She looked at the top of her game. Was her precious city having this effect on her, or the piece of demon soul that pulsed inside her? This situation was off the reservation, even for him.

"Ruby, is it? I, uh … I hope you don't mind me asking, but … I've seen you around. Are you free later?"

Drayvex's thoughts scattered as the voice buzzed like flies in his skull. Irked, he flicked from Ruby to the squirt behind the counter, and felt his mood plummet. Oh good. This again.

"Am I … free?"

"Yeah, for a drink?"

Ruby seemed genuinely taken aback by the weedy boy's advances, which only heightened his irrational irritation. He drummed against the wall behind him with pointed tips, digging deep for control. *You're out of your depth, deadbeat,* Drayvex shot at him. *Get fucked.*

"I don't really do this, but, if you like?" The boy fumbled with the stack of cup lids in his hands, a portrait of weak and needy as the cups on the counter steamed. Someone behind Ruby huffed.

Chapter 3

It took her a few seconds to catch on. But as she finally joined the land of the living, Drayvex watched her face morph into a look of surprise, and then something else as she attempted to laugh off the advance. "Oh. Oh, really? That's, um ..." Her gaze fell to the steaming cups on the counter.

He hadn't meant to get involved. But as the deadbeat edged closer towards her, a buzzing insect intruding into her immediate space, it was almost a knee-jerk reaction. A territorial flex of mental muscle that was both satisfying and unsettling. And as the server's head smashed into the counter between them, it *almost* looked as though he'd slipped and lost his balance. Clumsy boy.

Ruby jumped at the sound of head meeting wood. But as the boy put a hand to his head with a red face and the brief commotion died, her eyes flicked towards the door.

She was judging him. Peering his way with those big green eyes. Her cheeks were flushed, and she looked mortified. Whether because it had happened or because it had happened in front of him, he didn't know. Drayvex met her gaze head-on.

Petty, said a judgemental voice.

He flashed her a wicked smirk, committing himself. Once again, as in times before, he questioned why the Hell he should give a damn about such things. The answer still escaped him.

Smothering his frustration, he pulled at the door, holding it open for the girl who approached. She shot him a look as she passed out onto the street, and he bit down on his response. Go on, he jabbed, say it. I dare you.

"I take you're *not* here to sabotage my social life?" Ruby asked, doing her best to sound sweet and unassuming as she secured her cups in their tray.

Please, Drayvex thought, drawing level. Your social life is dying a hard death without my help. He smothered the remark, narrowing his eyes at her as they moved through the city. Instead, he went with, "Patience is a virtue."

Her face fell blank as she stared at him, forgetting to look where she was going.

"What?" he snapped, feeling her rub under his skin. "Do I *look* like a damn saint to you? Are you high?" Drayvex knew that his bleak mood was not Ruby's fault. But no matter how hard he tried to shield her from himself, from the never-ending darkness and rage pulsing through him twenty-four-seven these days, it had nowhere to go but out.

To his utter bewilderment, Ruby faced forward and laughed.

Drayvex rolled his eyes to the sky. Hell, she was high. "What is it?" he sighed, undecided on whether being laughed at was perplexing or insulting.

"I don't know," she murmured, her voice getting softer. "I guess this will always feel weird, huh? You, me. Coffee."

Tell her about Saydor.

"I need to ask you something."

Drayvex tensed, her sudden change in tone making him suspect he wouldn't like her question. "Then ask."

It was a while before she spoke again. "Did you do something to my mother? She was dead, and now she's …" She screwed her face up, fighting something he couldn't see. "Well, I'm not sure. But she has a pulse. Did you …?"

Ruby left the question hanging, but Drayvex filled in the blanks. Something inside him squirmed, that restless thing that protested whenever he picked his own best interests over hers. But he hadn't, though.

Had he?

Drayvex caught himself and rejected the thought. No. The last time he'd let her twist his resolve, she'd almost wound up dead. Every single thing he stood to gain from this was for *her* benefit. The two points she checked in with daily kept her on his radar while still allowing her to breathe with relative freedom. Her best interests were not deprived.

Ruby slowed to a stop, falling out of step. Steeling himself, Drayvex stopped beside her and looked into her waiting eyes, holding her gaze. "No, Ruby. Bringing anything back from the dead is not child's play." He moved around until he was standing opposite her. "I had to break every rule in the book to bring you back, while also covering my tracks and coming down hard on anything else that dares do the same under my rule. Your mother is really not a priority for me."

Chapter 3

He knew this was the way forward. And still, in the seconds that hung between them, as he watched her break at his words and then rebuild herself, he glimpsed each glistening shard, as though he was suddenly inside her mind. The clarity was jarring and alien.

And then, mercifully, gone.

Drayvex had tried and failed, had in fact exploited many less extreme methods of raising prickly humans from the afterlife before finding other uses for what remained. And she could never know about either.

"I was dead?"

He considered her words. Technically dead, but still within his reach. "Yes."

Her lips parted, but no sound emerged. Ruby looked as though she was choosing her words carefully. "Well, I'm grateful that you risked so much for me. I *am*. I just ... I don't know." She moved her coffee tray into one hand and ran the other through her tumble of hair. "I assumed."

Drayvex sighed and moved in close, knowing that his timing would only be worse if Saydor himself was poised to strike them from above. Humans flowed around them in impatient swerves as the two of them stood face to face, far from alone. And yet, for all he saw in this moment, they may as well have been. "Ruby, I need to you listen."

She stilled at the sound of his voice as he spoke softly into her ear, still as a human can get. "What is it?" Her voice was low.

He slipped an arm around behind her and rested it lightly against her back, partly to blend with the locals but also in anticipation of her reaction. She flinched at his touch but didn't resist. "On the day he killed you," he said, "Saydor escaped."

At the mention of his name, Ruby stopped breathing.

Drayvex kept going. "Now, I don't know where he is. I don't know what he's planning. But the one thing I can say with absolute certainty is that *when* he discovers you survived, he will come for you. And he will do everything in his power to get his hands on you."

As her wide eyes came to rest on his, she uttered one single word. "Why?"

He felt himself grimace and didn't bother to hide it. Why lie when the truth was so simple? "To hurt me." Because Saydor had discovered the one big, exploitable, Ruby-shaped weakness Drayvex had. Because Drayvex had been unable to walk away from her, and unable to kill her. And now, they were bound.

"And ... how would he do that?" Her voice was steady, but her heart was running away from her. The tray in her hand quivered. Not here.

"We should keep moving," he murmured, hearing the faultless composure of his voice. "Don't you think?" It was the kind of smooth that took years to perfect, to tweak to a fine art.

Ruby stared at him, her eyes wide and unreadable. Ironic, considering the two of them. Considering he was supposed to be good at reading a face. His claws slipped down, extending in an age-old reaction to physical stress, until he felt the tips resting against her back. Drayvex pulled back his hand.

Without saying a word, she took a deep breath and turned. And without missing a beat, she walked off.

Chapter 4

Drayvex trailed Ruby from a distance, keeping his eyes fixed on the splash of red in the city that almost seemed to fold around her. And it was clear to him then that she could navigate this terrain with her eyes closed.

Claws twitched at his sides as the tension rolled off him, senses sprawling in a city-wide net that dragged in everything at once—the dregs of humanity, the vast basic multitude, the shining beacons of the exceptional few that said *come and get me*, and the skewed minds of the hundreds of his kind that hunted within these twisting walls—and knew that it was futile. But the pain of holding so much, of reaching so far, was almost a release; was preferable to trying and failing, and thinking and over-thinking, and trying, and failing. A moment of sensory overload when everything became a blissful nothing.

"Have a nice day."

Drayvex let go all at once. They were at Ruby's flat.

Pushing aside the vague stabbing in his skull, he looked over towards the vagrant propped up on one side of the building. The coffee Ruby had unloaded was in one hand, and as she smiled and made for the double doors, the figure drew the cup into the folds of material that cloaked them almost entirely.

Drayvex stopped for a moment as he passed, looking down on the human-shaped thing inside. Although technically the second tracker in order of creation, it was point A in terms of Ruby's daily commute. She disappeared in the middle. But as long as she made it to point B, then in theory, all was as it should be.

He met her in the lobby, waiting for the lift.

"I knew it," she said, turning to glance behind her as he arrived.

Drayvex folded his arms, narrowing his eyes at the confrontational lilt in her tone. "That you have a big sign above your head that says 'eat me'? Hardly a revelation."

Ruby visibly tensed, her shoulders rising before she spun on him and glared. At least, it looked like a glare. But something heavier sat just below the surface, out of reach. "That there's a reason you're here." She was actually leaning forward into his space.

The button on the lift glowed and flickered, tiny imperceptible flashes. "Yes. It's called *time management.* You should try it sometime." He hadn't realised he was also leaning forward, equally confrontational, until her scent hit the back of his throat in a sharp waft, almost on top of him. And then he couldn't *unsee* it. The pulse in her throat. The curve of her jaw, the set of that delicious mouth, always running away with itself.

Drayvex tried to switch it off, aware that his teeth were larger now than a moment ago.

"You should have been straight with me sooner," Ruby uttered, accusing. "Would you even be telling me about this now if you didn't want something in return?"

The lift pinged open. Her words flecked his hardened skin like a caustic substance. It was true that he'd been putting this off for far too long. It was also true that he had his eye on her dodgy book of secrets. But all the same, the insinuation was a label he didn't care for.

Drayvex had not even been aware of the book until yesterday. It had been there on her desk, open for all to see.

Ruby stepped back and stared at him with a guarded expression, no doubt taking his silence and moulding it to fit her low, low expectations.

Chapter 4

Squeezing her cup, she turned and stepped into the lift, putting her back to the wall as she tapped the keypad with unnecessary force.

He slipped in behind her, maintaining the condemning silence that he knew was bothering her, purely out of spite. But as the doors slid closed, and he watched her gaze fall upon the spot on the mirror where his reflection should be, he wavered, her startled expression coaxing a flicker of a smile.

Warring with himself, he fought to cling to the heavy silence. "No one knows why," he muttered, losing without dignity. "One of life's fun little clichés." Ruby turned from the mirror, a dubious look sliding towards him in the compact space, and he sighed, done with whatever *that* was. "Ruby Red. So stubborn and misguided."

Drayvex shot forward in one blurring motion, stopping in front of her almost immediately, and placed a clawed hand on the wall behind her.

Ruby had not been ready for such a manoeuvre. And as he got up close and personal for the second time, she seemed at a loss for words.

"The question is," he said, his voice so low it was almost a growl, "are you going sulk in a corner and wait for that spineless, low-born ingrate to take your life from you, piece by piece? To pick you apart inch by agonising inch until you beg for death? Or are you going to make yourself useful and fight back?"

Her heart was working hard, but he kept going, determined to hammer the point through that impenetrable skull.

"Because I don't have all day, and when I'm not being brilliant at the throne of Vekrodus, people *happen* to notice that I'm gone. When I'm here, it's usually because of this one small, infuriating—"

It was so sudden and unexpected, his body reacted as though it was under attack. But as Ruby launched herself forward and seized the day, he managed to not open her up all over the floor.

For a moment, as that unruly mouth crushed against his, something hot and charged passed between them in an invisible current, pinning him to the spot. His teeth lengthened, claws curving and piercing through the flimsy metal wall under his hand. And then Drayvex was overwhelmed by a string of clashing instincts. The primal, the carnal, the curious unknown, twisting in a confused snarl of hunger that tugged at him from somewhere deep, begging him to yield.

The lift pinged and slid open.

Ruby froze against him, still somewhat attached. Her eyes sprung wide, and as fast as she'd arrived, her back was flat to the lift wall. She suddenly looked horrified, her mouth hanging open, as though someone had taken over her body and made her watch.

Unmoving, Drayvex stared at her, swallowing the slick of venom secreting from his throbbing fangs. The gesture had been so simple, so staggeringly *human*, that the act had rendered him into a state of non-reaction.

"I-I'm sorry. I don't know what came over me".

Ludicrous.

"That was a mistake." He could have killed her simply by reacting. She'd have only had herself to blame.

Ruby hesitated for a moment longer before ducking under his arm and scurrying out of the lift.

Drayvex heard the doors slide closed behind her. The very idea that she'd subjected a demon of his calibre to such a basic human impulse would be offensive on multiple levels if he was anywhere near his right mind. It was a dangerous place for any demon to be, let alone a demon with his name.

If you were in your right mind, you would have killed that girl long ago. But what do I know? I'm only *you*.

Extracting himself from the metal wall, Drayvex opened the doors and shadowed behind Ruby. He never did anything by half. Not even, it seemed, insanity.

Ruby was very deliberately not looking when he reached her at the door, fumbling with a set of keys. "You should be more careful," he deadpanned behind her, still somehow making her jump. "Not all mistakes can be fixed." And because he knew it would set off a chain reaction, he leant in and ran the tip of his tongue down the back of her neck.

Right on cue, she gave him a flaming blush.

* * *

Chapter 4

Ruby pushed into the flat and went straight for the bathroom, leaving the demon in her dust. The thought of leaving Drayvex alone in her flat was second only to the awkward situation of feeling herself unravel in front of him.

Closing the door behind her, she placed her half-drunk coffee on the closed lid of the toilet and leant into the bathroom mirror, expecting an impostor. There wasn't; just a slightly wild-looking version of herself staring back. She splashed some water over her face, letting the cold shock her, and rubbed a hand over the burning trail he'd traced down the back of her neck, feeling it linger.

She was the prime target of a powerful maniac with inhuman strength and no morals. But as if that didn't put her in over her head enough, she had just made out with another.

Catching her lip softly between her teeth, Ruby's mind slipped sideways. Maybe it was the way he locked on to her with laser focus in that all-or-nothing way, or the way that he pushed all her buttons when he wanted her to push back, but Drayvex had a way of stoking things deep inside her that even she didn't understand.

Ruby stepped back from the sink and dried her face before smoothing her hair. Whatever the reason, she would not let it happen again.

When she stepped back into the lounge, Drayvex was nowhere to be seen. Not pacified by his glaring absence, she slipped off her shoes and padded across the room. It was only when she reached the kitchen and spun on her heels, cursing him under her breath, that she realised she'd walked straight past him.

Drayvex was sprawled across the sofa like he owned it, her grandma's threadbare diary open in front of him, resting in one hand.

Ruby's breath caught in her throat. He'd found it. Forcing herself to continue breathing, she moved across the room towards him, drawing out each step. "Make yourself at home," she mumbled, tension dragging in her muscles. How long had he known about the diary?

His gaze slid towards her, the only part of him that broke his perfect stillness as she approached, looking up from the stained pages. His face was that frustrating mask of neutrality he wore so often, but his eyes were more open. A soft blue-grey, they were non-threatening, inquiring, despite her earlier spontaneous performance. She cringed.

"About the lift—"

"Where did you—?"

As they spoke at the same time, the room plunged back into silence. Then the mask was gone. What was left in its place was far from neutral, and Ruby gave an involuntary shiver as something crept down her spine. It was suspicion and dissonance, and heat.

Drayvex smiled, a weapon more than a gesture. "After you."

Ruby's eyes lingered on his mouth, those glistening points. She'd wondered for a long time what those lips would feel like on hers. But it wasn't *normal* to know what she knew, to see the monster in the dark Adonis, and still wonder. Now she knew. "That's my grandma's personal diary," she said, chickening out. "I'm pretty sure it's not meant for you." Her voice sounded stronger than she felt. Not willing to lose any more face, she approached where he lay and held her hand out for the book.

A moment passed, and she held herself in place with stubborn hope. If Drayvex didn't want to comply, there was no way on this planet that she could make him. It was a frustrating thing, to feel so utterly powerless in the presence of one person.

With a furtive look, he unceremoniously placed the open book into her hand. She grabbed for it with the other as it wobbled.

Ruby scowled at him, her gaze running down the length of the creature on her sofa, and rested on where his feet touched the cushions. Her nose tingled in indignation. Looking for a distraction, she tugged at the subject that neither of them seemed to want to talk about. "So, Saydor is alive. Not dead." She said the words and felt her stomach drop.

"Yes."

"But doesn't know that *I'm* alive?"

Pause. "Your guess is as good as mine."

Ruby looked at Drayvex once more and met him dead in the eyes. She was searching for reassurance. Something less vague and terrifying than

Chapter 4

what she'd just heard. She found none. "And he could be anywhere? We've got no idea where he is?"

Drayvex didn't answer, but his silence spoke volumes. His entire posture seemed to change in the blink of an eye, becoming tense and coiled. The gaze that pierced through her from the sofa had turned black. "No."

"Why?"

"To hurt me."

Was he angry at her? He couldn't possibly blame her for being collateral damage, surely. "So how do we stop him?" She struggled to keep her voice steady.

"You're looking at it."

A moment passed. Ruby tore her eyes from the yawning abyss on her sofa and looked down at the open book in her hand. Her confusion melted away as she stared at the pages. Drayvex had handed her the answer.

She ran a finger over the elegant scrawl, stopping to rest on the ink drawing in one corner.

"The Lapis Temporis." His voice was suddenly close to her left. Ruby straightened as he tested her reflexes. She sucked in a breath, keeping her eyes fixed on the drawing, ignoring the warm glow that burnt down her left. Her skin prickled in both anticipation and deep, instinctual warning.

"The stone of time is our best hope of crushing Saydor." Drayvex's voice was compelling, a deadly undercurrent dripping off his words. She gripped the book in her hands, looking at its pages without seeing. "We find this, and it no longer matters which stone he's hiding under or how he plans to use you as a tool in his never-ending quest for infestation."

Unable to stop herself any longer, Ruby spun to face him. The light of the day framed him as it poured in from the window behind, giving him a glow that softened his hard edges in a strange juxtaposition.

Drayvex reached out towards the open book with one clawed finger and rested it on the drawing. "We find *this*," he proposed, "and not even the gods themselves will stand in our way."

Ruby suppressed a shiver. "That sounds too good to be true," she said slowly, struggling to form a response. "What does it do?" How many stones were there, exactly? And how did her gran know of them?

Drayvex withdrew his claw from the page and flashed her a smile with teeth. "The Lapis Temporis is the reset button that every mook and their mother would sell their soul to possess. And you're going to make sure I find it first."

She blinked. A reset button on life? She couldn't even begin to wrap her head around the terrifying consequences of such a thing. No single living being should have access to that much power. But as she finally processed his words, her mind lurched. "I am?"

Drayvex held out a hand and curled his fingers inward in a loose claw. Ruby tensed, staring with clueless expectation at that hand. As she watched, black strands almost like smoke materialised from his palm. They rose and gathered together, wisps of darkness that grew and twisted as one until it sat, an oily black flame flickering and brushing the ceiling of his tipped fingers.

Ruby hesitated, nearly withdrawing as he moved it towards her, and then changed her mind. She wasn't scared of the dark. It was the things that lived in the dark she feared, not the darkness itself.

"Your gran was nobody's fool." He held the twisting ball of smoke above the book, and Ruby remained glued to it, mesmerised by the way it moved. It was as if the darkness itself was alive. "She knew that her life's work would eventually fall into unsavoury hands, and so she took precautions."

As Drayvex tipped his hand to one side, the darkness spilt onto the book, pouring out like a roiling liquid.

Ruby held herself in check with wide eyes as the smoke spread across the pages, obscuring the words under dark translucent coils. Some parts were visible, if she squinted, but only for the briefest of moments. The more she strained to see the words under the living darkness, the less she saw. Her temple throbbed in protest.

She blinked, confused by the disorienting smoke. It covered everything but the diagram.

"The book is warded," Drayvex offered, answering her unspoken thoughts. "No demon will get anything worth their eyeballs from these pages."

Chapter 4

Huh. Ruby scratched her head, her mind blown by the fact that her warm, good-natured gran knew how to ward against demons. In truth, Ruby herself had landed on the same conclusion: that her gran had spent a good portion of her life piecing together the contents of this vast, confusing book. But to hear Drayvex vocalise what she'd barely wrapped her head around was a trip. She nodded at the smoke. " And this is ...?"

"A basic imitation."

She looked up at Drayvex, her mind racing. He was watching her with that same expression she'd seen too many times before. Soft and calculating, deep in thought; eyes that were a cold blue, lost in the small mechanics of a bigger picture she had no place in. And yet, entirely focused on her in a way that made her feel that, yes, she did wield some power after all.

"You, however," Drayvex waved his hand in a dismissive motion, "have no trouble reading this book from cover to cover." The strands of darkness dissipated in an instant, writhing and breaking apart to clear the pages.

Ruby stared down at the swirls of ink. The words on the page popped out at her, the style familiar to her now after her many sleepless nights poring over her gran's precious words.

"In fact, I would go as far as to predict that *only* you can read it."

It took a moment for that to sink in. "Why would you think that?"

Drayvex shrugged. "You're human and dying. You want to keep an entire species out of your business. Knowledge is power, and power is everything. What do you do?"

Ruby was speechless. Her response stuck in her throat.

"You restrict such power to your bloodline."

Her response hung on her lips, suspended in the silence that followed in the wake of his revelation. It was smart, she couldn't deny him that. But would her gran have really been so black and white?

Ruby folded down the corner of the page, marking the place, and closed the book with a snap. Feeling the corners of her mouth pull into a small smile, she bit down on her lip. "You need me to translate."

Drayvex folded his arms, tilting his head to one side. Dark strands of hair fell across his piercing gaze, a gaze that was intently focused, as though trying to see into her soul. "Translate?"

She dropped the book, letting it fall behind her onto the sofa. "It's coded."

"Right."

So he really couldn't read it, then. Something squirmed in her stomach. "And if I say no?"

Drayvex didn't move a muscle as the words slipped off her tongue, as she squirmed under the impassive gaze she was pinned under. This wasn't just a solution to their mutual problem. This was a weapon on a whole other level. And she hadn't forgotten who she was talking to.

When he finally released her, Drayvex took a deliberate step back and smiled. There was nothing about it she liked. "This *is* plan B, Ruby. I suppose it depends on how badly you want to live." And with that, the conversation was well and truly over.

Ruby stood in the middle of the lounge, more conflicted than she'd ever been as the demon before her came undone, becoming that same roiling vapour she'd seen before, and slipped out of the open window.

Rude, she thought, rubbing her arms. Just once, she'd like to decide when they were done talking.

Chapter 5

It took Ruby all of five minutes to start digging into the diary. It had always been fascinating, and despite her reservations, it wasn't long before she got lost within its pages.

She was losing light, the fading day turning the contents of her apartment a dusky orange. Pushing her cold box of noodles to one side, she leant over her desk and squinted at the pages before her. Picking apart her grandma's code was a muddled combination of guesswork, reaping the rewards of previous headway and frequent trips down memory lane.

She had got distracted more than once by her gran's strong opinions on her dad. And although there was no love lost between Ruby and 'the scoundrel who had ruined her daughter's life', she had to wonder if there was more to the story than a man who had walked out on his family.

Regardless, she was making solid progress. But the longer she stared at the words, the harder it made her head pound.

Glancing at the little clock on her desk, she pursed her lips and reluctantly called it a day. The afternoon had just disappeared.

Collecting up her notes, she slipped the loose papers inside the book and slapped it shut. She would take it to work. Maybe if she got five minutes to herself, the change of scenery would shed some light.

Ruby paused as her thoughts tweaked, her gaze drawn to the little ball of light she was currently using as a paperweight. The mysterious object had shown up in the glass dish on the same day as Drayvex. It was palm-sized and light and glowed like a little moon, but when she picked it up, it became the sun. The first time it had sprung to life in her hand, she'd dropped it. The sound of it crashing to the floor had terrified the people in the flat below her.

Something buzzed on her desk. Placing a hand on her thumping forehead, Ruby lit up her phone and frowned. A text?

'HEY RUBE, IT'S ME. DON'T ASK HOW I GOT YOUR NEW NUMBER, YOU WOULDN'T BELIEVE ME. BUT I JUST WANT TO MAKE SURE THAT YOU'RE OKAY AND THAT YOU CAN CONTACT ME IF YOU NEED TO. DAY OR NIGHT. YOU HEAR? I KNOW THINGS ARE WEIRD BETWEEN US RIGHT NOW, BUT WE'RE GOING TO GET THROUGH THIS. PROMISE. YOUR BESTIE X'

A lump rose in Ruby's throat as she read Sandra's text. She wanted to believe that they would be okay. Hell, she needed a friend now more than she ever had. But Ruby had pacified Sandra with a lie, and then Drayvex had turned up on her doorstep like a spectre of bad tidings. How would Sandra react if she knew Ruby had lied? That she was working with the demon they were hunting to save her own skin? Would Sandra see it as a betrayal?

Ignoring the way her heart squeezed, she closed the text. These were small things compared to the larger truth. Ruby was being hunted by Saydor, a demon that had even Drayvex in a vice. And there was no reason that Sandra should die at that psycho's hands. Scooping up the diary, she headed off to prepare for her night shift.

She washed two painkillers down with the dregs of a cold cup of tea, all the while asking herself why she was pushing herself this way. She didn't quite know, although she did know it wasn't because Drayvex was expecting her to pull a magic combo out of thin air. Maybe it was the puzzle of it she enjoyed, the stretching of her brain. But Ruby suspected it was, at least in part, the way it made her feel close to her gran.

Her final reason, which maybe should be her primary reason, was that

Chapter 5

Ruby didn't want to die. In the event they took her alive, she wouldn't want to live. But not dying was her vehement first choice.

As she pulled on her work jacket, her gaze snagged on the little, ornate box on the bedroom floor. Triggered memories twitched, trying to break out of the mental box she'd shoved them into. Her back to the fence, heart bleeding. Fastening a heavy bracelet around her wrist.

Shoving these images back down, Ruby bent and plucked the little box from the floor. She peeled back the flaps, and there it was; Sandra's special bracelet. It looked like any other charm bracelet, silver and feminine, almost dressy. But this bracelet had saved her life. There was something about it that *repelled* demons.

Carrying the box over to the bed, she perched on the edge and reached inside. She was not prepared to go down without a fight. She would protect herself—

A jolt shot up her arm like lightning. It wasn't quite pain, but almost-pain, like an echo of someone else's suffering. As it hit her, it split her in two, cracking her mind down the middle and plunging her into an entirely new place.

It's dark, and she is not herself. But she's still present. Still present as the darkness flashes off and reappears, as the almost-pain thrums through her, competing for space in her head. Her head and heart are not her own. But they are familiar. Calm and chaos. A black abyss.

She's losing her mind.

Ruby ripped her hand from the bracelet and threw the box. It hit the wall and bounced to the floor, lying still on its side, the silver chain spilling out of its open top.

Her hands were shaking, eyes still glued to the bracelet—a bracelet that had once protected her. It was almost as though it had *rejected* her. Why?

Inching down to the ground with an outstretched hand, Ruby moved towards it. She pulled back halfway, stomach curling. Thinking better of it. Closing her eyes, Ruby inhaled in one deep, grounding breath and then headed for the door. This was Drayvex's doing. She knew it, just as she knew she was going to be late for work.

Syn was quiet. The night was still young, and that meant that she still had time to think.

Syn was the kind of bar that had a guest list and VIP passes. It was the place to be if you had some cash to flash, and the place to be seen if you didn't. Ruby didn't belong here. There was no doubt of this in her mind. She did, however, know how to speak to the rich, how to coax their money from their tight fists. This was all thanks to her previous, previous boss, a man who, despite owning an art gallery, seemed to spend his money as fast as he earned it. "Go fish," he'd say to her, expecting miracles. And sometimes, she'd brought home a big one.

Ruby went straight through to the back room when she arrived. The makeshift office space was cool and dark, and most of all, quiet. She dropped her bag in the corner and slipped behind the desk. Her mind needed to be busy. She knew where it would go if she let it wander.

The faint pulse of a heavy beat seeped in through the walls, a steady, repetitive rhythm that was a balm to her swirling mind. Shivering in the cool, she slid a neat stack of documents along the desk towards her and dug in. She clung to the work as she sifted through paper stacks, keeping herself busy. But it wasn't long before other thoughts crept in.

The Lapis Vitae had been all her gran spoke about. For the first chunk of entries, it was almost a fixation.

Ruby's hands stilled over her work. But her gran had found the stone of life. She'd done exactly what she said she would, and it wasn't enough.

Ruby pushed on. Grabbing a branded pen from the pot, she set to work on the books. Her gran had been scant on details. Even after decoding the section Drayvex had pointed her to, the book was obscure. 'The eyes of a blind seer'? How was that helpful?

She slammed down her pen and smoothed a hand up towards her messy bun, gripping it in frustration. Focus, Ruby. Unbidden, her gaze slid across the office to her bag.

If the list of dates at the front of the diary were to be believed, her grandma was the only female relative on her mother's side in a long line to live past the age of forty-five. And she'd died hours after giving Ruby the stone of

Chapter 5

life.

The thoughts chilled her. Her gran setting out to find a legendary item of demonic origin. Finding this dark power and then, what? Using it to live a long and fruitful life? Had she known that would happen? Or had she simply been desperate to change what she thought was her future?

Jumping to her feet, Ruby headed for her bag and rummaged inside for the diary. Just five minutes, no more. Then she would have to work. Pulling the leather-bound object from the folds of her bag, she crouched on the floor, holding it in her hand. Maybe Drayvex could shed some light on her weird family history. Would he want to help?

The door opened, and Ruby jumped out of her skin.

"Ruby, have you got a sec?"

Ruby shoved the book away and rose to face her colleague, who was looking rather harassed. "Sure, Anna. What's up?"

"Can you watch the bar for five? I need to make a phone call."

She puffed out, catching her breath. "Yeah, of course."

The figure in the doorway made a show of slumping in relief. Her raven hair swished around her in a blanket. "Thanks, you're a lifesaver!" As she ducked out, Ruby followed behind.

The bass-heavy music flowed through her, rumbling in her chest as she entered the modern, club-like room. Ruby crossed the space and slipped behind the bar, taking a moment to scan the crescent-shaped space beyond it. The room was cast in soft blue lighting, and the few bodies mingling were shadows and shapes in the crepuscular light.

A chorus of laughter rose above the music, and her gaze drifted over to the group across from her. She chewed on the skin of her lip, her disordered mind wandering. If she surrounded herself with people, would that keep her safe from Saydor? Or would it just endanger those around her?

"Your best scotch, on the rocks."

Ruby turned to the languishing voice and turned on her smile. "Of course." She reached behind her for a tumbler and filled it with ice.

"Make it a double."

She reached for the bottle and adjusted her measure. Placing the drink on the counter between them, she slid it towards the man who had spoken. "Anything else?"

The man across from her reached for the tumbler and pulled it against him, cupping it in a possessive way. "No. Put it on my tab." He looked like he'd just rolled out of bed, his dirty blond hair wild and unkempt, his crumpled suit two sizes too big. But there was a sharpness to him that Ruby couldn't quite place that contradicted his attire. A sort of lethargic grace.

Ruby pulled the book out from under the counter and flipped it open. "Sure. What's the name?"

The man looked up from his drink and smiled, a jagged pull of his features that made her feel uncomfortable in her skin. "Oh, I'm not in the book, dear. My tab is *special*." His voice was oily, and it slid over her in uncomfortable ways. He leant across the bar, moving in towards her, and suddenly, Ruby could smell the tang of his breath. Her stomach rolled. "Anna knows. You should talk to her." And with that, his eyes were consumed in a wave of black.

It was like a camera shutter, there and then gone again. But Ruby couldn't tear her eyes away from his, could not conceal the horror on her features. A demon, here. Right under their nose.

He must have seen the recognition on her face because those eyes widened for the briefest of moments, taking her in. Then, they narrowed to cold slits. But there was a spark of something there too, a sick sort of amusement. "So the little bird knows the score." He was in her face, boring into her without blinking.

Ruby's heart was hammering in her chest. Her mind raced as she tried to think her way out of this. What did he mean, Anna knew? How long had they been catering to the whims of demons here?

When he pulled back to his own side of the bar, that same smile returned. "I feel like we're going to be *good* friends. Don't you?" He was pinning her in that same way that Drayvex often did when he was trying to intimidate her. "What's your name, little bird?"

Don't panic. He doesn't know who you are. Don't panic. "Gina."

"Ruby, thank you so much."

Chapter 5

Ruby's stomach dropped.

"I see you've met our newest investor," Anna chirped. "Not been giving you too much trouble, I hope?"

Tearing her eyes from the demon at the bar, she spun to face Anna. No. Tell me this is some kind of sick joke, she thought, pouring as much as she could into her eyes.

"*Ruby* and I were just getting acquainted. But I feel like I already know her so well."

Anna's face dropped as she met Ruby's gaze. And that was when Ruby saw it. The recognition and the bravado, and the shame on her colleague's face. Anna was fully aware of what was going on. And she was going with it anyway because it was good for Syn.

Ruby couldn't stand it. "No problem, Anna," she blurted, moving like the wind. "I'll leave you to it." Not stopping to look back, she ducked under the bar and power walked across the room towards the cool, quiet office.

She crashed through the door into the adjoining hallway and stopped, breathing deep, gasping lungfuls. Willing herself to stay calm. Okay, so this demon now knew her name. That didn't mean he knew who she was. It didn't mean that he was connected to Saydor. Right?

The door clicked open behind her. Ruby froze. Her eyes slid down to her pockets in the painful silence, and panic surged in her veins. She had absolutely nothing on her she could weaponise.

"You're not a little bird," that oily voice cooed from down the hall behind her. "You're a spider."

One moment she was standing in the middle of the hall, the next her back was slamming into the wall. Her breath left her all at once as the impact shuddered through her.

"I remember you now, Ruby. I know who you are."

The demon's hand clasped around her throat, an iron grip hard enough to hurt. Regardless, she struggled against him, desperately scanning for a way to defend herself.

"I was there."

She stilled against the pressure, processing his words. They were like a trigger.

Bringing up a fist, Ruby swung out, aiming for his jaw. But the demon dodged her blind jab with ease. He squeezed her throat, and she choked, hands flying to her neck. She couldn't breathe.

"Listen here, little spider." He was spitting his words now, the slick in his voice gone. "I'm going to keep your secret, and you're going to keep me sweet. You're going to do everything I say for as long as I say. And I don—"

The pointed objects that burst from the demon's chest were vicious and surreal. The demon screamed out as they pushed deeper still, his grip on her throat faltering as something followed through.

His blood hit her in flecks. Ruby simply stared, numb. Forgetting how to feel, how to react.

She gasped as her aching throat was freed, her vision swimming. Rubbing her neck, she forced herself to focus.

Drayvex was standing behind the demon, dangling the dripping lump that was the demon's heart out the front of the chest. "I can't leave you alone for five minutes," he murmured, his voice low and simmering with soft heat.

And then, it was gone, with a sound that Ruby would never forget.

The gaping hole in the demon's chest was the size of a fist. She could see through to the other side. She could hear something dripping onto the floor. And with a pained look, the demon let go of her and crumpled at her feet.

Her relief at seeing him standing there was almost painful. She buckled, folding over herself as she attempted to pull herself together. Swallowing was painful. Breathing was painful.

Straightening, Ruby turned to where Drayvex loomed beside her. He was definitely a sight for sore eyes. And it surprised her then that despite all the poison that lingered between them, despite the pain and the betrayal, the demon he was, that his presence made her feel safe.

The heart was still beating in his hand. Ruby eyed it dubiously. "Is it still alive?" Her voice was weak.

Drayvex squeezed the pulsing lump in his fist in one brutal contraction, crushing it into a pulp that oozed down his hand and splattered to the floor between them.

Ruby jerked backwards and met the wall. The body at her feet twitched in a violent spasm.

"Not anymore."

She stared at Drayvex, lost for words. She couldn't make out the colour of his eyes in the dim, but she knew he would be watching her now that her slimy tormentor was dead. Clearing her throat, she looked down at the body on the floor. "You killed our newest investor," she said, an inappropriate giggle forcing its way up her throat. "My boss won't be happy."

Drayvex opened his hand and let the remaining lumps of heart splatter to the floor. He smiled, a wicked flash that he turned on and then immediately off. "I'm sorry, do I look like I carry spare fucks around with me like loose change?"

Ruby pursed her lips, fighting a smile.

I know who you are. I was there.

The smile dropped from her face. She looked from the body to the door, terrified that someone would walk in and catch them in some terrible assumed act. It was in that moment that her situation truly hit home. There was nowhere she was safe.

Her ears rang, heat climbing up her face. She may never be safe again.

Drayvex grabbed her by the arm, startling her with the sudden movement. It pulled her back. "We're leaving. Now." There was an air of command to his tone that made her sit up and listen, and Ruby was only too happy to let him guide her, grateful not to have to think. She nodded.

Aware of his hot grip on her arm, she couldn't help but look down to where his dark splattered hand curled around her, to the claws that rested against her shirt fabric. He was so careful around her. And yet, she knew those same hands had done terrible, unspeakable things.

By the time the door from the bar clicked open, they were long gone.

Chapter 6

Once again, Ruby was the small, human-shaped conundrum on every demon's mind. And if they didn't yet want a piece of her, it was only a matter of time before they did.

Drayvex slipped out into the night, letting his senses unfold into the wailing city around them. Human, demon, a jumble of one and a smattering of the other. The city at night was a demon's playground.

Waves of damp enveloped him in sporadic gusts, slipping away as a fine vapour before it could soak his burning skin. Shaking his head, he turned back to Ruby. She was staring at his steaming form as though seeing him for the first time all over again. He scoffed, knowing that this clichéd side effect was about as subtle as a sledgehammer.

His mind simmered as his eyes lingered on her, refusing to relinquish those hostile remnants that made it hard to be calm and rational. She would have some spectacular bruises.

Spitting at the ground in disgust, he grabbed her to leave, making a conscious effort not to slice open her wrist as he did so.

Lapis Vitae or not, her luck was ridiculous. Drayvex had only been near the bar on a whim. Because he'd had no logical explanation for the jolt that had ripped him a new one out of nowhere. It was a familiar pain associated with the demon-hunting scum of the Earth. And since the only unaccounted

Chapter 6

for part of himself was wrapped inside a living, breathing human, it had made sense to check on it. It had occurred to him after this that she still had had that fucking bracelet.

Ruby was preoccupied. He knew this because guiding her around the moving obstacles on the street was like dragging a weight behind him on a length of rope. Resisting the urge to jab her with something pointed, he scanned the expanse of the city.

The streets were well-lit and far from empty. Multiple targets, multiple distractions. The odds of another demon knowing enough to target her now had to be close to zero. Still, it had happened once. And that meant that their heartless friend had witnessed Ruby's death at the village and *not* taken the rigged portal back to Vekrodus. He had stuck around.

And was there really ever only one loose end? Life was rarely that simple.

Taking an impulsive left, he tugged them into an unlit side passage and spun to face her, gripping her by the shoulders. He could sense her discomfort at being in the dark, a place where he thrived. "Is there a quick back route we can take?"

When she didn't respond, Drayvex snapped his fingers next to her face, making her jump. The restless undercurrent that was poison in his veins was briefly overwhelmed by an impatient surge. "*Hey!*" he snapped. "Which way?"

"The backstreets," Ruby jabbed back, giving him a useless shove. "But it's too dark to see down there."

He could sense a demon presence nearby, prowling the rain-slicked street just beyond the mouth of the passage. Turning back to the problem at hand, he smirked and then questioned why he'd bothered. "We're not all blind and useless. You talk, I'll lead."

He slid an arm around behind the increasingly soggy Ruby and felt her shiver in the night. Something inside him coiled, a dual-pronged hunger that responded to her soft heat, and for a moment, he was back in that lift and tasting her mouth. He was the demon; but *she* was the wrecking ball. She was the one who had smashed open the door between them. And his perfect memory would not let it lie.

Her gaze slid towards him in the dark, and her heart sped up. "Fine. But keep your hand *right* there."

Drayvex baulked at the insinuation in her tone. "Excuse you?"

Ruby stilled against him. "Is that a problem?"

As precious seconds slipped away, he smirked at her veneer. She was just as screwed up as he was. He knew it, she knew it. "You tell me, Ruby Red. Is this a problem for you? Or do you need to get something *else* out of your system while we're here?"

As her eyes widened in the dark, Drayvex watched with unrelenting amusement as the girl he held curled inward. "I think I can *just* about hold myself together in Your Lordship's presence," she said with biting sarcasm.

Drayvex bit down on his throbbing fangs. No, she would not live that one down.

Ruby's memory was not as dodgy as he had feared. And as she led them down a path of back-streets and questionable alleyways, he memorised the route.

"There's something about your kind that baffles me." She paused, and Drayvex could almost hear the cogs turning in her insatiable mind. "Why do some demons change their face and others not? Is it a personal choice?"

Drayvex stared at the street light at the far end of the passage that was the home stretch. That was an easy one. "Shifting is a statement. Only demons with serious power can change their form. The shape itself is a personal choice."

His response met a pregnant silence, and he knew there were at least a dozen more pesky questions lined up on the tip of her tongue.

He shook his head, steering her curiosity towards safe ground. "Demons are either born or created. Blood is power. Purity of lineage is *everything*."

Ruby was holding her breath. "So where do you fall?"

Drayvex scoffed, irked by her oblivious question. "Please. Do you think they let any mixed-blood mongrel sit on the throne? My blood is pure."

He heard her breathe out all at once. "Wow, snobby much."

A demonic presence brushed against his senses.

Chapter 6

"So anyway, I think I've found something useful on the stone."

It was the same demon that had got close outside the club. Too close.

Drayvex felt his demon form bristle just under the surface. His claws curved and extended, darkness flexing within him. It didn't hurt to be thorough.

"Hey." They'd stopped in the alley's mouth, just inside the circle of light. The flat's entrance. "Watch it. Those things are sharp!"

Ruby's protests drew him back into his skin. He looked down and followed her gaze to where five curved daggers rested against her stomach. He cursed in demon tongue, and because his pent up frustration would not allow him to retract, he pulled back completely.

"Is everything okay?"

The presence had slipped away. Drayvex sneered. "Fine." Hot fingers of fury extended inside his skull.

Ruby moved around until she was facing him. "Really?"

She looked up at him, and the genuine concern in her gaze stopped him dead in his tracks. A kill switch stare. For a moment, he scrambled for words, any words, as she gave him a look that was meant for anyone else but him.

You're flying too close, whispered his mind. "Yes. Keep going." He couldn't disagree. But he had always known that she was the sun. Really, why turn back now?

Why indeed, said the snide voice, when black holes devour suns whole.

Drayvex closed his eyes, fingers twitching. First, he would silence Saydor. But eventually, he would find a way to silence himself.

He followed Ruby into the building's vacant lobby, where the cheap overhead lighting buzzed in persistent chorus. Ruby's face and arms were flecked with remnants of demon. His own splatters were rather less subtle, the one hand demon blood black from his hasty burst of temper. He could have done with making the rat squeal, but Ruby had always clouded his judgement.

"I said, I have a lead on the stone." She grabbed her damp hair with both hands and dragged it over one shoulder. "Well, I mean, I do, but I don't."

Drayvex stopped at the lift where she stood. Helpful.

"But before I tell you, I want to make two things clear."

He folded his arms, putting his back to the lift, and leant against the metal doors beside her. "Well, don't keep me in suspense," he pressed, flicking a forked tongue out in a restless snap.

Ruby blinked, momentarily distracted, before her entire face hardened. "The stone is for Saydor. No detours or dodgy after plans."

Drayvex smiled a slow smile, fixing his gaze on her as she laid out her terms. She had no idea who she was bargaining with. Regardless, as it stood now, they both wanted the same thing: that lowlife's death. "Ruby. I can assure you that removing Saydor from the equation is my *top* priority."

Her eyes narrowed as she picked his words apart.

"Next."

"Wherever this leads, I'm coming with you."

As her brazen words left her mouth, Drayvex didn't react.

"You don't get to grab and run. Not this time."

Drayvex stared straight into her big, green eyes and lost it.

Ruby jumped as he laughed out loud. "I'm serious," she said, sounding put out.

"No. You'll just get in my way, half-pint."

"Then show me how to fight back."

The smile slipped from his face as she dug her nails in. There was no way in Hell he was taking her with him. "Right. Because that's something I can teach you overnight."

"It's that, or you find your own way to the Lapis Temporis."

Drayvex glared at Ruby as she tested his fragile patience, his form burning with a fresh fervour. "Really? You want to do this *now*?"

"What better time than when fleeing for my damn life?" She folded her own arms, matching him pose for pose as her voice grew louder. "Today, a creep extorted me at my workplace. I'm not waiting around to become meat between the teeth of your demon pals tomorrow."

Drayvex suppressed a flinch at her flippant remark, his true form warring for ground. He squared up to her, knowing that it was futile, that she was

Chapter 6

going to make him the villain all over again, and that he would embrace it to keep her from killing herself in such a pointless way. "And you think that tracking down an ancient demonic power that controls time itself—a *power* that every demon with a brain cell would kill to possess—is safer than staying here?"

She fidgeted, and her damp shoes squeaked against the floor. "There is nowhere safe."

"That's the smartest thing you've said so far," he spat, moving to circle her in a slow, stalking motion.

"But if there *was* ..." Ruby unfolded her arms and stared straight ahead at the lift doors, her posture softening with her voice. "It would probably be next to the demon who has the entire race in his damn pocket."

He stopped behind her and sighed. "Wrong. I have more enemies than you can possibly comprehend."

"But only one that matters. You said yourself, he may already know I'm alive. And if he does, he knows where I am."

Drayvex rummaged around for a smart comeback, a way to say that he had no idea how to protect her from *himself*.

She spun to face him, and in that moment, she was that beacon of ridiculous hope that he would never understand. The same unwavering optimism that had convinced her to fight for a doomed world with nothing but her wits and the will to succeed. "I have to push back." She took a step closer until they were face to face, toe to toe. Her heart was the prominent sound as she met his gaze, and her eyes spoke volumes. "You've got to let me fight back."

He contemplated her with sullen acceptance. Was that what he was doing? Keeping her in a cage to ensure his own peace of mind?

Drayvex reached out towards her, acting on compulsion. Ruby tensed beneath his hand, her eyes glued to him as he carefully brushed a few strands of damp hair off her face. She wanted him to understand. He did. "If that's what you want," he murmured, lingering for a moment on her cheek, "then so be it."

As he dropped his hand, he heard her breathe out all at once. But instead of stepping back, he reached out towards her with thin strands of darkness. They stretched out and curled in the air, rising to wrap around the girl who completed his soul until she was made of a darkness that suited her more than she would ever admit.

"But you should know," he said, his voice low and carrying the weight of his words, "that there is nothing more important to me than protecting my position on the throne." He watched her process those words as her heart raced, hating what had to be said, but needing to get through to her. "If I ever have to choose between you and my name, then you're on your own."

It took her a moment to respond. But when she did, there was steel in her gaze that he'd never seen before. "So be it."

Drayvex watched her, unsatisfied.

"Tell me," Ruby said, walking around him and back towards the lift. He let her go, the curling tendrils of darkness around her becoming light and translucent as they faded. "What's the plan for the stone?"

He pushed a nagging feeling to the back of his mind. The Lapis Temporis, stone of time. They had all the time in the world to find it—and none whatsoever.

The war room glowed with the green hue of emerald flames. They burnt in their brackets, glancing off his lightless flesh and illuminating the rows of books on their shelves, bound in an assortment of skins. He wouldn't find what he wanted within those pages.

The plan, on a basic level, was simple. Use the stone to go back in time to one of those moments he'd had Saydor writhing on his back, and grind him into an amorphous paste. On a realistic level, it was less simple. But if he had to take a back-door route to killing that flaccid worm, namely by finding a relic lost to demonkind for near on a millennium, then so be it. That's what he would do.

Drayvex scanned the map projected above the vast circular table, barely glancing at the strands of magic that depicted Vekrodus in its sum glory as he reflected on Ruby's cryptic words.

'The book says that we will see the Lapis Temporis through the eyes of the blind

seer. I don't know about you, but I don't know any of those.'

He twisted a single red strand in the air between his fingers as he picked the words apart. *The* blind seer. The one and only. Perhaps a magic user as ancient as the stone itself.

He had wild a hunch that this blind prophet was far closer to home than he had dared to believe.

"My Lord, if I may?"

Drayvex side-eyed his fork-tongued advisor without turning from the spread. He nodded once, allowing her to proceed.

She bowed with a hunter's grace, ingratiating herself with an unhurried sweep, before stalking over to the map. Reaching across the table, she manipulated the strands of magic with two clawed fingers, tweaking the violent city slums until the area rippled and burnt a hue of red to rival her own flesh. "There is a rising tension in the east. Specifically," she tapped the map, "here."

The demon beside him hovered, poised for instruction. He didn't have time for this shit. "Deal with it."

Myna nodded once, almost a bow, before tapping the map once again. It fell still. She didn't leave. "My Lord."

Her presence was a headache. Drayvex snapped the strand he held, sending it across the tabletop. It hit the map with a crack, causing the whole projection to shudder and reform. "What is it?" Drayvex let his mood bleed into his tone, a warning she would do well to heed.

Not only one of his chosen advisors and a talented spy, Myna was an attention-seeking harlot. She had toed every single status-separating line between them to an art form to get what she craved from him, and Drayvex had always used this to his own ends, depriving and feeding her scraps of mindless affection as he saw fit. Today, he had more important things to deal with than playing minder to his advisor's fragile ego.

Myna didn't answer, and her insolent silence rubbed against his already well-worn composure. Feeling a violent urge bristling inside him, Drayvex turned slowly to face her. In his true form, he was darkness made flesh. All savage reflex, immeasurable hunger and ruination.

Her black eyes glittered with secrets as she let them slide up to his chest, as close to making eye contact as she dared. All sharp edges and curves, she was built for all kinds of battle. Wasted, perhaps, in a bloodless role, but her eyes were even sharper than her claws. "News. The good kind."

Drayvex struck out hard and fast, grabbing the demon by the throat. He pulled her in close and squeezed. "What happens when you make me ask twice, Myna?" he snarled, feeling her twitch in his grip.

" T-trai-tor."

He stood unmoving for a long moment before letting her drop to the floor. Traitor.

Myna had the good sense to stay down. "Apologies, Your Grace," she rasped. "I meant the traitor scum was seen entering a portal at the cross-exchange."

Drayvex tensed as her words hit home. His tail flicked in restless frustration, his mind moving fast. If Saydor had been seen now, after all this time, then it was because he wanted to be seen. That in itself was anything but *good news*.

"He was not alone. One demon remained to scramble the portal."

"I fail to see how this worthy of my time."

Myna managed a cold smile as he lingered on her. "We have that demon in our custody." Her fangs glistened as her lips stretched wider.

Drayvex turned his back on the demon on the floor, a small smile growing in response. Finally, something to break. "Well, we wouldn't want to keep our guest waiting," he murmured, heading for the door. "Give them a warm welcome. I know our bloodletter will be just *dying* to meet them."

The Grand Eye was exactly where one would expect to find him—in the highest room of the tallest tower.

The door creaked open as Drayvex entered, revealing the sparse, circular room that contained the demon he sought and little else. He'd left straight for the north wing, making the small but necessary detour on his way to the holding chamber. Business before pleasure, always.

The demon was hiding from the naked eye. He would no doubt have been

Chapter 6

aware of Drayvex's next move before Drayvex himself had decided to make it. Who would have thought that the mystic eyes he'd loaned this desperate creature at the start of his Demon Lord reign, eyes that once inside the skull of a seer quickly paid dividends, would eventually be a key part in tracking down a stone of power? Certainly not he.

Drayvex closed his eyes and reached inside himself for power, letting it bleed out until the air itself was charged and crackling. Then, with a single spark, he lit it like a match.

A pop sounded from the far side of the room, followed by a muffled yelp, and the Grand Eye fell into existence.

"There you are," Drayvex purred, crossing the room towards him.

The squat seer scrabbled to his feet, getting tangled in his robes. "Wait. My Lord, you don't have to take them." He waved his knobbled hands out in front of him as Drayvex approached, sinking smaller with each step. "I-I can serve you better if I can see! What is it you seek?"

Drayvex stopped and looked down on the demon, tutting with exaggerated slowness. "Come now, Lorazo. You knew this day would come, did you not?"

The demon's otherworldly eyes glowed electric blue in the dark of the room, the face they looked out from a mask of horror. "Just a little longer, My Liege! Have mercy!"

He paused and then uttered a single low command. "You will give me what is mine." Without giving his seer time to think, he struck out fast, aiming for the eyes.

The demon screamed as Drayvex plunged his fingers into his sockets, holding his struggling head in place with the other hand.

"Besides," he added, Ruby's words echoing in his head. "You're not blind if you can see." And this blind seer's eyes had seen *everything* they needed.

Chapter 7

The keys to the flat jangled in the corridor as she locked the door, the sound amplified tenfold by her fear. Leaving was a bad idea.

Ruby pocketed her keys and stood facing the door, staring, as her mind unravelled. It was unhealthy to act as though nothing was wrong, as though she wasn't in hiding from a supernatural killer. A monster that had already used up one of the nine lives she never knew she had. But what was she supposed to do, cower in her flat?

Just then, her thoughts stopped dead. She stood, goosebumps rising on her flesh, ears straining against the considerate corridor hush that was once a comfort, and felt something skitter down her spine.

Ruby span on the spot. Too late.

The intruder shoved her the second she turned. Her back made a thud as it hit the door. Her mind flailed, useless, as an imposing figure cornered her.

The point of a blade was placed against her throat. "Lesson one." The strong velveteen voice stilled her frantic heart, recognition slicing through her terror. "You will always be slower and weaker than your demon opponent."

Ruby breathed out in a hard stream. No longer blinded by fear, she looked up and found that endless, fixing stare of blue steel. She could feel it now,

Chapter 7

knowing that her life was no longer on the line. His signature heat. In fact, he wasn't just warm; he was burning.

She pinched her lips together, temper flaring where her fear had been moments ago. "Thanks for the pep talk," she snapped at him. "Don't quit your day job." The fact that he had her so thoroughly pinned just made it worse.

Drayvex's response was wordless, a self-satisfied smirk appearing on that arrogant mouth. She felt the tip of his claw against her throat and knew that one slip was all it would take. One impulsive swipe. But her mind was elsewhere, on the otherworldly creature pressed against her. He wasn't overly built, but Ruby could tell, in that moment, that he was *all* muscle.

She caught herself and knew that she was flushing. "Get off me." She gave him a useless shove. What was wrong with her?

Drayvex let the smirk slip from his face, and his eyes softened, the blue becoming warmer. "Demons will drag out a kill for a long as they can," he said, ignoring her, and his serious tone was as compelling as his almost perfect stillness. "Your fear adds to the flavour."

Ruby's stomach twisted. "Lovely."

He flashed her a wicked smile, one that he immediately switched off. And as she met his gaze, he held her prisoner with a single loaded look. "But they all have a weakness."

Ruby couldn't tear her eyes away, the look they shared piercing through into her soul.

"You just have to find it."

Out of nowhere, Sandra's words echoed in her head; the vow she'd made to Ruby that she would topple Drayvex off his throne and strike him down. Something lanced through her, sharp and fast. Did *he* have a weakness?

"If I ever have to choose between you and my name, then you're on your own."

She hoped it was well guarded.

Drayvex pulled away, and the temperature dropped.

Ruby peeled herself off the wall and adjusted her jacket. The light ball in the front pocket bounced gently off her ribs.

"Where do you think you're going?"

She glanced at Drayvex across the corridor, ignoring the disapproval in his question. He wouldn't understand, she thought, double-checking the lock on her door. People threw themselves at his feet, hung on his every word. She, Ruby, had to fight just for the right to stay alive; for everything she had. "Maybe I still have a job, maybe I don't. But at the very least, I have to see Mum."

A moment of silence passed before she finally looked back at Drayvex. He was leaning against the door opposite hers with his arms folded. "Do I need to remind you," he drawled, his gaze narrowed in that calculating way, "who insisted on being involved in this stone of time business and accompanying me *wherever it leads?*"

Ruby frowned as he quoted her out of context.

"I'll take that as a no."

Oh, one day.

He stood up straight, flexing his curved talons like a panther. "So drop your trivial human rituals and make yourself useful. I have a lead."

One day she would find a way to wipe the smug right off his face. And that would be a good day indeed.

They didn't go far. In fact, Ruby was getting a serious case of deja vu as Drayvex led them through the city. When they stopped halfway down a particularly narrow passage, she realised that it was as she had feared.

She glanced around her, wrinkling her nose. "Please tell me we're not going *through* the wall."

Drayvex didn't respond. Instead, he held out his hand, a wicked glint in his eyes, in a gesture that sparked a whirlwind of memories.

Ruby hesitated. Then, as before, she threw caution to the wind and took his outstretched hand.

The second time Ruby stepped through a solid brick wall was no more pleasant than the first. It was like pushing through warm clay, and it made no sense to her brain. The only difference between then and now was that this time, she'd known what was coming. And right on cue, when they stepped out on the other side of god knew where, the world span around her in loops.

Ruby lost her balance as the ground became soft and her legs even softer, falling forward in a blur.

A strong arm caught her mid-tumble, slipping around her middle, pulling her back. "I've got you. Just *breathe*."

Ruby leant against the demon who secured her, her back to him, trying to settle her turbulent stomach.

"And don't spew on me."

Her eyes flew open as his soothing tone turned to blatant disdain. "Screw you," she mumbled, waiting for the world to snap back into focus.

The first thing she saw when it did was that they were standing in a huge meadow. The expanse was splashed with colour that swayed with the slightest of breezes, along with the greenest grass she'd ever seen. It was beautiful and, well … earthly.

"Where are we?" said Ruby. The only thing she could see other than grass and flowers was the ginormous tree they were standing under.

"Close to home."

Huh. So they were still on Earth.

Ruby jumped as her phone buzzed, and felt Drayvex tense against her, and around her. Suddenly very aware of how close they still were and how warm he was making her, she coughed awkwardly. "I feel fine now."

It was wrong how comfortable she was getting around him. How safe she felt when he held her this way. He was still a killer, still the demon who put his own needs before her entire species. But he wasn't playing fair.

A few seconds passed before Drayvex released her, and she took her first few steps into the meadow.

Remembering her phone, she tugged it out of her pocket and lit up the text.

'HEY RUBE. ARE WE OKAY? ARE YOU OKAY? PLEASE TALK TO ME. I NEED TO HEAR FROM YOU. YOUR BESTIE X'

Ruby sighed, her heart squeezing. She couldn't keep ignoring her. It was cruel. Shoving the phone back in her pocket for later, she took a deep breath and turned to face Drayvex. "How did you know to come here?"

Drayvex was leaning against the tree, pieces of light dappling him through the branches above. At her question, he smiled a skewed smile. Cupping a hand in front of him, he muttered in a language she didn't understand and produced an item out of thin air.

Ruby stared in horror at the objects dangling from his fingers by fleshy strings. Eyeballs. Pink and lumpy, and staring at the floor.

Tearing herself from the gooey specimens, she swallowed against the rising sensation in her fragile stomach. "Dammit, Drayvex. What the Hell is that?" Ruby knew what they were. What she had meant to say was, why are you carrying a pair of eyeballs around with you like a psychopath?

Like a psychopath. There was clearly no 'like' about it.

"Come now, Ruby," he cajoled, his voice slick. "Don't tell me you don't recognise our blind seer? His sacrifice was truly *eye*-opening."

She spun back to face Drayvex, flinching as the eyeballs startled her all over again. He was enjoying every second of this. "You-you've got to be kidding me." She stared at him, struggling to find the words. The eyes swung gently beneath his claws, the irises a brilliant blue. "Please tell me that you haven't ripped some poor person's eyes from their head over my gran's questionable riddle."

He fell deadly still. Ruby froze in kind, unnerved, as he looked straight through her. One moment he was devil may care, the next the devil himself. It was like watching the sun disappear behind a swathe of black.

Ruby wasn't sure she wanted to look behind her. Inching around to follow his death stare, she scanned the meadow and spotted a woman.

The woman was not close by, but even from where they stood, Ruby could tell she was beautiful. She was crouched low, bent over something in the grass. Her hair was purple and braided back into several plaits.

"What is it?" she asked in a low voice, turning back to face him.

Drayvex was glaring at the woman, his eyes cold and black. The look of pure hatred on his face was jarring, and Ruby knew, in that moment, that she was losing him fast.

She shivered in the soft sunlight, fingers of ice creeping over her skin. She had no idea who this woman was. But she could almost see the great and

Chapter 7

terrible Demon Lord Sandra spoke of with such fear and loathing emerging in front of her. The face that he hid from her.

Ruby turned back to the woman across the meadow and baulked. She was looking up towards them, the same black expression almost mirrored on her features. It was eerie to see on her face, on a woman who, to Ruby, looked as though sunlight radiated from her very pores. But there was a savagery about her as well.

The air seemed to crackle around them. And then, he was gone.

It wasn't clear who moved first. But as the two beings met in the middle with an unearthly crack, it became clear to Ruby that neither being was as human as they appeared to be

Fear and adrenaline pulsed through Ruby as she watched Drayvex and otherworldly stranger strike out at each other in vicious tandem. She had never seen anything move the way he did. He was rage and fire, and impossible, deadly grace. And despite the fact that he undoubtedly represented the darkness in this ungodly spectrum, she was hypnotised.

Drayvex feinted, giving the warrior woman no choice but to act, throwing up spheres of colour that glistened like the skin of a bubble but deflected like iron. He pushed her again and again, alternating between attack and feint, as though testing her for weakness.

The woman dodged flaming black missiles like a ninja, throwing up glistening barriers when she couldn't move fast enough. The meadow was really paying the price.

Ruby held her breath as glistening shards of light missed Drayvex's shoulder by mere fractions, leaving scorch marks in the grass behind. He made it look easy, but she had no doubt that this lethal-looking light she was throwing out had his full attention. If a cheap bedroom lamp smarted, then these would have no mercy.

It quickly became apparent to Ruby that this was not a fair fight. This woman was fierce. A skilled fighter with a bloodlust that seemed on par with Drayvex's. Despite this, it was clear that she couldn't compete. He was slowly closing in, as calculating in a fight as he was out. Ruby wondered then if he was toying with her, the way he said demons do.

His claws were long and sharp, black as the patches of skin spreading like a living darkness up his hands, his arms. Ruby knew this was his true form emerging. She'd glimpsed it once from behind on a distant hill, just before becoming a puppet of the enemy. Saydor.

As she watched Drayvex now, she knew without knowing how that he was fighting that change in her presence. He hadn't seen *her* that day on the ridge, just his foe. But she had seen him standing in the pit, and she wanted him to show her now. It was crazy, but maybe she would ask him. And just maybe, he would allow himself to be vulnerable and open around her for the smallest of moments.

She never saw it coming. The massive arm that grabbed her was like a giant snake made of rock. Ruby screamed as something lifted her off her feet from behind and squeezed her against it. Its chest was equally hard behind her, and before she could fathom what was going on, she was encased in crushing stone.

She couldn't breathe. Her vision quickly tunnelled, ribs straining.

Shards of stone exploded above her head, raining down. The thing that had caught her wailed in bass, its voice rumbling through her body. Still, it squeezed.

"*Stop!*" A distant female voice. There was panic in her words. "Leave him alone." And suddenly, she was right there up close, arms raised as if to pacify. "Lunx, drop her."

Ruby squirmed as a sharp pain lanced through her.

A resounding crack like the lash of a whip echoed throughout the meadow.

Ruby gasped as she slid free, air rushing back into her lungs at the protest of her crushed ribcage. Her captor cried out, making the earth shake with each thundering step. She landed on the grass, catching herself with waiting palms, and flinched as something heavy thudded to the ground next to her.

"You bastard. I'm going to disembowel you and use you as a doormat!"

Ruby stared at the severed stone arm twitching on the grass, the screams of the woman floating over her head. Almost in a daze, she looked up and felt her eyes widen.

It was a stone man. A literal mountain of a man made entirely of stone

Chapter 7

towering over her, stamping its massive feet. Missing an arm.

She felt something grab her from behind, and for a second, she was falling off the ground. Panic flooded her confused senses, and she swiped out.

"Easy, killer. You're fine."

Ruby blinked hard as Drayvex's face swam into view. They'd moved. A few feet away, the stone man was stamping and whining like big child, leaving indents in the grass where she had just been.

Ruby's stomach twisted. She was dragged back as Drayvex grabbed her under the chin, turning her head one way and then another. She pulled her best 'what the hell is going on?' face, resisting the urge to slap his hand away.

He audibly breathed out, his ashen eyes fixed on her. He returned her silent question with a look that was a fleeting jumble of conflicts.

"I'll be back for you, filthy demon. You can count on that."

Drayvex's expression turned black. Her gaze remained locked with his as his eyes darkened, and the war for control that she saw waging in those inky depths turned her to stone in his burning grip. "You should keep your beast on a tighter leash, *shcrenta*." The threat that dripped from every word he spoke made her insides curl. "Now I'm going to tear you *both* limb from fucking limb."

Ruby baulked. They were going to kill each other. But why?

Drayvex dropped his hand from her jaw. The claws on it extended.

"I-I know you."

The silence that stretched amplified the slightest of breezes, broken only by a soft whining, and it took Ruby a moment to realise that the woman was talking to her. Throwing caution to the warm wind, she peeked out from behind her demon shield and looked for the voice.

The woman a few feet away was tall and lean, with the build of a fighter. Crouched on the floor beside her was the stone man, frozen in the act of being ushered away. Her long purple hair wasn't her only unusual feature, and her eyes glistened like liquid gold as she fixed on Ruby. She was stunning in an unearthly way, and Ruby felt inferior just looking at her. That was when she noticed the ears. They were pointed.

"The lake," she offered, her voice thawing. "That was me." And then, she smiled. "I'm Tira."

Ruby pulled back behind Drayvex with a jerk, her mind and pulse racing. The beautiful whispering in the park lake. Surely not.

"Are you okay, girl?"

Ruby could feel the heat Drayvex was throwing off hit her in waves. Painfully aware of the coiled demon before her, she ignored the elven woman and looked up at him, resisting the urge to shrink from his black gaze. "Say something," she murmured. Panic began to claw up her throat. "Please." Help me understand.

"Don't move."

The two words he uttered were not what she'd expected. But no sooner had they left his tongue than nightmarish tendrils exploded from his form. Ruby flinched despite the warning as the lethal-looking coils shot outwards. She needn't have. They were the eye of a terrible storm, untouched by the black stands of chaos that ravaged the space around them.

The woman dodged as though her life depended on it. The stone man was not so quick.

The gunshot crack that rang through the air was followed by a scream of primal fury. And as Ruby stared in wordless horror through the tendril-sized hole in the stone man's head, she realised she could see straight through to the other side.

The woman launched *towards* them.

She dived through the shafts as Drayvex drove them towards her, shards of light sparking in her palm. She contorted in mid-air as they punched out at her head, her chest, her form flickering with a translucent light where tendrils punched through her without touching. And as she jumped and soared overhead, the shard of light she gripped burnt with an angry tenacity in her palm.

The elven woman swung the light down towards Drayvex in a shining arc.

Ruby realised her intention too late. As the woman reached out towards her from above with the other grasping hand, Ruby could do nothing but twist in vain.

The elven woman was going to grab her and run.

***

The pixie bitch was really scraping the barrel, pulling out the light tricks in one last desperate strike. It wouldn't keep him down. But of course, that wasn't her intention.

He should have seen it coming, that this do-gooding harpy of nature would feel the need to meddle with Ruby's welfare. And as the blade of pure light sliced in a perfect arc down towards him, Drayvex made a split-second decision.

Grabbing Ruby, he spun and pulled her into the path of the blade in one swift movement.

The diving fae shifted gears. Her entire form switched from war face to panic in the blink of an eye as she twisted in mid-air, altering her course to avoid a collision.

Ruby braced for an impact that would never come.

Drayvex knew that a fae would rather die than kill one of their precious human pets. And as she shot past them and crashed to the ground, breaking her fall behind with what he hoped was her face, he heard the ground split beneath her. *I will destroy you*, he pushed, directing a few hundred years worth of fury and bile at the creature within the clouds of pluming earth.

Retracting his tendrils, he turned to approach the fae.

A small thud on his chest stopped him in his tracks. Drayvex looked down and deduced that the girl standing before him was not on the same page. In fact, her face told him that he would be paying for this stunt for some time to come.

"You used me as a shield?" she hissed, directing a death stare his way while jabbing him in the chest.

He tilted his head, watching her with grudging amusement. Of course, it sounded truly villainous when you put it like that. "Ruby Red," he said, "do you not trust me at all?" The blade that had been speeding towards his face would have taken him out just long enough to leave her wide open. Ripe for the plucking, and in fae spite, lost to him indefinitely.

She took a step back and folded her arms. "*Should* I?"

Drayvex narrowed his eyes at her rebuke. The smart answer, of course, was no. But it grated nonetheless. Was it unreasonable to expect some sort of minor internal dilemma? "You're right," he quipped, giving her a false smile. "Choices are for those with options. My mistake."

"Trust is a two-way street," she pushed, her loose hair catching in a lazy breeze. "Do *you* trust *me*?"

Drayvex ignored the mouthwatering scent that drifted his way and stuck in the back of his throat. He stared at her, facing his own question. The answer was no. Categorically and unequivocally not. Trust was a luxury that a Demon Lord could never afford.

Ruby smiled in a way that he'd never seen before. It was a small, knowing smile, and he didn't like it. "Then how can you expect it in return?"

Drayvex glowered at the girl before him, lost for words. He was going to take that smart mouth and—

"Let the human go, demon. I won't allow you to touch her again."

Drayvex bristled, her dogged persistence getting under his skin. His true form flexed within its caged confines, dangerously close to exploding into being all at once. Breathing in and summoning every ounce of control he had left, he turned to Ruby and flashed her a pained smile. "Give me a moment."

Ruby watched him in dubious silence.

The enemy was on her feet. She was looking worse for wear but fired up for round two.

Stepping forward, he put himself between Ruby and the interfering shrew in his way, burning with an intense loathing. "Manners," he tutted to her, hearing the growling duality to his words. "Why don't you try asking *the human* where she wants to be?"

The fae raised her eyebrows before her lip curled into a snarl. "Save it," she spat. " I won't ask again."

Drayvex flexed, drawing coils of black, shimmering power from his core

Chapter 7

to his pointed fingertips in a passive-aggressive display. "I know your breed are a race of brawn-and-no-brain, but you, my dear, are truly fucking moronic."

"You fetid—"

"Wait."

Drayvex rolled his eyes skyward as the voice from behind stepped up to stand beside him. His attention gravitated towards Ruby, splitting in ways that only she inspired. Mercy.

The fae's septic yellow gaze left him and lingered on the girl beside him with renewed interest.

"I'm sorry about your friend, but he's right. I don't need saving." Ruby smiled briefly, making it look like hard work. "Thanks, though, I guess."

The fae's expression of pure horror was utterly priceless. It wasn't 'my homeworld is a flaming trashfire' horror, rather 'blink twice if you need help'. But Drayvex savoured it all the same. His gaze flicked beyond to her 'friend'. The motionless mountain of rock had become a part of the Earth aesthetic.

"What-what did you do to the girl?" The fae glared at him, scrambling for her dignity. The open disgust on her face was almost as satisfying to witness as the horror that preceded it. Rage aside, theirs was a species that was as stoic as the dead. But Ruby was really pushing this creature's buttons.

"Now that we've established how useless your presence here is," he drawled, "are you ready to meet Mother Nature? I'm sure she'll be waiting on the other side with open—" He paused for effect, hammering each word into what he knew would be a festering wound. "Oh, that's right. There is no place next to mother dear for deserters who abandon their people to die."

Drayvex watched her expression change as he bated her, pinpointing the exact moment that she gave up on her brainless Ruby crusade.

"You'll pay for this, Demon Lord." Her grip tightened on her gleaming weapon as she stared at him with pure, unrestrained loathing. Her shoulders tensed, stance lowering.

"Do you nature-huggers have a Hell?"

She moved faster than he'd seen any fae move. But instead of launching into round two, she was gone without another word.

Drayvex spat at the ground in disgust, glaring at what was left of the ruined expanse of green around them. Once a coward, always a coward.

His gaze slid sideways to the girl who was so out of her depth it was ludicrous. Out of her depth, and yet, she was giving him attitude. Her face told him exactly what she thought of his theatrics.

He narrowed his eyes at her, mirroring her filthy look. If he was going to finally finish this fae business after so long, he didn't need the big walking target on his back that was Ruby distracting him with her fragile mortality.

Maybe this was for the best.

"Who was that?"

Drayvex felt his mood flicker. None of your business. "If you think I'm about to give you a damn history lesson," he growled, "think again."

Ruby glared at him, her gaze lingering a moment before slipping away. "At least tell me why we're here." She breathed out, her words almost a sigh.

Drayvex's thoughts slipped from one mortal enemy to another. He ran his tongue along the tops of his extended fangs as his thoughts strayed into Saydor territory. "Because, Ruby, these preternatural eyes have seen a thousand dark treasures." He held his hand out before him. "And now, we know that the one thing we need is still here on Earth."

Ruby's eyes grew in size as he uncloaked their gory compass again, the eyes materialising on the palm of his hand.

Drayvex looked past them to the girl beyond and smiled a slow smile. "They're close by. Just waiting to be found." And soon, he would go back in time and make sure that he, Drayvex, was the last thing Saydor ever saw; the last thing on his mind as he crushed the breath from those lungs and extracted sweet agony from that final dying breath.

Chapter 8

The closer they got to the sea, the more she could smell it. They weren't just in a meadow; they were near the coast. She was sure of it.

Ruby felt the steady thump-thump of the light ball bouncing against her ribs as she trailed Drayvex through the green wilderness. She didn't know why she'd felt the need to bring it with her. She didn't even know what it was. All she knew was that she was drawn to it like a moth to a flame.

She sucked in a breath and reached into her jacket for the globe. It burnt under her touch. Almost dropping it as she pulled it out, she tugged her sleeve over a hand and dropped it onto the material. It was time to get some answers.

Ruby drew level with the demon in her midst and hesitated. Her gaze was drawn to where Drayvex walked in silence beside her.

Something inside her shifted. An unpleasant tunnelling gripped her. It was almost as though she was … drowning. She was a small stone dropping through an endless sea of darkness, but she was right here, her feet planted on the earth.

Something was wrong.

Ruby held out the light ball in front of her. Her hand was shaking. Its pale glow was back to that dull, milky gleam it gave when she wasn't touching it.

It gave her strange comfort as she held it through her sleeve.

Ignoring the rushing in her head, her ears, she focused on Drayvex. "Why did you leave this at my flat?"

Everything inside her fell still.

As Drayvex glanced at her, her stomach flipped. His eyes were still black as night. His nonchalant gaze fell upon the object in her hand and lingered, and for a moment, he looked as though he was about to say something.

His expression didn't flicker as he looked away. But the darkness in his eyes yawned wide.

Unnerved, she pushed on. "It's strange," she said, determined to provoke a response out of him. "Because I could have sworn that you *take* my things. So when you give me something, I can only assume that you're having some sort of break with reality."

Ruby watched as the corner of his mouth pulled up, breaking the unreadable mask he so often used against her. After a moment, Drayvex glanced back at her. Pale wisps bled from the edges of that black gaze, like dawn breaking through a starless night. "It's a luxlor," he conceded, glancing away again. "You'll want to keep it close."

The wind was picking up. She shivered as a breeze tugged at her hair. "I do. Want to, I mean." The gentle incline beneath their feet felt somewhat final as the horizon loomed just ahead. "Why do I?"

Drayvex was focused on the eyeballs in his hand, the irises almost glowing now, dangling from their cords by his claws. But he looked and sounded as though he was somewhere else entirely as he answered her. "Because you and it are the same. Neither the darkness nor the light can claim you as its own." He paused, his soft, low voice sending shivers down her spine. "That makes it a weapon you are uniquely qualified to wield."

Ruby hadn't processed that they'd stopped until she'd replayed his answer several times in her head. A weapon. But that meant he was *arming* her. She stared at it, his words swirling in her mind. "What do you mean, we're the same?" she murmured, holding the luxlor before her at eye level. He was being cryptic. What was he holding back?

When Drayvex didn't answer, she looked up to find him. That was when she saw it. The sea, stretching out before them to meet the sky. Ruby couldn't help but smile as she was transported back to a simpler time, to Crichton, the little village she never knew was home until it was gone.

Drayvex made an impatient snort. "Of course, it was never going to be that simple."

Ruby blinked at the churning grey, inhaling a lungful of sea air and holding it like a balm. She breathed out all at once. "What wasn't?" She looked over to where he stood beside her, the edge of the cliff just a short shuffle away.

There was a bleak humour in his smile. "It's here," he said, turning towards her. The darkness in his eyes was back, all-consuming.

She shook her head, trying to ignore the smothering panic that was rising up, filling her head with black like a leak in a dam. Splitting her mind. "You mean, um ... you mean the Lapis Temporis?" The whole reason they were here. Wherever *here* was. "Where is it?"

The smile dropped from his face. "Ruby."

The sensation all left at once. Once again, it was blissfully quiet. She closed her eyes and sucked in a breath through her nose. "Hmm?" she voiced, distracted.

There was a long pause before he answered her. "Are we ... compos mentis?"

Ruby's eyes flew open. Condescending was Drayvex's default setting. It was the careful edge to his cutting remark that made her want to push back. "Why wouldn't I be?"

His eyes were ashen grey as he probed her with a sceptical expression. "You were shouting."

She stared, unblinking. She looked down at the luxlor, the tips of her fingers protruding from inside her sleeve, almost touching its surface. "Oh. Well, you were saying?" she pushed, ignoring him. "About the stone?" Whatever was happening to her now wasn't important.

Drayvex narrowed his eyes, not bothering to conceal his suspicion. "We made it," he murmured, piercing through her. "X marks the spot."

Ruby shifted under the ocular assault. "I don't see it."

He smiled without humour, the points of his teeth on full show. "Oh, it's here." He stepped towards the edge of the cliff, practically hanging off the edge of the world as her anguish spiked, and he looked down with brazen nonchalance at the drop below. "It's hiding from plain sight, behind magic as ancient as the power it contains."

Her heart sank. Oh. "So, in other words, dead end."

"For you, perhaps. But not for me." With a sharp flick of his wrist, the eyeballs disappeared from Drayvex's hand. She watched them blink out of existence, her mind lagging and struggling to keep up with her eyes. "If I shake a few trees, so to speak, something useful is almost certain to drop out. It's only a matter of *where*."

Ruby inched towards the edge of the cliff where Drayvex perched, her heart hammering. "Okay. Shake how?" She was not going to fall. She was not going to fall.

"I'll invoke a storm of power within the vicinity of, say, ten miles. Force our hidden stone to kickback and reveal its location."

"Huh." It almost sounded logical, the way he put it forward, even though she had no idea what he'd just said. Doing her best not to look down, she sidled up beside him and focused everything she had on the demon. "Is there anything I can do?"

Drayvex looked down at her then, and the hard look on his face surprised her. "No. I'll do this one alone once you're gone."

Ruby felt him shut her out, felt the solid wall he was erecting piece by piece—she caught herself. That was impossible. She was *seeing* it with her eyes. "Why?"

"Because," he asserted, his mouth now the only part of him that was not impossibly still, "when you pump raw power into the atmosphere to see what pushes back, there is always collateral damage."

Even through the heat that bathed her where she stood, fiercer in the places where they almost touched, she went cold. "Hang on a sec. Are you saying people could get hurt as a result of this?"

"If *people* happen to be in the way, then yes, it will smart." His fangs inched down, the tips lethal points as he casually dismissed her species as collateral damage.

Chapter 8

Ruby didn't know how she kept falling into the same trap, again and again. But here she was. "What made you think I'd be okay with that?" she almost whispered, meeting his gaze head-on. Drayvex didn't deserve the benefit of the doubt. And yet, she gave it to him every time.

He didn't answer her. Instead, he folded his arms, holding her with a remorselessness that squeezed in her chest.

"Do it," she said, crushing the milky ball in her grip. "But I'm staying."

Drayvex held the tense silence for a long moment, smothering the chill of the wind with his increasing heat. After what felt like a lifetime, his mouth turned down, giving Ruby only the vaguest hint of a conscience. And that was where it started and ended. With her.

She held firm, raising her eyebrows in a silent prompt. Her fingers were numb from squeezing.

"I won't risk you over something so banal," he replied in a low voice.

Ruby broke the look first. She ran her other hand through her hair, pushing away the suggestion in his words. It was cold comfort. "You may not care about the locals here, but I do." How could she make him understand?

Suddenly, the luxlor slipped from her grip. Reacting without thinking, she dived for it as it sailed over the edge. What followed was instant regret.

Too late. Ruby swiped out for the plunging stone as her top half fell over the edge. Her scream was ripped from her throat. Eighty feet of gravity and air. That was all that stood between her and the smash at the bottom.

She heard him curse. She felt him grab for her, his claws piercing her skin as he caught her by the wrist and halted her fall. She bit down on her lip, ignoring the sting as she briefly dangled, one foot still on the edge of the cliff. She was looking down. Oh fuck, she was looking down.

As her fingers finally closed around the luxlor, it flared to life. The flash of light it threw off was almost blinding. It was like a little sun. It seared into her palm as she gripped it tight, fighting the urge to drop it.

Ruby felt Drayvex go limp around her wrist. A surge of terror washed over her. Slipping through his grip, she grabbed out blindly as she once again fell over the drop. No!

Drayvex grabbed for her again. He snagged her for a second time, tugging her with a sharp jerk.

Ruby fell in the right direction, tumbling to the ground face first. As she hit the grass, the luxlor rolled from her grip. Its light spluttered out, plunging the world back into gusty shades of grey.

"Do you smell barbecue?" Drayvex muttered, his tone dry. "Oh, that's right. That's me."

The smell of damp earth filled her nostrils as she inhaled sweet breath after breath where she lay. Following his voice, she pushed herself into a sitting position on the grassy bank, her limbs shaking and useless.

Her arm stung as she used it. Wincing, she studied it.

Blood trickled down her arm from where his claws had pierced and dragged down her skin, smearing in ways that made it look far worse than it was. Dismissing it as the lesser of two evils, she looked up.

Ruby's gaze was drawn to Drayvex, who stood next to her with a face that told her he was so over her human crap. But it was his hand that really caught her eye. It was full-on demonic. His black clawed hand was slightly larger than it had been before, the dark flesh splattered with angry charred patches of paler skin and the only remnants of a hand that had once looked as human as hers.

She felt the shock reverberate through her as it hit her. The light had burnt him. Stripped him back like he was nothing. "I'm sorry. I didn't—"

"I have to say," he deadpanned, his tone sending little tremors down her back, "of all the beings that have tried and failed to kill me over the centuries, no one has ever tricked me into destroying *myself* before."

She looked up at him in horror. She would never. "Drayvex, I ..."

"Points for creativity, Red. But you'll have to do better than that."

It took Ruby a moment to realise he was yanking her chain. She breathed out in a sigh. Jackass.

"Wait." She blinked stupidly as a thought occurred to her. "Why I am I apologising?" She pulled herself to her feet and stood facing the charred demon who had plucked her from certain death. "This is on you. Why would you give me this dangerous weapon, knowing what it can do to you?"

Chapter 8

"Ruby." Drayvex dismissed her with an impatient wave, grimacing as he used the wrong hand. Her eyes followed it, glued to the piece of him that was demon through and through. "Forget the damn luxlor," he said, drawing out every word with hard precision.

Ruby's eyes flew up to meet his. His voice carried the weight of centuries of ungodly authority as he gripped her shoulder with his good hand.

"Put away those shining morals for five minutes and think of *yourself*."

Ruby pulled a face as she dangled, weightless, on the other side of his intense stare. She fought against him, even as she slipped into those endless smoky depths, her will bending. A nudge here. A whisper there. She would think of herself. But ... why?

"Satan knows, they're not doing you any favours."

She wrestled with the thoughts, foreign but right. All she could see was those eyes. He smelled like ashes and that rough pleasant scent she'd inhaled on his planet. Her thoughts were not right.

Ruby broke the surface for air, rising above muddy waters. Her thoughts were not right, and she found clarity. He was trying to sway her with his mind.

Feeling a seething calm pulse through her, Ruby focused on the demon before her. "Don't ever do that to me." The cold voice that came from her mouth didn't sound like her own.

To her utter amazement, Drayvex let go of her arm and stepped back. He watched her, a bleak expression settling on a face that suddenly carried the weight of a lifetime of unfathomably dark deeds. "You have no idea what he will do to something soft and bright like you."

Ruby's breath caught in her throat as his words pierced her like ice. Was she fighting for the freedom to choose or the freedom to die?

"If you did, your priorities would be very different, I assure you."

She sighed, a shaky breath that carried all her anger away with it and left her feeling small and scared. Maybe Drayvex was right. Maybe if she knew what lay in wait for her at that monster's hands, she would be no better than anyone else.

He would have her choose herself every time, consequences be damned.

But here and now, she still had her humanity to fight for.

Ruby looked at Drayvex and dug deep for courage. "Give me twenty-four hours," she murmured, knowing that he would hear her even though her voice was barely audible. "I'll study Gran's book, see if it has any answers. If I've found nothing by then …" She paused, feeling as though she were on the edge of a cliff once again. "Then we'll try things your way."

She could see the reluctance in his eyes, see the disapproval settling on his face as he tested her proposal over and over in his mind and found it lacking.

"Give me your word that you'll wait. Please." He wanted her trust. He would have to earn it.

Drayvex glowered at her as she held firm. He folded his arms, straightening into an imposing form that suddenly seemed to take up more space than before.

Ruby found herself hoping beyond hope that what she wanted meant something to him. After all, she was working with the a Demon Lord. His concept of humanity was a thin veil at best.

"Fine. So be it." He leant forward, close enough for his hot breath to stir the fine hairs on her forehead, and shook his head. "I hope you know what you're doing."

As Drayvex disappeared behind her, Ruby breathed out and gave a small smile. She dropped it as she accepted the mammoth task before her. She had no idea what she was doing.

"Let's move," said Drayvex, his voice already far away.

She hoped her gran had more to share with her. Because if she didn't, then she had next agreed to do things his way. And that wasn't worth thinking about.

* * *

The release that followed from abandoning his damaged human skin was instantaneous. The light may have scorched his hand, but the burning had continued to spread over him like an invisible plague, an all-consuming itch that could only be scratched in one way.

As his twisting horns pushed their way out of his skull and settled in their rightful place, for a split second, their usual weight was unfamiliar. Drayvex was aware he'd been spending more time than ever playing human on Earth. The realisation was a blow from behind nonetheless.

The arched fortress doors were flung wide before he reached them, the horde of demons on the other side throwing down the usual show of self-preservation at his arrival.

Do tell us. The voice in his head was practically spitting. How long can you expect to split yourself between two worlds and remain in one piece?

Drayvex scoffed as he entered the cavernous hall, his footsteps on the stone echoing in a room that would hear a pin drop. What could he do? There wasn't a single creature alive that he would trust with her fate, bar himself.

"Oh, My Lord. You're here."

Drayvex reluctantly looked down, irritation prickling, as the demon who'd stepped into his path bowed before him. Oh, what he wouldn't give for a strong black coffee. "Speak. *Now.*"

The demon shifted, somewhat retaining its sub-par bow. "Myna requests your presence at the hold, Sire. She has ... information you seek."

His attention did a u-turn as his advisor's name was mentioned. They'd broken Saydor's lackey. "Dismissed," he growled, speaking to the messenger, knowing the room would react. Information was information. No matter how paltry.

Drayvex vaguely acknowledged the guard as he approached the room where a traitor's blood painted the walls and the floor. The large guard bowed his head and reached for the door, pushing it wide before him.

The sour stench of demon blood assaulted his senses as Drayvex stepped into the dark room. He heard the door close behind him, and a vicious smile crept onto his face unchecked. "Room service."

As he spoke to the semi-conscious lump pinned to the table before him, he felt a deep anger flicker at the edges of his being. Anger at this whole mind-screw of a mess that had dragged a girl from Earth through all sorts of steaming piles. Enemies that had no business with any other being than him.

"Tell Lord Drayvex what you told us."

Drayvex clenched and unclenched his fist as he attempted to smother the flames that consumed him. He couldn't afford to lose his shit right now. Only cold, unfeeling logic would get the job done.

He stepped forward, moving with unhurried slowness towards the bloodied figure stretched across the table. Reaching out in a flash, he grabbed the demon by the head, snapping it round to face him with a sharp twist.

The demon hissed, flinching as his spine took the strain. He was missing an eye and most of his teeth. But the one he had left bore into Drayvex with a manic mingling of loathing and despair.

"Lie to me," Drayvex hissed with soft menace, squeezing the tips of his claws into the demon's face. "See what happens." He felt the demon shudder and pulled himself back from the edge, the urge to lose himself in violent retribution making his teeth slick with venom. Oh, how he would love to make an example of this piece of walking dreck.

The demon breathed out in one wet, rattling breath. "The Master," he said, straining. "H-has business on Earth. Placed eyes and-and ears inside a human city, searching." He coughed, spraying dark blood with each hack.

Drayvex ran cold. Blood pooled and spilt down from where his claws pierced the demon's face, flowing freely now as his grip tightened of its own accord.

"Wait. I know no more." The demon jerked and hissed in his grip, frantic now. "He never t-told of what he seeks. Just personal bu-business, he said, not—"

As Drayvex's hand crushed the head of the demon, unwittingly silencing it forever, Drayvex was a million miles away. They were out of time.

Retracting himself from the demon soup, he felt a calm urgency pulsing through him. They were out of time, and he knew exactly what needed to be done.

Chapter 9

It was an invisible vortex. She could see it swirling in the air, see the devastating effects of its reach, but she knew she shouldn't be able to. At the same time, the chaos danced at her command.

She was standing in a scorched meadow. It was night, but the colours of the flowers around her were as clear as day. She *was* the darkness. And she would not let him win.

The chaos at her fingertips was not her own. But as it ripped through the unassuming village nearby, she felt the weight of it register somewhere at the edge of her being. And as the night pushed back, making the gorging vortex swell to bursting and its liquid stain her mind in a wave, it was burnt away. Because she'd found it.

The second reckoning.

Ruby awoke with a snort. For a moment, she stared blankly at the white walls. Her heart hammered, eyes swivelling as she tried to piece together where she was. Who she was.

As the fog of sleep cleared, she breathed out in a sigh, slumping back against the hard plastic chair. Of all the weird dreams she'd had of late, hands down, this one had to take the crown.

Her gaze drifted over to the bed where her mother lay, oblivious in her angelic stupor. Barely past breakfast and Ruby had fallen asleep at her bedside. A small smile formed as she took her mother's hand, rubbing her eyes with the other. She'd never been able to cope without sleep. Pulling all-nighters had been more Sandra's forte than hers. To make matters worse, she wasn't much better off than when the night had started.

A chill drifted over her as her wild dream lingered, vivid every time she closed her eyes. She shivered.

"I won't risk you over something so banal."

Drayvex's words were a frustrating contradiction of an answer. But there was no doubt in her mind that his plan would come at a steep price.

Ruby didn't know where they would go from here. Her twenty-four hours was almost up, and she had scraps to show for it. But somehow, the idea of becoming a monster was worse than dying at the hands of one.

A hard tapping sound snapped her out of her reverie. Head spinning, she turned towards the door just in time to see a clawed finger disappear from the top glass panel.

Running her hands over her face, she paused for a moment more, collecting what little remained of her sanity. Then, she left her mum behind her and headed for the door.

He was waiting for her just outside the room. "How do you *always* know where I am?" she muttered as the door clicked shut behind her. Was it a demon thing, or had he put a tracking chip in her favourite shoes? She wouldn't put it past him.

Drayvex regarded her in a remote manner as he lounged against the wall beside the door. "You're predictable," he said in a toneless voice.

Ruby frowned at him, mildly insulted. She would show him who was predictable. But as she took a good look at the demon propped against the hospital corridor, she realised that something was off.

It wasn't a physical thing that she could put her finger on. Drayvex was different to when they'd last met. A little harder, a little sharper. Coiled with effortless poise that one could almost mistake for idle. But Ruby knew better.

"It's not been twenty-four hours," she said, defiant. They wouldn't change

Chapter 9

the outcome, but she wanted them all the same because they were hers.

Drayvex watched her with a slate grey gaze, silent and still as a nurse bustled past them with a trolley and disappeared into a room down the hall. He didn't blink once. "I have a theory."

Ruby fought the urge to squirm as her instincts screamed at her. "Oh?"

"You're going to help me test it. Right?"

It didn't sound like he was asking. She pushed back. "You have new information?"

He continued to pierce through her with his gaze. "I found it, Ruby. The place where it hides in plain sight." There wasn't a hint of humour on his face.

No sooner had the words left his mouth than a cold realisation hit her. Surely, he wouldn't have. She stared at him, suspended. "Wait. Did you ... go back last night?"

Drayvex pushed off the wall and straightened in one fluid movement. When he turned to face her, she knew the answer before he'd even spoken. "Yes."

Ruby blinked at him, amazed at how easily that word rolled off his tongue. "After giving me your word that you would wait?"

He folded his arms and tilted his head, as if daring her to question his judgement. "Yes." Short and sharp.

"And people got hurt? *My* people?" Her voice was rising. This was not the place for a supernatural argument, she knew. But god, this was a whole new level of callous for him.

Drayvex pulled a face, breaking the stony set of nothing he'd maintained up to this point. His fangs flashed at her, their tips sharper than she'd seen before. "Honestly, who knows?" he jeered. "A village of nonentities in the middle of pissing nowhere really isn't at the top of my priorities."

Ruby flinched as his words hit her like bullets. Her dream, or rather nightmare, flashed back at her with visceral clarity. Her power—*his* power—ripping through a village. Her hand flew to her head, fingers weaving through her hair as her mind span. Either that's one hell of a coincidence, or ...

A man on a walker shuffled past them, eyes like saucers.

Or her dream was not a dream at all. Not a dream, but a memory.

Drayvex was watching her. She was aware of his gaze boring into her before she'd even looked up. She'd had many a strange and unexplainable experience since Drayvex had found her again. Rejected by the bracelet that had once saved her life. The darkness in her head that was sometimes present and sometimes not, but always there when *he* was around. Connected to *him*.

Had he done something to her?

Ruby stepped forward, right up to the demon that was throwing off ridiculous heat, not just physically, but from the black look he was now giving her. Pushing all thoughts of devilry to the back of her mind with great effort, she glared up at him. Now was not the time to open up a second can of worms. Making an effort to lower her voice, she continued. "You blew through them like they were nothing."

"You're welcome," he spat, mirroring her volume. He was unholy fire and fury, beautiful and terrible. But she would not let him trample her without a fight.

"I'm *welcome*? How the Hell do you figure that?"

Drayvex pushed forward, claiming what little space she'd left between them and bathing her in his heat. His eyes were black and utterly fixed on her. "Because, Ruby," he murmured, a vicious edge to his now smooth voice, "no other human on this entire fucking planet has a Demon Lord doing their dirty work. And when that degenerate swine is dead, and your perfect life has resumed its perfect droll, it will be because *I* paid the price that you would not."

Ruby stared into those dark, abyssal eyes and felt them swallow her whole."You paid it, or they paid it?" she asked softly. There was nothing but darkness in there. She had been wrong about him once again.

She watched her words bounce off him without taking effect. That humourless smile felt nothing. His charm was just an act.

She tried again. "I trusted you. Does that mean nothing?"

For a flicker of a moment, she saw Drayvex drop his guard. It changed his entire face in small ways, and Ruby knew that she'd hit something beyond the steel walls. The smile slipped from his face.

"Tell me why."

Drayvex remained motionless for a moment more before grabbing her in a sudden motion. She flinched in surprise as a frustrated hiss escaped his lips. "Because he knows, Red," he murmured, low and precise. "He's combing your precious city with his spies, looking for *you*." The hand that gripped her squeezed her arm with barely controlled compulsion, holding her hostage. "Saydor is making his move. And that changes everything."

Ruby met his chaotic gaze and felt the opposite settle in her bones. "Not for me." She felt a slow chill run through her despite his hot grip. He would never understand what it meant to be human.

"Ruby?"

The sound of Sandra's voice sent skitters of shock reverberating through her. Eyes wide, Ruby peered beyond Drayvex, down the long corridor. Her muscles seized, freezing her to the spot.

Sandra stood a few doors down, her hand still gripping the handle of the door that snapped into place in her wake. She was staring at the two of them like she was witnessing the end of the world.

Ruby's throat constricted, her body kicking into panic mode. This was not happening. Surely to God, this wasn't happening. She stared at Sandra, wordless as Drayvex's hot grip burnt against her arm, his fingers twitching in small, restless movements that told her he knew exactly who was behind him. Could her luck get any worse?

"Sand," she whispered, feeling like a deer in the headlights of an oncoming truck. "This isn't what it looks like. We're not togeth—" She stopped herself, cringing as the words left her mouth. Lying wouldn't help her this time.

The tension in the air was thick in the bustling hospital silence, the enclosed sterile space now feeling grossly inadequate for the three of them to share. Drayvex slowly inched his head around towards the door where her best friend stood. Her best friend in all the world, who hunted demons like rabbits, and had the biggest one of all in her sights.

Barely throwing her the crumbs of his attention, he remained with his back to her, giving her a callous side-eye that sent chills skittering down Ruby's spine. The same could not be said for Sandra, who was now entirely focused on Drayvex. The demon who had become as much a part of Ruby as the scars that adorned her and reminded her she was alive; a Demon Lord whose reputation was matched only by his will to destroy anyone and anything that stood in his way.

Sandra and Drayvex fixed on each other like mortal enemies. Ruby's fearful mind kicked into overdrive as the two sides of her life collided. Who would win in a fight? Of course, it would be Drayvex. Without a doubt and without mercy. He would crush Sandra like she was nothing. But Sandra wasn't nothing; she was everything.

Unless Sandra had found a weapon to bring him down. Ruby's breath hitched as her mind conjured horrors. Was that her *in* to the hunters club? The head of the Demon Lord on a spike? No doubt, she would be welcomed with open arms.

The sound of the stairwell door wrenching open made her jump to attention. She looked towards it, swinging to close with a final crunch where Sandra had stood. Gone.

"Dammit," she muttered under her breath. Ruby tugged against Drayvex, pulling her arm free from his grip. There was no resistance.

Sparing him a fleeting glance, Ruby took off down the hall and wrenched the door open, throwing herself through after Sandra. The look on his face was one of open disgust.

"Sand, wait!" she called, panting as her voice echoed in the stairwell. " I was trying to protect you."

Sandra was at the bottom of the first set of stairs. She'd stopped, her back to Ruby as she shook her head in a small motion. "How long, Rube?"

Her friend's soft voice carried a melancholy that made Ruby's heart squeeze. She trudged down the steps towards Sandra, unable to drag out the moment any longer. Would being honest have really helped here?

She stopped at the bottom and stood, staring at Sandra's back. "A little while." Oh, how she wished she knew how to make all this go away.

She heard Sandra exhale, a hard sigh. That was all the warning Ruby had.

Chapter 9

Spinning on the spot, Sandra turned and grabbed Ruby's arm. Ruby jumped as she went for the sleeve, ripping it back.

When Sandra saw Ruby's bare arm, she moaned out loud. "Oh, Ruby…" As her pink-scarred face morphed into abject horror, Ruby realised what she was looking for. The scarring that should be there on her arm, just like Sandra's. "What have you done?"

Ruby scrambled around inside her mind for something, anything, that would justify her perfect skin. That would justify the pain and suffering she had bypassed because Drayvex had pitied her on that day. She came up short. "Sand, I-I didn't ask for that."

Sandra looked close to tears. "What does—?" She took a breath and screwed up her face, sounding affected. "Oh god, this is all my fault."

Ruby tugged herself free, covering the offending arm. Sandra didn't understand. She, herself, didn't understand this thing that was her and Drayvex, growing like a swathe of deadly nightshade over her life. So how could anyone else?

"What does that bastard have over you?"

Ruby tensed as her tone switched gears. The soft anger in Sandra's voice was unlike anything she'd ever heard from her. "Have?" Ruby stared at her, putting the pieces together, hardly daring to believe what she was insinuating. "What, like my soul?"

Sandra's fierce gaze bore into her, a fresh gleam of emotion glistening in her eyes. "I know you, Ruby," she said, grabbing her by the shoulders in a motion that made Ruby jump. "You're a good person. And that sick son of a bitch has a body count that puts our biggest killers to shame. You want to know why?"

Sandra paused, leaving Ruby pinned by her own fears. She didn't want to know why.

"It's not because he has to or because we're the cows in his parlour, feeding his depraved subjects." Her voice lowered, becoming harder. "It's because he *gets off* on it. The suffering and the violence. Taken just because he can."

Ruby opened her mouth to speak, but nothing came out. She blinked back stunned tears. Her knee-jerk reaction was to defend him, even now.

To say that it wasn't as black and white as that, that she'd seen a different side to him. That he fought for her when it mattered most. The words were ash on her tongue.

"... *it will be because I paid the price that you would not.*"

"Those are just the ones we know about."

Ruby was under no illusions about what kind of person Drayvex was. But it was so much worse than she could have possibly imagined.

Sandra's eyes suddenly lost their heat, becoming wide and fearful. She grabbed Ruby's hands and held them in her own. "Tell me what you gave him, please," she begged. "I can help you. *We* can help you."

Ruby sucked in a breath, caught on the edge of a moral precipice. *We.* She felt the emotion she'd been stifling trickle down her cheek. "I ..." She licked her lips. If she was his prisoner, then it was because she had walked herself in and shut the door behind her. "It's not that simple, Sand."

"They can protect you, you know. From him." Her eyes were pleading. "Join us. Help us *end* this."

Ruby felt the shock reverberate through her as she processed Sandra's words. She made it sound so heroic. "You mean, kill him."

Sandra gave her hands a squeeze of reassurance.

Drayvex was a lot of things, murderer being just the tip of that mother of an iceberg. And even if Sandra's hunter pals could back up such a farfetched claim, it would no doubt be well deserved. So why did the very thought of betraying him make her sick to her stomach?

"I'm sorry," Ruby murmured. And she was, to her very core. She felt like a traitor, protecting the monster as it devoured everyone around her.

She watched Sandra close her eyes and felt something inside her break. As Sandra pulled away and stepped back, she didn't look up again.

"Sand." Ruby baulked, feeling her slip away. "Aren't you going to hear me out?"

Sandra didn't move as she spoke. But the sigh that escaped her slips was world-weary. "Say your piece, Rube," she said. "Make me understand."

Ruby stared at her, panic starting to squeeze her chest. They were doing this right here and now? No friendly coffee between old mates, no small

Chapter 9

talk to soften the hard truths?

When Sandra opened her eyes, Ruby flinched. The way she was fixed on her now reminded Ruby of Drayvex. It was a hard, no-nonsense stare, and it was wrong on her face.

Ruby breathed out, picking her words carefully. What she wanted to say was that Drayvex and the Demon Lord were two very different creatures. She'd suspected as much before watching him switch at the meadow, and now, it was clearer than ever that the Drayvex she knew was not the Drayvex everyone else had the pleasure of dealing with. Instead, what came out was a rather lame, "he's not like other monsters."

Sandra didn't even blink. "No, he's worse."

She cringed. "That's not what I..." Dammit, was she really defending him at the cost of her friendship? "All I know," she said, speaking softly as she stared into the eyes of her friend, "is that when the eyes of the world aren't watching and expecting, he's an entirely different person."

The pause that followed was unbearable. Then, without responding, Sandra turned and started to walk towards the next set of stairs. And, heart breaking, this time Ruby let her go. It appeared she did not understand.

* * *

The door to the ward clicked open, and her scent sanctified the airless cage where he waited, clamouring with the menagerie of noxious hospital odours for his attention. Drayvex turned from the city to face her.

Ruby looked like hell. Not just because the telltale remnants of her failure lingered as pink circles around her eyes, but because she was glaring at him like she could quite happily murder him. It came as no surprise, given that her meddling snake of a friend had no doubt been dripping poison in her ear. The little dead hunter. Clearly quite the judgey bitch.

But unfortunately for Ruby, she wasn't the only one that had reached the end of her tether. And Drayvex would not be slighted twice.

He fixed her with a withering stare as she crossed the room, listening to her heart pound in her chest like she was running a marathon. He took a slow drag, the cigarette he stole from the skinny nurse spewing into the room. A bitterness crept in as he wondered how a creature so small and weak had clawed so much power over him. How someone he could have killed a thousand times over by now could twist him into so many knots without breaking a sweat.

Ruby stared back, eyes glistening and furious. She stopped at the bed, leaving the shell that looked like her damn mother between them.

Drayvex wrestled with his own indecision, caught between the need to indulge the volatile, hateful snarl inside him and wanting to protect her. He didn't really blame her. In a mercenary sense, he expected nothing less than to be cast off without a second thought when the moment suited her, in this case in her desperate attempt to resurrect her Frankenshambles of a relationship with the hunter. He would do the same in her shoes. But this was no ordinary girl. She was *vânători* scum, part of the sadsack organisation that had dedicated their lives to putting him down like a dog. And that would not do at all.

"Whatever you're about to say, don't," Ruby spat, warning him with a weary glare. "Just don't."

Drayvex let a slow smile creep across his face. He let go of the cigarette, keeping it weaving in mid-air around invisible fingers with his mind as the smoke swirled. "Ruby. Don't feel bad," he cajoled, knowing that he would regret pushing her away but unable to stop himself. "Kowtowing isn't a completely useless skill to have. You do seem to have a taste for low hanging fruit."

Ruby sucked in a breath, shaking her head in as she side-eyed the floating fag. "What the hell is wrong with you?" she snapped, trying and failing keep her voice quiet. "That's my best friend."

He glared across the room at her, feeling his fangs fill the space inside his mouth, knowing he would never take the high road. No matter what she expected of him. "Is that what you call it?"

She blinked. "What?"

Drayvex stepped forward, reaching the bed and its occupant lying between them. "It's cute how willing you are to abandon yourself for her approval. But she needn't worry." His claws extended, almost with a mind of their own. "We're not *actually* together, right? It's one big coincidence. No damaging demon affiliations here."

Ruby's anger briefly morphed into a cringe as he caught her off guard. Then it was back. "Dammit, Drayvex. Every time you push, something I love breaks!" She blasted her words out, the dark corners of her mind spilling into the air between them. "You have no idea what it's like to stand here with you and feel like you're betraying your entire species; like you're fighting on the wrong side." She slammed her hand down onto the bed between them. "Why do you always have to make it so damn *hard* to defend you?"

He heard the cigarette drop behind him. He felt her words burrow like splinters and seethed. Oh, *he* had no idea? He led the entire demon race. He was on permanent damage control when around her. Every demon that saw them together became evidence to destroy, but no. He had *no* idea.

I thought you said she *wouldn't* slight you twice, dripped the voice in his ear.

"I'm going to clear things up for you," he said dispassionately, making up his mind. *"Don't* defend me." Drayvex leant over the bed towards her until they were face to face, looking her dead in the eyes. "We are not friends. We are not enemies." He felt a chasm between them widen and kept going, ripping wide in a final, self-destructive shudder from which there would be no return. "We will never be a casual fuck, or a convenient alliance."

All the anger had drained from her face. But there was no putting the blood back in the body now.

"We are *nothing*. So the next time you feel the need to need to defend your association with me, do us both a favour and don't fucking bother."

Ruby was giving him that look. The soft concern that was so out of place, it was unnerving. He stared back, giving her nothing, ignoring the way her anguish tweaked at him. Mercy, he could barely stand to look at her, and still, she had something over him.

He hated that so much.

Chapter 10

Ruby knew in her gut that this was it. That this time, for sure, he would leave her to drown, and she would never see him again.

For the past two days, she had expected her death on every street corner. She had skipped her morning coffee runs and chatted with a friendly nurse over the phone about her mother's lack of progress. When bills came in, she had navigated the city like a clumsy ninja, heading straight for Syn to beg for her job, only to discover that they were being shut down.

Ruby stared into the depths of her overpriced latte, a million miles away, as she contemplated her fate in the corner of Koffee. She didn't have money to waste right now. But somehow, the small comfort of her favourite coffee shop was more than worth the price and the risk of being found.

She sighed, her frustration with herself and with Drayvex peaking for the umpteenth time since he had left her in the ward. Clearly he hadn't been eavesdropping on her and Sandra, or he'd have heard her rejecting the hunters. Of all the sodding times he'd chosen not to be a lurker.

Ruby laughed under her breath, smiling to keep herself from screaming. She dug her nail through the tissue napkin on the table, flaking pieces of shredded paper over the edge. Okay, so she had not handled things well. Her trail of self-destruction had been swift and brutal, pushing Sandra away for good before proceeding to move on to Drayvex.

Chapter 10

She took a sip of her coffee, savouring the taste. She hadn't thought it was possible to offend the great and terrible Demon Lord. There was simply nothing in that empty chest cavity to target.

Ruby froze as her gaze fell upon the TV screen on the far wall. The TV was on mute. But the green landscape behind the silent reporter was familiar—eerily so. As the picture changed to a scene of devastation, the headline in bold screamed out at her. 'Freak weather cripples Irish coastal town'.

Her stomach gave a sick sort of squeeze. Freak weather. Her cup hovered at her lips, her grip unsteady. Oh god, he was a monster.

Ruby tore her eyes from the screen as guilt gnawed at her. She'd known this for a long time. She couldn't fall back on ignorance. She paused as her gaze snagged on the young server behind the coffee bar. He was watching her from across the room.

She frowned as he hastily fell to drying his cups, placing her own back on the table. Jeez, it was the same server that had asked her out. She looked back down at the table, regretting indulging her need for comfort and familiarity.

The sound of the chair across from her scraping along the floor was enough to finish her off. Ruby scrabbled backwards on the padded bench, panic surging through her sleep-deprived mind. She wasn't ready to die.

She was on her feet and ready to run. But when she looked up, her strength left her all at once.

Drayvex stood across from her, one hand on the back of the chair facing hers. Breathing deeply, Ruby took in the demon before her, slumping forward to lean on the table as relief made her weak. He'd sought her out. Why?

Without speaking a word, he sank into the seat opposite, his movements slow and measured, as though they had all the time in the world.

One of us does, Ruby sniped to herself, her stomach churning. She met his smoky gaze, simmering and devious, and understood that they had hit a crossroad. A crossroad that would lead her away from this madness—this snarling, ravenous unity that was the two of them—or *through* it.

She held his gaze, reluctant. She was okay with being nothing. She didn't need him to see her, or want her, or even respect her. What she needed was for Sandra to forgive her. He tilted his head in an open invitation, strands of sleek, dark hair falling across his forehead. His gaze pierced deep into her soul, daring her to make a move.

In that moment, she could read those eyes like the pages of her gran's diary. *What are you, Ruby Red?*

The thought that hit her next was a cold fire. She didn't want to be enemies. Anything but that. It burnt through her with a fierce chill, making up her mind.

Ruby tore her gaze from his and, committing herself to *through*, she retook her seat. The sounds of the coffee shop filled the space around them as she took a long swig of latte from her cooling cup. She didn't rush, taking her fill and wiping her mouth before putting the cup back on the table. She looked up and beyond the demon to the server with the wandering gaze and caught him staring again. And finally, when she could no longer stop her own from being pulled like a magnet towards him, she focused on Drayvex.

He was watching her with that perfect stillness, and Ruby wasn't sure he'd moved at all since taking that seat. But there was an intensity to his gaze that she seldom saw. It was like he was picking her apart in his mind and rebuilding her, trying to figure out her deepest, darkest secrets.

Ruby wet her lips and took the plunge, knowing he was stubborn enough to maintain this until closing time. "I lost Sandra a while ago," she said, breaking the extended silence. "But it wasn't until I saw her again, after Crichton fell, that it truly hit home." She leant her elbow on the table, her heart heavy. "There's this rift between us, you see. It started with her hunter dad, and when a demon left her fighting for her life, it changed something inside her, and I don't think I can ever fix that." She paused, collecting her thoughts, her mind skipping back in time. "The other day, when she saw us together, well. That was just the final nail in the coffin."

The bell above the door chimed, and Ruby turned to look, expecting the worst. It was a woman, child in tow. She breathed out, looking back towards Drayvex. "I was overwhelmed when I said those things," she confessed, her

Chapter 10

voice soft.

Drayvex hadn't reacted to the door. She wondered if he didn't need to use his eyes to see, or whether he no longer cared either way.

Following a hunch, she pushed on. "Even though they may be true. But your ego isn't the real issue here, is it? Your problem is Sandra."

Drayvex narrowed his eyes. In that moment, she wished she knew what he was thinking. She would go as far as to say that this had not gone the way he had expected.

Ruby saw her in and took it. " I don't think she'll be coming to check on me again in a hurry. In fact, I'd be surprised if she hasn't dropped me completely and gone back to her new friends. So you really don't need to be a dick about this. Sandra is gone."

For the first time since walking in, Drayvex gave her the smallest of tells, the corner of his mouth turning up in a smile that was barely there. His eyes were steel blue, and Ruby took that as progress. What would she do without those eyes, those small windows into a dark, complex soul? She caught herself. Did demons even have souls?

"Do you want to finish this?"

His voice startled her, unfamiliar after such a length of nothing. The question sounded genuine. "Yes," she said, knowing that *this* was Saydor. "Let's not let a good slaughter go to waste." And just like that, the elephant was back in the room. This time, her elephant.

Ruby bit down on her lip, wondering when, if ever, she would be able to quit while she was ahead.

***

Drayvex had no idea how it was possible for such a small human to give him such a behemoth of a headache, but the girl was out for blood. No doubt, it also had something to do with the bastard Earth sun, beating down in a blaze of taunting light onto the clearing. Well, screw you too, he cursed it as it threw its poison over his flesh, a sensation not dissimilar to a thousand stabbing, acid-tipped needles. It would not beat him.

The moment he'd stepped through the portal, he'd caught the stench of fae in the air. If that deplorable pixie wasn't a hundred miles away by now, that could only mean one of two things. She knew he'd be back and was waiting to kill him. Or, the more likely scenario, she hadn't found what she was looking for.

Drayvex narrowed his eyes as a hostile suspicion surged through him, hot and fresh. *Get in my way*, he pushed out into the atmosphere, knowing she would almost certainly be close enough to hear it. *Go on. Make my day.* There was no such thing as coincidence.

Ruby's vow of silence was both exactly what he needed and infuriating in ways he couldn't fathom, not least because she was using his own tricks against him. His gaze slipped sideways to where she walked just behind, seemingly lost in her own head. His extending teeth were competing for space. And as he became more aware of them, he focused on the small, battered dwelling in the distance. Did she know just how much she stretched his fragile patience?

Drayvex had left Ruby two Earth days ago with no idea of what to do with her. Her closest friend was a member of the biggest demon-hunting operation that her world had seen. If Ruby wasn't already reporting back to HQ, then it was only a matter of time before she stabbed him in the back. He had even equipped her with the means to do so. He had allowed her to get close. Consistently, ridiculously close.

There were countless reasons why he should have nipped this in the bud by now. Nipped *her* in the bud. But when Ruby had gone dark, when she'd stopped visiting her mother's bedside or checking in with the vagrant outside her flat—when he no longer knew if she was alive or dead—they all ceased to matter. Drayvex had to make sure she was okay.

And when he'd seen her, he'd wanted to offer her a choice.

And then, and then. A line of deadly dominoes. But no matter which way they fell or what her expectations were for the future, there was one thing he could say with absolute certainty: she would *not* outlive him.

When they reached the small, run-down house at the top of the hill, Ruby stared at it like he'd lost his mind. He watched her, amused, despite his dismal mood. It was the last place one would look for a stone of power. Only one story and missing several windows, it was a structure that looked as though it posed a threat to the stone, never mind those who tried to take it.

"I don't understand." She frowned.

Drayvex feigned shock. "Oh, it speaks."

Ruby pulled back her hair as she turned towards him. It burnt a deep red, glistening fire under the rays of the sun. "I have plenty to say. You want to hear it?"

As she sassed him in a way that no other being alive would dare, his fangs gave a pleasant throb. His gaze fell to her mouth, and a carnal thought licked at the edges of his mind. He could think of far better uses for that insolent tongue of hers.

Drayvex pulled his mind from the gutter. He knew she was referring to his unforgiving methods, and she would not get an inch from him. Besides, the last thing he needed was to give 'sleeping with the enemy' a whole new meaning. "Is it relevant to this disasterpiece of an undertaking?" he sniped, putting her in her place as his skull continued to split itself in two under the sun. "Because if not, may I suggest you shove it somewhere warm and dark, and instead focus on not being a has-been demon's chew toy?"

Her mouth hung open as she processed his rebuttal. Then, with what looked like every ounce of her light-dwelling patience quota, she slowly folded her arms and stood, expectant. "Fine. Are you going to get on with it then?"

Drayvex breathed in through his nose, digging deep for the little patience he possessed. Mercy. Giving her a black look, he got straight down to business. "This wreck of a house isn't real," he said, smiling with teeth. "What you see is a glamour. An illusion to keep undeserving halfwits from using the Lapis Temporis to elevate their status and existence."

Ruby's focus switched from him to the house and back again. "Is it … solid? Could someone live there and be none the wiser?"

Drayvex stared at her, perplexed. Really, *that* was her first thought? "They could try. If they're unable to sense the magic, chances are their brain would be soup long before anything else killed them."

She wrinkled her nose, her large green eyes flicking back to the house.

"You brought the luxlor?" Drayvex went straight for the mark.

Ruby paused before reaching into her jacket. The luxlor was wrapped in a scrap of cloth, and as she held it out towards him, he couldn't help but wonder if that was for his benefit.

He pushed it back towards her with a pointed gesture, and he felt her jolt as his hand brushed hers. "Use it on the house."

She blinked at him before looking down at the glowing object in her palm. "I don't know how."

Drayvex watched the confusion play out across her features, intrigue creeping in as he wondered what she was truly capable of. The girl of light with darkness in her blood.

He moved around to stand behind her, and as if sensing his intention, she held herself still. "It will respond to your touch," he murmured, speaking into her ear. "But unless you take control, it will never listen to you."

"Okay?" she said, making it sound like a question. "And how do I make it listen?"

Drayvex reached around Ruby from behind, going for the luxlor, and felt her shiver. He tugged at the cloth with the tip of his claw, and she obliged, removing all but the cloth between the luxlor and her palm. "Don't fear it. Embrace it." He spoke the words like a mantra, caressing them and giving each word the impact it would need to empower her. "Feel it wash over you, and know that your will is absolute."

As he watched her breathe out and slowly pull away the final piece of cloth, he once again found himself questioning why he would want to give power to a creature he would never fully trust, a human who could turn on him at any given moment. She would be so much easier to control if she remained small and weak.

The moment the luxlor touched her skin, it burst to life. For a small moment, it spilt out into the air in an aimless spread, and Drayvex flinched as it came within inches of his flesh. Before it could reach him, it shrank back.

Chapter 10

The answer was surprisingly simple. If *he* could control her, then so could every other reprobate she encountered. And that would not do.

Ruby was a natural. Light poured from the luxlor in a concentrated beam, pointing at the house that was not a house, making it ripple.

Suddenly, the veil shuddered. Ruby almost dropped the luxlor as the run-down shack disappeared all at once. She grabbed it and righted the beam, staring with wide eyes. Drayvex watched her jaw drop as she took in the structure before them and smiled with satisfaction. Of course, his theory had been spot on.

The temple before them stood tall and wide, blazing a blood red under the Earth's sun. Elevated on a platform of stone, it stood out like a jewel against the drab grassy backdrop of Nowhere, Earth, seducing those with power to its doorstep with what he knew would be a cave of infernal treasures. Its stacked roofs had vicious, overhanging eaves that looked like jagged teeth, and on the ground, the embellished doorway yawned, its maw the devouring jaws of a hungry beast. Even on a disgustingly bright day such as it was, shadows clung to every crevice and nook, stubborn, pulsing darkness feeding off the malevolent energy that radiated from within.

Drayvex could feel it from where they stood, washing over him. He smiled as it made itself known, allowing himself to indulge in a moment of triumph. The Lapis Temporis was inside. And Saydor would soon be a stain on demon history.

Suddenly, he tensed. What he saw on the doors of the temple sent a ripple of unrest through him. It wasn't the big, screw-off lock that had caught his eye. It wasn't even the large stone guardians that stood on either side of the temple, poised to annihilate any who tried and failed to open the lock on the first attempt. It was the second keyhole, right next to the first dark magic lock; the taunting second that told him he would never be able to win.

The second lock was of light, but it didn't just require any light magic. It needed old Earth magic, the kind that was now almost extinct.

They needed the power of the fae.

Chapter 11

She could feel it rising like a restless thing, the hungry darkness inside her head.

Ruby struggled to focus her remaining will on the luxlor, waiting as he left her hanging. She wet her lips and carefully manoeuvred her body around to face him without disturbing the beam. "Are you even list—?"

The look on Drayvex's face stopped her dead in her tracks. She was getting to know that look well by now. It never meant anything good.

Ruby followed his black gaze back to what she had decided must be the devil's own temple and squinted at its monstrous beauty. The temple was terrifying to behold. Spectacular in a Gaudi kind of way, and yet somehow, like nothing of this world. Parts of it resembled the various temples she'd seen on budget holidays with her mum, but like a child's collage of all its favourite things, lumped together and forced into a disjointed whole. The other parts were unlike anything she'd seen, and they triggered silent signals of primitive fear in her brain. She had no idea what she was looking at, but her subconscious just *knew* not to ask.

Before she could find out what his problem was, he was gone. She felt the rush of air from behind as he took off at his own speed and then saw him at the foot of the stone steps.

"Don't be shy," Drayvex called, his voice carrying in strange ways. "There's plenty of room for three."

The sound of it sent a shiver down her spine. His tone was sly and seductive and held an aggression that she didn't understand. He didn't sound like he was talking to her. The dark presence in her head was angry. It battered the inside of her mind like a caged thing, a second presence that was both familiar and beyond alien. Overwhelmed, Ruby glanced down at the blazing ball in her hand.

She gasped. It wasn't blazing at all. It was a swirling ball of black; and it was *freezing* to her touch.

She almost dropped it as she stared at the transformed luxlor in horror, panicking as her concentration slipped through her fingers like water. A thick, black smoke had begun to pour out from where the light had once beamed, twitching, writhing strands. What the hell? She looked towards the temple, fearing the worst, but it never even flickered.

Ruby hastily slipped the object back into her jacket, watching the temple, waiting for it to disappear. It didn't.

"The warrior fae are *many* things." Drayvex's eyes were a deep crimson as he stalked back and forth at the bottom of the stone steps. And as he spoke the name of the species that she had come to know through him for one reason alone, it clicked into place. He was baiting the woman from the lake. "But watching from the shadows while a human does your leg work..." He tutted, slow and deliberate, coming to a stop all of a sudden. Black streaks crept up his clawed fingers, spreading up his arms like cracks of darkness and bleeding out.

Harsh whispers screamed in her ears, echoing and bouncing with ferocity in her head. Tentative, she began to close the stretch between them, moving towards the blood-red temple. The grass went swick, swick at her feet.

"I suppose we'll add lazy bitch to that growing list, shall we?"

Tira appeared out of nowhere. She flashed past like a golden bullet, landing a few feet behind Drayvex on all fours. She twisted, poised and ready, glowing with an intensity that made Ruby wince. She almost seemed to be drawing the brilliant sun from the sky, as dark, angry clouds rolled in faster than Ruby had ever seen. "How dare you!" Tira spat in an ethereal voice, straightening and pulling out a long, golden rope. It flicked before her with a crack, sparking as it hit the ground.

Ruby blinked. Not a rope; a whip. A whip made of light. Forgetting how to breathe, she looked at Drayvex—and her heart stopped as she took him in.

A pair of twisting horns dominated the top of his head. They were black and imposing and layered with rows of small spines that ran down their entire length in vicious curves. He looked somewhat bigger, although Ruby was now questioning her sanity as patches of moving shadow clung to him, pulsing and swirling as though alive.

If Tira could pass for a celestial being, then Drayvex was a hellish god. And he was changing right before her eyes.

Ruby stopped walking. This had been what she'd wanted, to see Drayvex for who he truly was, up close and personal. Now, she wasn't so sure.

A long black tail snaked down from behind and slithered across the floor like a deadly snake. It was covered in the same scale-like spines that were on his horns. "Did I touch a nerve?" he mocked, his voice carrying a soft, growling duality that hadn't been there before. His claws splayed out beside him, longer than she'd ever seen them.

Drayvex and the fae woman had fought in front of her before. This time, it felt different. For one, Drayvex had always been so careful to keep his true form in check around her. For whatever reason, he'd resisted using it the last time he'd fought Tira. Now, he was stripping away his human form with casual abandon.

Tira was also different, practically supernova. If she'd had this power before, why hadn't she used it?

An uneasiness spiked in Ruby's veins. The darkness bled inside her mind like a poison, staining it endless black. Something was wrong.

"Did you think I wouldn't notice?" A sickening crack echoed out from where they stood as a row of spiny protrusions pushed out from Drayvex's spine down his back."That I would lead you to the temple, break the lock and watch while you fill your filthy fae pockets with whatever your heart desires?"

Chapter 11

The sky was now dark and dreary, and Ruby realised with a jolt that the sun had quite literally been sucked out of the sky. Her mind span as she watched the two beings flex. What was going on? What did the fae have to do with this?

"You will never break that lock, wretched creature," sneered Tira, spreading her arms out to either side of her in a slow arc. The whip in her hand trailed down to kiss the floor. "I would rather die a hundred times over than give *you* what you seek." And as she spoke those final words, she smiled.

Something inside Drayvex exploded outward.

Ruby stumbled backwards as ebony flames span in a fiery maelstrom around him, blasting out and then up into the sky in a flash of darkness. It briefly hit her in a wall of heat, even from the safe distance where she stood, and as the black flames reduced to a simmer, licking at his skin, they surrounded him like an aura. He was quite literally on fire.

Ruby flinched as his answering laugh chilled her to the bone. Drayvex was definitely bigger, she was sure of that now. The flesh of his arms was now entirely black and gleaming, defined with lean muscle that was more obvious than ever before. But her eyes were drawn most of all to the lethal, hook-like spines that scattered sparsely down his forearms.

"I could kill you a hundred times over," Drayvex mused, pausing as though the thought appealed to him. "But why give you one hundred chances to escape me when I can kill you once and make you feel the pain of *every. Single. One?*"

As Drayvex was speaking, Tira lifted the whip, and on his last word, she surged forward, bringing it down hard where he stood. Ruby's stomach squeezed.

At the last moment, Drayvex disappeared. The light whip hit the ground with a vicious crack.

He reappeared behind Tira in a blink and hit her from behind. The ball of pulsing darkness slammed into her back and sent her screaming to the ground.

As he moved with a slow arrogance towards the writhing figure, Ruby realised that Drayvex was now barely recognisable from the suave, human-looking version of him that she had come to know. His feet were large and clawed—large enough to crush any part of her with little to no effort—and his legs were black and muscular. Smooth like his arms, around the scatterings of spines.

The smothering darkness inside her hissed, coiling and thrashing. Violent in a way that it hadn't been before. It was more than she could handle.

Drayvex stopped when he reached Tira, and in a flash, she was whipped from the ground by nothing Ruby could see. "No one will remember you," he said, his dual voice toneless and almost sounding bored. She dangled in the air in front of him, clutching at her throat in silent anguish. "No one will avenge you. The last of an unremarkable species."

Ruby saw what was coming and, in that single endless moment, was pulled in two different directions. Her instinct chose Drayvex.

"The whip," she screamed across the space, watching it twitch on the ground of its own volition. She would never reach it in time. She was way too slow.

Drayvex turned a fraction towards her, his black eyes staring as though he'd just remembered she was there.

Tira dropped a hand from her throat, catching the whip as it jumped towards her, and with everything she had, she cracked it at him.

Ruby had expected Drayvex to drop her and protect himself. He didn't.

Drayvex brought up his tail in a black whip of his own, putting it between them. The light whip cracked against his flesh, blazing as it connected and coiled.

Ruby flinched as it hit. Her mind cracked in two, splitting down the middle as, for a long moment, she was plunged into a world of pain. An echo of someone else's. Of his pain, she realised with a jolt.

Drayvex held firm as the whip wrapped itself around and around his tail, and Tira sneered, a smugness there even as she continued to choke and twitch in the air. Then, after what felt like an endless time, his tail thrashed out with one powerful flick.

The whip was ripped from the fae's hand. And as it landed on the grass a

Chapter 11

way away, her movements became more frantic.

"You-you need ... me," Tira choked, seething. "You'll ne-never op ... open the d-door without m-me."

The smell of burning flesh overpowered Ruby, and she almost gagged. Black, oozing welts ringed his tail, cutting through the skin down to the muscle. The wound dripped, staining the grass with blood the colour of darkness. In that moment, Ruby felt as though she'd caught a true glimpse of what Drayvex was really capable of. The demon who would rather take a direct hit than let his prey escape. Because that, she thought, numb, was what Tira was now.

Tira dropped her hands, letting her neck take the strain. Quick as a flash, she lashed out with blades of light that seemed to form in her palms out of nothing.

Drayvex was faster. Almost as though he'd expected this, black tendrils burst from his dual form and grabbed her like she was made of paper. They wrapped around her endlessly, binding her tight.

That was when the remaining pieces fell.

Ruby stared at Drayvex, the demon he was through and through. Her brain struggled to acknowledge that it was him, that Drayvex and the demon were the same person. Thing. One and the same. Beautiful and savage.

The more of his demonic form Drayvex embraced, the less she'd wanted to look at him. Not because she couldn't bring herself to, but because her safe, human instincts were screaming at her. It felt wrong, like something bad would happen if she took in his true form, that she would shrivel up to nothing if she looked him in the eyes. Now, as she stared straight up at the face that only vaguely resembled the Drayvex she knew, dancing with shadows and malice, she felt true fear.

"I'll let you in on a secret," said a smooth, basal voice that was darkness itself. The tendrils around Tira squeezed. "I don't care."

The darkness inside her head battered the inside of her skull. The darkness that was Drayvex. She gripped her head, clenching her teeth to stop herself from screaming. His fury was a force unto itself. She couldn't stand it.

The shadows that moved over him were just like the patches of darkness on the temple. She wondered then how much of the darkness in her head was Drayvex and how much was the temple.

Drayvex moved in close to Tira, and without knowing how, Ruby knew that he was about to bite her. But they needed the fae. Tira had said so.

"Wait," Tira choked. "I'll wo-work with yo-you!"

"You'll die screaming."

Ruby keened, her head pounding. She fell to her knees, a scream escaping through her teeth. His hatred and bile knew no bounds. It was burning her from the inside out. She felt the grass and smashed her head against the ground. She smashed again. Make it stop.

All she could hear was the blood rushing in her ears and the high-pitched ringing that pierced through her mind. She tasted blood and felt her tongue sting. She knew she was screaming; she could feel it in her throat. The darkness enveloped her like a wave. Those eyes burnt in her mind. Rage like madness consumed her.

Smash.

She would make it stop. Make it end.

Chapter 12

If it could go wrong, then it already had.

Drayvex stood, glaring a hole in Ruby's apartment door. His fingers curled, edging towards the fist that would punch the flimsy door off its hinges and open it wide. At the last moment, he thought better of it. She would not thank him for his impatience.

Sighing, he carefully manoeuvred the unconscious girl in his arms so he could rummage through her pockets. She would be out of it for a while.

When he found the key, he let himself inside and locked the door behind him. The sound of her screams echoing through the clearing had pierced his mind with a harrowing urgency. With that had come unwelcome clarity.

Drayvex moved towards the sofa and placed her down across its length, tossing objects in the way behind him. Where her skin had just been pressed against him, she glowed with warmth. In every other way, she was ice. He remained on the floor next to her, reluctant to leave.

The temple they'd unearthed was not just any temple. This had become abundantly clear the moment he'd come to his senses, revelling in his full demon glory. He couldn't pinpoint the making of this pivotal decision, to strip away the skin that barely contained him on a good day, and yet, there was no creature in existence that could force him to do so against his will.

Drayvex studied Ruby as he quietly seethed. Only the ancient ones had the power to pull such a sadistic stunt with such ease. They were thought to be long extinct, but the power they'd left behind lived on in many ways. It wasn't mind control. They couldn't add anything that wasn't already there, festering away under the surface of a mind. It was persuasion. The subtle fanning of incorrigible flames. And Drayvex was beyond furious.

Her chest rose and fell in jagged movements, her sharp intakes of breath stirring the air around them, making it impossible for him not to breathe in her delicious scent. Her skin was pale, too pale. Drayvex mithered over her condition, unable to shake the memory of her head slamming into the ground again and again.

The idea that he'd lost himself so entirely in her presence was galling. But was he really expected to believe that the human who'd already seen so much of his world—who'd suffered at the hands of many a demon degenerate and refused to dim her light—had simply taken in his true form and lost her mind?

Feeling his restless frustration peak, Drayvex rose and leant over Ruby, bringing up his hands. He placed one on her leg and another on her moving chest. Muttering a simple incantation, he drew power down his arms to his hands and felt it flow from him into her.

The soothing warmth took effect almost immediately, and as her breathing slowed, he felt her begin to thaw. Drayvex's temper was legendary, a side effect of being Lord Evil incarnate and a fact usually far beneath his concern. But there was a piece of him inside her. And he wondered now, as he watched over her, his insides in a turbulent state of flux, how much of that Demon Lord fury had bled through to her.

He didn't want to leave Ruby on her own. She'd seen a lot in a short space of time. She would need reassuring, should she not have taken leave of her senses, that even though he was a diabolical hellbeast, nothing had changed. But he didn't trust himself around her when he was so furious.

The very idea that he now had to mind his fucking temper, manage himself indefinitely so that he didn't blow her fragile human mind, was the universe at its finest. Consequences in spades.

Drayvex rose to his feet. A deep-seated rage simmered just below the

Chapter 12

surface, barely contained as he raked his thoughts for a way forward. That hideous shrew was still breathing because *he* had allowed her to flee. Because he couldn't keep her contained and stop Ruby from braining herself. It was one or the other.

He always surprised himself when he chose Ruby over whatever vital, selfish need filled his head at the time. But then, this entire operation was for her. Denial would only get him so far. Although it silenced the intrusive thoughts that slipped through the cracks, thoughts that he was—

Drayvex stopped. He watched Ruby, now looking more like she was taking a peaceful nap, and flinched. He was nothing like his mother. He didn't want to indulge such damaging thoughts. But he'd have to be blind not to see the horrifying similarities now.

Was this how *she* had started?

He grimaced, pushing all meaningless thoughts to the far corners of his mind. Their plan had failed. Saydor would soon come for the girl. And Drayvex would have to be ready when he did, or she would pay for every single one of his mistakes.

* * *

Ruby shivered as she woke, a full-body shudder that felt like she'd been ripped out of a safe place and flung into the cold.

She opened her eyes and stared at the ceiling, goosebumps spreading down her arms. She'd been so warm and comfortable just a moment ago. She grabbed for her blanket, unwilling to rise to a cold room—and froze mid-pat.

Ruby sat up fast. The room span.

Resisting the urge to barf, she let herself flop back down and waited for her eyes to focus again. Was she hungover? And for Pete's sake, why did she never seem to make it to bed?

Groggy, she let her mind drift as she adjusted to being awake. What she needed more than anything was coffee. A nice strong, black…

The thought of her next caffeine fix triggered a slew of memories. They came at her with a sluggish urgency, appearing and then making way for another and another. Coffee at Koffee with Drayvex. Pointing the luxlor at a shabby, abandoned house on a hill and getting a satanic temple. Watching him go head to head with the fae, watching him strip back the layers of his humanity like a business suit and revealing what lay beneath. The rage and the darkness that followed.

Ruby lurched off the sofa, almost losing her balance as everything came flooding back at once. Just like that, the ignorant bubble between asleep and awake she'd been floating in had popped.

She stumbled towards the window and yanked it open, grateful for the rush of fresh air that poured in. Her limbs shook beneath her as she gasped it in, heart racing, her eyes closed to the world. She let the tumble of city sounds drift around her, and the cool, moist breeze tickle her face.

As time passed, and she began to shiver once more, Ruby felt the panic and the overwhelm slowly trickle away. She would not leave the flat. She would shut herself in, and dammit, she would make the world and its nasties come to her.

Leaving the window open, Ruby turned, putting her back to the glass. So they had failed to find the stone. Or they had found it, but the temple wouldn't let them in. Or they could get inside, but it had something to do with the woman in the lake. A woman who was quite possibly now dead by Drayvex's hands.

She ran her fingers through her hair and found a tender spot near her forehead. She winced. Silver lining, though; Ruby now knew why Drayvex had always been so careful not to change around her. Careful, that was, until it no longer suited His Lordship, and his fury had filled every corner of her mind like a violent, sentient poison.

Ruby shook her head, in a state of utter disbelief that this was her life. Craving the comfort of coffee and sugary food, she shuffled towards the kitchen and pulled out the old machine. She didn't want to think of Drayvex.

Her phone rang from across the room. Ruby frowned, placing the coffee jug on the counter, and turned towards the sound. There weren't many people who had her number.

Chapter 12

She crossed the room, her heart racing. Could it be Sandra ringing to make peace? Grabbing her phone off the sofa arm, she swiped to answer, not bothering to look at the caller ID. "Hello?"

"Oh, hi. Is this Ruby Peyton?"

Ruby's heart dropped. "Um, speaking." She squirmed. Should she really be so quick to confirm her name to a stranger right now?

"Hey, Ruby. My name is Martha. I'm calling from Silver Orchard down on West Willa Way. How are you doing?"

She hung on the line, a tense silence stretching before her. "Can I help you?"

The breezy female caller paused for a moment before plunging back in. "I'll keep this brief, Ruby. I was given your contact details by your previous employer. We're currently looking for bar staff, and you come highly recommended. Are you available to come down and have a chat this afternoon?"

Ruby swayed on the spot, reeling as her mind screamed *trap*. But she was jobless and drowning in bills. Could she really afford to turn it down? A wave of panic rose up in her chest all of a sudden.

"Ruby?"

She swallowed and cleared her throat. "Sorry, yes. Yes, I'll come as soon as I can. Thank you."

"That's great! We'll see you soon."

Ruby hung up the phone, her chest constricting. She didn't *want* a job right now. What she wanted was to hide out here in her flat indefinitely. If Drayvex couldn't stop Saydor from coming for her, then no one could.

She swallowed, staring vacantly at the cheerful faces of her and Sandra on her phone screen. But of course, she had no money coming in. And eventually, if she lived that long, she would be homeless on top of everything else. Homeless, vulnerable. Easy to pick off.

Ignoring the way her chest constricted, Ruby closed her eyes and mentally prepared herself to leave the flat. She had to take the gamble. It was the only way forward.

The city was different today. In reality, Ruby knew that the only thing different was her. But rational thinking did little to settle her frayed nerves as she navigated its streets.

She shivered and zipped her jacket up right to her chin. The luxlor pressed against her from her pocket, the bulge now slightly visible under the stretched fabric.

It didn't help that the sensation of being watched had followed her from street to street ever since she'd entered the city's centre. The luxlor would protect her from demons if she could get to it in time, she countered. At least, that was her hope. If all else failed though, slamming it against a demon's head would probably leave a mark. It was as light as a feather, but when she dropped it from a height, it sounded like a cannonball.

Ruby tried to blend in as the lights changed to walk, and the crowds around her spilt out onto the crossing. So her previous employer had secured her a job interview. The chances were that would have been Anna, if it was indeed a real job offer. She wondered if Anna would have something to say about their creepy mutual friend. A small smile crept onto her face. Their *dead* creepy friend.

The smile slipped as her thoughts turned to Drayvex. Eyes that haunted her flashed over the old memories, over his once familiar face. Stop it.

As Ruby hit the pavement on the other side, an uneasiness crept into her muscles. She would have to go through the old precinct to get to West Willa Way. She fought the urge to turn and look behind her, paranoia seizing her mind as it came up on her left. It was an area that was seldom busy.

Keeping her hands close to her pockets, she swallowed and pushed through the doors into the empty shopping precinct.

Her footsteps echoed on the hard, shiny floor, announcing her arrival to all inside. Cringing, she picked up her pace. A potent mix of fragrant scents wafted up her nose as she passed a spice shop with a single customer inside. Once again, her thoughts drifted against her will back to Drayvex. She saw the beautiful harbinger of death with the savage face of her future nightmares. And she saw the aggravating jackass that always knew better, whose presence was like a hurricane blasting through her life—his reaction

Chapter 12

of utter revulsion to the spices. If *she* thought they were strong, then they would probably destroy his nose.

Why was it that her thoughts always seemed to circle back to him? She squeezed her eyes shut. Would she ever again be able to look at that half of him without seeing the other?

One moment Ruby was power walking towards the far exit, the next she was knocked senseless.

The blow came from behind. It smacked into the centre of her back, scrambling her brain. As she hit the floor face first, she felt her nose go pop. An electric pain shot across her face, and a flood of warmth gushed from her. It splattered her mouth and the cold floor beneath her in a horrifying wave.

For a moment, Ruby lay there, stunned. All she saw was red.

The sound of unhinged laughter drifted across the precinct. She froze, terror gripping her where she lay. It came from behind her, and then to her left. To her right. Moving too fast for any human.

Ruby scrabbled on the floor, trying to find her feet. Not yet. Please god, not yet. She grabbed at her bloody nose, squeezing the flow.

A strong hand ripped her from the floor. She landed against the nearest wall, and her breath left her all at once.

"Make a sound, and I'll kill every last meat sack in this construction," slid a strange, gravelly voice.

Ruby gasped in through the sharp pain in her chest. The demon before her looked somewhat human. Unlike the demon from Syn though, this one looked more like an aggressive drunk. As he smiled at her, his teeth yellowed and pointed into tiny daggers.

She tried to run, but he pushed her back with one hand, barely using an ounce of his strength. His hand came up to her throat, and the points that now rested against the soft skin of her neck pricked as he applied just enough pressure for her to feel it. She froze, one hand still desperately trying to stem the flow of blood from her nose.

"Ah-ah. Stay. Good human." The demon pulled out a phone with the other hand, mumbling to himself as he checked something on the screen. Ruby's other hand slid slowly towards her pocket. She found this an odd sight, a demon with a mobile phone, but it didn't distract her. She glared at the demon, resenting being spoken to like an animal waiting to be slaughtered.

It was in moments like these that she could truly appreciate how strange it must be for someone as vicious as Drayvex to treat her with any kind of compassion. As a human, it was something she just expected. He often fell short. But she'd never met another demon like him.

"Right." The demon snapped the phone shut, turning on her. "Time to go, my sweet little steaklette."

Ruby's hand reached the bulge of the luxlor in her jacket. Fry, you son of a bitch, stabbed her thoughts.

Without warning, the demon shoved her away. He slid backwards, a look of horror on his ugly face.

Ruby gasped, arms flying out as she slipped on the red smears on the floor. She stumbled backwards, meeting the wall in a few confused strides. He was looking at her neck.

"Oh, no no no no no," he moaned. "That is *not* what I signed up for!" The demon hissed, stamping his feet on the ground and then staring again in renewed horror. "He didn't say you were the Demon Lord's *pet*. Huh?"

Ruby blinked at the agonising demon. What?

"Oh, no. Ain't nothing you can give me to make an enemy of him. Balls to that!" The demon let out a string of curses, stepping back further, looking around frantically as though he expected to be annihilated on the spot.

And then, as fast as he'd arrived, he was gone.

Ruby's hand slid to her neck, over the bumpy scar that had appeared on that nightmarish day. She dropped her hand, a painful mix of relief and annoyance flooding through her. That was the second time she had been called that now. It was time they had a chat. And so help him, Drayvex would answer every single one of her questions.

* * *

Drayvex could feel the rising unrest of the gathering multitude below, hear

Chapter 12

their hollow drivel as he made them wait. Left them to stew in their own filth and despair. Judgement day had arrived. Those who had failed him would soon be dead. And if they'd all betrayed him, he would kill every single one of them.

The cavernous throne room was barely sufficient to hold every self-serving worm who enjoyed his protection. But Their Lord did commandeth, and so come Hell or high water, they had made it so. Because the only thing they valued more than their favourable existence was their own hides.

As Drayvex stepped out onto the platform where his throne towered over all below, a sudden and complete hush rang out across the entire hall. If only, he thought, he could silence them permanently. His life would be almost tolerable. He closed his eyes and fought back a twitch of a smirk.

The gathered masses fell into a bow that fanned down the room, and as he walked straight past the throne, his advisors taking their place on either side, he was aware of every single snatched glimpse as he made slow and deliberate strides across the platform. His head was elsewhere.

Drayvex stopped and stood, staring them down with a loathing that squirmed deep in the pit of his being, leaking through into the cold detachment that he rarely had the patience for anymore. Everything was personal when it came to Saydor. The demon had made that clear on the day he'd dragged Ruby into his petty war for dominance. The day he'd used her to hurt him.

"Rise."

At his command, the sea of faces before him straightened as he released them from their obligatory show of deference.

"It has come to my attention that some here have forgotten where their blood lies." Drayvex paused to let his words sink in, his voice containing a soft menace that carried the depth of his rancour so much better than volume. "Look at you. Dripping with duplicity, and yet still you expect more. You make me sick."

There was a shift as a restlessness rippled through the demons in his service. Every single one of them had sworn their fealty and talents to him long ago. It had barely been enough then, let alone now.

"So as a gesture of your *everlasting* loyalty, you will all prove your allegiance to me again, right here and now."

Without needing to be told, Myna clicked her fingers from beside the throne. "Bring it!" she roared with commendable authority.

Drayvex heard the scrape of stone against the hard floor and knew he would soon know, one way or another. Saydor could run. He could hide. But he would not win this. Drayvex would tear all the worlds apart if he had to. And when he found him, stone or no stone, Drayvex would erase him from existence.

No one would remember him. No one would mourn him. Saydor would become the nothing he'd spent his life running from.

His thoughts slipped further, straying to a place he was trying to avoid. He was so far from anything that should remind him of the girl, so far from her light in more ways than one, and yet it made no difference. Had Ruby woken up yet? Had she done any damage with her clumsy actions? Had *he*? Should he really have left her alone before knowing the answers to these questions? He frowned.

The moment the demons before him saw what he had planned, their disquiet escalated to a commotion. Their petulant protests buzzed in his ears, dragging him back to the matter at hand. The stone basin ground to a halt next to him, the large guard that had pushed it bowing hastily and scurrying off the platform.

Drayvex felt a flash of temper surge through him and let it devour him. They would bend to his will, or they would snap.

With the clench of a fist pumped to bursting with power, he grabbed the entire room with well-honed mental prowess. A thousand hearts, gripped within the squeezing fist of his mind. A thousand lives, his to take or spare. "You will swear," he snarled, leaning into the exquisite pain of power stretching towards its limit, "or you will die."

The demon horde fell to their knees in an almost perfectly synchronised submission, opening up the vein he demanded of them and filling the room with a familiar sour stench.

Drayvex watched the sea of black droplets float through the air, compelled

Chapter 12

by ancient magic towards the stone basin of truth. Only when the first drop of blood hit the stone did he let them go. As he did, a sense of unrest swept over him, an unfamiliar sensation. He burnt it away.

Blood swearing was basic but powerful black magic. It was the only effective way of securing a demon's loyalty, if such a thing existed. Saydor was paranoid to a fault, and Drayvex was confident that the swine would have demanded this from those turncoats that claimed to be his. If Saydor had claimed any demons within these walls, those closest to Drayvex and most useful to a runaway Demon Master, Drayvex would soon know about it. It was impossible to swear oneself to two demons at once.

Drop after drop hit the basin in a black rainstorm, pooling and expanding outward. Any moment now.

The feeling of unrest persisted, her face clear as night in his mind. An erratic slice of pain reverberated through him, flickering and confused.

He heard the sound of bodies exploding, demon panic. The magic sorted the corrupt from the loyal, spreading those who had already sworn to another in bloody chunks over those who stood nearby. Drayvex heard it all, but all he saw was her. Her face burnt into his retinas.

Drayvex motioned to Myna without glancing her way and felt her reach his side. Was this to do with the piece of himself inside her? Did it really work in that way? Was that her pain?

Uh, hello? spat the contemptuous voice of his sanity. Priorities?

"My Lord?"

"Finish this," he uttered dismissively. "I have something I must attend to." He needed to know.

Chapter 13

Drayvex entered Ruby's flat through the window, slipping between the smallest gaps in the seal and pouring himself inside. The flat looked empty.

From the moment he reformed, becoming a solid thing with refined senses, he smelt the blood. It hit the back of his throat and triggered a predatory response that sent his venom ducts into a frenzy.

His muscles locked, tension flooding through him as his earlier unfounded fears took root again, shooting to the worst possible conclusion. Something had got to her. Game over.

Drayvex burst into blistering heat, a jolt of something raw and savage lancing through his mind. If he had to tear this entire fucking city apart piece by piece, he would find the one responsible. And he would flay them alive.

When he finally bothered to use his other senses, he located Ruby's heartbeat in a nearby room. It was jarring, and as he stood by the window, listening to her steady breathing, the shuffle of feet on a soft floor, he concluded that he was losing his damn mind.

Drayvex stalked across the flat, slipping up to the room with the closed door. Leaps of conjecture were for weaklings. Not for the likes of he, who had maintained the position of Demon Lord for centuries by staying five steps ahead at all times. *She* did this to him. She made him utterly batshit crazy.

The door was flung open wide. Drayvex stilled on the spot, his reflexes coiling.

Ruby emerged from a cloud of steam, almost colliding with him as she left the room in a hurry. Almost; until she tripped over her own feet and finished the job.

As the girl who had taken over his life and screwed it 'til it bled landed in his arms in an ungainly tumble, Drayvex attempted to hold his warring instincts in check. Instincts that pushed him right to the edge of civility. He could definitely smell blood. If he didn't know it was hers, he'd have assumed she was hiding a body.

As he caught her and tried to disengage from kill mode, Ruby looked up at him with wide eyes—and a swollen nose that answered at least one unspoken question. Yes, that would do it. Gods, one day her clumsiness would kill her.

The last time she'd sprung away from him so fast had been the last time he'd forced her to confront the truth about him. A short, sharp shock that was an uncharacteristic mercy in one big way. He had let her leave with her life. Today, the only mercy he had to offer was to put her out of her misery.

There were traces of fear in her eyes as she avoided his gaze, a wariness that lingered in her stance and in the space she put between them. Both were normal, logical human reactions to the hellscapade their previous engagement had become.

Drayvex had expected all this and more from the girl who had not only witnessed a Demon Lord in full glory, but embraced the full fury of his wrath. But the anger he also saw in those depths was unexpected.

He stared at her from across the space, eyes narrowing as he watched a tangle of emotions dance in her eyes. The fires of anger would no doubt get a human through most things. It had a way of consuming a mind and its problems that was freeing on multiple levels. That was, until it took on a life of its own; a raging inferno of hatred and bitterness, sucking in everything around it. If anyone could relate to that, it was him. Angry, fine.

But angry at him?

"Do you have something you need to say?" Drayvex tilted his head to one side as he watched her, wrestling with himself as he attempted to appear as human and as non-threatening as he had on that first day they'd met. It was harder than it should have been. For one thing, he'd been trying to regain his composure since he'd arrived. His reaction to Ruby's 'death' had been a revelation. An unnerving snarl of backlash that, in that brief moment, was destruction and blood, and he knew it would never have been enough. It was all wrong.

The blame he could see in her eyes would have been enough by itself to put him in a bad mood.

Ruby wrinkled her nose, and even through the reflexive wince, she looked as though she was bracing herself for something unpleasant. "Yes, actually." She looked up, and finally, she met his gaze. Her voice was soft and didn't match the fierce tangle of conflict in her eyes. "I need you to be honest with me."

A strange compulsion took him as he watched her struggle with whatever consumed her, as he heard her heart race. He wanted to reassure her, to smooth over the sharp edges that those interfering old hags had dredged up and dragged them over. He was unworthy of her trust, but he wanted it all the same.

Drayvex folded his arms, holding himself in one piece through sheer force of will. "Speak your mind, Red."

She hesitated. "You won't lie to me?"

He felt his fangs pushing against him as he got the sudden sense that he would not like her questions. "You may not get the answers you want," he said, snaring her and holding her with a new intensity, "but they *will* be the truth." Brutally so, if needed.

Ruby nodded, her face dubious as the world slowed, and they held each other captive with a shared look.

Drayvex felt an impatient impulse as he watched her waver on the edge of two minds. It was frustrating to watch. Like a spinning coin, she would fall one way or the other. She would either embrace what could not be unseen,

Chapter 13

unfelt, or she would not.

Making up his mind, he threw caution to the wind.

As Drayvex crossed the space between them in a blink, Ruby let out a squeal, alarm flashing across her features. The only thing that had changed was her. She, who had experienced more than any other human alive. And tiptoeing around her was not going to help.

"What? Demon got your tongue?" he scoffed, feeling his fangs exalt as he let them go.

Ruby stared at him, almost open-mouthed as the seconds stretched around them, her face unreadable and blank. Then she folded her arms and squared up to him.

Drayvex tried not to smile as she took the bait. Her previous fear had been replaced by the kind of insolence that usually drove him mad. Mad because she infuriated him and because no one had ever challenged him in the delicious way that only she did.

"What's this?"

His smile slipped as Ruby pointed at the mark on her neck, the mark that told the demon world that she was his. She would not like the answer to that one.

"And why do I keep being told that I'm *yours*?"

Drayvex was speechless. Where had she heard that? He reached out towards her, towards the mark in an absent gesture. Was that the source of her anger? She resented the claim that placed her below him?

She tensed as he brushed a black-tipped finger over the small scar on her neck, his mind drifting back to a version of himself that had been as furious as he was clueless to the chaos he would willingly endure for this creature. "That," he murmured, choosing his words carefully, "is my mark. It tells any demon with a shred of self-preservation that you are mine and mine alone."

Ruby blinked. "Why ...?" She took a step back, and he let her. "Why would you do that?" Her voice was barely more than a whisper.

Drayvex sighed. I was trying to kill you. "It was an accident." He flashed her a toothy smile, the irony of them being the culprit not lost on him. "Don't overthink it," he said, watching her from his peripheral vision as he began to wander the edge of the room. "It's not a life sentence. Use it, ignore it. It means nothing to me."

It wasn't a lie. He was exponentially more powerful than Ruby would ever be. They were from different worlds, and in both worlds, he was the hunter supreme, and she was the food. Drayvex was the superior species by far. But that did not make him superior to *her*.

She followed him around the room with her eyes, turning her body to face him as he worked a lingering restlessness out of his system. "It saved me today," she said. "The mark."

Drayvex stilled on the spot. So her injury wasn't self-inflicted. "When?" he snapped. "Where?" His words came out unintentionally rough as visions of Ruby fighting for her life brought his temper flooding back with a new lease for life.

Ruby flinched before pulling a face and gingerly touching the bridge of her nose. "Never mind that." There was an edge of bravado to her voice that made him regret his own tone. "Can I continue?"

Drayvex closed his eyes and summoned every ounce of precious sanity he had left. One way or another, she was going to be the death of him.

* * *

"Speak your mind."

Ruby kept her eyes on the demon stalking through her flat, reluctant to ask her next question. It was more of an accusation, really.

Drayvex's whole demeanour had changed in the blink of an eye. She regretted telling him about her demon scuffle. Her nose throbbed in protest, along with her pounding head. Would he still want to be forthcoming with her, or would he shut her down?

"I can fix that, you know."

She hesitated over his words, the detour of conversation. Of course, he'd have clocked her injury the moment he saw her. It was not hard to miss.

Pulling her hand from her face, she slipped towards the sofa, towards Drayvex, sinister and beautiful in her lounge. Both versions of him were, in their own way. Goosebumps spread down her arms, despite the glow she could feel from all the way over where he stood. He would not distract her today. "I know you've done something to me," she said quietly. "Mark aside. I just don't know what."

Ruby hadn't known how she would feel when faced with Drayvex once again. She had expected to feel like her insides were outside. Vulnerable, overwhelmed. She had expected to see the face that she just couldn't shake every time she blinked, the one she associated with the blistering rage. She had even expected the barrier that it had put between them. But what she hadn't expected was to hate it as much as she did. She had no idea how to smash through that, but she wanted to, more than anything.

Drayvex turned towards her, impossibly still even as he did so. The look in his eyes sent a chill down her spine. Did she really want to know the answer? "That's not a question." His voice was soft and dark and sent a different kind of shiver running through her.

She trailed her fingers over the fabric of the sofa back, her makeshift shield, stomach churning. "No, it's not." She took a breath and steeled herself. She was stalling. "Sandra's bracelet. You remember? The one I told you saved my life."

Ruby watched his expression flicker. He hadn't expected that. "That *vânători* scrap."

She ignored the inflexion. "It hurts me to touch it. It's almost like it's rejecting me." She watched him as she spoke. She saw the flicker of understanding that was there and then not. It briefly crossed his features, the smallest of uncontrolled reactions.

"That's not a question either." He was going to make her spell it out.

Ruby forced herself to move, her fingers grazing the sofa fabric as she walked around its length. "And there's something in my head. A presence, a darkness. I feel it when you're close, when your eyes are black." She felt it now. A restless shadow, licking at the edges of her mind. The monster in her head. Unnerving, but not like at the temple. Never as vicious or as all-consuming as when they had stood before that terrible building. "It's taken me this long to realise that it's you." Her voice sounded a lot stronger than she felt. She was moving towards him now, slow steps that filled her with a building dread. But she had to face him. They had to face this. "Why?"

Drayvex straightened as she approached, confronting her. His face was impassive, but she knew that his thoughts were swirling. She just *knew* these things, without any sense of how or why.

"Tell me what you did to me," she demanded. She stopped a few feet away.

This was a two-way thing. She knew that, even as she pushed and did all the taking. But she needed more from him than she could give back right now. Ruby hoped he understood that. She was trying. But his next answer would be everything.

Drayvex stared at her for a long moment. His claws were back. They twitched on his folded arms, gleaming black hooks. His eyes were simmering with something she couldn't read as he considered her demand. And yet, at the same time, they still managed to feel cold. Removed.

Eventually, he broke the silence. "What did I do to you?" To her surprise, he laughed. It was an easy, humourless sound, nothing like the harsh, mocking laughter she was used to. He moved in closer towards her, and Ruby held herself still. "I saved your damn life." There wasn't a hint of humour in his ashen eyes. Just heat and sincerity, and a cold, careful edge. She felt them snare her, piercing into her soul.

Drayvex's fierce heat bathed her. Sometimes it was more of a glow, but today he was on fire. Slivers of purple burst through the storm of his gaze in ribbons, fighting for dominance. "When your heart stopped, I took a piece of myself," he said, his low tone almost conversational, "and I put it inside you."

Ruby had forgotten how to breathe. She had forgotten how to think. And as he trailed the back of a finger down her jawline like the wings of a burning butterfly, she struggled to keep her thoughts from scattering. It made perfect sense, why Sandra's bracelet now hurt her. Why she sometimes felt him in her mind. The fury that had levelled her out of nowhere as he tore into the fae. They were connected.

Drayvex watched her, almost ridiculously nonchalant as she floundered, lost for words. "No, that doesn't make you a demon," he said. " Yes, there

Chapter 13

will be side effects. No, I don't know what they are. Don't ask—"

"W-why would you do that?" Ruby's breathing accelerated as her thoughts raced ahead at their own speed. "I have nothing to give you. Nothing of value. I can't ever make that worth your while, I—"

She stopped short and flinched as Drayvex grabbed her by the shoulders in one sharp jerk. "You think I kept you alive because you're *useful* to me?" His face was so close, they would be breathing the same air, if she was still breathing.

Ruby blinked. He was angry. Just like that, beautiful and furious. "I ..." What other reason could there be?

Drayvex sneered, giving her a close-up view of his rows of fangs. "You are the opposite of useful," he growled. "You are the bane of my fucking existence. There is nothing you have that could possibly make it worth enduring *this*."

Her heart gave a painful squeeze. "Then why?" she shouted into his face, his caustic words and the pain in her face fuelling her. "If I'm such a plague on your perfect life, why not just let me die? I was already there—"

"Pass," Drayvex snarled. "Hell knows, I'm still trying to figure that out."

Ruby stared at him, stunned into brutal silence. He stared back, eyes wild and dark. Neither of them moved or spoke. The weight of his confession dragged at her, and the prickle of her eyes betrayed her as angry tears welled.

Suddenly, his eyes softened. In that moment, there was an edge of desperation there that she had never seen before. "Ruby, you don't un—"

"Please go."

Drayvex stared at her, his frozen aggression saying one thing, his eyes another. She couldn't breathe. She needed him gone.

He looked as though he was about to fight her, to launch into a different kind of dispute as she fought a battle of her own and tried not to show him how much he'd hurt her. But after a moment, he stepped back, and the walls went up.

Ruby turned her back on him. Please just go. She squeezed her eyes closed.

She didn't hear him leave. Rather, she felt his presence, and then she didn't. And as soon she was finally alone, she felt herself deflate.

Hot anger flashed through her before she could slip towards self-pity, fuelling her with something stronger. Screw Drayvex, she thought, and screw Sandra. The only person she could count on was herself. Never had this been clearer to Ruby than now.

She would fight for herself.

Chapter 14

Ruby lingered outside the entrance to the flat, letting her head rest back against the side of the building as the sound of a distant guitar lulled her. Her eyes closed as she disappeared inside herself. The reality of her situation had not yet sunk in. She knew it must be that because no one in their right mind would be this hopelessly numb in the face of defeat. Not when defeat meant her best option was a quick death.

Maybe she should take up smoking in her final hours.

She took a deep breath as an old memory snuck up on her. Her mother, leaning out of the window, smoking a sneaky fag. The guilty look on her face when she was caught red-handed.

Ruby giggled and then faltered, letting it trail off with the fading memory. She was not as numb as she would like to be.

It was still early, but already the streets were filling with early risers, those, unlike her, with jobs and lives to maintain. Her trail of thought slowed as she noticed the same old beggar sat just a little way down from her. She couldn't see a face inside the layers of blankets, but the folds had turned towards her. She was being watched.

No coffee today, she thought, giving the smallest of smiles. She pushed off the wall and strolled without aim or direction, following the pavement. She was going mad within those same four walls of her flat. She wouldn't go far. Just a quick breather. Then she would come back.

Ruby was lost in thought as she trailed through the city, taking a boring square route around the building that would bring her back around to the entrance.

"You are the bane of my fucking existence."

She flinched as Drayvex's voice intruded with enough force to make her falter. No. He would not take up space in her head today. Her heart dragged, despite her resolution. She could block him from her thoughts, but she couldn't stop herself from feeling.

Ruby had never truly known why Drayvex had come back to protect her. But she knew that she would release him from whatever misguided sense of obligation had ultimately brought him back.

"Why?"

"To hurt me."

She bit her lip too hard and felt the skin break. Had Saydor overestimated her worth?

Ruby stopped in her steps as a strange sensation shuddered through her. It almost felt as though she was being watched. She shook her head, ears straining to listen behind her. Speak of the devil, and he shall appear.

She sighed, knowing that they had let this go on for too long. "Go away, Drayvex. I have nothing to say to you." She wasn't really mad at him. She was more mad at herself. Drayvex had always been upfront with her about who and what he was. It was she who chose to ignore that, time and time again. Maybe because she was drawn to the danger. Maybe because he made her feel powerful. Or because the dizzying highs were worth the crippling lows.

She spun on the spot, expecting to see him there. The face she saw instead caught her off guard.

"Hello. It's Ruby, right?"

Ruby's hand shot to her bulging pocket. She hesitated, fingers hovering over the luxlor's surface as she stared at the man behind her. It was the barista from the coffee shop.

"I'm sorry, I didn't mean to startle you. I-I recognised you, and I wanted

Chapter 14

to introduce myself."

Her heart pounded as she processed what was going on. Oh. My. Days.

Ruby breathed out, withdrawing her hand. What would have happened had she zapped him? Did the luxlor affect humans at all? "Oh. Hey."

Coffee guy moved towards her, a nervous smile on his face. "I'm Ned."

She groaned internally as he stopped beside her, his hands in his pockets. She did not want to get cosy with Ned.

"I'm so sorry," Ned whispered in a completely different voice. "He has my family."

A lump of ice slid down her back. What?

Ned struck out hard and fast. He grabbed and spun her, wrapping an arm around her neck.

Ruby screamed, but her voice cut off as he squeezed tight. She thrashed against him, fierce panic flooding through her as he blocked off the air.

"Forgive me."

She felt his hand press against the back of her head. As a sea of black dots swam in her vision, she knew she was done for.

It's over. We tried.

Ruby clung to the remnants of sweet darkness as her senses returned in a rush of brutal clarity. No no no, please god, no. Her eyes flew open.

For a moment, she stared without seeing, her blood laced with a fear that sunk its claws deep. But when her brain clicked into gear, her eyes grew wide.

Everywhere she looked, Ruby saw bones. Hundreds of skulls were embedded in the ceiling, arranged in patterns that were clearly part of the décor, with walls of bones lining the edges of the spacious room. Small skull pyramids sat stacked on the floor at intervals, strange and eerie. But what drew the eye most of all was the large bone chandelier that hung from the ceiling, a macabre centrepiece that demanded her full attention. It was like nothing she'd ever seen. The structure was made up of pieces of all shapes and sizes, with leg and arm bones dangling from the bottom like streamers. Each curved arm looked like a spine, and at the top of each sat candles. A room of death in art.

Ruby shivered. Not just because she could never unsee all those staring faces that were part of the furniture, but because it was *cold*. She could almost see her breath. The stone floor beneath her was probably cold too, but since she could no longer feel anything through the chill that ran to her core, she could only assume.

Panic throbbed in her veins as she stared around her. She was sitting on the floor, her arms bound behind her to a solid object at her back. Where was she? Her breaths came hard and fast, and she struggled to keep them under control. She had no idea. Nothing about her surroundings felt familiar or safe.

Ruby thought that the bones around her were human, but that didn't make her feel any better. She swallowed back the sob of hysteria bubbling up her throat. No, she was better than this. They would want her to panic; *he* would want her to panic. The yellow devil. Nostrils flaring, she sat in the gloom and attempted to collect her wits.

Ruby closed her eyes. Breathe in. She was not just any human; she was the daughter of a fearless officer of the law. Breathe out. She'd worked side by side with the notorious fiend who ruled the demon world. Breathe in. A few months ago, she'd played a part in preventing the demon apocalypse.

The distant bang that echoed from the far end of the room sent her pulse into overdrive. Her gaze flicked to the door in the far wall. A door that was now opening wide.

As a familiar figure stepped into the room, Ruby stopped breathing. Paralysed mind and body, she stared wordlessly as the monster closed the door behind him and began to cross the space towards her. His sinister whistling etched itself into her mind. Never again would she want to hear a cheerful tune on anyone's lips.

When he came close enough that she could make out the details in the horribly familiar shape, her fight or flight response finally kicked in. Ruby yanked helplessly against the bonds at her wrists, throwing herself as far forwards as she could go. It wasn't far. She was bound tight.

The laugh that filled the eerie room dripped down her spine and made

Chapter 14

her contort in silent anguish. "Well, well, well. We meet again, child."

Saydor stopped a few feet away, and Ruby couldn't stop herself from looking up, against every instinct screaming at her.

There was nothing remotely human about this creature, aside from the fact that he stood on two legs. His frame was large and somewhat round but in a contorted sort of way, as though he wasn't quite solid. His flesh was a bruised yellow, with clusters of black veins bulging at intervals beneath the exposed skin she could see, and that face—well, it was like looking at some kind of hellish, humanoid piranha.

Ruby stared into the eyes of the beast and shivered. His oily black gaze was fixed on her, and there was a wild hostility there that was jarring.

Saydor held her for a moment longer before breaking into a vicious smile that stretched on endlessly. "Do you like this deplorable place?" he simpered, moving towards her once again. He drew in a long breath through his nose and made a show of breathing out. "Ah, one could almost say that it's *home from home.*"

Ruby turned her face away as he laughed at his own inside joke, tearing her eyes from the rows of vicious fangs in that shark-toothed smile. "Where am I?" she whispered, her voice oddly calm.

Saydor stopped in front of her, staring down at where she was bound at his feet with detestable hubris. As though he was convinced that this was where she belonged. "Do you not recognise the handiwork of your own wretched species? This is a place of worship, my dear." He spread his arms wide, and her eyes were drawn to the small hooks at the ends of his fingers. "A living token of human greed and hypocrisy."

She tried to process the words and failed. This place hadn't been built by demons?

He dropped his hands, and suddenly, all she could see was red. The eyes of the skulls around them began to bleed, dripping red trails that splattered down onto the floor from the walls, the ceiling. The sound of blood crashing down was deafening.

Ruby shrank back against the pillar as blood fell like rain from above. It soaked her with warmth, staining her skin, her clothes. She closed her eyes and bit down on the whimper that wanted to escape. There was no way out of this for her. She should have stayed at home.

Suddenly, his oil-slick voice was in her ear. "You all want to be saved," Saydor hissed, flicking a cold tongue into her ear with a snap. She flinched, her nerves already shot. "Heinous, god-fearing fleshbags that repent on your deathbeds. But I'll let you in on a secret, girl."

Ruby swung her head away from his mouth. She kept her eyes squeezed closed as the warm, wet drops ran freely down her face and soaked into her clothes.

His voice oozed in her other ear. "Your god has nothing on me."

"*Enough!*" she cried out. The word blasted from her in an angry, terror-fuelled directive, echoing around the room and leaving total silence in its wake.

That sinister laugh was the first sound to break the stunning quiet.

Ruby's eyes flew open, a knee-jerk reaction. The room was empty. More than that, the blood was gone, the bones the same pale yellowish colour as when she'd first laid eyes on them. She sucked in a breath and looked down to check herself, scrabbling to sit upright. Not a drop.

"You're full of nasty surprises, aren't you?"

At the sound of his voice, she looked up. Saydor was standing over her once again. His tone tried for conversational, but the dangerous edge to his soft words made him miss the mark. Had the walls really bled, or had it all been in her mind?

As he threw out a clawed, webbed hand, Ruby was unprepared for the invisible force that came at her. It yanked her to her feet by her throat in one rough motion, holding her pinned as the bonds at her wrists pulled tight behind. She gasped against the invisible pressure.

Saydor was so close, he could have used his own hand to hold her. She could count the number of pointed fangs in his mouth, smell the nauseating tang of his breath that hinted at his unsavoury diet. "Tell me," he purred, smiling with the charisma of a hungry piranha. "How did you do it?"

Ruby stopped struggling and held herself still. It was no use; she was just hurting herself.

Chapter 14

"The venom of the hartva should have turned your blood into a gelatinous dessert." He gestured towards her with a hand, and she felt the pressure at her throat swell and fade. "But here you are. The little fleshbag that just won't die."

The invisible force withdrew all at once, and she gasped, falling slack. The hartva. Was that what the demon that had killed her at Crichton was called? Those black, fathomless eyes bored into her as she struggled in her mind for the words. She wasn't special. She didn't have powers or supernatural luck. It was Drayvex that had saved her that day. They'd won the battle. And then *she* had almost lost the war.

Saydor's tongue came out in an impatient flick. "His Infernal Lordship is awfully determined to keep that fragile heart of yours beating. To keep you *close*." He growled the words into her face, and Ruby's stomach turned. Her ears rang as she tried to focus. "Why?" He spat the word as though it were a bitter taste in his mouth. "What makes a mere human worthy of the protection of a Demon Lord?"

Ruby stared at the repulsive demon in her face, her mind still trying and failing to provide her with an answer he would accept. Why had Drayvex made it his business to keep her alive? Honestly, she had no idea. The part of her that had never fully been able to let him go all those months ago wanted to think that it was simply because he gave a damn. They had been through a lot, survived together. Was it so much to think that it actually meant something to him?

But of course, Drayvex had revealed more to her than he'd meant to the last time they'd spoken. She was the stone of obligation around his neck. That was almost worse than being enemies.

The impatient hiss that hit her ears ran straight through her, and she flinched at the sound. "My dear," Saydor growled, putting a claw against her pulsing throat. "If you don't talk willingly, then I will have to make you." She sucked a breath in through her teeth as he pushed the tip into her skin. "Are you useful to me, or are you not?"

"You are the opposite of useful."

Ruby felt the sharp sting as it pierced her. Go to Hell, she thought, glaring with defiance at the creature before her, doing her best to ignore the smothering fear suffocating her. She was going to die here, and they wouldn't even have to bury her.

Without warning, Saydor grabbed her by the hair. He pulled at the roots, snapping her head back, and her scream echoed and bounced off the walls of the bone chamber.

Ruby saw red. She'd never felt so powerless. But when she felt a cold finger slid over the scar on her neck, she froze. Would Saydor know who had made it, like the demon in the precinct? Would it change her situation, or would it expedite an already hopeless outcome?

She couldn't see his face, but she could almost hear the cogs turning in that skewed mind. Head tilted back at a painful angle, she breathed in ragged pants as he held her there, unmoving and silent. Ruby didn't know what history lay between Drayvex and Saydor. But it was clear to her from the little she'd seen that the hate ran deep on both sides.

Something sharp lanced down her throat in a swipe, narrowly missing the scar. She twitched against him, but he tugged her head back. A frustrated noise escaped her lips.

A warm oozing rose where he'd scratched her. Saydor's cold, serpent-like tongue ran up the length of the oozing trail at her throat, a cold, wet slug, and Ruby's stomach squeezed.

For one never-ending moment, the room was silent. Her breaths came and went, the only audible sound, until the chuckle that slid out of his mouth stopped them completely. Every muscle in her body locked in place.

"Well, well, well. I do believe we have a winner."

Ruby gasped in fleeting relief as Saydor let his hand fall from her hair and pulled himself back completely. Her relief was short-lived. What now?

Saydor licked his lips, making a show of doing so as he stared at her like a piece of meat. And as that wide, toothy grin grew to an obscene size, all she could do was stare back in alarm. "That sly devil wants to keep you all to himself. And I know just why."

Ruby squeezed her interlocked hands behind her back. Saydor knew something that she didn't. And she wanted to know, too.

Chapter 15

It's over. We tried.

The words pierced his consciousness like a poisonous barb out of nowhere. Drayvex bared his teeth, disgusted that such a thought had even entered his head. If they hadn't won, they had failed. And failing was not an option.

Drayvex hovered at the door to the Magus Nox, indecision plaguing him in a relentless pulse at the back of his mind. He hated how weak she made him. Despised these festering sensations inside him that would not be willed away. But it could not be denied that he had made a spectacular mess of damage control.

The Magus Nox was the only room to contain a private portal within the castle walls—*his* portal—and the well-set guard that patrolled the immediate area was frozen in place at the door, the very picture of subservient. But Drayvex could hear the heavy thud, thud of her gutless heart as he lingered in the corridor, wavering between the mindless killing that would take his mind off, well, everything, and the human that he was avoiding.

Drayvex trained a black gaze on the twitchy guard, a deep rumble of a growl rising from his chest out of frustration. His guards were not used to indecision, not from their Lord. He held her in a withering stare, watching the minute slips in her perfect composure, tasting the scent of her agitation as it filled the corridor. He could not afford to be weak.

The urge to rip her a new one hit him in a violent, biting impulse. He took it out on the door. As he lashed out, it burst open on its hinges, swinging inward in an arc and smashing into the wall. *Do your fucking job*, he blasted at her, venting at the terrified guard with his mental voice, before stalking into the room and slamming the door behind him.

The vast, stretching room hummed with dormant power under the thin layers of dust, cloaked in a darkness that was incomplete, as the globe bathed everything around it in its dormant glow from the centre of the room. Finding an alternate way into a temple of ancients that *didn't* give his mortal enemy a length of rope to hang him with would take too long. But there wasn't a scenario he could live with that involved partnering with that nature harpy. The only useful fae was a dead fae.

Drayvex slipped down the length of the room with deliberate slowness, moving past the row up on row of tomes on their shelves that stretched down and went up into the far ceiling. How much time did they realistically have? If he wasn't with Ruby, he couldn't protect her. If he wasn't on Vekrodus, maintaining his title and claim to power, he couldn't stop Saydor from making his move on the throne. He sneered, the storm inside him furious as he considered this impossible stalemate.

It should be obvious which one of these took precedence. He had warned her she would always come second to the throne, and she had accepted this as word. And yet. And yet.

There is another way, offered the dispassionate voice of his fractured mind. Use the girl as bait. Lure out the spineless cretin and then crush him.

Drayvex rebuked it. No.

I'm glad we can afford to be so picky.

He flicked his forked tongue out in a sharp snap, irritation flaring as he argued with himself. Yes because having Ruby there as a big fuck-off target while fighting Saydor had worked so well last time. Pay *attention*. He passed the globe and kept going, the portal at the far end of the room pulling him closer, a magnet to his restless energy. He couldn't protect her while protecting himself.

Chapter 15

When Drayvex reached the portal, he stared into its shuddering depths, the subtle licking of the darkness swirling in his mind, slowly consuming him. He really wasn't in the best frame of mind to be seeing her. But he was drowning in what he couldn't do. And putting off his Ruby problems had never worked in his favour.

Reaching out towards the fragile skin of the portal, he let her location fill his senses and pushed through into the void.

The city was unchanged in its commotion of corpses and automatons. Drayvex walked among them, humans and their routines, sleepwalking through their fleeting life. He could only guess at such oblivion.

As Ruby's flat came into view, he swung between letting himself in through the window and giving her the tedious illusion of choice. He doubted whether she would open the door to him. It didn't matter either way. Welcome or not, he wouldn't be leaving until they'd neutered the raging shitstorm hanging between them. Regardless, he chose the door.

Drayvex drummed his claws against his folded arm as he waited with patient impatience for Ruby to open the door. After what felt like an endless stretch of silence, he shook his head and burst into an impatient column of smoke.

As he slid under the door, it occurred to him that there was something missing from this picture: the subtle rhythm of her human heart. He reformed on the other side and stood in her empty flat. Screaming Hell, he was going to murder her himself.

To say he was distracted was the understatement of the century. Drayvex should have known that she would feel the need to run headlong into whatever dangers she could find in his absence. After all, they'd been doing this dance for some time now. His earlier outburst would have only fuelled that ridiculous, obstinate desire to do the opposite of anything he told her to do.

Hissing in frustration, Drayvex came apart in a violent flurry of dark coils. Twisting through the empty flat, he launched himself at the dodgy seal of the window and poured out into the sprawling city.

Ruby wasn't at the hospital. And as he drifted over the masses, he stewed.

Blistering temper aside, he had meant what he'd said to her. The girl had been the bane of his recent existence. She was the hydra that multiplied every time he'd tried to remove her from his life. Nothing about this punishing slogfest between them made sense.

Ruby wasn't at the coffee shop. In fact, she didn't seem to be at any of her usual haunts. By the time he'd circled back to the flat, the nagging dread he'd successfully smothered was taking root faster than he could kill it. Did she honestly think he would leverage her life in that cheap way? Fine, yes, he was a demon. No, his past choices had not done him any favours. But Drayvex had thought that at this point, it was painfully obvious how much he needed her to live. Was it so hard to read between the fucking lines?

Drayvex stood at ground level, taking in everything around him in a sprawling mental net. She was a needle in a haystack of haystacks, one glistening mind in an entire conscious sea. If she was still here, she wouldn't have the kind of time he'd need to sift through.

He switched tactics, moving towards the tracker sitting at the entrance to the building. As he approached it, it didn't react. Drayvex ripped it off the floor, pulling it in close by its folds of material.

You know it looks like a human, you crazy fuck?

Drayvex barely heard the detached voice of his saner self as he made a mental connection with the listless figure, taking the tracker's most recent observations into his own mind; a rush of motion and colour that imitated real memory.

Ruby had barely made it around the corner from the flat. The tracker had followed her to the edge of its pitiful limits and watched from afar as she had addressed *him* with cool disregard, clueless to what was really behind her. The boy who'd already injected himself into her life —the flaccid worm from the coffee shop who had been unworthy of her attention—was her undoing.

He pulled out in a sharp jerk, doing significant damage to the tracker that dangled in his grip. Seething, he made eye contact with the woman across from him who was frozen to the spot and felt his bloodlust rising in kind. Saydor had been cunning to use a human. A small, weak, unassuming

Chapter 15

creature.

"He has my family."

Drayvex felt a hot, pulsing anger surge through him, the sensation mingling with his wretched guilt in a destructive cocktail. Your family, he thought in a vicious stab.

Muttering a brief incantation, he let the fabric fall to the floor as the tracker inside its folds came undone and disappeared. The woman's terrified eyes never left his.

Don't worry. I'll give them your regards.

* * *

Ruby stared at the creature before her, unable to stop herself from uttering the words that she knew she would ultimately regret saying. "Tell me." She swallowed, straightening as she leant against the hard object at her back. "Tell me why."

Saydor's smile became soft and secretive as he fixed on her. His blood-red eyes were practically glowing with excitement. "Why, my dear. The answer is in your blood."

Ruby's mind slowed. "My-my blood?" That wasn't what she was expecting.

The demon was watching her every tiny movement. She shifted, the bonds at her wrists rubbing, and fought the urge to shrink away as his fangs extended. "It appears our mutual oppressor has not been forthcoming with you. No matter. I will tell you everything."

Cold coils of apprehension gripped her as he spoke, his words finding and hitting a chink in her wall. Drayvex was never forthcoming with her. What was hiding from her now?

Saydor began to slowly circle her, a cat toying with a lame bird, his footsteps crisp on the stone floor. She wished he would just get on with it. This slow, drawn-out routine was torturous. What was his game? What did he know that she didn't? Was he going to kill her, or just pull her apart and leave her screaming in the dark?

"The blood running through your veins is cursed with dark magic," he oozed, his voice bleeding from the space behind her. "I can taste the raw power running through you, and it is *exquisite*." As he moved into her peripheral left, she followed him with her eyes, frozen in place. "You are a human keg of untapped potential. A living weapon. Quite the asset, even for a demon of status. He was shrewd to put his mark on you."

The cheerful manner in which he spoke of her so-called curse was a jarring contrast to the panic and anger that swirled inside her. She wasn't a weapon. She was a person, not a thing.

"Of course, it's also slowly killing you."

The words rolled off his tongue as though he was confirming the weather. Ruby's world stopped turning. A numbness hit her in a full-body, knockout slug. It stole her breath. It wiped her mind.

Saydor stopped in front of her. He was no longer smiling. In fact, the monster before her was all business.

"Excuse you?" Ruby stared ahead into the bone cavern without seeing. She was dying?

"Yes, I'm afraid your meagre human lifespan has been significantly clipped. But you needn't suffer while you live."

Ruby's eyes flicked up to where Saydor gloated a few feet away, snapping into focus. She could barely feel the emotion that clouded them in a salty sheen. Her mind was oddly disconnected from her body. He was lying.

"He's using you. Abusing you as he furthers his own ambition. He will continue to do so." Saydor's manner changed, and his words became urgent and sharp. The lash of a whip.

He appeared in front of her in the blink of an eye, and she flinched as he leant in close. Saydor's words were so fast and basal, they were almost a growl. "I could keep you here against your will. Bleed you and break you, and wait for you to heal before starting all over again. Of course, I could."

Ruby closed her eyes, trying to stop herself from spiralling. She couldn't breathe. Liar. Drayvex had never once taken her blood.

That you know of, pulsed an errant thought.

That awful laugh reverberated in her brain as he sounded off next to her.

Chapter 15

"But where would be the fun in that?"

Ruby dug her nails into her palms, squeezing her hands into fists.

"Work for me."

Her eyes flew open. She stared at Saydor, at the demon in her face, wondering if he, or maybe she, had gone mad. "What did you just say?" she whispered.

The smile was back. That stomach-turning, nightmarish maw that made her want to be anywhere in the world but where she was now. "My dear, you must know that the World Destroyer can't give you anything that I can't match." He reached out and ran a cold, clawed finger down the side of her throat, dragging the tip over the scar. "Turn your back on Drayvex and work under me."

What was going on? Ruby could only stare at him in horror. Was she really being ... recruited?

"I will keep you safe from any—" He paused, and the wicked gleam in his crimson eyes was that of pure delight. *"Backlash."*

Ruby shivered at the word. Backlash. She could only imagine how Drayvex would react to such a betrayal. Would he let her stand with the enemy, or would his violent retaliation destroy them both?

"I will also make sure that all your human needs and desires are fulfilled for the remainder of your significantly shortened life." Saydor breathed inward in a slow stream, his eyes closed as he hovered close to the drying trail of blood down her neck.

Ruby's stomach swirled as fast as her head. If she said no to Saydor, she would be condemning herself to a world of pain. A never-ending cycle of fear and agony, all in the dark. She was supposedly dying, but it would not come soon enough. If she said yes ...

"I'm a reasonable fiend, Ruby."

Ruby's shaky breaths filled the cavern, the only audible sound as she stared at Saydor in desperation. If she said yes, he would surely use her against Drayvex. Turn her into a weapon, point her at him and make her do awful things that tore her apart. But she wasn't brave like Sandra. She *was* scared of pain. Of dying in a place the light never touched.

But Drayvex would be quicker, colder. Stronger. Maybe he would put her out of her misery.

A wet sort of sound pulled Ruby back to the monster before her. He was growing tendril-like tentacles, bursting out of him like aliens in a horror film. They were like Drayvex's, only lighter and dripping with a thick, green substance that smelt like the bowels of Hell. "I'll give you some time to come to your senses."

His growling voice filled the cavern of bones, and Ruby could swear that every single skull vibrated to his words. She screwed her eyes shut and thought of home. Her cosy little flat with the wonky oven. The bed that creaked as though she was getting busy whenever she moved.

"I will be seeing you *very* soon, my dear. Do not think you can run from me."

Ruby's eyes flew open as he launched himself at her, turning to a bright green smoke as he hurled himself at her face and smothered her.

She tried to scream and choked. Her grip on consciousness slipped, and she was dragged into the dark.

Chapter 16

Ruby came around shivering behind an alleyway dumpster. She felt like trash.

She winced as she moved her stiff neck, pulling her knees up to meet her chest, and hugged them against her. She sat like that for a moment on the hard concrete, listening to the city traffic; existing in a limbo-like place between curling up to die and deciding to live, just so she could die on her feet.

For a brief moment, she lost herself. The girl in her skin was almost a stranger. An empty shell of a person who looked whole but was hollow inside. This scared her more than anything. So it was with the last vestiges of her broken spirit that she pulled together what pieces of herself she could find and dragged herself to her feet.

She would not be rolling over today, it seemed.

The luxlor was gone. She registered that somewhere in her mind as she dragged herself through the lively city. It was but one of many complaints she had.

Ruby had caught sight of herself in the reflection of a shop window and shopped short. The scratch that ran down her neck looked worse than it felt. The blood had oozed out and smeared down in a line where her captor had dragged his fat tongue, running over her collarbone and soaking into the top of her shirt. It was drawing a few eyes. Her wrists were red raw where she had been bound, made worse by her struggling, and her entire body ached as though she had the flu. All she wanted to do was find somewhere safe to drop because if she didn't do that soon, she would drop where she stood.

It was because she was distracted by these things that she walked straight past her flat's entrance.

Ruby about-faced and stumbled through the double doors into the main reception. She'd barely made it a few steps in before they burst open behind her. She spun to face the doors, her heart bursting out of her chest.

Drayvex stood in the doorway, his dark eyes fixed on her. The doors clicked shut behind him.

She tried to catch her breath, staring back at the demon who made her chest ache in so many ways. His presence had once made her feel safe. In a manner, she was still glad that it was him. She had learnt the hard way that no one could be trusted. It may as well be the devil she knew.

He moved without warning, shooting forward in a blur. Ruby panicked as he appeared in front of her, stumbling backwards in a knee-jerk response. She knew her nerves were shot.

Drayvex's eyes paled, darkness skittering away. He froze on the spot, raising a hand in front of him in a casual truce. There was a measure of caution to his gaze and something she couldn't place. But she could also see the wild fury that seethed in their depths. He was radiating heat, his presence an oppressive, tangible force. "Okay," he murmured, clearly pacifying. He lowered his hand, his mouth pulling into a hard line. "Take it easy."

Ruby was tired, both physically and emotionally. She didn't think Drayvex would hurt her. But her mind was screaming 'demon'. She didn't know how to switch it off.

"Satan alive." He shook his head, his teeth pointing. "You really know how to drive a demon out of their fucking mind. You know that?"

Ruby baulked as he rebuked her. His words were hard, but his voice was soft. "I—" She paused as her thoughts stuttered, shivering in the empty reception room. Surely, if anyone was out of their mind, it was her.

As Drayvex looked back up towards her, she caught a glimpse of something raw, burning amid the tightly controlled tempest behind his gaze. He sighed, and slowly, moving as though she were a flighty bird, he slipped towards her. "I didn't think I'd get you back in one piece."

Ruby let him approach. And when he was right in front of her and giving her a not so casual once over with eyes that missed nothing, she felt herself slipping towards old feelings. Maybe it was the almost possessive lilt to his words, tugging at her in strange ways. Or the indignation curling on his lips as he hovered on the mess of her throat. But she wanted so badly to trust him.

"Quite the asset, even for a demon of status. He was shrewd to put his mark on you."

"But several pieces would have sufficed?" Ruby murmured, her head swimming.

"It was an accident. Don't overthink it."

She watched uncertainty flash across his face. "Well, last I checked, humans don't function well in pieces." His tone tried for light, but the careful way he spoke needled at her anxiety. He slid out of focus as her vision blurred.

She swayed on the spot, weightless and floating for a moment as she lost touch with her surroundings.

"Upstairs," Drayvex said in her ear. And she realised that he must have caught her because she was no longer cold.

To Ruby, it felt like she'd simply blinked. In reality, she knew she must have passed out because one moment she was swaying in reception, the next they were inside her flat.

Her head snapped up, jerking in panic as she took in her surroundings.

"Easy, Red. Nothing is going to get past me."

Ruby stilled at the sound of Drayvex's voice. She registered that she was sitting on the carpeted floor in the lounge, her back against the wall. She looked up, following his voice to where he stood before her, arms folded, and met his piercing gaze.

"Because I will turn them inside out and make them serve you on their hands and knees until their organs splutter and die."

Her heart stuttered against her will. She took him in a reflex that felt like breathing. There was something off about him, but it was his eyes that really stood out. They weren't darkness, nor were they light; they were both. It was as though night and day were warring for ground, and neither one could conquer the other.

She sucked in a breath, still caught in his gaze. "Promise?" The word tumbled out before she'd thought it through.

She saw the corner of his mouth twitch. "I'm not joking."

Ruby ran a hand through her tangled hair, feeling the last bit of fight she had drain out of her aching limbs. She got the feeling that he was waiting for something. She let her head droop to rest on her knees, registering for the first time that she was finally back home. "Neither am I," she mumbled.

She stayed like that for a handful of minutes, just listening to her breathing and trying to relax. It was so quiet. Peaceful, even. And she had almost forgotten that Drayvex was still there until a glass of water was placed on the floor beside her.

Ruby tensed, staring at the clear liquid from the corner of her eye. It was odd that *he* was also quiet.

Feeling steel inside her all of a sudden, she made up her mind and spoke into the room without looking up. "So apparently, I have a dark affliction. It's a blood curse." Her voice was eerily matter of fact, and she wondered if the demon could sense just how close to the edge she was. "It's supposedly killing me. But you already knew that. Right?"

Drayvex didn't immediately answer, and she fought the urge to look up and place him. The water sat, magnifying the fluff on the carpet.

"Is that what he told you?"

Irritation flared within her. Despite her resolution not to look up, she did. Drayvex was leaning against the sofa a few feet away, lurking like the ominous, out-off-place shadow every room had. "Can you just be straight with me?" she snapped. "For once?"

Chapter 16

She immediately regretted following through. But instead of hitting her with the usual passive-aggressive display of ego, he simply narrowed his eyes. "Drink," he commanded.

"Excuse you?"

"You heard me. Water. Now."

Ruby was speechless. She picked up the glass from the floor and cradled it to her stomach, eyeing him with fresh suspicion. "Did you know?" She squeezed the cool glass in her hand, her breathing ragged. "That my blood is a weapon that my body can't handle? That—"

"Yes, I knew."

She faltered as his smooth words hit home. Her heart sank. Of course, he knew.

Drayvex folded his arms and watched her with a measured look on his face. "When you bled all over the shadow lantern in my castle, I put two and two together." His voice was low and as matter of fact as hers, and the smooth confidence she heard there, even now, galled her. "Because if *I* didn't power it, then it could only have been you."

Right. "But you told me it needed blood." The pieces fell into place as she said it out loud. "Oh ..." She felt cheated.

He lingered at her throat, his eyes flickering. "Not blood. Power."

Ruby heaved herself to her feet, using the wall for support. "And you kept this from me because ..."

Drayvex tilted his head to one side as he watched her get to her feet, his eyes in flux, as though they were unable to make up their mind what colour they wanted to be.

"... It was easier to take what I wasn't aware I had?" She finished her sentence, knowing that her heart would break if he said 'yes'. It was stupid, really. But if Saydor was right, then Drayvex had never stopped using her.

As he looked at her from across the room, his expression darkened before he laughed. "Sure. I suppose I deserve that."

Little jolts skittered over her skin as his voice tweaked something deep inside her. He deserved so much more. And that wasn't denial.

Just then, Drayvex seemed to change without moving as he straightened faster than she could follow.

As he moved towards her, her mind and body span into a frenzy. Placing her free palm against the wall behind, she stared him down, her chest rising and falling. Just say it.

Drayvex stopped in front of her, oozing dark majesty from his very pores, and she couldn't stop herself from taking him in. How many times had she done so since he'd inserted himself into her life? Her senses never adjusted. And as he reached towards her and grabbed her by the chin, she was reminded of this once again.

Ruby flinched as he tilted her head up and commanded her full attention. His hot grip was loose enough that she could pull free. But instead, she simply stared into those stormy eyes.

"I don't want your blood." His words were slow and clear and laced with a patronising distaste that lingered in the air between them. "If I did, you wouldn't be in any state to be having this conversation. Trust me." He flashed her a humourless smile and a set of fangs that were nothing like Saydor's but equally monstrous.

She was barely breathing as he inched in closer, his face a mask of cool determination.

"What I want," Drayvex said, "is for you to drink some damn water."

Ruby's mind span. Her face burnt where he held her, but she wouldn't have looked away even if he wasn't. Where was the rage? The demon that flipped like a switch, that stopped at nothing to claim every ounce of power he could get his hands on? Surely there was more to it than that.

Drayvex was fixed in place as she tugged herself free and proceeded to down the entire glass like a petulant child. And it wasn't until she put the empty glass on the floor at their feet and shot him a glare that he spoke again. "That wasn't so hard, was it?"

She bit her lip, chewing on the skin as she tried to figure him out. Did she believe him? Could she really allow herself to think that she was walking around with dangerous magic in her blood, and the demon who had taken everything from her in his previous quest for power *didn't* want a piece?

"It doesn't make sense that he would let you go." Drayvex's eyes slipped down once again to the mess of her neck. She felt the darkness in her head flex. "He had his leverage. He even had a nice little bonus, all neatly wrapped in one convenient, human-sized package." His voice had taken on a dangerous edge, and Ruby felt herself tensing under his black gaze. "What does he want?"

"I know what he wants." She sucked in a deep breath and squared her shoulders. "Saydor wants me to join him. To turn on you and go willingly. But it's a trap because—"

"Mother of … " She didn't catch the entire stream of curses that tumbled out of Drayvex's mouth. But as he erupted like a volcano of profanity, she realised that the rage had not been gone at all. In fact, right now, it was more present in this room than ever.

* * *

Drayvex felt any precarious composure he'd managed to maintain up to this point shatter with violent force. Fingers of rage gripped him in a vice as Ruby's words rebounded in his mind. His skin squeezed as he struggled to contain the demon seething inside it. Of course, that putrid lump of demon filth didn't just want to stick the knife in. He wanted to twist it and jump on it for good measure.

He hadn't expected her to answer his ambiguous question. But it was clear to him now that Saydor was playing a very different game to him. "Well, someone's just dying to be noticed. Oh, that's *right*." Sarcasm bled into his words as he vented out loud. "That would be the spineless nobody playing keep-away. Probably bored as fuck at this point."

She would never choose Saydor. His fangs throbbed as they extended and filled his mouth. The notion was ridiculous at best. At worst, the sad-sack delusions of a low-born underdog.

"He's going to come back for my answer." Ruby's cool voice sliced through his unwitting descent. "He'll take me either way."

Drayvex let his gaze slide back to the girl before him. She looked like she'd been through Hell. But it was clear to him from the way she held herself, the way she was reacting to his presence, to things that used to barely phase her, that Saydor had got in her head.

He breathed out, making a conscious effort to regain what was left of his brittle composure. "No. He won't."

Ruby stepped back and leant her back against the wall. "How do you know?" she murmured. Doubt creased in the corners of her eyes.

Drayvex watched her for a long moment, wavering. They were running out of options, and Saydor had forced his hand. He needed her to come back to Vekrodus with him. His domain was the one place an ex-Demon Master would have to be utterly deranged to break into. The difference, of course, between her cooperation and resistance was abduction. Again.

He shifted his weight. Having to move consciously, being aware of his every twitch, was a drag. Almost painfully so. But he wanted her to see that he was not a threat to her, even if it was a comforting lie. "I'm taking you with me—"

" I'm releasing you."

Drayvex stared at her, into those big, green, crazy eyes, as she spoke over him. He raised his eyebrows at her, a flash of impatience causing him to bite down on his tongue. "Go on." It leaked into his voice regardless.

Ruby blinked up at him, her heart beating at twice the normal speed. "I don't want you to be tied to me through obligation. So, anything you feel like you owe me …" She stopped and sucked on her lip, worrying it with her teeth. "What I mean is, we're done. I'll take it from here."

Drayvex stood immobilised under her gaze, for the second time in his life, lost for words.

Well, I didn't think you could possibly screw this girl up any more than you already have, said the snide voice of his sanity. But bravo.

He breathed out in a slow stream, her words stoking his deep frustration. He was in Hell. A Hell that he didn't rule, made specifically for him and only him, that he could never, ever escape from. "Screw this."

Ruby flinched as Drayvex moved forward and placed a hand on the wall behind her. He leant in close, taking her full attention without fully trapping her in. She tensed at the sudden proximity, and something inside him coiled

Chapter 16

in response.

"Let me make something clear," he said, hearing the soft growl to his words. "I, and only I, get to decide when I'm done here. So take your head out from whatever warm, dark space it's residing in and *listen* to what I'm about to say. I'm only going to say it once."

Ruby's heart was working overtime. Her blood flowed just beneath her skin, colouring her face and neck in delicious ways. Her soft heat bathed him with just inches between them, his fangs aching to plunge into her soft flesh as the floodgates opened. But it was too late to throw on the brakes. All he could do was sound off at her and try not to eat her.

Drayvex leant over her, glaring down at her in a way that would have most demons curling in on themselves. "We." He gestured between them with a curl of a careful claw, brushing past her face. Her eyes were glued to his, wide and almost transfixed. "This."

Her mouth was distracting. The way she sucked on her lip was almost an invitation. Focus.

"This clusterfuck of an accord makes zero sense."

She opened her mouth, her face changing as though she was about to say something. Drayvex placed his free hand over her mouth, stifling whatever unruly garbage she was about to spout at him. And as she gave him a comical look somewhere between surprise and 'how dare you', he gave himself the green light. If he wasn't on such a roll, he would have laughed out loud.

"You know, it goes against everything I stand for." He felt his tail push past his guard, and he let it slide down unchecked. "But I didn't raise you from the damn dead because your blood is preternatural rocket fuel. I'm not leveraging your life, hanging over your head until you pay me back threefold. And if I had *obligations* to anything in this tedious existence, it wouldn't be you."

Ruby tensed beneath his tail as he brushed it past her leg

"I did it because I want you alive. I want you to waste your existence on your pointless human garbage, and I *despise* that you've made me say this out loud." Drayvex spoke every word with barely held restraint. It had been far too long since he'd killed something. He smiled without humour. "But you have to push, so here we are."

Neither of them moved for what felt like an endless moment, caught in a time loop. But it was Ruby who broke it first.

She lifted her hand and slowly, with a touch that was barely there, placed it on his arm. Little jolts of electricity jumped under his skin at her touch, and he felt himself tense in response.

Drayvex complied as he picked up on what Ruby wanted, letting his hand fall away from her mouth. If he could run at this point, then he would be pushing the sound barrier.

"Okay," she said, heat spreading across her cheeks.

He watched it fan, briefly mesmerised, before tensing. "Okay ... what?" Okay, I hear you now that my head is no longer buried up my arse? Okay, I'm going to drink until the demon in my flat goes forth and multiplies?

"Okay, I'll go." She took an audible breath. "With you."

Drayvex felt a portion of the tension he'd been holding slip away as she agreed to come quietly. "Wise move," he breathed into her ear, triggering a full-body shudder that she failed to stifle. He smirked.

The expression slipped as his thoughts took a different turn. He had thought not so long ago that working alongside one bitter enemy to kill another was the only option he couldn't live with. He was wrong.

Chapter 17

Ruby lay on her back, counting the individual ribs of the vast domed ceiling far above. They were black and gold, somewhat ornate. The shapes gave her eerie flashbacks to being trapped in a room full of bones. She squinted her dry eyes, trying to catch the detailing, and felt goosebumps slip down her arms. Surely to god, they were far too big to be real bones. Surely.

The room they had entered on the other side of the portal was enormous in length and height.

She heard Drayvex make a sound similar to the times she'd stubbed her toe on the bed frame, and she turned her head from the ceiling to find him.

He was standing in the centre of the room, poring over a large, swirling globe on a raised plinth. When she looked his way, his eyes slid in her direction, becoming a glare that accused her of a hundred different crimes without saying a word.

Ruby sat up straight, her muscles aching with the effort, and wrinkled her nose in indignation. "What is it?" she sighed. What could she have possibly done now?

Drayvex shook his head and turned back to the globe. "The smell of you is ridiculous. That's what. I'll never get it out of this room."

She stared at him, blinking in amazement. This had been *his* idea. "You—"

She folded her arms, suddenly furious, burning a hole in the side of his head. *He* was ridiculous. "My god, you're unbelievable."

He swept a clawed hand over the surface of the globe, and the coloured strands of inky liquid followed his touch. "*My Lord* will suffice. But by all means, don't let me hold you back."

"Bite me," she fumed before realising her mistake.

Drayvex stopped mid-swipe, his finger hovering over the now pulsing strands of liquid-like colour. The smile that formed at her words was unsettling. "You really should be careful what you say." His voice slid over her in strange ways, and she fought not to squirm. "A demon will take you at your word."

Ruby grimaced. He was a jerk, but he was right. She got to her feet, letting her eyes wander absently over the impressive walls of books around her. "If I'm dying anyway, does it really matter?"

The entire room was bathed in blinding red as the globe shone like a crimson beacon. She threw a hand over her eyes, shielding them as it pulsed once and threw the room into a dingy darkness.

"Don't do that." Drayvex's voice came from directly beside her in the dark. Her heart skipped a beat. He sounded unimpressed.

Ruby sucked in a breath. "Do what?"

"*You* don't get to give up. Not after what you've put me through."

The room flared back into light as the torches that lined the walls burst into flame all at once. She blinked at the sulky demon beside her and realised he was holding the luxlor in one hand. "I, um ..." Always so dramatic. "I was just deflecting."

Drayvex stared down at her with moody grey eyes. "Mhmm." He looked like he was ready to drag her to Hell and back.

She suppressed a shiver. One could argue that she was already there.

Ruby jumped as Drayvex dumped the cool luxlor into her empty palm and brushed past her. "You dropped this," he muttered.

It wasn't cold for long. Within seconds of being on her palm, it began to glow with heat. Springing into action, she tugged open her jacket and dropped the ball into her inside pocket. How did he find it?

Chapter 17

Ruby span to find Drayvex. "Where did you get this? I thought I'd lost it when I was …" She trailed off when she realised he wasn't there.

Drayvex was on the move, and he was leaving her behind. "Are you coming, or do you live here now?" sniped the voice that echoed down the long room.

She closed her eyes and took a deep breath. *Give me strength*, she thought. *One of us is going to kill the other before the day is out.*

The smooth, searing ball in her hand rolled from palm to palm, scorching her skin in invisible trails as she tilted them back and forth. Her brain hurt, and she wasn't sure whether that was down to the past hour's intense focus on a single object or Drayvex's relentless appetite for punishment.

Ruby stopped rolling the luxlor and held it still on her hand. The light glared with a fresh intensity, not spreading outward or escaping but sitting under her tight control. She breathed out in a puff and dropped it onto the wiry grass beneath her with a thunk. "Damn," she said, falling onto her back and looking up at the cloudy sky above. "I think it finally likes me."

They'd been to this particular area of land a few times now. She didn't know exactly where they were, but they were somewhere near the coast. It was chilly but not freezing, and there were scatterings of sheep that wanted to be as far away from them as possible.

She heard Drayvex scoff from somewhere nearby. "And that is why you'll never be any more than a lackey. If they like you, you're doing it wrong."

Ruby rolled her eyes at the sky, ignoring his snide comments. She could now pull the light in any direction she desired, mould it to her will and contain it within the glassy globe it came from—in small part because he had made her do it again and again until she thought about nothing else but ramming it down his throat.

It had become clear to her that Drayvex was withholding … well, a lot, she suspected. What she did know was that they were on fae watch—and that somehow, he knew Tira would be here soon.

The slight breeze that ruffled her hair was nice, and as she lay on the hard grass, her eyes getting heavier by the second, her thoughts drifted to her mother. Had she known that Ruby was cursed? No, Ruby didn't think so. They'd had a good relationship. She squeezed her hands together, feeling her nails bite into her skin. Overwhelm crept in, slipping over her in a smothering blanket. Even so, how do you tell your only daughter that she will not grow old?

Something sparked in her mind, triggered by this harrowing thought. The diary. The list of names and dates she'd found, relative after relative dying young. Was ... Ruby stopped breathing. Was her whole female line cursed?

The flex of darkness in her mind wasn't her own. She turned her head to one side, looking towards where she knew Drayvex was lurking by the stone wall. He was watching her. As she met his gaze, already fixed on her, her mind fell blank.

Ruby couldn't pinpoint when it had happened. But it was only now, as she stopped to take him in, that she realised she no longer saw the savage creature made of living darkness and malice. Drayvex was Drayvex.

He wasn't close by. But he almost looked like he was lost in thought himself. The picture of stillness, his hard edges didn't look so hard in this moment, and she had to remind herself that it was here on this very land that not so long ago, he had destroyed the lives of all locals living nearby for the sake of a lead on the stone. Ruby took a deep breath, filling her lungs with fresh coastal air as she marvelled at how one person could be such a contradiction.

"Ruby," he said, snatching her from her thoughts. "Saydor wants you on your knees." His rich voice was soothing, almost hypnotic. "You must know that."

Ruby had no idea how to answer that. "I don't know what I ..." She faltered. "I mean, I suppose."

"It's because you're a threat."

She blinked at Drayvex, looking for signs that he was telling some kind of cruel joke. He looked as though he was being serious. "Don't make me laugh," she muttered, looking back at the sky. Her, a threat to the big, bad Saydor? Hilarious.

Chapter 17

"He told you you're a weapon, didn't he?" It was a question, but the way he spoke, it was anything but.

Ruby's mind span as her imagination ran away with itself in the silence. If she was a weapon, then who, or what, would she be made to kill?

"Did he also tell you that you can wield yourself?"

Ruby stared up at the grey sky, no longer seeing what was up there. Now she was listening.

Drayvex's voice had a gained smugness. The kind of smug that knew it was right and revelled in it. "Of course he didn't. He wants to break you and take your power for himself. He wants you weak and scared and *pliable*."

Ruby sat up straight and turned towards Drayvex. What was he getting at? That she could, what, use her own cursed blood as a weapon?

He smiled at her then, a wicked smile that was somewhat secretive, and it took her breath away. Beautiful and monstrous. "Because, Red, there's nothing that pisses your enemies off more than when you turn your designated weakness into your strength."

"My strength ..." Ruby stared at Drayvex, utterly stunned. Drayvex had always had a ridiculous level of control over her. When he tore her down, she felt small and pathetic. But when he gave way to her, humoured her, empowered her in a way that only he could, it made her feel invincible.

There was literally nothing she could think of that Drayvex stood to gain from telling her this. Maybe he really did give a damn after all. He had all but said so.

She took a shaky breath, her heart squeezing in strange ways. "Will you show me how?" Her voice sounded small as she stared into his eyes. This rising sensation was like nothing she'd felt before. It terrified her to her core.

Wait. She could not have feelings for Drayvex. No, no, no.

He stared at her as she faltered, a narrowed, calculating gaze that picked her apart.

This was all wrong.

* * *

The way she was looking at him was all wrong. He had just equipped her with the raw materials for Ruby v.2—once again putting *her* needs before his own—and her look of dismay stopped him dead.

The words that had come out of her mouth were 'show me how'. But Drayvex wondered what was really going on in that crazy head of hers. Her eyes were suddenly begging for space, as if the almost ten feet between them was no longer enough.

"Is there any point if you're dying anyway?" he echoed, his voice flat. It was petty, taking shots at Ruby when his attempts to reach her fell short. He knew this. But rejection had never been his forte.

Her face changed in an instant. He had caught her off guard. She looked away, self-conscious as he weaponised her own words, and when she looked back, there was a measure of hurt in her gaze. "Did I do something wrong?"

Flaming Hell. He couldn't do right for doing wrong. He closed his eyes, a wry half-smile forming. "Forget it—"

A familiar earthy scent drifted towards him on a breeze, and in an instant, Drayvex switched gears. The faerie was here.

He pushed off the wall and straightened, his senses in overdrive. His physical form responded to the presence, setting him on a knife-edge, and he fought to keep his current skin in one piece. This would not end well. But it *would* end in their favour.

Ruby reacted to the sudden change, pushing herself to her feet. "What is it?" she asked, scooping the luxlor up from the grass.

The way she held it, containing the light within its spherical shape without even registering what she was doing, held him for the briefest of moments. She had taken to light magic like she was born for it. Would she be equally welcomed by the dark?

Drayvex dragged his focus back to the one thing that mattered. "She's here." He slipped towards Ruby, looking at the land behind her. "Are you coming or staying?" His tone was all business, but the turbulent part of him that he'd come to associate with Ruby was already having misgivings.

"Are you going to go all Lord of the Demons on me again?"

He stopped beside her as they drew level, glancing sideways at her. She was pouting at him, her defiance almost successfully masking the anxiety that lurked just beneath. Yes, that was a problem. It was clear that Ruby still had a rather sizeable bone to pick with him. He couldn't really blame her, but it needled all the same.

"If there's any sense left in that shrivelled hive of a temple mind," Drayvex intoned, trying to keep the irritation out of his voice, "then no." The ancient beings would not interfere with him again and live to tell the tale. If he had to spend the next century annihilating every piece of lingering consciousness of the god-like creatures that had screwed him twice, then he would.

Ruby frowned at him. She opened her mouth to respond and then changed her mind.

He clenched his jaw. *I can't read your damn mind, Red.*

"I don't know what that means, but I'm coming," she said eventually.

She was hiding something. Drayvex could see it in her eyes. He looked at the stretch of coarse green ahead of them, her blatant secrecy rubbing at him in a different way to the stench of fae in the air. "Fine," he growled. "You will stay close. You will stay where I can see you. Got it?"

If anything could keep him grounded at the temple, it would be her presence.

"Yes. Jeez."

Drayvex shot her a look, scowling at the oblivious creature beside him. Mercy, what was he saying? They were done for.

I think you should let me do the talking. That was what she'd said as they approached the unearthly fae stench that hung in a concentrated smog across from them.

Ruby was looking at him now with doubt written all over her face, as though *he* was the volatile variable and she was the rational head. The nerve of this small, weak creature was astounding.

"Don't think," he drawled, fixing on the three lone trees at the end of the far cliff. "You might hurt yourself."

She pressed on, undeterred. "You've almost killed her twice now—"

"I'd be very careful about my next words if I were you." *Three* times she had wriggled from his grasp. To say the reminder was unwelcome was an understatement. There was a special level of Vekrodus hospitality reserved for spineless curs like this.

Ruby paused, the soft threat in his words briefly stopping her in her tracks.

The trees were dead. Brittle and black. Burnt by magic?

"My point is," she said carefully, undeterred by his rancour, "that Tira is more likely to want to help me than you." She paused before adding, "Don't you think?"

Drayvex turned back towards Ruby, his fangs extending with a mind of their own as the magic-drenched atmosphere overwhelmed his senses. She fidgeted under his scrutiny as he narrowed his eyes at her in distaste, refusing to look away. How long had she been on a first-name basis with his pissing enemy again?

He ran his tongue along the tops of his teeth. He was reluctant to admit that Ruby was right. But if she was anything other than a constant thorn in his side, it was a wildcard. One that, if she was literally anyone else on this planet, he would be using to full advantage.

Drayvex turned to face her. Her green eyes searched him, stripping him back with a single look. Like flesh from bone. He flinched. He could almost feel her in his mind. "You want to lead?" He folded his arms, expectant, while she silently implored him. "Then be my guest. She's hiding in the trees."

Ruby blinked at him. "Really?" She narrowed her eyes in a curious way, as though looking for the hidden message in his words. "You'll let *me* take point? Willingly?"

He fought his answering smirk. "Make me repeat myself. See where it gets you."

She cursed him under her breath, living life on the edge, before smiling sweetly at him from behind her hair. "My Lord."

Drayvex bit down on the throb of his fangs as she ingratiated herself with saccharine scorn, a dual-pronged hunger making them slick. You know exactly what you're doing, you incorrigible witch, he mused with a carnal edge. One day soon, she would push back, and he would devour her whole.

Moving slowly, he leant into Ruby so that his mouth was close to her ear. "Next you'll be throwing yourself at my feet," he purred, flashing her teeth that glistened with venom. "You had me thinking you don't have a subservient bone in your body. Clearly, you've been holding out on me."

Drayvex had expected his words to trigger some sort of delicious reaction. But it was far more spectacular than he could have hoped for.

As a terrific blush burst across Ruby's cheeks, she bit her lip and tore her eyes away, turning towards the trees with a hasty twirl. "Keep dreaming," she threw at him before marching off towards the edge of the coast.

He smirked, letting it linger for a moment as she walked away. It slipped the further away she got until all that remained was the pliable stretch of nothing between success and failure.

If Ruby couldn't pin the bitch down, then he would pull her apart piece by piece and pump her full of darkness until she begged him for death. Then, and only then, would he offer her a way out. There would only be one.

Chapter 18

The three trees lined up at the end of the cliff looked out of place. Black and bare of leaves, they stood with eerie stillness as she approached. As a rogue breeze tugged at her hair, Ruby realised they were unaffected by the wind. They may as well be carved out of stone, she thought, eyeing them with trepidation.

Ruby felt goosebumps spread down her arms as a beautiful voice whispered through her mind. *Come.*

Just like that, she went cold. The heat that had lingered in her face, the fever as Drayvex had spoken in her ear with all the velvet charm of the serpent of Eden, drained out of her. She glanced behind her, back to where she had left him. Gone.

"A-are you there?" she addressed the fae woman, wrapping her arms around herself as she faced the trees. How could someone be *in* the trees? "I just want to talk."

The wind continued to whip around her, licking the tips of her ears and nose with an icy tongue. *Speak, my child.*

The lyrical voice echoed like a wind chime. It was the opposite to having Drayvex in her head—the dark, wilful presence that took up space in her mind and refused to be ignored. Instead, her voice was like a light summer breeze.

Chapter 18

Ruby slipped forward until she was within an arm's length of the middle tree. Up close, the bark almost looked charred. "We don't know each other. You certainly don't owe me anything. But ..." She took a deep breath and, with a pounding heart, plunged in. "I'm hoping that you'll help me all the same." She placed her hand on the trunk of the middle tree. She almost pulled away again in surprise. The bark was warm. "We both have a demon problem. Do you understand?"

A few seconds of loud silence rang out as she waited for some kind of response. But when the tree on the right began to glow, Ruby gasped and stumbled backwards.

Drayvex was right. Tira was *inside* the tree. Like squeezing out of a narrow doorway, the fae emerged from the glowing tree and stepped out onto the grass. The trunk fell back to black the moment she was no longer touching it.

Ruby's mouth fell open as she stared at the ethereal woman standing before her. She exuded radiance and power, and her skin had a lustre to it that almost made it appear to glow in itself. She was dressed from head to toe in golden armour, with long purple hair that fell as one braid over her shoulder to her stomach.

Tira stepped forward, and Ruby fought not to step back away from her. She was a different kind of intimidating to Drayvex. It was almost hard to look at her, ordinary as she felt in this moment. "What's your name, girl?"

Ruby fought to keep herself together. "It's Ruby."

She felt Tira's golden gaze pouring over her like a beam of light. "Ruby, I will help you. Have no fear."

Ruby's mind stuttered as she replayed those words. Wait, did she already know what they needed? "You will?"

Tira's gaze roamed the area around them before falling back on her. "The bigger they are, the harder they fall," she said, her voice almost reverberating as her tone gained a sinister undertone. "The World Destroyer is no exception."

The words tweaked in her stuck mind. World Destroyer? She had heard that before, when ... Oh, wait.

Ruby shook her head. "Uh, not that one," she said weakly, kicking herself. She should have seen that coming. "Another demon. Saydor."

The fae before her switched in an instant. "Your company with that deplorable creature is willing, or you don't want to be free of his—?"

"Saydor will use and discard me if I don't get into that temple and take what I need to fight back." Ruby angled away from Tira, who was leaning in towards her with a fierce look. Ruby herself couldn't explain her relationship with Drayvex. She wasn't about to try and explain it to a woman who had tried to kill him.

Comprehension seemed to dawn on the fae as her face became a beautiful, unreadable mask.

"Will you help me get in?" Ruby asked in a soft voice. Please comply, she begged. She struggled to maintain eye contact. "You also want in. Am I right?"

"You are working with the Demon Lord." It wasn't a question, and Ruby got a distinct sense of disappointment radiating from the ethereal being before her. "When you say *you*, you mean you and—"

"Correct."

The voice that materialised behind her was darkness made flesh. Ruby suppressed a shiver. She felt his heat at her back and looked at Tira, who was now glaring at the space behind her.

As Tira's hand shot to the weapon at her hip, Ruby felt an urgent need to intervene. "Wait—don't draw!" Ruby turned herself so that she was between the two fractious beings and raised her arms on either side. "Please."

To her left, a furious fae who was one provocation away from launching herself at Drayvex with full force. To her right, a demon radiating Demon Lord arrogance from his every pore, who looked as though he would rain Hellfire down upon them at a second's notice.

Ruby felt the precarious situation they were standing in teetering. "We all want in," she declared, commanding the attention of the two beings a thousand times stronger than her. She was so out of her depth. "We can't do it alone. Are you not capable of tolerating each other for one moment for the sake of . . ." She paused. She had no idea what a fae would want. "Uh,

Chapter 18

larger goals?"

The silence that rang out between them was deafening. She glanced at Drayvex, who was as still as the eerie trees. He was utterly fixed on Tira. Ruby looked to her left. "Also," she added, her voice breaking just a small amount, "I really don't want to die."

Tira's blazing golden eyes fell upon her. "No promises," she snarled, making the hairs on Ruby's arms stand on end. "But we can try."

She breathed out. That ... actually worked.

"Such altruism. Give the fae a godhood."

Ruby shot Drayvex an exasperated look. Jerk, she thought, shooting it at him as though she could propel the thought into his mind. Contain your personal garbage.

And when he glanced at her, the smallest of smirks cracking the stony set of his features, it shook her to the core.

The temple was both exactly how she remembered and far worse. Ruby stared at the monstrous patchwork building before her, feeling small and afraid. Was this what it felt like to stand at Hell's gates, a horrible eternity stretching out before you?

Drayvex was on edge. She could feel him splitting her mind, the darkness wild and restless. A coiled spring just waiting to snap. She risked a glance at him and realised he was watching her. She didn't like the look in his dark eyes. "Don't run," he said, his voice low and dead. "No matter what."

Ruby stopped breathing. He was being strange. "Why would I run?" Her voice was stolen by the wind, but she knew he would hear her all the same.

Drayvex paused before answering in the same lifeless tone. "This place brings out the worst in me. And you won't like what emerges."

She stared into his jet black gaze, fingers of fear creeping over her at his warning. Her mind stuck. Did he mean his full demon form or something more?

"Is there something wrong with your eyes, demon? The door."

Drayvex bristled as the fae woman provoked him from the base of the steps. His fangs inched down, their points sharpening, the lips that contained them curling into a sinister smile. "Give me an order again, *Shcręnta*, and I will cut out your tongue and make you choke on it."

Ruby didn't know what was more unnerving; the jarring extent to which his voice had changed or the fact that he was still looking at her as he threatened the fae. Venom dripped off his every word. But there was an unquestionable authority in the *way* that he spoke, and it reminded her of her first demon encounter. They'd been chasing her until he arrived, and then they'd thrown themselves at his feet in deference and called him My Lord.

Tira's face became savage, and for a moment, she looked as though she was about to bite back.

Panicking, Ruby summoned every ounce of conviction she had and cut between them. "Let's get this done, shall we?" she said in her best no-BS voice. "This place gives me the creeps." And with that, she started to make her way towards the doors. It was like babysitting the gods—terrifying and utterly ridiculous.

The doors at the top of the steps were enormous compared to the rest of the temple. A set of double towering stone slabs, they were carved with all kinds of morbidly intricate depictions. Shadows danced in the smallest of carved crevices and collected in the doorway corners, pulsing in a way that made her feel queasy. If the temple brought out the worst in Drayvex, would it also bring out the worst in their unwanted guest?

On either side of the temple, larger than the doors even, were winged beasts carved out of blood-red marble. They leered down in tandem, eyes fixed on her wherever she seemed to be. As Ruby stared up at one and let it consume her, ice water running through her veins, she once again felt that primal fear. *Run*, warned her mind. *You shouldn't be here.*

Drayvex stepped up beside her, taking a place on her left, and she dragged her eyes towards him instead. The entire surface of his eyes was endless black. "We get one shot at this," he said, his voice containing an eerie calm. He held out a hand in front of him and watched it with a slow, thoughtful musing.

The clawed fingers of his hand were black. But as he twitched them,

Chapter 18

strands of slick, oily darkness materialised in the air around them. They spread outward in sluggish clouds like ink dropped in water, tangling down his fingers and merging in the palm of his hand. Ruby watched with a sort of mesmerised horror as the darkness of his fingers spread down, a silent wave that turned the flesh of his hand, then his arm a gleaming black.

"We must unlock them at the same time." Tira stepped up on her right, eyes blazing, a miniature sun glowing in the palm of her hand.

Ruby turned back to Drayvex, her heart pounding. "Or what?" she asked, failing to hide her apprehension.

She felt his eyes slide towards her, the restless presence in her head stilling for the briefest of moments. "Or security kicks us into next week." He looked then, up towards one of the marble guardians.

Comprehension dawned as she followed his gaze. She didn't want to know what two monsters made of hellish marble were capable of. "No pressure," she panic-joked under her breath, "but I left my ID in my other jacket."

Ruby had gotten pretty good at reading the smallest of changes in the demon beside her. So when the shape of his mouth shifted, she knew that her cringe-worthy banter had not been wasted.

"This place is a pretentious snoozefest, anyway," Drayvex said, flexing the fingers that now cradled a swirling, knotted ball of chaotic darkness. As the energy around him changed, causing the hairs on her arms to stand on end, he fixed on the lock. "Open sesame."

The burst of light and darkness that followed was a shocking clash of brilliant contrast. A ball of darkness hit a door right in the centre and expanded briefly, swelling and then contracting, as though the stone was drinking it in. At almost the exact same moment came an eruption of blinding light against the other door, expanding out and then converging inward in the exact same pattern.

The silence and nothing that followed was excruciating. Ruby felt herself subconsciously edging forward. The tension was almost more than she could bear.

She felt something hot coil around her ankle and stilled. Stunned, she looked down. It was a long, black tail.

As she looked up at Drayvex, he shook his head in the smallest of reprimands. She looked back down. The sensation of such an appendage coiled around her tweaked her curiosity. There were small, horned protrusions scattered down its length, but the flesh looked soft. It was like a glistening black snake, and the more she stared, the more she saw the fine, scale-like patterns on the surface.

The resounding gunshot click that rang through the air was alarming after such a long period of silence, and Ruby's heart almost stopped completely.

"It is done." Tira's voice contained a soft reverence, and Ruby realised it was the first time she had ever sounded soft in any way. She looked up at the ethereal creature on her other side and felt the squeezing of muscle around her ankle as Tira slipped towards the temple doors. Drayvex eased up almost immediately, but Ruby was shocked at the power behind such a thing. She supposed it would almost be like a fifth limb.

"What's the hurry, pixie?" he asked, the dark edge to his voice making her anxious. "Hot date with a willow tree?"

Tira stopped before she reached the door. She looked at them both and blinked, as though she'd temporarily forgotten who she was with. She narrowed her eyes then, and Ruby could almost see her weighing up her options.

The hot pressure around her ankle withdrew completely.

Tira flexed, her hand hovering over the hilt of a gleaming sword at her hip. "Where are my manners?" she all but spat. "I forget I'm in the presence of vermin royalty."

The darkness in Ruby's head thrashed, violent and unconstrained. In an instant, she was plunged into a disorienting double vision as Drayvex took a step forward, ebony flames licking at fingers tipped with deadly curved blades. A pair of imposing horns had pushed through on the top of his head, and as she stared at him from behind, heart held fast in an icy grip, she knew that things were spiralling. The terrible hissing sound that came from the demon hit her with an almost physical force. "Allow me to remind you of your place."

Chapter 18

Tira whipped out a small silver sword and sneered, pulling it up and holding it poised towards him.

"Wait!" Ruby flailed. Not now. They might still need the fae to get the stone. Moving fast, Ruby stepped in front of Drayvex, facing him down. A jolt of fear lanced through her as she looked up at him, half expecting to see the demon inside. They were so close.

Drayvex looked right through her as she appealed to what was left of his reason. The look of pure loathing on his face almost stopped her in her tracks.

"This isn't over," she urged him, speaking low and fast. "We might still need her." And because the storm inside her lulled for an instant as she spoke, she put her fear behind her and reached out, curling her hand around his wrist.

Drayvex stiffened, turning to stone beneath her. She didn't know what Tira was doing at her back, and in that moment, she didn't care. Ruby knew it was reckless. But as his lightless flesh burnt under her touch and the ebony flames that danced over his fingers bathed her arm in heat, all she saw was him.

"You hear that?" Drayvex's fathomless gaze was still looking straight through her to the woman behind. "You owe Ruby your worthless hide." The flames at his fingers ebbed and died.

Ruby breathed out hard, suppressing the warning chills that his tone incited.

"I'd be on my knees right about now if I were you." And without another word, he strode towards the large double doors, leaving Ruby to collect what was left of her nerve.

She stared out at the expanse of brownish-green blades, the temple at her back. Tira had remained silent, and the heavy scraping of stone on stone that filled the air had a sort of finality to it that she couldn't quite place. She shivered in the cool breeze.

"Earth to Red."

As the impatient demon needled her from the doorway, she ran a hand through her tangled hair and span for the door. That, at least, sounded a lot more like the Drayvex she knew.

Tira stared at her from outside the entrance as she passed, her narrowed golden gaze searching, picking her apart. Ruby gazed back, trepidation squirming inside her. Of course, Tira wouldn't understand their relationship. No one did.

Ruby stopped next to Drayvex, who was standing just inside the doorway in the shadows between two worlds. He flashed her a heated look, the dark of his eyes briefly becoming a tangled storm of red and black. "Close means close," he reproached her. "Are you capable of that?"

She blinked at him, briefly lost for words, before finding her tongue. "My self-control is as good as yours," Ruby sniffed. And then, leaving the outside world behind her, she stepped past him and into the monstrous temple beyond.

Chapter 19

The temple of the ancients was a small city-sized trove of dark wonders, a distorted hall of one thousand rooms, stacked and squeezed into a dwelling the size of a large human house. There was some serious sorcery at play within these walls. Drayvex could feel the raw power oozing off every surface and congealing in the air around him. And his senses were screaming in agony.

He gave the cavernous rotunda a shrewd once-over, making a mental note of the ojeki demon stalking the back half of the room. What he needed was to shed what remained of this skin and bathe in the delicious concoction that assaulted him. But of course, he couldn't do that in Ruby's presence. And her presence was the only thing stopping him from ripping that pixie bitch limb from limb and making the fae extinct once and for all.

Ruby was a stable point of focus in a volatile snarl of total hedonistic abandon. The irony of this was almost too much.

Drayvex turned and looked behind him to where she stood, and breathed out in a hard stream. Her face was quite the picture of cautious wonder. What he wouldn't give to slip into her thoughts as she eyeballed the demonic-but-not-quite-demonic temple surrounding them.

As if sensing his gaze, her roaming eyes landed on him. He stared at her for a moment, contemplating, as the fae walked in behind her like she owned the place. She stared back, her eyes reflecting unspoken emotion.

Drayvex summoned her with a tilt of his head. The weight of his horns did little to ease the incessant noise in his skull. He wondered how she felt about them. "Change of plan," he murmured into her ear. His voice was beginning to reflect the strain of his internal struggle. If this bothered her, she didn't let it show. "You're on pixie watch."

Ruby's eyes grew wide. "Hang on," she said under her breath, inching back to look him in the eyes. "What?"

He gave her a stony-faced look. "I need to know what *it* wants. And I need to know how it plans to screw us over. Go interrogate it." If his suspicions were correct, there would be no room for error.

She blinked, staring at him as though he'd lost his mind before she sighed in a weary huff. "You know," she whispered, "not everyone is a selfish overlord who's only out for themselves."

Drayvex felt something inside him shift. Oh, you poor, sweet thing. He curled his demon hand around the top of her arm, being careful not to puncture her, and leant in, pulling rank. "Just do it." So fragile. So defiant.

Ruby glared at him, and if looks could kill, he'd be well on the way. "Fine. Get off me."

Drayvex pulled back, fighting a grimace as the ringing in his ears escalated to a piercing shrill. If anything could slip under the guard of an ill-tempered fae, it was her. Sweet, unassuming Ruby. The virus that would not be killed.

He saw Ruby wince and narrowed his eyes at her. "What is it?"

She pulled her palm from her head and looked up at him, blinking. "Headache. I'm fine." She blinked then, her eyes softening. "Are you … still with me?"

He slid his gaze back to where she stood, burning on all kinds of levels. It seemed like a wasted question, seeing as neither of them had moved. But Drayvex knew she was digging deeper. Seeing more than she should, as always.

For a moment, he hesitated, fleetingly vulnerable as she worked her ridiculous power. As if that wasn't enough in itself, he could have sworn he actually felt her brush against his mind. "Let's just get this shit over and done with," he said with as much snap as he could muster, shutting her out. He didn't know what was worse: the pot-stirring ancients that were poisoning his mind or Ruby's x-ray vision.

Drayvex had known from the moment he set foot in the temple that the power pieces in the room would be kept at the back with their guard. Regardless, he wanted to be thorough. And as he slipped in and out of various rooms on various levels and took stock of what treasures each had to behold, he rewarded his patience with some of the ancient ones' finest pieces. The glowing red dagger on the plinth before him just begged to be soaked in the blood of his skin-walking enemies.

Drayvex reached out and took it from its raised platform, placing a small vial of his blood in its place as payment, and tucked the dagger away. He was wise to the ancient ones' tricks, of course. Every item that he took would demand a piece of himself; one more string on the puppet masters' axle. But some things were worth an extra string or two.

Someone or something would go to town with his pure blood in a decade or so's time. Or maybe they wouldn't, since the only fae left in existence would soon be a nasty smear on the grass.

The whispers in his head intensified as thoughts of revenge consumed him; voices that were not his own. His form slipped in a temporary loss of control, and he focused on the voices drifting across from the other side of the vast hall.

"Is there something in particular you're looking for? Maybe I can help." Ruby.

"There is but one item in this cavern of trickery that I seek. It is the one thing that matters now. My bid for a better tomorrow."

Drayvex pulled himself back together and left the small room. He tasted his blood as his fangs competed for space and spat it on the floor in a black glob. The ojeki demon hissed at him from the back of the rotunda.

"What does it look like? Describe it to me." Ruby's persistent voice carried across the space.

"It is beautiful to behold. I will know when I see it. But tell me, girl. Would you really stand by as this creature gorges itself on the power within these walls, hoping that it will remember to save you? Is what you seek so important?"

As the pregnant silence expanded to bursting, he forced himself to unclench his jaw and stalked into the next room, cursing the poisonous fae in every tongue he could think of. So speaketh the prophet of Mother Nature, he sneered, his thoughts barbed. The spineless fae deserter; a creature who made a deal with her people's executioner for a *beautiful* item in this room.

"That's not what this is."

"You know what I think, girl? I think the demon has its claws in you deep."

Drayvex listened to the pixie running her disgusting mouth across the hall, only half-seeing the miniature light and dark lock on the gaseous creature on the plinth. He owed Ruby minutes of her life that she could never get back.

"It's Ruby. And you've made it clear what you think. But the only thing I need protection from is Saydor. That's why we're here."

Drayvex entered the next room, smirking at the poorly concealed frustration in her voice. It was a logical assumption to make, that this was a normal, healthy demon-human relationship, and that he was in control. But the idea that Ruby found this as irrationally irritating as he did tickled him.

"I believe you believe that, Ruby. But do you know why this demon is known as the World Destroyer? It's because he bought the title with blood. Genocide."

"Please, stop."

Drayvex felt the angry pressure of his fangs as they filled with venom. Predictable. Boring. Fucking yawn. Distracted, he stared at the fragment of stone floating above the small plinth and felt something click. Was that ... a stone of power?

"What are you looking for?" Pixie bitch.

"That's ... You know I can't tell you that." Ruby.

Not a complete stone, but a broken half. There for the taking.

Chapter 19

"Would you know if you found it?"

The Lapis Voluntatum. The stone of will.

"Well, no, but ..."

A pure, white, gleaming chunk, this stone hadn't been corrupted by a single mind. He shot a burst of dark magic at the lock on the stand and took the incomplete stone from the platform, replacing it with the knife. Jackpot indeed.

"As I thought. Tell me what you know."

Drayvex's split attention merged as the fae pushed back. Feeling a hot wave of destruction rise up and lick at his twisting mind, he fought not to crush the stone in his grip. His flesh was turning black, but that was no longer his main concern. *Oh no, you don't.*

As he appeared behind Ruby in a blink, her shoulders tensed. "Ruby knows very little, I'm afraid," Drayvex lamented in a low drawl. He smiled at the fae creature with plenty of fang, giving her a preview of her eventual cause of death. "Does a faerie really need her tongue to cast magic? I'll bet she doesn't even need her hands."

"You putrid—"

As the fae whipped out her pointy toy and swung it upwards, Drayvex was quicker. He punched out around Ruby with black tendrils, wrapping them around the fae's throat and arms, immobilising her.

Ruby span to face him."Drayvex, don't. I wasn't going to—"

"It doesn't matter. I know what it wants."

The struggling fae in his grip stopped. She glared at him, teeth bared. "Do t-tell, World Killer," she sneered through his squeezes. "Tell us wh-what a creature of th-the light wants."

He could feel Ruby's eyes on him. Practically feel the judgement radiating off her. She didn't see what he saw—the ugly, twisted hag behind the faerie façade—and the responding resentment this triggered was enough to make him want to rip the creature apart on the spot. Bathe them both in pixie blood.

"The Lapis Temporis is your *better tomorrow*," Drayvex said, his voice hard. "But I'm afraid it's already spoken for."

Tira's eyes widened, and Drayvex saw a flash of fear. "No, d-dem0n. I seek not—" She choked as he squeezed her tighter. "Not your sto-stone."

Filthy liar.

"Stop, you're going to kill her!"

"A glamour. I see-seek a glamour!"

Drayvex saw red as the temple voices joined the fray. "You'll have to do better than that," he snarled, lashing out at her captive form with more tendrils. He wrapped them around her chest and heard the satisfying crack of bones, then a cry that reverberated around them. "I'm not some second rate, two-bit demon you can lie to and discard. I will *break* you inside and 0ut."

"Just stop!" Ruby grabbed his arm and made a poor attempt to dig her nails into his hard black flesh. "What the Hell is wrong with you?"

He let a growl rise from his chest as he switched his attention to her and watched her flinch. "Stay out of this," he snapped, out of patience, time and precious sanity. "This doesn't concern you."

Her eyes widened as she took him in, and for a moment, he saw a flash of fear.

Somewhere deep inside, tangled within the snarl of hatred and predatory instinct, he knew there would be remorse. It was not something he could reach.

"Tell me what we need." She breathed in slowly, looking him dead in the eyes. "To find the stone."

There wasn't much of him left that cared. Drayvex was more demon at his point than anything. The whispering in his head was unholy screaming. But the pieces of him that remained gravitated towards her. He glared down at her, the speck that would not be told, and found himself indulging her. "We pacify the ojeki demon and make a deal for the stone."

Ruby nodded to herself, breathing in deep. "Right."

Once again, Drayvex knew he should have seen it coming. But as she ducked between his tendrils like a little ninja and headed with purpose towards the demon at the back of the room, he swiped out with one to grab her. He swore as he remembered that he couldn't touch her with them, narrowly missing her arm. "Not smart, Red," he snapped after her, feeling like he was being ripped apart as he fought to hold fast to the last remaining pieces of his human guise. "Don't be a fucking idiot."

The fae in his grip was changing colour. She was losing the fight. Her life was his to take, and it would be so easy to squeeze her until she burst. To screw the stone. Screw Saydor. The girl who was destroying his life piece by piece. To tear off his enemy's limbs and beat the fae with them until she was a stain on the temple floor. Exquisite, even.

Drayvex slammed the fae down into the floor head first. "Dammit, Red!" he shouted after her. "You think that bloated fool Saydor is your biggest problem? Think *again*." He was going to murder her. If he could get there first.

The moment he got within grabbing range of Ruby, he yanked her back by her jacket collar. The seven feet of ojeki demonic muscle before them jabbed out with long, clawed fingers, swiping the air where her throat had just been.

Stepping between Ruby and the pale, horned creature, Drayvex whipped out the gleaming object he'd selected to exchange for the Lapis Temporis and offered it to the enraged ojeki. "*Voss*," he said in a smooth voice, slipping into a familiar tongue. "*Skµervo.*"

The demon stiffened, falling still as Drayvex held the magic-soaked item out to it.

"Yes?" Drayvex's voice slipped into a low rumble. Trust me, you do not want to try me, beast.

Neither he nor it moved for a long moment as they squared up to each other. Then, finally, the ojeki reached out and plucked the offering from his hand. He heard Ruby breathe out behind him and flicked a forked tongue out in irritation. "Not a word from you," he said, addressing the human behind him.

Ruby huffed out and wisely kept her thoughts to herself.

The demon inspected the glistening object between two fingers and then slowly raised its arm and pointed behind it. A room in the far distance pulsed a deep red.

There you are, he thought, narrowing his eyes at the door.

* * *

The ojeki before them was quite something. Taller than either of them, it was a wall of white muscle, with hands and elongated snout splattered with ominous red. Its horns were like prongs that curved up and met in the middle, also tipped with red. She stared into its black, inhuman eyes as it pointed behind it. Something behind glowed red. Her stomach squirmed.

The sound of a scuffle behind her was enough to break the stare. Ruby turned towards the sound and felt fingers of ice grip her.

Drayvex was stalking towards the red room, dragging a semi-conscious Tira on the ground behind him by the nightmarish coils he controlled. Gruesome red marks ringed her neck where the coils had been before, leaving infected-looking welts.

Ruby opened her mouth, a protest hanging on her lips. Whatever she was, Tira didn't deserve to be treated this way. They'd only got this far because Ruby had convinced her to play nice.

"Whatever you're about to say," Drayvex said, cutting her dead, "do us both a favour and don't." There was a soft, growling undercurrent to his words that made her pause.

With effort, she pushed it down, fighting not to wince as the piece of him inside her thrashed in her mind like a caged animal. Drayvex was losing it. She studied him, an anxious gnawing picking away at her. It was impossible to ignore that it was now spot the pieces of him that still looked human, and not the other way around. Her eyes kept finding those horns, protruding from his skull like some kind of unholy crown. They needed to get out of this place before he destroyed them all.

Smothering her guilt and trying not to look at the beautiful, savage woman struggling meekly on the floor, she went to catch up.

The red glow faded the moment they entered the room. And that was the moment all Hell broke loose.

Ruby stared at the platform. A wordless horror grew inside her, and she

Chapter 19

felt that sliver of hope she'd clung to all this time shatter. There was nothing there. She struggled to breathe.

She heard a crash that pummelled her eardrums, and still, she continued to stare. Someone had beaten them to it. They'd lost. Saydor couldn't be defeated.

It was the resounding scream that finally ripped her away. She spun towards the awful sound, to where Tira slid down the wall. She was gripping her chest, cracks spidering out through the stone around her. "I told y-you, demon. I didn't t-take your stone—"

"Stop talking."

Ruby felt a tingle of warning as he spoke. His soft, subdued tone was a terrifying contrast to the raging darkness pounding her skull. "Wait," she whispered.

A burst of red shot across the room in a violent spurt. Tira screamed, choking. Forward on all fours. Her blood sprayed the floor between them. Her tongue lay on the floor at Ruby's feet.

Ruby gagged. Her vision tunnelled. Blood everywhere.

Drayvex stepped forward. "You may have her fooled, but I see what you really are. And it's pathetic."

Ruby looked up from his feet to the vicious, scythe-like claws that twitched at his sides and put two and two together. He was going to execute her.

"No, wait!" she cried. She wasn't thinking. She was pure instinct as she stumbled towards the bloody fae, slipping on the wet floor. As the beautiful devil she no longer recognised moved faster than she could follow, Ruby threw herself in front of Tira and hoped he would stop for her.

For a horrible second, as Drayvex drove his claws towards her stomach, Ruby thought he would go through her. And as they collided and her brain scrambled, Ruby drifted on her own frequency.

Death by Drayvex. At least it was quick.

Chapter 20

Ruby's triple vision slid back together in a blink, like the lens of a focusing camera. It took her brain a little longer to catch up.

The pale demon lay on the floor in an expanding black pool just beyond the doorway to the room, as though it had approached them and then paid the price. The flapping 'o' of its neck was brutal and surreal. She shifted against the wall of the splattered room, confusion clouding her mind, and winced as her body protested. Wow, she felt like she'd been hit by a bus. Again.

"I hope that hurt," said a scathing voice to her right. "Hell knows, you deserve far worse."

Ruby froze. She spun off the wall to face Drayvex, eyes wide as it all came flooding back. She'd tried to protect Tira. By some miracle, she hadn't ended up as a kabab. But by damn was he solid. She took a breath, her stomach squeezing in anticipation of his next answer. "Did she get away?"

Drayvex moved faster than she could follow. One second he was lurking in her peripheral like some ominous black cloud, the next he was right in front of her. His eyes were no longer black but blood red. "What the Hell do you think? Yes, she got away. Why would you do something so fucking stupid?"

His tone was the bite of a whiplash. "*Why?*" she bit back. "Are you out of your mind? I'm not going to stand there and—"

"I almost killed you."

"Well, that's nothing new, is it?" Ruby spat, embracing a newfound pettiness. She could feel the heat radiating off the demon in waves. With the horns and tail, Drayvex had never looked more like a demon in his human form. It made arguing with him even more reckless, knowing how close to the edge he was. If he went full demon again, she would be in trouble. But all she wanted was to find something pointy and jab him with it.

Drayvex bared his teeth in a look of utter disgust, and her gaze was drawn to them in that acute, primal way only pure instinct could command. When he laughed, it was a sound she was certain was to make her feel a fraction of her true height. He smiled, a slow, unfriendly gesture. "I hope that thieving pixie was worth sacrificing your life for. There is no plan C."

Ruby felt a surge of annoyance flare up inside her. He was so certain that Tira had taken it. She'd been practically catatonic when they'd entered the room. She looked down at the blood-splattered floor. "You know what I think?" she said, dragging a hand through her hair. She paused, her gaze sticking on the rogue tongue lying across from them. "I think you're hate-blind. Do you actually give a damn whether this is Tira's fault, or do you just want an excuse to add her name to your long list of victims?"

"Say that name," Drayvex said, his voice low and dangerous, "one more time."

Ruby stared at him. She chewed on her lip, more furious than she ever remembered being. "Who, Tira?"

In an instant, Drayvex unravelled. He devolved in an angry swarm, ripping himself into smoky black ribbons that tangled and collected in mid-air before her. Ruby barely had time to suck in a breath before he launched himself at her, a cloud of pulsing, living darkness heading straight for her face.

As he connected, everything around her went black. A rushing sound filled her ears, and she felt herself stumble backwards and meet the wall.

Suddenly, her head was filled with images, sounds, places she'd never been. They flashed before her eyes with vivid clarity. Gruesome, visceral.

Bloody. It was a war that she had never witnessed. Enemies that were not hers. All clashing under a blood-red sky.

I told you once before, thundered Drayvex's voice inside her head, *and now I'm telling you again. These are the backward savages that chose war over truce.*

Ruby tensed against the wall as demon and fae killed each other around her on a grand scale. A distant memory of her own tweaked at her. He'd mentioned this before.

They are the same light-born stiffs that were woefully inadequate. If they are victims in any way, it is of their own boundless stupidity.

She saw Tira's face then, beautiful and fierce, as he pelted Ruby in a relentless psychic attack. He'd slaughtered them all. All but the one who chose to live. And she had haunted him ever since.

So the next time you feel like siding with my mortal enemies, he said, scathing, his voice reverberating inside her skull, *the next time you have an opinion about my rule, let me know in advance so I can brain you with it.*

Stunned, Ruby watched the figures around her begin to dissolve and turn to black smoke. He's out of his mind, she thought, her nails digging into the grooves she could feel in the wall behind her. Her breaths dragged as her thoughts raced to catch up.

"No," he said out loud. "I'm the only one who's not."

As Drayvex's face swam back into view, and with it the rest of the temple room, Ruby stared at him in utter disbelief. He could read her mind now? Were there any boundaries left between them that he *hadn't* eviscerated? Her hand slipped down into her pocket.

He was watching her with that same cold, calculating look. Crimson eyes narrowed as they dissected her with as much finesse as a butcher. "What, no witty comeback? No smart-ass comments? I'm speechless."

Ruby felt her anger at the demon seep into every part of her as he bated her, as he flicked his forked tongue out into her face and grazed her cheek. He thought he'd won. He was in for one Hell of an awakening.

Drayvex pulled away, stepping back to stand before her with an effortless superiority that fuelled the fire inside her. Only he could make doing nothing look like a power move. Her hand curled around the luxlor in her

Chapter 20

pocket, and she felt it sear against her palm.

With a curl of his lip, he turned away from her. She could almost hear his scathing voice in her head. *It's no fun when the food doesn't play back.*

Ruby pulled the glowing sphere out of her pocket and lifted it before her, fire burning in her veins. You can eat this, she thought, reacting on seething impulse.

The beam of light that shot past his shoulder hit the wall beyond and exploded. Shards of smooth stone flew out in a cloud with an echoing crack that lingered as the pieces fell.

Drayvex didn't even flinch. But as he turned back towards her with hostile slowness, the dust settling around him and coating the floor, the fire in her veins turned to ice.

Ruby had a second of clarity, of instant regret, before he shot towards her in a blur, coming to a jarring stop right in front of her. As he leant in, she froze to the spot. Heart hammering, her eyes rolled up to find his. She knew this was a mistake the moment their eyes connected. She was looking into a swirling vortex of darkness and crimson streaks, and now she couldn't look away. The air between them crackled, heating where they almost touched, where he claimed all the space. She held his fierce gaze, fixed in place out of deep fear and a stubbornness that would one day get her killed. He stood equally motionless, glaring back until she couldn't stand it anymore.

"Was that meant for me?" Drayvex uttered, his low voice carrying a smooth menace that sent skitters of fear and thrill shooting through her.

She should diffuse the situation. Pacify the ungodly creature before her. Swallow her pride and kiss the devil's feet. Maybe he wouldn't completely destroy her. But that fire inside her was connected to her tongue. And it would not bow to him. "I was aiming for your head," she said.

Something flashed in his gaze, and her insides twisted in response. It wasn't the wrath she'd expected.

Ruby was unprepared for such a look. The shock that coursed through her subsided as her body instinctively responded. Angry and confused, and more than a little aroused, she looked at his mouth, sucking at her lip through her teeth.

One second they were toe to toe, the next their two bodies were pressed together in a simultaneous movement that left her wondering which of them had moved first. There was no doubt, however, as to which of them was stronger. Ruby's back hit the wall again, and her hand flew out for balance.

She could see it mirrored in Drayvex's eyes. The carnal hunger, the lust. His conflicted desire for her coursing through him. There was something powerful and wrong between them, and she knew without a doubt it would chip away at her humanity; that it was something that would consume her until there was nothing left but raw, animal need and selfish impulse.

Ruby wanted the beautiful monster before her. Except Drayvex was no ordinary fling. He was the king of the demons, and he was going to destroy her from the inside out. Ruby was going to go to Hell for this, and she didn't even care.

With Drayvex pressed up against her, the temperature soared. Her thin top clung to her chest as he bathed her in his fierce heat, pinning her in a satisfying way. His mouth crushed against hers, his lips searing velvet. He wasted no time, slipping his tongue inside her with quiet insistence, and she let him dominate her.

He tasted of sweet sin. Ruby felt her walls crumbling, and not for the first time, something clicked into place inside her mind. That same static calm, as the piece of him inside her aligned with its whole.

One kiss, and she wanted more. His hair looked just as soft as his lips. She lifted a hand in slow motion as their tongues danced, his fever making her brave. The urge to run her fingers through that midnight tangle was too much. Ruby slid her fingers through those sleek strands, enjoying the way it felt against her fingertips. As they met something hard and ridged, she tensed. Horns.

Drayvex paused against her as she brushed past them. He shuddered as though they were sensitive to her touch, a soft growl rumbling in his chest. The sensation of power she felt in that moment almost knocked her off her feet.

Almost in direct response, she felt something hot wrap around her calf,

Chapter 20

his tail snaking up and around her thigh in a binding grip. And just like that, her power was gone. She was the prey once again.

Ruby dragged in precious breaths as they came up for air, staring into each other's eyes. The darkness had been reduced to wisps in Drayvex's gaze. The dominant colour was that blue-purple explosion she rarely saw, and she couldn't help but wonder what it meant. But she had no trouble whatsoever translating the wicked gleam in those eyes. She was done for.

Before she knew it, their lips were locked again. The temperature inside the small temple room was off the charts, and her pulse was frantic. Utterly at the mercy of the demon she embraced, the feeling that came with it was pure, nerve-shredding exhilaration. He was going to destroy her.

Something sharp pricked her tongue, and her mind stuttered. It took her a moment to remember that Drayvex had fangs.

Drayvex seemed to taste her blood at the same time she did, tensing against her. Then his tongue ran down the length of hers, and he made a soft sound of satisfaction against her lips. "Fuck," he murmured, his voice tinged with regret. "You taste divine."

Ruby felt shock course through her as he tasted her like a good merlot. She'd known that Drayvex's diet primarily consisted of living, breathing humans for a long time now. But Ruby had got very good at ignoring his extreme diet, his murderous tendencies, the things that made him a terrible person. Because if only by association alone, it made her just as terrible.

But now that she could see it again, she couldn't switch it off. Couldn't stop herself from wondering how many people had suffered at his hands, just in the past month alone. How many people had met their painful end because of this beautiful mouth?

Ruby put her hand on his burning chest, her anxiety beginning to spiral. Drayvex was an unapologetic killer. He was the forbidden high that, for every hit she took, cost a piece of her soul. It was too much.

Drayvex didn't respond when she pushed on his chest. But as she gently pulled her mouth back from his, he relinquished his hold.

Ruby sucked in a breath and looked up at the demon she was still entangled with. If they got much closer, they would be merged as one person. Lord, give me the strength to resist him, she prayed. "I can't do this," she said softly, insides twisting as she held his reckless gaze.

The heat never left his eyes as he looked down on her with all the wild calm of a growing storm. "Ruby," he chided, his voice light and teasing. "I'm not going to eat you."

Ruby almost regretted her decision as he placated her. There was an easy kind of patience to his tone that she'd never heard there before. "I…" She hesitated, lost in eyes of endless depth. "I need to get some air."

For a long moment, neither of them moved. Creeping fingers of anxiety slipped across her mind as the seconds passed and they both burnt. Then, after what felt like an eternity, without speaking a word, Drayvex retracted himself completely.

The moment she had the space, she slipped out from between him and the wall and started for the temple doors, leaping over the oozing mound that blocked the doorway in one graceless jump. This was the right thing. It was the right thing, and she would keep telling herself that until she believed it.

Chapter 21

The idle figure sprawled on the grass a stretch from the temple stirred as he approached. Ruby turned her gaze from the faint glow of the approaching night, listening to the sound of his loud and deliberate footfalls as he made his way towards her and stopped beside her. She didn't fully turn her head, instead seeming satisfied by the glance she'd stolen of his boots, before looking back up at the star-strewn dusk.

Drayvex exhaled, his frustration spewing out into the comparative cold as a jet of tangled vapour. He glared at her in the false darkness, struggling to hold onto the poisonous rancour that usually kept him warm. The effort it took to stay mad at her was exhausting. He gave it his all anyway.

Without speaking a word, he joined Ruby on the ground and fixed on Earth's sky. Now that he was far enough away from the temple that he could think without wanting to claw his own eyes out, he could be objective. The missing Lapis Temporis had nothing to do with Ruby's dodgy decisions. For one, both light and dark locks on the plinth had been broken when they arrived. But the fact that its tree-hugging thief was now beyond his reach? That he had been robbed of his final chance to end a feud that had plagued him for centuries? That was *all* on her.

Drayvex ran his tongue along the tops of his agitated fangs as his senses reeled. They were all drawn to the girl beside him. Her soft heat, her mouthwatering scent. The way the space between them crackled with unknown energy. The thump-thump of the one thing keeping her alive.

His mouth pulled into a wry smile. No, not the *only* thing. He wondered if that was why his thoughts seemed to curl around her in obsessive patterns—because he was never truly free from her presence. There was always a part of him drowning in her light.

You wish it was that simple, drawled the disconnected voice of his fractured mind.

"Not knowing what I want is part of being human." Ruby's voice sliced through his thoughts. He turned his head, eyeing her with fresh suspicion as she took a whack at the heavy silence between them. The way her mouth pulled into a half-smile as she spoke was almost apologetic.

Drayvex wanted to laugh. The irony was painful. He was crossing so many lines of late, they were starting to blur together. He turned back to the sky, dismissing her dismal attempt to salvage some safe middle ground. Good luck navigating that smoking crater, he thought with dry humour. They had well and truly nuked it to Hell.

"Being human is all I have left. Does that make sense?"

Her voice wavered as she spoke, and he heard her shiver in what he assumed was the night chill. He never felt it. But the vicious stab of satisfaction he took from her misery would have been enough to keep him warm by itself.

"Will you please say something?"

The frustration that tinged her words was oddly amusing. He smirked and then glowered, annoyed that she'd bated him out of his own gloom. "Idle chat's not really my thing," he said, dismissive. "But no. You've never made any sense."

Ruby sighed next to him. "Fine." She paused, holding her breath as the cogs in her mind turned at high speed. "Have it your way."

Drayvex glared at the anaemic Earth stars. Yes, it was his way, every time without question. Without fail, or something paid with its life. Until *she* came along and screwed him over in her sleep. The girl who tasted of power and darkness, but in every other way, was light. A taste that was now burnt

Chapter 21

onto his tongue. He added it to the growing list of things that were slowly driving him insane.

"So I have some thoughts."

Mercy. He closed his eyes, ignoring the dual hunger the memory of her taste triggered within him. Was she usually this relentless, or had they swapped roles? "You don't say," he murmured, pulling out the chunk of will stone and turning it over in his hand.

"I know things didn't go our way today. But there is still something left within our control."

Drayvex could hear the apprehension in her voice, the way it suddenly changed. He could feel her anxiety in an unnerving echo, and he tensed, his own spiking in response.

He heard Ruby shift on the grass before sitting up straight. He kept his gaze fixed dead ahead, barely seeing the stars littering his vision. "I want to make a deal with Saydor."

Drayvex almost crushed the broken piece of stone in his hand as she spoke words he never thought he would hear.

"If I go willingly, on my own terms, I can report back and infiltrate—"

"No." He heard the hard edge to his tone and knew it expressed a mere fraction of the aversion and utter revulsion that surged through him in a knee-jerk response.

Ruby paused, her heart picking up speed. He could feel her gaze like a physical weight. "You know he's going to get me either way, right?" Her own voice grew hard, matching his. "We can use—"

"Absolutely not." Drayvex sat up straight and turned with barely held restraint to give her an incredulous look. He dug his claws into the soft earth, fighting to subdue a turbulence inside him that had nothing to do with the temple. "Did you bang your head when we collided?" He curled his lip and fixed on her, unsure as to how well her vision worked in this half-light. "You're not even trying anymore."

She turned towards him in the growing night, fully spinning her body to face him. "Is that your opinion?" Her voice was soft and laced with something he didn't like. It almost sounded like determination. "If so, maybe you should keep it to yourself before I decide to brain you with it."

Drayvex suppressed an uncomfortable stab as she reminded him of his earlier fit of temper. He'd let her get under his skin, and that had been a mistake. One that had led to … other mistakes. "In my defence," he muttered, "you're really annoying."

He couldn't deny that kissing Ruby had been the biggest one of all. Making out with your prey was acceptable foreplay. Ordering food just to watch it swim in its juices was plain weird. Still, it was not a mistake he had learnt from. And Drayvex knew he would probably do it again.

"That's not a defence." As Ruby got to her feet, he knew she meant business and that he would have to change her mind—or tie her down—to keep her from doing something stupid.

Drayvex rose in one swift motion, consumed by a sudden driving need to pacify the girl. Yes, he was pissed off with her; with her hot and cold bullshit. With her ridiculous expectations of his self-control. But it would be a cold day on Vekrodus before he lost her to that swine. Over his dead, rotting corpse. And he was about as far from the afterlife as one could get.

Drayvex slipped towards her and stood before her, a restless energy making his claws curve out and down in the pseudo darkness. The way Ruby was *almost* looking at him told him her vision was limited.

Sending power to his fingers, he conjured a small flame, creating the closest thing to light a demon could muster. Her eyes fell to the flickering flame, and he watched it dance in the reflection of her gaze as he considered and dismissed angle after devious angle. He could come down on her as hard as Hades, and still, she would find a way to slip his guard.

Stay, he thought as he watched her, the simplicity of such a request stilling his frenetic thoughts for a brief moment. Drayvex dismissed it almost immediately. He was losing his edge along with his damn mind.

Settling on tenuous middle ground, he flashed her a fanged smile. "I suppose I *could* have handled some things better," Drayvex conceded, the words sliding off his tongue with new purpose. "As tempting as it is to cave your skull in with your own unwanted opinions."

Ruby blinked at him, staring for a moment, before narrowing her eyes the

Chapter 21

smallest amount. "That was ... almost an apology." She crossed her arms over her chest, huddling in the night air. "Okay, what do you want?"

Drayvex tilted his head to one side, watching her with a steady gaze. "I want you to stop being a martyr and let me deal with this steaming wreckage."

She stared at him, her face unreadable. "So now you want to chat?"

He narrowed his own gaze, calculating, a small smile pulling at his mouth. *Keep running that smart mouth, Ruby Red,* he thought. *See where it gets you.*

Ruby blinked, her expression changing. Surprise flickered across her features.

Drayvex's smile grew. Yes, it was as he thought. They had their own private frequency. "I have a plan," he said.

She shivered as he spoke, the timing divine. "I thought you said there was no plan C."

His smile dropped, mood plummeting. There was always a plan C. He had just never intended to use it.

Drayvex watched her, forgetting for a moment that he was annoyed with her or that she was single-handedly destroying his hard-earned reputation, lost in the flames that flickered in her gaze. What would he do to keep her out of Saydor's hands?

The answer was resounding. It no longer surprised him.

She must have seen something in his eyes or maybe felt the echo of a cold, dark mood spreading like a black hole. Ruby shifted, chewing on her lip, her eyes softening. "Listen, about earlier. I don't want—"

Drayvex carefully placed a clawed finger over her lips. "Save it," he said, cutting her off. "What's one smoking crater when everything around you is burning?"

Her face pulled into a frown. He watched her, already several steps ahead as he solidified the new plan. He didn't need to hear her say it. He was the double-edged sword that she would never fall on. The devilish impulse she would never act on. The familiar enemy who would devour her in every way.

Ruby was the mistake that he would keep making. Pleasure and pain, intricately woven into one torturous fabric. And it was clear to him now that only one of them had the balls to embrace both sides.

The three burnt trees at the edge of the cliff thrummed with foreign magic, power beyond his grasp. He felt it push back as he tested it with his own, its angry and unrelenting resistance. It was just as before.

Drayvex let his arm drop, cutting off the flow of power all at once. Knock knock, he mused, confronting the ugly ultimatum. It's time to make yourself useful.

Placing his hand on the scorched bark of the middle tree, he addressed the fae within. "How many pixies does it take to light a torch?" he mused, speaking in a slow drawl.

Drayvex shook his head, a humourless smile on his face as he goaded her. What he was about to do may be beyond all sanity and reason, but he needed the nature stiff to comply. Business.

He tried again, stemming the poison that oozed from ancient wounds in his enemy's presence. "I know you're listening. I want to have a little chat." He kept his voice hard and civil, drawing on centuries' worth of Demon Lord duplicity. Of buttering up rivals and playing the long game. "No humans, just you and me. It'll be nice and cosy."

A non-existent wind disturbed the trees, rattling their dead branches, and as they clacked together like finger bones, stripped bare by the disease it housed, he knew she was indeed listening to every word he said.

Drayvex let a small smile play on his lips. "What are you so afraid of, faerie? That I'll persuade you to step out, only to slit your throat?" He laughed, a harsh sound that carried in the night. "You forget who you're dealing with. Such pathetic actions are reserved for the mindless lackeys who crawl at my feet."

He grazed a claw over the blackened bark of the tree, his mind in several places. He was aware of just how much now hung on this nasty little meeting. He knew that he would do whatever it took to make it work, even as that selfish impulse threatened to undo him. That voice that said, turn back.

Chapter 21

She will never know what happened here. You can thank me later.

Drayvex let his hand drop away. "You have my word that I won't harm you," he said, a cocktail of caustic activity burning in his veins. "And my undivided attention."

The trees fell still all at once, unaffected by the sporadic gusts raking through their branches. He narrowed his eyes, waiting to see what the last fae in existence was really made of.

The heat that emanated from the tree before him was of the same magic that kept him out. He couldn't see it, but he could feel it like a toxic river, and within seconds, it was spilling down the sides of the trunk and collecting at his feet. Disgusted, Drayvex stepped back.

The fae that stepped out from within the middle tree could easily have been trying to destroy him with the power of her mind for the way she was glaring. Considering this was far beyond her capabilities, the effect was lacking.

Drayvex stepped towards the ill-tempered creature planted at the foot of the trees, moving with slow, measured authority. She never took her eyes off him, and as he stopped in front of her and reached inside his pocket, she fell into a battle stance and tensed.

The pixie's septic yellow eyes lost their rancour for a fleeting moment as he pulled out the blackened slab that was once her tongue. She caught herself then, her gaze shooting back up to him and burning a hole in his head.

What's the matter, he thought, taking vicious pleasure from her contempt. *Demon got your tongue?* He held it out to her, testing his self-control as he let a wasted opportunity to goad her slip by.

She stared at him, refusing to look at the lump of dead muscle in his hand. Her lip curled, body frozen in the same battle stance. It was almost as though she didn't *trust* him.

Drayvex watched her, the satisfaction twisting inside him only a brief reprieve from his black mood. "Take it," he uttered, feeling it melt into revulsion. "Before I change my mind." The shit he did for that little redhead.

The creature before him seemed to sense there was something else he wanted. Or maybe she was just that desperate to curse him in her backwards language. But the speed with which she grabbed for the tongue almost set off his kill reflex.

He fought back a snarl, his teeth on edge, and breathed out into the night. Give me strength, he thought. Stupid is as stupid does.

Drayvex met the yellow gaze of his enemy head-on, pushing through the drag in his veins, the voice that insisted it was not too late to turn back, and spoke with smooth assurance. "I want to make a deal."

Chapter 22

"Tell me about your planet." Ruby leant out of the large open window, taking in the clusters of angry grey swirls in the dark sky of Vekrodus. It was a stark contrast to the blazing red stars that had been there on her last visit. Exotic red sands and sky maelstroms. What else was out there?

"Then will you tell me about yours?" The enthusiasm of the greebo behind her was infectious.

She smiled, turning away from the alien view. The thin veil at the window fell back into place. "If you like."

The little room had not changed a bit. Small yet oddly spacious, with a pale fur rug in the centre and several small, square nooks set into the walls. Each nook held something strange and intriguing. The floor itself was clammy and warm, and Ruby had touched it to make sure, fuelled by a vague memory that she could barely grasp.

Ruby had been in a very different place when she was here last. For one, she'd just lost the two people in the world who mattered most to her. Now, she wanted to know everything. More so, since Drayvex had told her they would not be here long.

"What's out there?" she asked, gesturing behind her to the window. "Beyond the desert." She edged towards the rug, intent on running her fingers through the long fur.

There was a brief thoughtful pause before he obliged. "There is the Veinous Gara forest. It eats weak demons and absorbs their goodness for the sake of the whole. Everything that grows in the forest is part of the same living network, and it all feeds as one. Krick has never been there, but others say it is quite something."

Ruby stilled at the foot of the rug, hardly believing what she was hearing. A carnivorous forest? "Does it, by any chance, glow red?" She pictured the forest Drayvex had taken her to in her mind, small details now screaming out at her with fresh perspective. The trees had been covered in pulsing black lines. She had likened them to veins.

This world was beautiful and deadly. Just like its ruler.

"As it happens, yes. Was that a guess?"

She turned to glance behind her, looking for the funny creature named Krick. He was standing towards one side of the room, a puzzled expression on his tiny face. As tall as her knee and all gangly limbs, he was pretty much a walking twig. "Um, I've ... heard things too."

Seen things would be less of a bare-faced lie. But the truth was, she had no idea how he would react to the truth. Sandra had not reacted well.

Ruby knelt down and reached out towards the pale rug. As her fingers slipped into the long fur, her heart squeezed with the memory of grief. Mind slipping backwards, she gripped a handful of fur in one hand.

"Is it my turn?"

She took a breath before relinquishing the rug and getting back to her feet. "Go ahead," she said. She gave the room and its contents a quick once over before heading towards the door.

Krick was immediately by her side. "A-are we leaving?" he squeaked.

Ruby reached the door and pulled it open. "He said I have the west wing. Right?"

The little greebo hesitated. "Y-yes, but—"

"So I'm counting on you to tell me when we're no longer in it." She looked down and smirked, tickled by the look of utter panic on his face. It was followed by an immediate twinge of guilt.

Chapter 22

"Oh, good grubs. Yes, okay. But, My Lady?"

Ruby flinched. "Ruby, please." For the love of god.

Krick's eyes widened. "No trouble, I beg of you. If anything were to happen to you on my watch, My Lord will punish me for an eternity."

Ruby stared at him, lost for words. "Did he say that to you?"

He pulled a face, his little features twisting. "My Lord said lots of things. That I'm to keep you safe and content. That I'm to keep you out of trouble. That if anything were to happen to you while he was gone, he would—"

"Okay," she said quickly, relenting. "Okay, no trouble. Cross my heart." Ruby already knew that Drayvex was a maniac. But this was on its own level.

When they exited the room, Ruby stood for a moment in the large, dimly lit corridor, looking one way and then another. After a moment's thought, she chose the opposite direction to her previous escapade. She knew exactly where that went, and she did not want a revisit.

The wide corridor was lit with clusters of small black flames. She wondered, as they were black, how they were giving off any light at all. The walls were bare but intricately carved in ways that made certain parts pop.

"My Lord treats you favourably."

Ruby's stomach flipped. She looked down at her small guide, hesitating at the sudden turn. The obvious answer was 'yes', but it felt like a trap.

"It is not in his nature. Are you different to other humans?"

She breathed out, realising that she had been holding her breath. "Is that your question?"

He blinked at her, completely oblivious to her internal dilemma. "Yes. Krick is curious."

Ruby stared down the endless corridor, towards the black, unlit mouth ahead of them. Why did Drayvex elevate her above all other humans? He didn't seem to know himself. "Not really. I don't know. We just sort of..." She stopped. Anything she could say next would sound ridiculous.

All she knew was that she wasn't better than anyone else, or the chosen one, or uniquely talented; she was just Ruby. And a blood curse that was slowly killing her wasn't going to change that.

Krick's eyes grew bigger. "Sort of what?"

She licked her lips. "Collided." And he was the damn freight train that punched through her life. Had she forgiven him? With her mouth?

She cringed. Nope, nope, nope. She did not want to revisit that right now. She felt the heat rising in her face and quickly changed the subject. "Okay, my turn."

Krick looked disappointed. "Ask away."

Ruby stopped walking as a room approached on her left. She thought about her question as she shuffled towards the closed door. "Tell me more about Vekrodus," she said. "Please." She hadn't forgiven Drayvex, not by a long shot. She was just giving him the chance to redeem himself.

"There's also the crimson waste, a stretch of rocky, dusty nothing. The land is barren, and it's the perfect place to challenge your nemesis to a fight to the death."

Ruby stood, fixed in place with her hand on the door handle as she processed Krick's words. The crimson waste.

"Scavengers that survive in the waste pick off the weak and injured. So you really don't want to be there unless you're strong."

She tried the handle. It clicked open. She wondered if Drayvex never bothered with locks because no one here would dare cross him. "Is the crimson waste red too, like the sand?" She'd had lots of time now to process the whole 'other planet' idea. Still, hearing Krick speak about this alien world in such a casual way was something she struggled to wrap her mind around.

"Why, yes it is." She glanced down at him and saw him scratching the side of his long head. "How did you know?"

She smiled. "Oh, just a hunch." With such a name, it would be a shame if it wasn't red.

Ruby swung the door open wide and almost closed it again. She blinked, doing a double-take as she stared open-mouthed at the view before her. Mushrooms, as far as the eye could see.

"Oh, I wouldn't go in there if I were you," said Krick, grabbing onto and

Chapter 22

tugging her finger.

Mushrooms of all shapes, sizes and colours grew over every available surface, both on the floor and what she could only assume were the walls and ceiling. She half angled her head down to Krick, unable to fully tear her eyes from the bizarre view. "What …?" she tried. "Why-why mushrooms?"

Krick tugged on her finger once again, and she allowed herself to be led away. "They are sleeping," he said simply, as though it was the most obvious thing in the world. "My Lord keeps them docile, as they are bad-tempered when they possess all their senses."

Ruby gave him a dubious look. Right, because that didn't sound dodgy at all. Trying not to linger on whether Drayvex was keeping mushrooms with attitude sedated against their will, she closed the door and kept going.

More rooms. Some almost mundane and some weirder than weird. It was almost as though this was the part of the castle that things got dumped in to deal with later. But no matter how much she wanted to believe that even Drayvex's house had a clutter corner, she had no doubt that every single object in this enormous building had its place and purpose. And that everything was *exactly* where he wanted it to be.

The corridor and its many rooms ended, opening up into a larger, hall-like room that looked like it had been ripped straight out of a gothic church. On the wall directly ahead of her was a humongous, multi-panelled window that ran from floor to ceiling. It looked as though it was there to catch the light, except Ruby knew that Vekrodus had no light. On the floor in the middle of the room was a symbol she had never seen before. It had been carved into the stone floor, the shape and complexity of it running in tiny trenches and leading away as one down the length of the room to the window. A channel.

She glanced behind her to where Krick stood, feeling her face mould into a question. She took a breath to ask him about it, but he got there first.

"Blood," he said, and shook his tiny head in a way that spoke for itself. "Ancient magic."

Ruby hesitated before deciding she didn't need to know any more to piece this room together. From one satanic temple to another, she thought dryly, slipping out of the hall and leaving it behind.

Back in the flame-lit corridor, she noticed a route that branched off to the right. Huh. She licked her lips, wondering why she hadn't seen it before. Not a dead end after all. She started towards it, slipping into the passageway, her eyes widening in the dark.

"Oh, Ruby, wait. That's beyond the wing!"

As Krick's voice sounded from a ways behind her, she skidded to a halt. "Thanks for the notice," she chimed, struggling not to roll her eyes. She turned and froze, stopping mid-turn. There was something up ahead.

Ruby's heart pounded hard and fast. They were shaped like a woman, curving in all the places Ruby herself wished she curved, with thick, muscular limbs. And her skin was *red*.

She stared at the creature across from her, unable to peel her eyes away. A pair of curled horns sat on her head, but only one of them was complete. The other looked like it had been snapped off halfway down. A long tail snaked down to her feet, where a curved black stinger sat on the very end.

"Nononononono." Krick's voice was barely a whisper. "This is bad."

Just then, the demon's head turned. Ruby knew that she was in trouble, and as she looked up into that sharp face and met a pair of glistening black eyes, her body reacted accordingly. Every hair on her body stood on end. Adrenaline surged through her.

It happened so fast. One moment she was frozen to the spot, the next her life was flashing before her eyes.

She screwed her eyes shut, turning her head away as the demon hissed and moved in a lurch to cross the space between them.

The almighty crack that resonated down the passageway made her flinch, the sound hitting her like the impact that never came. When Ruby opened her eyes, they widened at the scene before her. It was Drayvex—and he was pinning the red woman to the wall by her throat.

The ungodly black demon before her had lingering vestiges of the Drayvex she knew. Still, it was a shock to the system.

But it wasn't the only thing that alarmed her. She looked down at herself, mind careening, and saw the floor through her body. She was completely

Chapter 22

transparent.

"Did I give you *permission* to enter the west wing, you insolent whore?" snarled a basal voice that was only half-familiar. "Or are my orders now above the *great* Myna?"

Ruby could hear her choking in his iron grip. She looked at Krick instead, who was glowing blue. His hands were extended to either side of him in what looked like concentration, and it was in that moment that it clicked. Her current state was his doing.

"I … My … Ugh."

"Something to say? Speak the fuck up."

Despite her resolve not to look up, she did. She heard the female demon gasp as Drayvex loosened his grip enough for her to breathe.

"Y-Your Eminence, don't … I c-can explain!"

"What, pray tell," he growled with smooth menace, wielding every word like a weapon, "takes precedence over the flawless fealty I expect from my closest advisers? Tell me. I'm *dying* to know."

The demon twitched in his grasp, indecision playing out across her body. "Forgive me," she wailed. "I s-saw vermin in these ha-halls." She tried to turn her head, her eyes roaming to the corridor where they stood.

Ruby felt sick. Could they still see her? Should she run, or hope Krick had it handled?

Drayvex paused, looking down on the demon like a cat with a struggling mouse in its jaws. "You saw what?" She heard the condescending edge to his tone and wondered how he would handle this.

The demon named Myna gasped for breath as he squeezed, and Ruby ignored the sickening pop that followed. "A human. I saw a human!"

Ruby heard a tiny gasp next to her and followed it down to Krick. He looked like he was about to collapse.

The hard laugh that echoed down the corridor sent little skitters running down her spine. "A human," Drayvex deadpanned, "in *my* halls." He leant in closer, his imposing horns almost touching the wall. "The food, walking around like it owns the place *without* being eaten." He was mocking. She knew this was the way forward, but it tweaked at her all the same. Rude.

"My L-Lord, I—"

"Are you sure you're quite well, Myna?" His voice had turned slick, and it slid over her in strange ways. "I can have you replaced if you're no longer sound of mind. We'll make it nice and quick."

"No, no, I li-live to serve. Punish me!"

Ruby had to give it to him, he was good. It made her feel better about all those times she'd been duped by him in the past.

A tugging on the hem of her jacket pulled her attention away from the unfolding drama. Krick motioned with his head, two sharp jerks. It was time to go.

She glanced once more at the two demons, her stomach squeezing. Boy, was Drayvex going to be mad at them. She would do what she could to protect her little friend.

The moment they were round the corner, her form re-emerged all at once. Pausing only to scoop an exhausted Krick from the floor, Ruby got her bearings and made a hasty exit.

As they entered the little room that had almost become familiar, she pushed the door closed with the nudge of a foot and placed the little demon on the floor. He was as light as he was thin, almost weightless.

"Hey," she said, looking down at the motionless creature on the floor. "Thanks. That was pretty impressive."

Krick only groaned. "Oh, I'm done for. His Unholiness will—"

As though summoned by name, the door swung open behind them with a drawn-out creak. Krick jumped in a whirlwind of tiny limbs, scrabbling towards her and shielding himself behind her legs.

Ruby turned to face Drayvex as the door swung wide, her heart squeezing in her chest. She would not let him take this out on her small friend. He would have to blame her this time.

The demon eyed her with an impassive look from the doorway, his stony grey gaze carrying the brunt of his scrutiny. His silence spoke volumes.

She squared her shoulders, her skin prickling. With fierce determination, Ruby took the demon by the horns. "Before you say anything," she said,

Chapter 22

speaking with wary calm, "this was not Krick's fault. It was mine." She hated not knowing which way he would snap.

Drayvex closed the door with a final resounding clunk. "Right."

She followed him with her eyes as he stalked across the room towards her. She licked her lips. "He told me I was leaving the west wing, and I kept going anyway." Defiance leaked into her voice as she provoked him.

He stopped beside her, shoulder to shoulder, and turned his head towards her. A soft heat radiated from his form. "You don't say."

Ruby hesitated, confusion and doubt breaking into her thoughts. He almost sounded bored; except, that wasn't it. His tone tweaked at her in strange ways. Was he playing mind games?

She stared at him, searching the colourless grey of his unreadable gaze. "So, we're good?" Her voice suddenly sounded small.

Drayvex stared back, his usual intensity replaced with a dead nothing. "Yes, Ruby. We're *good*."

Ruby felt an irrational panic start to claw its way up her throat. She had expected to feel the hot side of his temper. To feel his wrath pounding her skull, to have to defend the creature who had been tasked with keeping her safe. But the eerie calm of the demon before her was far more disturbing than the rage she'd come to expect.

Krick jumped out from behind her leg. "My Lord, that's not—"

"Leave us."

Krick flinched as he spoke and glanced up at her. She gave him a subtle nod, trying to be discreet, and he bowed once to Drayvex before scurrying out of the room.

The moment the door closed behind him, Ruby felt it in the air. It was almost electric but in a different way than she had felt around him before. It was more than she could stand. "Is something wrong?" she blurted out, her tongue running away with her once again.

Drayvex side-eyed her as she fixed on him. In that moment, as their eyes met, she felt like she was drowning. It came out of nowhere, a tidal wave she couldn't escape from. Then he looked away, and it was gone. Ruby watched his fangs inch down, their pointed tips emerging from behind his lips. What was he keeping from her now?

"No more than usual," he said, his tone dismissive, before showing her his back.

She watched him slip towards the window, motionless for a moment as she hovered between two minds. Then, she followed behind.

By the time she stood before him, Drayvex had completely changed. "Get your shit in order," he said, the snap of authority in his voice suddenly jarring to hear. "We're leaving."

Ruby blinked at him, her gaze fixed on the sleek black strands that fell across his stormy gaze. "Wow, okay." She sucked in a breath, feeling like she had whiplash. "Where are we going?"

It was pointless to ask. She knew, and yet, she asked anyway. As Drayvex narrowed his eyes at her, she noted he was almost a different person to the one she had faced mere seconds ago. "Plan C," was all she got. And then he was gone.

Ruby chewed on her lip. What the hell was plan C?

Chapter 23

They were back at the clifftop with the three solitary trees, and Ruby couldn't even begin to guess why.

The sun was setting fast, taking with it the best of her sight. She pulled out her phone as it buzzed in her pocket, a hopeful note soaring in her chest. Had Sandra finally texted her back? It fell again when she saw the sender: her local pizzeria with all the latest offers. Sighing, she slipped the phone back in her pocket. Were they just not friends anymore?

"Forget her, Ruby. She's not your friend."

Ruby tensed as Drayvex's rich voice bled out from the darkness behind her. A stab of annoyance flared at his words. She wanted to defend Sandra, to correct him and tell him to mind his own damn business. But honestly, she couldn't.

She sighed, spinning on the spot to find him. "You don't have to sound so smug about it," she said, needled. "You're not even trying."

Drayvex was draped in the shadows of the dying day. Still, she could make out his features, and she waited for that skewed smile that always dug under her skin and sped up her heart to emerge and put her in her place. Instead, he slipped towards her, silent as the shadows themselves.

Ruby looked up and met his gaze as he stopped in front of her. She couldn't see the colour, but once again, panic began to claw up her throat as she got the distinct feeling that something was very wrong. Drayvex was not acting like Drayvex. As much as she hated his inflated ego, as much as that destructive, relentless—and quite frankly psychotic—whirlwind nature of his brought out all her own worst violent impulses, its lack thereof now almost made her feel like the world was upside down.

There was something else missing too. And it was only as she shivered in the evening dusk that she placed it. He was standing right next to her, but she could barely feel his heat.

Drayvex breathed out, a warm summer breeze that tickled her face. "If she was the friend you say she is, would she leave you at my mercy, knowing what she knows? That I could have my wicked way with you a hundred times over, and there would be nothing you could do to stop me?" His voice was low and flat.

Ruby shivered, reacting in a way that had entirely nothing to do with the cold.

"The little hunter with her eyes on the biggest prize imaginable." He went on, his voice gaining a soft edge of darkness. "She's traced trail after trail of sheer bloody devastation. Lost count of the bodies, dug into the wild and vicious whispers of my conquests and traced them all back to me. She's barely scratched the surface."

She was breathing hard. Stop.

Slowly, as if fighting some kind of impulse and losing, Drayvex reached out towards her, all of a sudden an inferno of heat. He traced a burning finger down the length of her jaw. "So where is she?"

Ruby's eyes welled up as his words hit her square in the chest. It wasn't a taunt. The way he spoke, it was almost a castigation.

"Why isn't she fighting the world and its fucking mother to get you back?"

Her heart felt weightless for a moment as he uttered those words with a fervour that stirred up dangerous feelings, as his hot finger lingered on her skin and then fell away. "I don't ... know."

"She's not your friend." Drayvex spoke with firm finality. "Let her go."

Sandra. She felt a pang of grief as it hit her. Ruby had well and truly lost her to her dad, hadn't she?

Chapter 23

She licked her lips, feeling like she was hanging on the edge of some invisible precipice. "Why are we here? I thought we were done with this place."

She heard him laugh under his breath, short and humourless. "If only." The sudden edge to Drayvex's voice caused her body to tense with stress. Then, following his gaze, she turned to look behind her.

The silhouetted figure that stood tall and proud by the trees was unmistakable, even from a distance. Ruby spun back to face Drayvex, frantic questions buzzing in her mind. "I don't understand." Why was the fae who had barely escaped with her life standing there as though she was expecting them?

He tore his gaze from the fae on the horizon and looked down at her, falling into a perfect stillness. The fading light was making it hard to read the demon, but she could see that his expression was as listless as his tone. "It's going to go a little something like this. You will go with *that* to its rainbow-coated pixie cave, while *I* hunt Saydor to the ends of the fucking galaxy and beyond, and pump him with all the molten fury of your sun."

Ruby's jaw dropped. Wait, what? She stared at him, speechless. "Have you lost your mind? You tried to kill her. You ripped her tongue right out of her head." She weaved her fingers into her hair. "Why would she do anything for us?"

"It's okay, Ruby," called a warm, beckoning voice from across the open grassy space. "You'll be safe with me."

She felt Drayvex bristle next to her, a strange sensation considering they weren't touching. Tira could hear them. "We came to an agreement," he muttered by way of explanation. His tone was sour.

Ruby stared at him. An agreement. "With her?" She heard the words, but they didn't make any sense. He may as well have told her the sky was green. They couldn't go five seconds without trying to kill each other. When had they come to an *agreement*?

He sighed. "Yes, Ruby. With the pissing fae. We are out of options."

Oh. She swallowed, her heart speeding up. She'd annoyed him. "I was just … surprised that you would want this, is all."

The moment those words had left her mouth, she knew they were a mistake. She felt him grab her in the dark, a sudden movement that made her jump. "What I want?" he growled, his hands burning against her upper arms as he held her in an iron grip. "Palm you off to my bastard enemy and get on with my highborn life? Is that it?"

Ruby blinked, stunned. "I—what?" She squinted at the shadows of his face, wishing she could read it. "No, that's not …" She took a breath. Get on with his life? Talk about dramatic. "That was bad phrasing. So this is like the park at Crichton?"

She was pretty sure he was glaring at her. "Same magic, different festering hole in reality." He let go of her arms, peeling his fingers away as though he was tempted to squeeze her like a bottle of ketchup.

Ruby shook her head. Saydor had a lot to answer for. She bit her lip, anxiety gnawing at the edges of her mind. "Is there nothing I can do then?" She felt resignation bleed into her veins.

Drayvex tilted his head in the gloom. She pictured him narrowing his eyes at her. "You can do as you're told. I might even keel over with shock."

She felt a smirk tug at the edges of her mouth. Very funny. She glanced behind her to the impressive silhouette on the horizon, then sighed. "Fine," she said, chewing on her lip. "I suppose it does make sense." She flexed her shoulders on the spot, trying to shake the awful feeling of wordless dread that was back and coursing through her.

As she turned to head towards the waiting fae, Ruby felt Drayvex's hand on her arm once again. She paused, turning back towards him.

Wait.

His voice filled her head, low and urgent. It was just like before, except the tone was all wrong. She simply stared at his face, its details lost to her.

Never tell the faerie about filenos. The piece of me inside you must remain between us. Got it?

Ruby forgot how to breathe. How was he doing that? Could she speak back?

Something warm brushed against her hand in the dark. She jumped, her hand reflexively curling around the thing that had been dropped into her

Chapter 23

palm.

Wear this on your wrist, he said. *It will subdue the demon inside you and allow you to pass through the barrier.* Never *take it off inside.*

A sensation close to horror swept over her as she processed Drayvex's words. *Filenos.* She didn't know the word, but it was clear as day what he meant. The piece of him inside her—it hadn't even occurred to her that the barrier would reject her because of it. Sandra's bracelet certainly had. She opened her mouth to speak.

He shook his head. She closed her mouth. Her heart pounded against her ribcage. *How long?* she thought. No response. She tried again. *How long will you be gone?* she thought at him, willing the words towards him.

Drayvex didn't respond, and Ruby twirled her hair around a finger in frustration. But as the restless darkness in her head stirred at her question, he eventually answered. *A while.*

She didn't know how to respond to that. Instead, she took a breath, and slipped what felt a lot like a bracelet blindly onto her wrist.

The flickers of restless darkness immediately vanished, along with the oppressive dread. She felt his presence leave her mind, dark flames extinguished by a magic she couldn't begin to understand. Was it just her in her head now?

"After you," Drayvex murmured, speaking out loud. She supposed that answered her question. Steeling herself, Ruby faced the figure on the cliff top and started towards her.

A light emanated from the beautiful warrior before her, a soft glow that somehow always seemed to come from behind her. Despite the tense situation, and the demon lurking somewhere behind Ruby, Tira gave her a small smile as she approached the eerie trees. She gestured towards Ruby with a hand, holding it out to her. "Come," she said. "This world no longer serves you."

Ruby frowned, the fae's choice of words striking her as odd. She span on the spot, putting the trees behind her. She could no longer sense Drayvex's presence with the bracelet on her wrist. It had always been more of a reflex than a conscious decision, to seek him out with senses she didn't know she possessed. It was only now, as her mind tried and flailed in the empty space, that she realised how much she'd come to lean on it.

He was right behind her. She breathed out in a stream, her pulse racing. She could see him clearly now, and she didn't like the look on his face; the grim determination in his ashen gaze. "You *are* coming back for me." She spoke slowly, suddenly unsure. "Right?"

Drayvex didn't respond. Instead, it was Tira who answered. "Not if I can help it," she said. The smile in her voice was unnerving.

Ruby span back towards Tira, realisation hitting her with the force of a knock-out punch. This was not a temporary solution. Frozen in place, she stared into the golden eyes of the creature looking down on her. Drayvex would never come back for her, because he couldn't.

Ears ringing, she stared at the blackened bark of the tree before her. Her throat began to close. This was not an on-the-spot decision. "Wait," she said to him, breathless. "I don't think—"

"Yes. You do." Drayvex's terse response came from behind. It was followed by a swift shove to her back.

Ruby toppled forward, landing on the middle tree. It swallowed her whole.

Chapter 24

Ruby landed on all fours on the softest grass she'd ever fallen on. Mind spinning, heart pounding hard, she vaguely registered the sweet scent in the air as she sucked in breath after breath. That jerk. How could he just cut her loose? Her chest constricted, tightening of its own accord. Did she not deserve a goodbye? Had she not earned at least that?

She pulled herself upright, kneeling on the grass, and sucked in the sweet scents around her. Honeysuckle? Her whole body on edge, she looked up to see where she'd landed—and her entire face fell slack.

She was looking down on the most beautiful valley she had ever laid eyes on. Kneeling on the peak of a hill, the vivid green grass sloped down before her and stretched out in endless, rolling hills, expanses of pink and white flowers carpeting the ground in a patchwork. The mountains on the far horizon touched the clouds, their very peaks swallowed by the sky in a rolling mist. Despite this, glorious sunshine beat down onto the valley in a warm embrace, making a distant river look as though it was made of pure, glistening gold. It was, in all senses, a whole other world.

There was a small pop from behind her. Scrabbling on her knees to face it, her hand reflexively dug into her jacket, where the luxlor was nestled against her.

"Peace, Earth child. You are safe here. Welcome to Moraea."

Ruby forced herself to take a breath, staring up at the beautiful creature before her. Her hair was draped over her shoulder in one purple braid, resting on the chest of her light golden armour. She was clearly built for battle. And despite the golden glow of her flawless skin, and those soft golden eyes that had a honey-like warmth to them, there was a coldness about her that set Ruby's teeth on edge.

She pushed herself to her feet, forcing her clenched hands open by her sides. "I can't believe you didn't kill each other. What could Drayvex have possibly said to you to convince you to provide sanctuary, after everything that's happened?" Silver tongue indeed.

Tira started towards her, and Ruby's pulse quickened in kind. "Ruby," she chided, her lyrical voice light and friendly, "my grievance with the World Destroyer has nothing whatsoever to do with you." She stopped in front of her, looking down with the faintest of smiles in the corners of her lips. "I've wanted nothing more than to snatch you from that deplorable creature's clutches from the moment I laid eyes on you. It was my pleasure."

Ruby felt queasy. She swallowed it down. Tira's animosity was understandable, justifiable even. Just like the strange ache of betrayal that Ruby felt now. "Well, thank you," she replied. "For taking me in." But in true Drayvex style, it was never that simple. How could she be mad at someone who went to such lengths to keep her alive?

Tira turned to look down into the valley below, before glancing behind her and setting a leisurely pace. "Follow me. Stay close."

Breathing out in a huff, she gathered her wits and followed behind.

The walk through the beautiful valley was a tonic Ruby desperately needed. She hadn't realised just how tightly wound she had got until she began to uncoil and feel somewhat like herself again. Meandering against the flow of the chuckling river, she trailed her fingertips over the soft stalks of corn-like reeds at the water's edge, lost in thought. Her mother wouldn't even know she was gone. Would she ever wake up and ask for her? Would Ruby ever see her face again, or was this her life now? Would Drayvex replace Ruby with some other poor girl who took his fancy?

Chapter 24

She scoffed, her last thought carrying a surprising sting. Good luck finding someone stupid enough to put up with your garbage, she thought, chewing on her lip. She looked down at the heavy object around her wrist, suddenly remembering that Drayvex had given it to her in the dark.

She stared at it, her breath stilling in her lungs. It wasn't what she'd pictured.

Ruby had expected practical and basic. The bracelet she was looking at was nothing of the sort. The dark, gleaming metal twisted and curled in delicate links that almost looked like thorns. She could probably use it as a weapon if she swung her arm just so. The deep scarlet gems that dotted its length were glowing in a way that reminded her of the exotic red flower in her flat that never died. It was truly quite something.

She ran a finger along the smooth, twisting metal, swallowing back a strange sort of tug. It wasn't her usual style, but it was striking in a way that reminded her of its equally dark and arresting owner. Was this really just a functional piece? Did demons give this sort of thing to anyone? She dropped her arm and looked back towards Tira. She would probably never know.

Ruby had been staring glaze-eyed into the distance for a while. It was only now though, as her racing thoughts stilled for a moment that she started to really use her eyes. That can't be right, her mind pushed. Surely they were playing tricks on her.

The stretch of enormous trees before them were scattered like the entrance to a strange forest, with little wooden huts suspended halfway up as many as she could see. They were built around the trunk of the trees, with some holding two, even three huts stacked high. But it wasn't the tree houses that had set her mind spinning—it was the people inside them.

She stopped walking, skimming over the figures that were moving in and out of the huts, climbing the trees, swarming on the ground. Groups of tall, beautiful creatures, carrying stacks of wood and bundles of vines back and forth.

"Spectacular, aren't they?" Tira spoke from a few paces away, pride and admiration colouring her voice.

Ruby stared at her, struggling to find her words. But Drayvex had *obliterated* the fae. It was only Tira that had got away. Right? "Are they …?" She blinked at them, trying to count. Too many.

"My people," she finished, an almost-smile on her face.

Drayvex was mistaken. They had clearly found a way to survive.

They were beginning to stare. Ruby shrank into herself as, one by one, those striking faces all stopped what they were doing and turned to face them in silence. She quickly got the feeling that they were judging her. She felt heat rising in her cheeks. One of them was coming towards them.

Tira greeted the waiting masses with a voice loud enough to carry. "Fair folk, we have a guest. I know that you will make her feel welcome."

A tall, handsome man with long, dark hair and an impressive scar slashed across his face stopped before them, bowing his head at Tira in greeting. "Tiraeth."

Ruby baulked as his amber eyes flicked towards her. The contempt she saw there was unmistakable.

"Malwen." Tira nodded back, but he was no longer looking at her.

"Forgive me," he said, speaking to Tira, but looking Ruby up and down. "But isn't this human the Demon Lord's pet?" The way he spat the word 'pet' made the hair on her arms stand on end. Ruby felt a protest rising up her throat. How dare you look down on me, you—

"Peace, Malwen. *Ymlacio*." Tira looked behind her to where Ruby stood, her purple braid swishing down her back. She gestured towards Ruby with an arm in an exaggerated movement. "This girl," she boomed to their waiting audience, "is as much a victim of the World Destroyer as we are." Her voice was almost a rallying call, and the answering rumble of agitation and hostility that echoed through the trees was truly terrifying. "She is one of us now."

Ruby felt the sound shake her right down to her core. In that moment, she was back in Drayvex's mind, watching the battle unfold between demon and fae. Two bitter enemies, one ruthless goal. She swallowed, agitation creeping into her muscles. She had fallen out of the frying pan, and straight into the preternatural fire.

Chapter 24

* * *

Drayvex stared at the single glistening strand that dangled from his fingers, the lingering remnants of her scent caressing his senses. The hair flashed red as it caught the sun, briefly catching fire and searing his vision, as though still linked to its wilful owner. Tucking it away, he looked down from the window at the human rat race below, grimacing as the amalgamation of other aromas in the room assaulted him. If he could capture the smell of a hospital, he would use it to torture demon deserters.

Dulling his senses, he turned from the window and gazed across the small room, towards the motionless figure in the bed. The final tracker was a loose end. One that no longer served a purpose.

Drayvex slipped across the room, moving at a human pace to the bedside of the thing that looked like Ruby's deranged mother. He found himself lingering on the face, looking for visual similarities that hinted at any sort of vague relation to her. The shape of the nose, the slope of the mouth. He quickly concluded that Ruby was adopted.

Your sentimental shit won't bring her back, sniped an impatient voice not unlike his own, the voice of his once saner self. *Just get it done.*

He clenched his jaw. *Choke on it,* he pushed back. Pulling back the sheets, he made a fist and punched straight through its chest. The lifeless shell beneath him jerked in a violent spasm, fingers twitching in a reflex it had never needed. As he closed his hand around the soft core of the spell and squeezed, the body fell still once again.

Drayvex extracted his hand from the tracker. The machinery it was hooked up to began to scream. Resisting the urge to wipe black gunk on the hospital sheets, he put his hand on the decimated chest and pushed power down from his core. The decommissioned tracker rebuilt itself on command.

In the time it had taken them to cross the space between his portal and the fae's, Drayvex had talked himself out of Ruby's exchange one hundred times over. One hundred and one times over he had countered, killing each selfish impulse with the most selfish one of all.

Pulling the sheet back up to cover the tracker, he stepped back and waited for the inevitable panic that would ensue. The truth was, he would rather amputate her from his life like a rotting limb than watch her walk into the jaws of Saydor of her own volition. If he had to do it again, he would change nothing.

The door to the room burst open, and two humans rushed towards the bed. Drayvex slipped out of the room as they fell about their fruitless task, barely seeing the warm bodies that swerved to avoid him in the cluttered passageway as he made for the exit. They would try and fail to restart her life. They would pronounce her dead, and when they couldn't find her daughter to break the news, life would eventually go on.

Life, bled the voice. Is that concept still familiar to you, or are you so wrapped up in *her* that you've forgotten who you are?

Drayvex bared his razor teeth at a scrappy woman who did not move out of his way in time. She scrabbled backwards with a wordless scream, causing a scene as she barrelled into the humans behind her.

He had not forgotten. He was Lord of the fucking demon multitude. But Ruby had never bowed to him, had never fawned or scraped at his feet. She'd made him work for every single prize he'd set his sights on, for every small smile and concession. It was all *too* easy to shed the only skin he'd ever known while in her presence. Her absence in his life now would not reverse the damage. The seeds of chaos she had sown within him had well and truly taken root.

The hospital doors parted before him as he left the accursed building behind him. The strand of DNA in his pocket sat waiting for his attention. When he was around the corner, and out of sight from the majority of prying eyes, he allowed himself to come undone. He became darkness itself, his physical form unravelling and burning everything away. Saydor could run. He could hide like the craven invertebrate he was. But he would eventually show his face, looking for her. And Drayvex would oblige.

Rising up and dispersing into the atmosphere, Drayvex felt the vast pools of loathing inside him ripple. He would pull the traitor apart limb from limb. Keep him alive and conscious, make sure he felt every ounce of agony. Feel

Chapter 24

every throbbing organ, every lump of his torn flesh sing as it became one with the throne he so coveted. Supporting the one true ruler of Vekrodus, for all eternity in a grisly mosaic.

Ruby would be just fine. It was better this way; for the both of them.

* * *

Ruby sat in the shade of the forest, perched on the knotted roots of a large tree as the fae buzzed around her and slipped her suspicious looks. She couldn't blame them for not trusting her. She was the unwanted guest who had cavorted with their worst enemy. But Tira had brought her into their fold, and because her opinion seemed to carry some weight, the looks she got remained only looks.

At some point after her arrival, Ruby had realised that not only was the sun still high in the sky, but the shadows on the ground around her weren't moving with the passing hours. When she'd asked Tira how long the days were here, she'd discovered that Moraea was in a permanent state of daytime. It was then with a jolt she'd realised that not only was this place a total contrast to the everlasting night of Vekrodus, but for both worlds, time seemed utterly irrelevant.

Tira cleared her throat.

Startled out of her thoughts, Ruby looked up to find her holding a wood-carved cup filled with water towards her. Grateful, she took the cup and drank deeply. When she came up for breath, she looked up at the creature before her. Her stomach twisted, reacting to what she was about to ask. She had to know how the fae were here.

"Forgive me," Ruby said, measuring her words with care. "But I was under the impression that it was only you ..." She trailed off at the end, unsure of how to finish. *That you were the last one standing.*

Tira stared at her, her golden eyes blazing all of a sudden under the cool shade of the forest. She looked down at the cup, her face distant, and Ruby wondered if she'd overstepped. "It was."

The soft triumph in her voice didn't match the words. It was only then that Ruby realised Tira was smiling. It reminded her of Drayvex, of the skewed way he smiled as he revelled in his victims' pain. Ruby was rooted to the spot.

"But I found a way to bring them back."

A chill ran down her spine. Bring them back … from the dead? "Oh?" was all she could manage.

The fae took a seat on the spongy ground opposite her, bringing up her knees and folding her legs beneath her. Looking straight into Ruby's eyes, the smile slipped from her inhuman face. "The Lapis Temporis was all I needed, Ruby."

Ruby felt as though she'd been smacked in the gut. No.

"And I couldn't have done it without you." She held out her hand towards Ruby then, an invitation. "Let me show you what really happened."

Chapter 25

Agony. It was hard to think, hard to breathe as the one named World Killer dragged me across the temple floor. Bound in coil upon coil of the abominations that spewed from his body, his poison burnt me, seeping into my system. I would never scream, never give this creature the satisfaction; but gods, it hurt.

"Whatever you're about to say," he threatened you, "do us both a favour and don't." He had us both right where he wanted us.

Ruby could see it all before her, clear as day, as though she were looking out from Tira's own eyes. Drayvex, merciless and inhuman. The vicious black coils that enveloped her bleeding through her skin. It was easy to see in that moment why she considered Ruby his victim. Except Ruby knew better. She'd been there of her own free will, and Drayvex wouldn't hurt her. At least, not intentionally.

My thoughts were not clear, my vision slipping in and out. But he dragged me into a room and demanded that I use my power on the lock. It wasn't until I turned my head and focused on the plinth that I saw it there. It was beautiful..

The Lapis Temporis was mere feet away. I was weak, and I knew I had but one chance to get this right. I had to be the first to get to it, but I knew the demon would not allow that on his watch. And thanks to the temple, he was at the height of his power.

The World Destroyer kept me prisoner as I struggled to my feet, his abhorrent coils remaining around my throat in a bind even as he withdrew the rest. I could feel his poison sapping at my strength. I could barely breathe. But you challenged him then, condemning his cruelty. For whatever reason, at your words, he retracted. I cannot explain what I saw in that moment, but I thanked the goddess for you.

Ruby swallowed back bile, her ears ringing as she processed what was being projected before her. She could see herself, the Ruby in the projection. It was her fault. Whatever was going to happen next was her fault because she had seen only what her human eyes could see. She had denounced Drayvex. And instead of doubling down, he had responded to her.

The demon and I opened our designated locks in a simultaneous blast of power. At the last second, I changed direction.

My timing was impeccable, but the World Destroyer was faster. He almost ruined everything. And as I twisted all the fury of the fae towards him, he lunged for me. The impact knocked my beam of light straight over his head and sailing in an arc towards where you stood.

I must admit, I am grateful in that moment that the demon was not yet done with you. It was never my intention for you to suffer for his sins. But as his attention turned to protecting you, I went for the stone.

A spreading horror had slowly been creeping over Ruby's body as she witnessed the *real* turn of events. Her limbs were heavy and dead.

Ruby stared at the image—no, the *memory* before her, lost for words. She'd been defending Tira this whole time. She'd clashed with Drayvex over her, risked her own life to protect her. He'd seemed so intent on painting Tira as the villain, so hate-blind and biased, that Ruby had chose to ignore him. And her humanity had cost them everything.

Once the Lapis Temporis was in my grip, I knew I'd won. There was nothing he could do as I activated the stone, except watch as I triumphed where he'd failed. A delicious moment indeed.

I had set it for a few minutes prior, so I knew I would have mere seconds to get myself together. Ultimately, I overshot, and as we entered the temple for a second time, I knew I must have the same conversations, make the same movements as I had the first time around so that the timeline did not diverge too soon. I knew I had to take in his poison again. Exactly as I had the first time.

So I let him take me, let him poison me once again as he dragged me to the room where the Lapis Temporis was once housed. To the empty plinth.

Once again, I underestimated the World Destroyer as he crushed me without hesitation, and once again, you came to my aid. I remember thinking, as you faced down the demon of demons, that I would find a way to repay you, no matter what. That I would not have you suffer any more at that creature's hands.

Ruby drowned in her emotions as she witnessed the stark truth. Tira was the one who had betrayed them. But Ruby could see it all spread out before her in a horrible pattern. It was she who had truly hammered those final nails in her own coffin. Her own, and quite possibly Drayvex's, whose enemies were gathering in secret and fuelling each other's hatred of the Demon Lord who thwarted them.

She sucked in a shaky breath, trying to hold herself together. How could compassion and simple humanity have led her so astray? How could doing the right thing have been the wrong thing to do?

"But I ..." Ruby ran a hand through her tangled hair, trying to stifle the frantic feeling inside her. She looked across towards the beautiful deceiver before her. A million questions still spun in her mind. Drayvex had been right all along. She'd never wanted to hear that jackass say 'I told you so' as much as she did right now. "I don't understand," she persisted. "How did you go from there to ..." She gestured around her with a hand, sweeping over the fae busying themselves throughout the forest around them. "To this?"

Tira just smiled. "Let's walk," was her light response.

Ruby swallowed. She was surrounded by bodies, and yet, she had never felt more alone.

"Are you well?"

Tira's mild concern reached Ruby from within her tangled thoughts. Pulling out of her own head, Ruby forced herself to smile. "It's just a lot to take in. Continue, please. I'll be fine." Just like the deep-rooted instincts that screamed at her to run when Drayvex got too close, they were telling her now to play along. It was all she could do not to scream.

Glowing specks of light floated through the air throughout the forest, glistening like gold dust. They increased the further in they went, making the area around them look enchanted. Ruby's curiosity had never come with an off switch, and as they drifted past her face, she fought to keep her mind on the thing that mattered most.

Tira walked beside her, intervening only when she wanted to change their direction. "The Lapis Vitae's power is complex and vast. When using its power, the one true path of the past becomes an infinite web of strings. A multitude of possibilities that will affect not only the present, but the future."

Ruby breathed in the sweet scents of the air, trying to calm her nerves. No one person should have that much power over life itself. She felt a twinge of guilt as she thought this. Had she not also sought to use the stone for her own gain? She was no better than Tira or Drayvex. Just far weaker.

"Finding the right strings to pull is where the problem lies," she continued, reaching out to cradle a little golden light before her with one hand. Her voice dropped in tone, taking on an undertone of melancholy. "Finding a way to pluck so many of my people from the jaws of certain death, to save so many lives at once, is challenging to say the least."

Ruby stopped walking. It sounded like she was still trying to resurrect them. But that couldn't be what she meant. The fae were walking and talking and scowling right before her eyes. "What are you saying?" she prompted. "I can see them all, right before me."

Tira let the little glowing light drift from her grip. She sighed. "What you see is the product of my desires, Ruby. They exist because they are between life and death, and because of the magics within this self-contained world. I am still searching for a way to make it permanent."

She felt her eyes widen, understanding dawning on her. "You haven't found the right path yet."

The fae beside her shook her head. "I have not. But it is only a matter of time before I find that bastard's weakness."

Chapter 25

Ruby breathed out, sending the little golden motes around her swirling through the air. Did that mean Drayvex was thwarting her on other potential timelines too? But surely it made more sense to stop the war from happening in the first place.

Her gaze fixed on the soft light that broke through the trees at the far edge of the forest. But her mind was reeling. "Can I ask you something?" she asked, tentative.

Tira paused for a beat, before responding with open warmth. "You may. Ask, child."

Ruby felt her heart speed up. "Wouldn't *preventing* the war with the demons save all your people at once?" Drayvex had told her he'd offered the fae a truce. If that was true, their rejection had been what sparked the war.

Tira's expression went from summer sunshine to blazing inferno in the blink of an eye. Her face fell, becoming a sneer as her golden eyes burnt with an almost blinding fire. "That is not an acceptable solution," she thundered, her voice reverberating through the trees. "The Demon Lord must not live. We will die before we make a deal with that devil."

Ruby felt herself shrink away from the creature as she became something else entirely. How could something that represented the light be so twisted with hate? It made no sense. She'd come to expect such reactions from Drayvex. But she had not expected such venom from a being that quite literally looked like the sun goddess herself.

"Apologies." The light dimmed in her eyes as she regarded Ruby, a sombre expression now on her face. "That was not aimed at you. Shall we keep going?" She gestured towards the far light breaking through the trees. "I have something I wish to show you."

She breathed out, steeling her nerves, once again forcing a smile. "Of course. No harm, no foul." She dropped it as soon as they started walking. There was no way this would end well. Not for any of them.

They broke through the trees at the end of the forest, and as Ruby stepped out into the brilliant sunshine, she reflexively shaded her eyes from the blinding light.

"Welcome home," Tira offered from beside her.

Frowning, Ruby lowered her hand and gasped. Home …

The enormous lake before her was a sight for sore eyes. It was like looking through a window in time. The fruit trees and flowers that bloomed around the water's edge were bright and fragrant, with pink cherry blossoms scattered over the surface of the water. It was a paradise she knew like the back of her hand, from the position of each tree, right down to the crunchy gravel path that ran around the lake's edge; and it made her heart squeeze with homesickness.

She turned towards Tira, unable to wipe the stunned expression from her face. "What is Crichton Park doing in your world?" She could barely take her eyes off it.

The small smile that grew on her fae guide's lips was a knowing smile. "Your park, as you know, was always ours. It was a gateway to here, and this is the other side of that gateway." She looked out over the water, her light golden armour glistening under the sun.

It struck Ruby in that moment that this woman was the brave warrior she'd dreamed of becoming when she was little. Beautiful and fierce.

"It is exactly how it was before the World Destroyer crushed your people like they were nothing more than insects beneath his feet."

Ruby flinched as Tira's words hit her where it still hurt, where it would always hurt. She saw him then, dragging her through the village as everyone around them was slaughtered by his kind. The Earth is screwed, he'd told her, almost sounding bored.

"It's okay, Ruby." Tira's smooth voice drew her back. "You can come here as often as you like. Moraea is your home now."

She was breathing hard. Looking down at the bracelet around her wrist, she unclenched her fists and stroked a finger over its smooth, dark curves. He'd also fought Saydor and taken the world back. Was it really too little, too late?

"Soon the fae will once again rise as one people. We shall declare war on the demons and that degenerate butcher they bow to. We shall bathe in the Demon Lord's blood, and finally take back the freedom that he stole from

Chapter 25

us."

Ruby's chest constricted as she fixated on the glowing red gems of the bracelet. What the Hell was she supposed to do now? "Right," she muttered. "*If* you find a way to make this permanent."

Tira bent down to the grass at their feet, plucking a mushroom from the earth, and popped it into her mouth. "*When.*" There was no doubt in her voice.

If Ruby found a way to warn Drayvex of the uprising fae, he would slaughter the entire race all over again. She chewed on her lip, baulking as she tasted blood. By doing nothing, she would be siding with the fae. Her betrayal of their fragile accord would have a steep price, of that she was certain. And caught off guard by an ethereal army, he may actually lose the fight.

Ruby stared at the glistening lake, the surface a sheet of glass. "I think I'll stay a while," she sighed to the creature beside her.

"Of course. Take your time."

She felt her knees buckle, and then the soft grass beneath her. There was no doubt in her mind that Drayvex deserved everything that was coming to him—every violent strike, every retaliatory stab in the back—for the sins that dripped off him like lies from his forked tongue. Tira had been good to her, welcomed her with open arms.

Ruby ran a finger over the thorns at her wrist. Her heart pulsed in her throat, pounding a guilty rhythm. She didn't want to betray Drayvex. He may well be a monster, but he was *her* monster. Her shallow breaths came and went, barely worth taking. But the fact of it was, she was going to have to betray someone. And he had betrayed her, and quaint Crichton, first.

Chapter 26

The girl before him was a perfect clone in every way that mattered. Sleek crimson hair tumbled down her back, framing the face that he could not escape, the big green eyes that were burnt into his mind as though by witchcraft. She would fool anyone into thinking she was the real deal, if only for a little while—or until she opened her mouth.

She was staring at him, and there was nothing in those vacant depths but lies.

Drayvex turned his back on the Ruby thing, the demon beneath his skin bristling. He'd had no illusions about the timing of this plan, that it would be as much a grate on his remaining sanity as an opportunity. Looking at this cheap imitation now, he knew that he'd been right.

He breathed in, and felt something stir inside him. Everything around him smelled like her. This flat had been her home ever since her village fell. Her scent was quite literally everywhere, and yet, it was far easier to deal with than the impostor who stood before him, with all of her presence and none of her fire.

Get your shit together, and get it done.

Drayvex bared his fangs in a sneer, for once in total agreement with the voice. This Ruby was not meant for him. She was meant for Saydor. And if he wanted her, he would have to crawl out of his pit to come and get her.

Chapter 26

"We're leaving," he said to the Ruby behind him, his tone hard. Business was business. Never let it be said that the Demon Lord was anything but committed to punishing traitors to his name. Committed and hungry for bloody retribution.

The city embraced its new Ruby as she weaved between crowds of listless humans on the street, her weaker but identical Ruby scent mingling with the stew of others around her. Drayvex trailed behind, following her movements from a distance he could close within seconds. Close in an instant, if he went *through* the masses, as opposed to around.

Suddenly, he could smell the swine thick in the air. The scent of him came out of nowhere, as though he'd just arrived. Saydor was here.

Drayvex zoned in on his flame-haired bait, who was wandering in an oblivious state on his orders. The real Ruby had been gone for less than two Earth days. Had he dragged his feet as before, they may have run out of time.

The inane babble of the humans around him faded as he focused his senses, blocking out anything that wasn't Saydor or the girl. Her heartbeat pounded in his ears, her shallow breaths rushing into her lungs and filling his head in stereo. Saydor's filthy scent burnt in the back of his throat, the demon's presence polluting the air, bleeding into everything surrounding. And still, Drayvex couldn't pinpoint his exact location. All he knew was that the demon was not alone.

It was starting to rain. He didn't feel it, just saw the drops as they registered in his vision. He was going to make Saydor pay. He would remove every bone in that bloated creature's body, spread out what was left like a welcome mat and order every demon under his rule to wipe their filthy feet on his useless bulk, before making him wish he'd never been born. Drayvex would crush him for ever touching the girl who carried his mark. It would never be enough.

One second she was going straight, the next she was angling off to the right. Disappearing into the crowds.

Drayvex followed her scent, blocking out all others as she veered, homing in on the creature that had got her attention. She was following his orders to perfection.

As the Ruby clone wandered into a shady passageway, unflinching in the absence of fear, or any other human emotion to speak of, Drayvex came undone. Unconcerned with the fleshy robots around him, he slipped into a black, vaporous form and edged towards the mouth, towards where she stood, keeping low to the ground.

When he saw Saydor waiting in the shadows, he plunged into a seething mental abyss. Not even in his incorporeal form—a form supposedly above all constraints of the flesh—could he hold back the blistering rage. It consumed him as he took in the monstrosity waiting in the shadows for *her*, bleeding into his every thought and impulse.

"My dear. I knew you would see sense."

Wasting no time, Drayvex pulled himself inward with a snap. The twisting black strands of his form pulled together then exploded outward, becoming something solid and steaming.

The low chuckle from inside the passageway slid over him like broken glass. "I might have known that Your Lordship would crash this party," Saydor dripped, his oily gaze fixing on him. That self-satisfied grin spread across his face, a face that was just begging to be pounded into a soupy pulp. "I don't recall inviting you."

Drayvex moved down the passage in semi-human form, his self-control dangling by a thread as violent impulses swirled in his mind. He would not be baited like some second-rate demon sidekick. "What?" he rumbled. "Not even for old time's sake?" He stepped around the Ruby clone, stopping in front of her as old habits died hard. There was no point in protecting her. The lights were on, but no one was home. "I seem to recall you being all too eager to debase yourself at my feet not so long ago."

Saydor bared his fangs, vitriol flickering across his face before it disappeared. "Still got that sparkling sense of humour, I see. That's good." An insolent smug spread as his eyes narrowed, those sunken black pits flashing red. "You must be getting tired of chasing me. It's not easy being inadequate, but one of us has to do it."

Drayvex's temper flashed. He punched out in a psychic attack, aiming

Chapter 26

straight for Saydor's chest.

He saw it in slow motion as he lunged: the demon that moved in his peripheral. The vicious smile on the scumstain before him. And as his psychic fist punched through the chest of the minion who'd thrown itself into his path, he sneered in disgust. Saydor had always had a way of inspiring underdog loyalty in Drayvex's feckless amoeba rejects.

The weak creature he'd hit screeched, coming apart in flakes of burning ash as raw power pumped into its body. Savage overkill.

"Poor Zandok," Saydor said in mock anguish, looking down at the grey pile on the floor. "Was that really necessary?"

Drayvex felt a hot, burning itch as he glared at Saydor, the demon that had sunk so low, he was barely worth the trouble they had gone to to seek revenge. Smiling in a humourless expression, he stepped forward to slowly circle Saydor. His skin burnt, the demon just beneath pushing to break through his current form. "I see we've sunk to whole new levels of low. Congratulations." His tone matched his mood. His voice became almost basal as the need for some small release won out. "Not content to just hide in the shadows, run from me like the spineless nobody you really are, you're now forcing weaklings to fight your battles."

"I knew it."

Drayvex stopped behind him and fell still. What the fuck now?

Saydor was smiling. Drayvex could hear it in his voice, even through the tightness of his foe's audible stress. "She's really quite something. I must applaud your skills. But you've left her wide open."

Drayvex's gaze fell to Ruby, to the thing that looked like her. Saydor knew. And he was right. Drayvex would never have left the real Ruby unguarded. She was watching him, her face smooth and calm. It mattered not. She had served her purpose.

His gaze shifted to the small gathering of humans collected on the street. They were gaining an audience. He moved around until he was face to face with Saydor, getting in his face. "*What* do you know, base-born?" he growled. "Say what you mean or stop boring me with your drivel."

The wet ripping sound from behind him pushed him right to the edge.

Turning towards the noise, he knew what he would find. Still, it hit him harder than it should have.

The demon behind her had punched straight through her chest. Her heart was in its hand, dangling straight out the front.

It wasn't her. It wasn't Ruby, he knew this—and yet it was. And as the light faded from her eyes right before him and her body slumped to the floor, it was as though the creature had taken a knife to his own chest and gone to town on what was inside.

The rage that followed drowned out everything else. For a moment, it was everything, as his vision tunnelled, ears ringing, power spiking within him.

The demon exploded into a fine black mist. A crack rang through the air, splitting the ground where its feet had been, spraying the passageway in a radius, taking her heart with it.

Saydor tutted from behind him. "Always so dramatic."

Drayvex spun in a flash, bearing down on the ex-demon master with a ready-formed flaming black orb.

The moment he turned, another demon shot out of the shadows. It was heading to block the attack with its face.

Drayvex was quicker. Seething with gasoline-like fury, he grabbed the demon with his mind, twisting its head and body in different directions. As the demon fell limp to the ground between them, he pushed out, black tendrils bursting from his form.

The sliver of fear he glimpsed in Saydor's eyes in that moment was a drop of blood to a starving demon. He hissed out as Drayvex lunged at him, raising his oozing green hands to fight fire with fire.

Saydor was too slow. The black, dripping tendrils wrapped around the demon, binding his hands to his chest as Drayvex replayed the Ruby clone's death in his mind. Stuck on repeat. Feeling the flames in his hand burn with the fury of his past mistakes, Drayvex brought it down hard on Saydor's face and rammed it down his throat.

The furious screams of agony that erupted from the sack of bile before him were music to Drayvex's ears. "Dramatic," he drawled. The bound

Chapter 26

Saydor thrashed in his grip as he howled. The flames burnt him from the inside out, and Drayvex kept it alive, pumping more power into him still, stripping him down from within. He hissed into the demon's ear, squeezing the venomous tendrils that bound him. "I'm just getting started."

A larger demon came at him from behind. The light faded from clone Ruby's eyes. The memory fed the unquenchable madness. Drayvex turned his head, laughing as a demon built like a tank dodged one psychic attack only to walk straight into the path of another. It hit the passage wall with a crunch and fell still. Large cracks spread up the wall, splitting through the building behind with speed.

Drayvex forced the thrashing Saydor to his knees as black smoke poured out of his nose. The pained look in his eyes was mingled with a mad fury. The demon's resistance was weakening, skin cracking. His body couldn't heal itself fast enough.

He felt Saydor try to shift forms and bared his venom-slicked fangs in a sick smile. *Leaving so soon?* he pushed. *But we're having so much fun.* To be bitten by another demon was a mark of shame. Grabbing the thrashing demon by the head, he yanked it back, exposing the throat. He would make sure to plunge nice and deep.

The crunch of concrete that ground through the air made him pause. Drayvex hovered over the bruised yellow flesh of Saydor's neck, listening to the sudden hysteria of the humans on the street.

Ignore them, commanded his inner voice.

He turned his head a fraction, holding the thrashing Saydor down with brute strength. The front corner of the building fell away, no longer attached. The humans below seemed to realise all at once that their phones would not save them.

It was a moment of hesitation. A second at most. But in the time it took for him to dismiss them, Saydor made his move.

The demon beneath him contorted with a snap.

Drayvex whipped back around, sending a shock of power flashing through him from his core. He cursed as Saydor's form collapsed inward, sending it wide. He was slipping through his fingers, quite literally.

The sound of concrete crashing to the ground smothered the screams of the humans out on the street. The tang of blood hit his senses, triggering a predatory reflex.

What a waste of good food. Saydor's smug voice oozed in his head. The cloud of green smoke spewed out into the air, rising and dispersing into the atmosphere. He was running. Again.

Drayvex hissed, rising up straight, burning. Ruby wasn't here, and she was still messing with his head. He scanned the immediate area, sensing that Saydor was still close by. Her roots clearly ran deeper than he'd dared imagine.

I know why you're hiding her from me, taunted Saydor, intruding in his head.

He tightened his mental defences, shutting Saydor out. Closing his eyes, he focused his senses and searched for the location of his presence. No demon was invisible. Not even Saydor.

"Face it." The demon's smug voice floated through the air. "It's because you know that she would choose *me*."

Drayvex's eyes flew open. Focus snapping clean in two, he saw red. "Pathetic," he snarled into the passageway. "You had Ruby right where you wanted her, and what do you do? " Whipping around, he sent a concentrated blast shooting up into the atmosphere in a blind swipe. It didn't connect. "You gamble her in a power trip. How's that working out for you, pretender?"

Saydor's presence was getting weaker. But his soft laughter echoed in the air. "I always get what I want, Drayvex. You know this."

Drayvex felt his presence disappear, and with it, his remaining shreds of self-control. His demon form pushed through with a crack that bounced off the surrounding walls, flooding his system with cool darkness. Saydor would get what he deserved and more.

Chapter 27

The water was warm. Her back to the lush grass, Ruby gazed up at the cloudless sky as she mindlessly trailed her fingers through the lake. Everything was still, but her mind was busy.

Time didn't pass here. Or it did, and she just wasn't aware of it. If she had to take a guess though, she would have to go with weeks. The Crichton Lake copy had become a place of great comfort during this time. It was the one familiar thing in a beautiful, eerie world, among beautiful, eerie people where she didn't quite belong. She'd found that no one bothered her when she was here, and that suited her just fine.

Ruby sat up and got to her feet. She stared across the vast lake, at the scattering of colourful trees beyond, and sighed. Turning on her heel, she headed back towards the shade of the forest, and with it, civilisation.

The forest had that deep, woodsy smell that she'd always loved. She weaved through the trees, knowing her path well now. As she passed a female fae up a tree, she nodded in her direction. The fae nodded back.

Ruby didn't belong here in Moraea, but it wasn't because they'd made her feel unwelcome. On the contrary, most of them had almost seemed to accept her at this point, to stop associating her with the demon that destroyed their lives and start treating her as an individual person. There were, of course, those few who remained suspicious. Their distrust was plain on their faces, frozen in place every time she passed. It never escalated.

The huts up the trees around her became less sparse the deeper she went, an entire village hidden in the apex of the forest. She kept her eyes down, on the path ahead. Her fingers found the cool of the bracelet as she walked and thought, thought and walked. Soul searching, for lack of a better word. Ruby had made a regular habit of it.

Sliding her index finger around the links, she looped them in a familiar fiddle, her thoughts straying to its owner against her will. Drayvex was there every time her thoughts drifted. She couldn't escape those piercing eyes. Had he destroyed the Earth yet in a cataclysmic battle with Saydor? Or had he shoved her through the portal and washed his hands of the whole thing?

Ruby looked down at the dark thorns encircling her wrist. Did he ever think of her from his throne-top perch? Would she ever not be thinking of him? She dropped her hand to her side. None of it mattered anymore. Yet they plagued her. Little itching questions that would never be scratched.

Sunlight poured into the forest from the far exit, dappling through the trees onto the springy green at her feet. Taking a deep breath, she left the forest behind her and headed out into the light.

The sun beat down onto the chuckling river, making it gleam like a precious gem. The forest village wasn't the only place the fae congregated. The more time Ruby spent in their company, the more she learnt from them. For example, the forest fae had chosen the forest because their power lay with nature. And the fae who lived in the mountains had *created* the mountains they made their home.

She was a good student, and her teachers were only too happy to blow her mind.

Ruby followed the river, ambling beside it against its flow as she looked for the marker. She pulled the luxlor from her pocket, absently cradling it in her palm. Strands of light reached for her from within the globe, reacting to her touch, but she wasn't interested in the light. Certainly not of late.

"Neither the darkness nor the light can claim you as its own."

She pictured herself in a dark room, trying to make it come to her.

Chapter 27

Drayvex's words repeated in her mind, the memory tugging at her again. At the temple, the luxlor had spouted darkness. It could only have come from her.

The strands of light in the globe flickered. Ruby shook her head, shoving it back in her pocket as frustration seeped into her muscles. Her every attempt to recreate that day had failed.

Spotting the jagged rock across from her that was her marker, she took a running jump and leapt the stream. She didn't know why she was so intent on summoning darkness now. It felt wrong somehow, like she was committing a sin. But deep down, she wondered if she did know. That maybe it was the thing that connected her to Drayvex.

She forced herself to breathe as fingers of anxiety crept across her mind. She was surrounded by light, standing in a world free from darkness and the problems it caused. And she was trying to will it into existence.

Ruby scrambled over the stones, slipping through the gap between the two rock faces. Regaining her footing on the other side, she gazed down from the mountains at the stone village below.

The houses that dotted the land were nothing like the huts built in the forest's trees. They were almost grand, built tall and reflecting the skill of each individual fae. Some of them were even painted in lavish colours. Amongst them were monuments, places of worship, and every time she revisited the area, shiny new things had appeared. Buildings constructed in a fraction of the time it would take humans to raise them.

The tiny rocks that were scattered about the mountain face made the ground beneath her unstable. Ruby watched her feet as she descended, using the jagged rocks to steady her balance. Handles for a clumsy human.

When she reached the bottom, she skidded to halt. Dust flew into the air around her.

"Ruby. How goes?"

She squinted through the dispersing cloud, fixing on the fae who had addressed her. A vaguely familiar face appeared as it cleared. "I'm well, thanks," she said, smiling.

The fae who might be Raena smiled back, putting the cover models on Callien City's vogue magazines to shame. Her slate-grey eyes lingered on Ruby for a moment, before she turned back to her work.

Ruby slipped away, heading aimlessly into the village of the stone fae. Beautiful people bustled about all around her, some acknowledging her presence as she passed, others meeting her gaze and snatching them away. It was getting harder to remember the faces, let alone the names.

She bit her lip, a familiar pit growing in her stomach. She had watched their numbers grow daily. Her discomfort grew along with them, each new fae battle-ready. Each one carrying vitriol towards the Demon Lord as potent as his was for them.

Ruby had asked Tira about the numbers. And Tira had explained to her then that the closer she got to securing her people's future, the further she could stretch her desires. The closer she inched to her goal, the more fae she could call to the wings.

She followed the dusty path, weaving between beautiful stone structures, trying to block out the milling crowds around her. Ruby owed Drayvex nothing. Tira—no, the *fae*—had been good to her. He didn't deserve her consideration, let alone her loyalty. But she just couldn't switch off.

Ruby found the outskirts of the stone village and kept going. What lay beyond it, she didn't know. It was as good a day as any to find out.

The luxlor tapped against her ribs as she walked. She ignored it, knowing that failing to produce what she desired would only worsen her mood. She immediately changed her mind. Reaching into her jacket, she glanced up at her surroundings, her fingers brushing over its cool surface—and stopped in her tracks.

The building she was staring at was isolated from the rest. It was almost shrine-like, the way it had been designed, and stained a glorious gold that shone like the real thing under the exotic fae sun.

Ruby's hand fell from the folds of her jacket. Her curiosity prickled. She had to get closer.

The small square shrine stood by itself. Isolated and standing just beyond the village borders, it was all but ignored by the fae living nearby. She stood

Chapter 27

gazing up close at its grand structure, taking in the intricate details carved into the stone walls. They looked like lettering. It wasn't a language that she recognised.

The doors were wide open. Ruby let herself inside.

Her footsteps bounced off the stone floor and echoed within the space as she entered. The inner was as gold as the outer, a single room almost empty save for one focal point. She felt a shiver run through her in the sunless chill and froze to the spot. The cold wasn't the source of her goosebumps.

The shining green beacon on the pedestal before her sat in the centre of the room, drawing her eye with effortless beauty. The light was coming from an object that looked a lot like a stone.

Ruby shuffled forward, almost in a trance, drawn towards it like a moth to a blazing turquoise flame. The stone was perfectly circular, with tiny beads of light that zipped around it like the rings of Saturn. It felt both wrong and right at the same time, and even she, as weak and human as she was, could feel the weight of its very presence filling the room. She could hardly bring herself to blink.

She stared at it, holding her breath. Her mind was firing on all cylinders. Surely, this wasn't … this wasn't the Lapis Temporis. The stone of time. Was it?

She fisted a hand in her hair. Her heart pounded against her ribcage. Surely, she hadn't just stumbled across it by accident. Just sitting there, completely unguarded.

Ruby felt a sudden weakness in her limbs as a clammy heat rose up into her face. She leant over, breathing slowly. They trusted her. It was the only explanation she could come up with, that the poor, broken human they'd adopted wasn't a threat.

Standing up straight, she turned and walked herself out of the building.

The sunshine was too much. Numb, she took a few paces back towards the stone village before she stopped and looked down.

Her eyes were drawn to the bracelet at her wrist against her will. She saw him clear as day in her mind, and it was a stab in the gut. Drayvex, the demon who haunted her nightmares, who held her heart in a vice. She was going to betray him after all.

Ruby couldn't breathe. She forced herself to take another step away, and another. He had slaughtered the entire fae race in cold blood just because they wouldn't fall into line. He deserved everything they would deal out and more.

She took another wooden step. Stared ahead towards the far village, a bitter taste spreading on her tongue. If she warned him the fae were coming, he would just kill them all over again. She would be condemning them to death.

She closed her eyes. Her legs would no longer move. Tira had betrayed them when she stole the stone for her own ends. She would slaughter the entire demon race if she could, and Drayvex with it. Kill them from behind, without warning. Because the end justified the means. She was no better than him.

Ruby swallowed. She herself was only alive because he had saved her. Given her a piece of himself, shrugged it off like it was nothing.

She spun on the spot. Her steps were heavy, but they carried her nonetheless, back towards the little gold shrine.

Standing in the doorway, she shivered once again as she lay eyes on the swirling stone of time. Even from a distance, looking into its centre made her feel dizzy. She moved towards it, hardly aware of her own actions. Standing before it, it bathed her in green light. Oh, what she would give to be anyone but herself in this moment.

Ruby reached out towards the stone, her muscles stiff, almost locking in place. But she *was* her. One way or another, she was about to condemn an entire race to death.

Let it go. It was time to make her peace and walk away. Let him go.

The ringing in her ears was sudden and loud. The air in her lungs felt solid. Intention became instinct. And everything that followed was a blur.

Before she knew what she was doing, Ruby was running. Out of the shrine, back towards the village as though her life depended on it. She had to get away.

Stone buildings flashed past her. Beautiful faces. Where was she going?

Chapter 27

She had no idea. All she knew was that she couldn't stop.

She burst from the village and began to scale the small mountain trail with an energy that stemmed from fear. Her lungs were tight, her legs screaming at her as she drove them up the slope. Her thoughts were a tangled mess. Keep going, keep going. Don't look behind you. You're going to die.

When she reached the top, one of the fae called to her from the base of the mountain. Ruby almost expired on the spot. Ignoring the voice, she pulled her jacket tight around the two solid lumps nestled against her and headed for the river that ran between the stone village and the grassy hills.

She got all the way to the exit before it hit her. Collapsing to the soft grass, she fell to her knees on the bank, shivering. She was going to kill them all.

Ruby made a sound that was half laugh and half sob. She was on that hill she'd first arrived on after being shoved through the portal. The portal from the three trees and the hidden temple.

She wanted to scream. It was getting hard to breathe. The middle of nowhere, that was where she would come out on the other side. It could be the other side of the planet for all she knew. She would have to take that chance. Steeling herself, she got to her feet and scanned the hill for the tree she needed. The tree that would take her back to Earth.

But wait. She sucked in a breath as a thought smacked her over the head. There was another portal nearby. One that was closer to home.

Driven by the sudden need to get home, Ruby tore off down the hill and back towards the river. If she was wrong, this would all end badly. She would be boxing herself into a corner, no doubt the corner she would die in. But if she was right …

There were no fae waiting to take her out at the river. Guilt pulsing through her, she pushed herself harder and headed for the forest.

As she tore through the forest, she became aware that she was attracting attention. Every part of her hurt. She kept going, too scared to stop. Why oh why was she so unfit?

One of the fae stepped into her path. Panic screaming in her mind, she swerved around him. Her elbow smashed into a tree as she tried to dodge him, and she screamed in pain.

"Child, wait!"

No time. Gritting her teeth, Ruby dug deep. Legs and lungs screamed along with her pulsing elbow. Regret. She was already swimming in it.

She didn't think they were chasing her. Then again, she couldn't afford to check, or she would run face-first into a tree. The light at the end of the forest was in sight. She wanted to cry with relief. At this point, the pain coursing through her drowned out her fear tenfold. If she didn't stop soon, she was going to be sick.

Ruby kept her eyes on the approaching light, on the forest's end. She was going to make it. She was going to collapse. She was going to make it, she—

"Ruby, wait!"

The familiar voice sent a fresh wave of fear skittering over her skin. It was Tira.

No, please go away. Ruby burst from the forest on the other side and into the bright sunshine. The Crichton Lake replica twinkled at her, beckoning. She stumbled to a halt, hands on her knees. Would this even work? It was too late for doubts.

"Ruby, what's wrong?" Tira's voice was getting closer.

Ruby tried to call to her, but she couldn't speak. Her lungs were broken. Glancing behind her, she saw the magnificent warrior woman pounding towards her, and her life flashed before her eyes.

Forgive me, Tira, Ruby pleaded. Then, without another thought, she ran towards the lake and hurled herself into its depths.

Chapter 28

She was sinking, and then she simply wasn't.

Ruby struggled in the water, kicking with limbs that felt more like weights than working legs. Her tired lungs begged her for mercy, sluggish panic pulsing in her veins. She hadn't thought this through.

Breaking through the surface of the lake, she gasped for air. The sun shone through her eyelids, blinding her. No, no, no, no. She was still here. She flinched as her eyes snapped open and then felt them widen.

The park looked exactly the same, but everything beyond it had changed.

It was like going back in time. Back to a time when life was simple, and her biggest problem was her hard-headed mother; except, its rustic beauty had all been stripped away. But it was Crichton, and it was beautiful.

Ruby almost sank again as a wave of relief swept over her. It had worked. It had *actually* worked.

She swallowed water as her tired legs failed to keep her afloat. A jolt of fear lanced through her. Oh no, not today, she thought, pushing through the pain and starting for the lake's edge. She had not come this far just to get this far.

Ruby Peyton: escaped hoard of battle-hardened fae with time stone, drowned in lake.

The last of her remaining strength went into pulling herself out of the lake. Dripping and shivering on the park grass, she tried to settle her erratic breathing. She felt like a criminal on the run.

Just then remembering the reason for all her troubles, she dove into her sodden jacket. The stone was still there. Breathing out, she pulled it from within the folds and held it in the palm of her hand. Guilt twisted in her stomach region.

Ruby sighed, pulling herself to her feet. How could she have done this to someone who had only ever treated her with kindness? She shook her head, shoving self-pity to the back of her mind. Ruby had certainly not stolen the stone first.

Tira would discover what Ruby had done, and she would come for her. The thought was enough to make her blood run cold. She had to find Drayvex.

The stone in her hand was no longer giving off any signs of life. In fact, it seemed to be utterly dead. She chewed on her lip, unable to shake the ominous feeling creeping over her. She stowed it back inside her jacket.

A noise from the lake behind her made her stand to attention. Ruby turned to face the water, her entire body stiffening as bubbles rose up from the depths of the lake. Something was coming up—or some*one*.

Ruby took off across the park as though her life depended on it. Surely to god, Tira had not already been to the empty shrine? Did time stop in there? She reached the gates and fumbled with the metal latch, fingers numb and clumsy. She was not sticking around to find out.

Exhaustion and fear took turns to overwhelm her as Ruby bolted through the old streets of Crichton. The park may still sit untouched, but the village beyond it had been ravaged. If she'd had time to process the sad, empty shell that it was now, she would no doubt be mourning its loss. As it was, she was emotionally stretched. How did you find a demon who could jump between worlds like train platforms? Tracking down Drayvex was going to be a nightmare.

Ruby slowed, looking down at her wrist as a thought occurred to her. The gems on the bracelet caught in the sun, tiny red fireballs. But did she not already have a strange connection to Drayvex?

Chapter 28

Looking for cover, she ducked behind a wall and fumbled with the clasp. The bracelet came away and fell into her waiting hand. If she could exploit their connection, then she would.

Dropping the bracelet into a soggy pocket, Ruby breathed in through her nose and out through her mouth. Then, closing her eyes, she let her mind wander to Drayvex.

Before long, she could almost feel the heat that he threw off in waves pelting her back. She could feel the way the tangled storm of his presence filled her mind, his hot breath on the back of her neck.

Goosebumps spread across her skin unbidden. She wondered how far her imagination would be willing to take things. Cheeks flaring to life, she flexed her neck, keeping her eyes closed. *Find me*, she thought at him.

She didn't know why, but she got the distinct sense that if she opened her eyes, he would slip away. Like trying to hold onto water. *I need you to find me.*

Ruby was suddenly very tired. She could feel the imaginary Drayvex slipping through her fingers. *I can't do this alone, dammit.* Alone.

Nothing happened. She bit her lip. She didn't know what she'd expected. Feeling stupid, she pushed off the wall and kept going. The hard way it was then.

Crichton was dead and silent. Even the wind seemed to be avoiding this place, she thought, trying not to look at the burnt shells of shops and cafes that had once provided her with comfort.

Something skittered past on her left. It flashed in her peripheral vision, there and then gone. She snapped her head around. What was that?

She jerked away from the main road, darting down into a side passage. Her heart pulsed in her throat. *Please understand, Tira*, she thought. The stone and luxlor hung heavy in her sodden jacket, weighing her down even more than her wet clothes.

Something skittered directly behind her. A strange kind of fear spiked in her veins. She'd never learnt to harness the dark. Swivelling on the spot, she stood and braced herself for impact. Tira *was* the light. And the luxlor would be useless against her.

Ruby caught the tail end of a—she blinked hard. A tail?

Panting, she swivelled back towards the passage. Did demons still prowl here? Shivering through a bone-deep chill, she gritted her teeth and steeled her nerves. She would get back to Callien and make a plan from there.

The beast that appeared in front of her came out of nowhere.

Ruby stumbled backwards, horror sinking its claws in deep as she stared at the thing. She hadn't heard it make a sound, and yet it filled the little passage with its broad shoulders and powerful limbs, a mound of black fur and muscle. Her breaths almost stopped as the creature fixed on her. It was crouched on all fours, but she had a feeling it was build to run on two. The soft growling that rumbled from its chest was a warning that paralysed her. Its face was a skull, long like a dog, and nestled within a black mane of fur.

Don't panic, she thought, her eyes wide. Her hand gravitated toward her pocket.

The demon moved with her, sinking low.

Ruby froze. She could hear Sandra in her mind, see her lying helpless on the floor. That was the moment that ripped them apart. The day that changed them both forever.

Tears swam in her vision as she stared at the demon; as she thought of what might have been, had she not left Sandra at the mercy of fate. Maybe Sandra would not have been so beyond her reach now.

Ruby was pure anger and grief as she whipped out the luxlor. The demon pounced, snarling in a chainsaw rev that shook her bones. Her past self would have cowered, waiting to die. Present Ruby fought her demons with everything she had.

She screamed as the blast of light engulfed the hulking demon and then herself, leaving them both blind. The last thing she saw as her body braced for impact was the demon veering off to the right. Its screeches bounced off the walls within the narrow space.

Ruby was still holding the luxlor out before her when the light faded. She blinked, staring down the empty passageway. And then, with mounting dread, turned to her right.

The demon was on its back.

Chapter 28

She lurched backwards, meeting the wall behind her. A numbness crept over her as she took it in. Its eyes were darting, smoking limbs twitching in the air. Helpless.

The luxlor burnt in her palm. She'd done this. *Her.*

The full-body writhe of a nightmare trying to find its legs was the wake-up call she needed. Ruby blasted it once more in a short sharp burst and broke into a sprint, powering through to the other side of the passage.

Her feet pounded the pavement as she slipped past empty houses in a blur. She wasn't the badass Sandra or her mother were. But she was far from powerless. Maybe it would be enough to get her to the city in one piece.

* * *

Find me.

The voice buzzed in his head, a self-imposed delirium that had no business sounding so much like her—or being so fucking loud.

Drayvex bore into the demon from across the chamber, spinning a silky strand of pure power between his fingers. Saydor's lackey. Strapped to the vertical rack, the bound beast was one he recognised. The toady turned turncoat. Drayvex didn't have to dig deep to be consumed by the rancour that this fetid creature inspired.

This one would serve as a reminder to all of what happened when you crossed a Demon Lord.

The mutilated demon fixed on him, its one remaining eye seething and wild. The other was splattered down its leathery muzzle in a gory trail, one of many delights the hellinger had inflicted on its hefty form.

Saydor could brainwash as many of these sorry specimens to his cause as he liked. The torches of Vekrodus burnt as black as his aura. He, Drayvex, owned demonkind. They all lived by *his* grace. They were pawns, their sole purpose to do his bidding. And if they wouldn't heel at his command, he would *un*make them, with pleasure.

I need you to find me.

Drayvex hissed as Ruby's voice attacked him. For a moment, he wavered, the plea in her voice spiking a restless need that had long become reflex. He knew it wasn't her. But it was a mental battle he was not winning, even as he stood in demon full glory. He couldn't focus with this shit going round his head.

He was trying to forget her. Instead, the voices in his head had been replaced by hers. The lack of control triggered a deep, heavy anger, and the familiar cadence of her voice sent a keen edge slicing through his thoughts. It gave him an insatiable thirst for violence.

He stepped forward and crossed the dark chamber towards the hellinger and his demon captive, needing to take back control. There weren't enough traitors and pissants on the entire planet to keep his mind and hands occupied indefinitely. But that wouldn't stop him from washing the planet in their blood.

The pale, gaunt figure with the tools of torment turned a fraction as he approached. White skin stretched taut across its skeletal face, fleshy flaps pulled tight across empty eye sockets. With no eyes and a mouth that was magically sewn shut, Drayvex didn't have much to go on. But as the hellinger probed him with mental feelers, it took a step back.

He knew it would. It was blind, not stupid.

The horned specimen strapped to the rack shifted, and Drayvex took a sadistic pleasure in the visible multitude of terrors that crossed its face in a one-eighty flip. "Allow me." Drayvex held out his hand in expectation.

The hellinger reacted to the glacial command without hesitation, placing the instrument in his waiting hand.

Drayvex closed his claws around the twisted metal and looked towards the demon. He smiled a sick smile, a heady cocktail of power and soft, seething rage pulsing through his being. "I want to play a game," he uttered, hearing the steel in his own voice.

I can't do this alone, dammit.

He bared teeth, fighting not to grimace. Do what? Even his delusions were deluded.

The demon let out a hiss. "Kill me."

Drayvex jammed the sharp end into the demon's chest.

Chapter 28

His captive cried out, baring the protruding daggers in its mouth. They were slick with dark blood.

"Keep it warm for me," he growled. Leaving the black-splattered instrument sticking out of its chest like a demon handle, Drayvex turned and headed for the door. Enough.

There was only one thing left of hers that remained. It was the one lingering tie that existed between them. He would burn it all away.

The block of flats gleamed without mercy under the Earth-sun, metal and glass catching in aggressive flashes, protesting the callous thoughts in his head.

Drayvex eyed the monstrous construct with a bitterness he knew was wasted on the inanimate object. The road between was teeming. Cars grated past in his peripheral, humans swarming around them; an ever-moving stream of mundane in the stagnant pool that was Callien city.

It was irrational to think that destroying this building would kill the voice that sounded so much like hers. Ruby was dead to this world. Taking out the place she'd called home would only fuel the madness, not kill it.

And the humans still inside? purred a voice in his head that was far too smug.

He glowered at the building, indecision giving way to resolve. Not his problem.

Drayvex reached out in front of him, turning his open palm face-up as the city bombarded his senses. Ten floors up, three windows from the left. He sneered, letting the rising power consume him. It was beneath him. And yet, in this moment, all he could think was that he wanted to purge it from existence.

The power that thrummed down his arm reached his fingertips as he summoned it forth. The humans that walked by ignored him to painstaking perfection. Instinct told them to stay away, an instinct that Ruby had been sorely lacking.

As Drayvex inched his claw-tipped fingers inward, the magic fought him. He pushed back, crushing the pressure in his palm in slow motion like an abandoned can tossed to the road.

The monstrosity of a building on the far side of the road groaned.

The thing that collided with him at full sprint hit him in the chest. The physical impact was feeble at best; he barely felt it. His mind, however, was obliterated.

Now he knew: he had truly lost his mind.

Chapter 29

It worked. Drayvex had heard her after all. She couldn't believe her eyes.

Ruby's relief almost crippled her as she connected with the demon on the street, her cares far away in that brief, suspended moment. He turned to stone beneath her, burning as she clung to him like he might slip through her fingers.

When Drayvex didn't move, her fear came crashing back with force. His reaction didn't make sense. And the more she thought about it, the more painfully apparent it became that he had not been expecting her at all.

It was too late for regret, and as Ruby withdrew herself all at once and stood before him, a self-conscious blush heated her cheeks. "Sorry. I …"

She stopped. The urgency of her situation pulsed in her entire being. But there was something about the way Drayvex was looking at her that derailed her thoughts. She tensed, reacting to his stress without even knowing what she was reacting to. It was almost as though he didn't *want* to see her here.

Ruby pushed the thoughts away. She squinted at him, unsure of how to proceed. She didn't have time for this. "What's wrong?"

Drayvex narrowed his eyes, pinning her to the spot. His gaze had changed from jet black to the palest blue the instant they'd connected. Now, they were black once again, and glistening with contempt.

She felt it smack her in the chest. Suspicion was something she'd come to expect by default. The lack of trust between them was mutual. But it was the edge of loathing she saw that dug at her. It didn't belong in those eyes, staring at *her*. It was all wrong.

"Will you say something?" Ruby heard the plea in her question as her composure slipped, but she was beyond caring.

He dropped his hand and slipped towards her, closing the small distance she'd put between them.

As Drayvex roughly grabbed her by the jaw with one clawed hand, she flinched.

She began to feel the crowds closing in on her, panic clawing at her as he penetrated her soul with a wild black gaze. She stared back, vulnerable and cold. Tira could be anywhere. Had his sentiment all been an act? Had he been glad to be rid of her after all? "I can't do this without you," she whispered.

Something seemed to click inside the demon before her as she wilted under his scrutiny. Ruby watched it happen. She watched his face change in a contrast that was both mesmerising and terrifying, darkness draining from his eyes as though someone had pulled a plug.

He dropped his hand, and she rubbed her chin, her mind reeling. What the Hell was that? Psycho.

"Satan's sake—what the fuck are you doing here?" Drayvex gaped at her, the snap of his tone reaching his eyes in red wisps. Eyes that, in total contradiction to his biting tone, were almost tender.

Ruby blinked at him. Nice to see you too, jerk. She breathed out a shaky breath, eyes darting to the people around them. They needed to get off the street.

It was as though he'd read her mind. One moment they were the obstacle in the middle of an ever-flowing stream of bodies, the next they were under the shade of a shop awning. She forgot how to breathe as the headrush stunned her.

Drayvex was also stunning. In an instant, he had become all business, that cool mask of nothing as handsome and pitiless as ever. "Now, speak."

Chapter 29

Ruby processed his soft command, trying to focus as the heat that rolled off his skin bathed her. Oh god, where did she even start? She felt her heart pounding in her chest.

It took her a moment to notice the thin wisps of darkness curling around her, but as she looked down at herself, she realised with a start that they were cloaking her in shadows. Concealing her. They were coming from Drayvex.

He leant in, his ashen gaze pinning her with an intensity that was unwavering. "Tell me everything."

Ruby swallowed her nerves. This was why she was here. She stared back, gathering her thoughts, free-falling in the storm of his gaze. She chose this. "Okay."

Drayvex remained fixed on her, the picture of still. And as his mouth pulled down in an expression that was louder than anything he could have shouted, he was also the very picture of impatience.

"Just remember how close I am," she said, speaking in a hush, "before you lose it."

She watched those astute eyes narrow at her in warning. His skewed mind had no doubt jumped to the worst possible scenario. He wouldn't come close.

"Did she hurt you?"

Ruby was taken off guard by Drayvex's words. They carried an unspoken threat that sent a cold shiver down her spine, even basking in his warmth. "No. No, that's not ..." She sighed. Here goes nothing. "I broke out from Moraea to warn you what was coming. And I'm certain Tira followed me here. Because ..."

Drayvex put his hand on the window behind her head. She heard his claws clack against the glass. "Because ...?"

She felt the dam break. And as he prompted her with the impatient patience of a demon on the edge, it all came tumbling out. "Because Tira took the stone. And she told me everything. She told me how she went back with its power and relived the temple all over again to control the outcome. Then she showed me what she'd done with the stone."

Ruby hesitated, watching the crimson bleed of Drayvex's eyes drown out the grey. The darkness in her head thrashed like the lash of a whip. It was too late to turn back now.

"I *saw* everything."

"What," he said with a growl, "did I tell you about that thieving bitch?"

She cringed as he spoke with a fresh edge, her guilt tweaking at her. The part of him inside her pulsed, smothering her mind in seething, rushing darkness. She put her hand to her head, her eyes drawn to his teeth. Had they always been that sharp? "There's more."

Drayvex sneered, giving her a full show. They were definitely bigger. "Don't tell me. The shit-show is missing its main event." He whipped his hand back from the glass, stirring the air around her face. His sarcasm on top of the thrashing darkness was more than she could take right now.

She wanted to scream. "Dammit," Ruby yelled, "you're pounding my skull."

The silence that followed was deafening. She bit her tongue, feeling awkward.

When she looked up at the seething demon, she saw he was glaring at her. With what looked like a fair amount of effort, Drayvex flashed her a pained smile. "Speak up, Red. I can't hear you over my bleeding eardrums."

It was Ruby's turn to glare. My brain is bleeding, she jabbed, hoping he could hear her thoughts.

Sure enough, his dark eyes slid from the window behind her, a bleak humour glinting as he took her in.

"Look, there's no easy way to say this—"

"Not here," Drayvex interrupted. He looked over his shoulder, towards the block of flats.

Ruby nodded. They needed privacy. And... She glanced around her at the people flowing past them, throwing them furtive glances. And they weren't going to get that here.

The flat felt empty and bland. Maybe because Ruby had spent the past god knew how long in a literal paradise, but it no longer felt like home. She

Chapter 29

padded over to the window, lost in her own head. Then again, Tira's world had never felt like home. Did she even have one anymore?

"You're scared. Why?"

Ruby started as Drayvex prompted her from somewhere behind. His voice was low, velvet-smooth. Was he trying to calm her? She breathed out, suddenly so tired. It was working. She turned slowly from the window to face him, unsure of how to answer.

He stared at her with a steady gaze. His eyes were a cool grey.

Because I screwed over an entire race to keep you safe, she thought, chewing on the nub of her nail. And I'm not sure it was the right thing to do. "Tira told me everything. And I took her trust and stabbed her in the back. Because..."

Ruby could feel the tension rolling off Drayvex like an extra presence in the room, the pressure filling her head. She wasn't helping either of them.

Just say it, Ruby. Say it! "Tira was using the stone to bring the fae back from the dead. All of them."

Something in the room snapped.

Alarm shot through her as she realised the sound had come from Drayvex. She felt it shoot through her skull, a reverberation that terrified her more than his darkness in her mind. And she saw the hellish black horns that had appeared on his head. "She was still trying," Ruby gabbled in a hurry, wishing she had the power to pacify with voice alone like he had. "It's not as easy as she first thought, which ... is why Tira is coming for me now."

"Mother of Chaos," he growled, trailing off with a string of what she could only assume were profanities of his own tongue. Then, all of a sudden, he stilled. It was jarring, as though he'd simply disconnected. "I should have known." And as his crimson glare fixed on her once again, he slipped towards her with an eerie calm.

"What?" Ruby braced her twisting stomach, looking up with a determination she had no idea she still possessed. She supposed they were both exceeding expectations today.

Drayvex stopped in front of her, the king of her nightmares, the monster all wrapped in a beautiful package. "You complained of a headache as we entered the temple. You were suffering from time lag."

She blinked at him, stunned. Time lag.

"Is there anything else you wish to share with the class?" he murmured, looking down at her with distant regard.

Ruby gazed up at him, almost nonchalant now. The worst was behind them. "There is one other thing."

She watched his eyes darken and narrow, his claws curve and lengthen as he folded his arms. "Spit it out."

Suddenly feeling sheepish, she reached into her jacket pocket and pulled out the stone. And as she lay it in the palm of her hand, she watched his eyes grow wide. She swallowed. "I stole the Lapis Temporis from right under her nose."

Chapter 30

The Lapis Temporis. It was unmistakable, even dull and lifeless in the palm of her hand, its dormant power reaching for his mind.

Drayvex dragged his gaze up from the stone to the world's smallest thief. She looked like she was waiting for him to explode. He did.

The laugh that erupted from him caught her off guard, making her recoil in a way that only made it harder to stop. Once again, Drayvex had done something disgustingly selfless in the Ruby's name. And once again, while left to her own devices, she had repaid him, and then some.

"You think this is funny? Think again."

Drayvex focused again on the girl standing before him. Small and infuriating and defiant. He swallowed a slick of venom, his previous conniption a speck on the horizon. He would never say it out loud, would never give her such power, but he had missed that unruly mouth.

And no, it really wasn't so funny. He could see the fear in her eyes, smell it on her as she chewed on her lip, waiting for him to respond. He ran his tongue along the tops of his fangs. Ruby was right to be scared. She'd taken a risk, cemented her allegiance to him, and in doing so, had made a powerful enemy.

Sobering, Drayvex took a step forward. He reached out towards the stone in her grip, hovering just short of touching it. Its glassy surface swirled, liquid clouds of green blooming in the palm of her hand. Fortunately for her, she also had a powerful ally.

Ruby tensed as he moved into her personal space, her eyes meeting his and holding them. Seeking reassurance.

He skimmed his hovering fingers over the surface of the stone, slipping down to meet the cool underside of her hand. He felt the fragile bones of her hand twitch under his fingers and then still. "I'm going to protect you, you know," he uttered with low conviction. He slipped his hand slowly under hers. "From every last fucker that wants a piece of you."

Drayvex watched Ruby swallow. Watched her struggle with his words and the casual way they settled with a permanent sort of weight. "You will?" Her voice was breathy.

He watched his fingers curl around to rest on her wrist, a calm descending over him that didn't match his wild disposition. They had always made strange bedfellows. It was just getting stranger.

She looked down at where they touched, where the curved hooks of his fingers rested against the thin membrane of her skin. Her pulse throbbed beneath the tips. The smallest of slips would rip her wide open.

Out of nowhere, a flash of memory intruded. The not-Ruby, her heart dangling out of her chest.

Drayvex held himself in check. "Is there not a piece of me inside you?" he reasoned, looking into those big green eyes. He let a wicked smile grow on his face.

Ruby's gaze glazed over as their eyes met. They slipped down to his mouth and then up to what he assumed were his horns, sitting heavy on his head. He needed to get rid of those. "Well ..."

"Does that not make your enemies my problem?"

Her mouth hovered open as her words got stuck. "I-I guess—"

"And what do you think I do to those who brand themselves my enemy?" He felt her then rather than saw her, a flicker of light in the darkness of his mind. Slipping straight through his mental walls and into his head. Any other time, it would have been stifling. "They die screaming."

Chapter 30

Ruby closed her eyes and breathed out. When she looked up at him again, there was a fresh resolve there that he'd rarely seen her indulge. "Okay." Then, just as slowly, she reached up with her other hand and traced a single finger down one of the claws at her wrist.

Drayvex stilled, muscles locking. The path her finger trailed was hypersensitive. Her touch was lightning, striking as many times as it pleased. It was always too much. He was hooked on the burn.

"But I don't want her dead."

He narrowed his eyes, giving her a calculating look as she glanced away, avoiding his gaze. Carefully extracting himself, he folded his arms. "Mmm, no. You don't have that luxury." The soft warning behind his words lingered in the air, a physical thing with dark essence. "That harpy won't show you a shred of mercy."

Ruby looked up, head jerking. She moved back towards the window at her back, hand running through her hair. There was a wild edge to her that reached him in a shockwave. Her restlessness seeped through his skin, bleeding into his pores. "You don't understand."

Drayvex stared at her, now on edge himself. Was that his, or because *she* felt this way? He glared at her, a stab of frustration lancing through him. What a damn mess.

The fight seemed to drain out of her all at once. "I chose the demon over an entire beautiful race I just discovered existed. What you do next is solely on me."

He flicked his forked tongue out in a snap. So I'm 'the demon' now, am I, dear? he thought, watching her with fresh suspicion. That sounds like a downgrade. His keen eyes followed her every small movement, and as she turned and shuffled from the window, she bypassed him completely.

Ruby sank down onto the sofa with a sigh. "Every fae you kill from this point on is blood on my hands."

He slipped towards the sofa, trailing his claws along the fabric as he moved behind her. "I see."

She tensed mid-hair swipe, her heart picking up speed. "You do?"

Drayvex smirked, reaching the arm of the sofa and facing her side-on.

She already had him bound in so many ways. If she thought she could blackmail *him*, extort the demon who practically invented extortion and save her own soul, she was as delusional as he was. "You want to have your prey and eat it."

Ruby blinked once, staring straight ahead at the wall. "I ... what?" She turned her head towards him and frowned. "You mean my cake?"

Drayvex wrinkled his nose. Please. "You see many demons raiding bakeries? No, I don't mean a pissing cake."

As her frown turned into the filthiest of looks, his fangs gave a pleasant throb. He fought to keep his mind on the matter at hand. Mercy, he needed help.

"You're not being fair," Ruby said, her tone telling him this conversation was over.

Fair, he thought, stepping around the sofa and stopping right in front of her, is for has-beens and failures. He smiled as though she could hear his thoughts. He wasn't sure. But her poker face was flawless as she looked up and met his gaze.

Suddenly, her eyes grew wide, and she froze. "My mum. Shoot!"

Drayvex felt every muscle lock as she sprung up from the sofa with a new urgency. The damn mother. Well, shit. She'd really got him on this one.

"How long have I been away? I hope she's okay."

Are you going to tell her what you did with mother dearest? teased a voice in his skull.

He stared at the girl before him, hanging between two precipices. He would rather stick a spoon in his eye and scoop it out. He needed Ruby close, not fighting him. No, the truth would not serve either of them.

You are one cold bastard.

Ruby's heart began to pick up speed again. She was looking at him as though her world was ending. "What's ... wrong with my mum?" He had taken too long. "Drayvex?"

The three succinct thuds on the far door had them both spinning towards the sound. Saved by the unwanted guest. His claws twitched at his sides. But who in the unholy bowels of Vekrodus would be looking for Ruby now?

Chapter 30

"I don't think—"

"Stay put. Do as you're told." Drayvex took a step towards the door, the demon just beneath his skin bristling. He couldn't smell demon; all he could smell was human. Their species wasn't going to save them.

Before he could get any closer, the human on the other side of the door let themselves in. The moment her scent wafted into the room in a concentrated blast, he knew who was coming.

Drayvex would not come second to her twice.

* * *

Ruby's initial reaction as Sandra stepped into her flat was of pure, unbridled elation. Then fear grabbed her by the throat as reality came knocking. It drowned out everything.

The moment Sandra locked eyes with Drayvex, her entire demeanour changed. She whipped out a gun, moving faster than Ruby could follow, pointing it at Drayvex's head.

Ruby darted forward, moving out from behind him to stand between them. She held up her hands in a pacifying gesture. "Sand, put it away," she pleaded. "Please."

Sandra didn't take her eyes off him. Her eyes were hard, her clothes dark and practical, fitted almost like a uniform.

Ruby could feel Drayvex burning behind her, sense the hostility that bled from him like a dark stain into the room. Her instinct prickled in warning. He was more dangerous now than ever. "The gun won't do anything." She lowered her hands, taking a half-step forward. "You know this." More than anything, it was just going to provoke him. It was an invitation he didn't need.

Sandra scoffed. "Oh, this one will hurt. Trust me."

A lump of ice slid down her back. What did that mean?

Drayvex laughed, a hard, mocking sound. She flinched as it sliced through her. "If it isn't the little hunter with the big mouth. Did Daddy give you that?"

The contempt in his voice was hard to swallow. But it was the responding venom that glistened in the eyes of her best friend that was hardest to take.

"What do you know of my dad, demon?"

"You stole it, didn't you? Good for you, wannabe." She could almost imagine the condescending smile that displayed a full mouth of fangs as he put on a show, confidence more than bordering on arrogance. "You show that prick who's boss."

"These bullets are made from the molten core of your planet. When I shoot you in the head, it will sting like a bitch. At a minimum, it will destroy your brain and poison your bloodstream. If I'm lucky, I'll be drinking champagne from your skull by tea time."

Ruby felt Sandra's callous words sink in and settle as though they were made of lead. She was bluffing. There was no such bullet that could hurt a Demon Lord that way. But Drayvex didn't correct her. And just like that, she was forced to consider the possibility that he was not invincible after all.

She didn't like it. Not one bit.

"How confident are you?" Drayvex's voice had become soft and deadly. If darkness had a voice, it would sound like him. Deep and rich, and cruel. "I suggest you don't miss." Strands of darkness slipped over her shoulder, emanating from the demon. Darkness that, unlike him, was cold as it brushed against the skin of her throat. "You fail to take me down in one shot, little girl, you'd better run. Because I will rip you limb from fucking limb."

Ruby stepped forward, crossing the room towards Sandra.

"I will *break* you in ways your basic human mind can't even comprehend. But by all means, do what no being, living or dead, has ever been able to accomplish. Take your shot. And then I'll take mine."

He paused, and his next words echoed through her mind. *I suggest you choose your next move very carefully.*

She bit the inside of her cheek, nose tingling. *I suggest you don't threaten me,* she pushed back. Did he really think she'd turn her back on him so easily? She wasn't like him. She stopped in front of Sandra, who was now,

Chapter 30

finally, looking at her. The gun never wavered.

Ruby stood staring at her once cheerful, bubbly best friend, her heart aching. How had they got here?

"Rube, please. I need you."

She sighed, the ache turning to a stab. "Put it down, Sand. We can talk about this." As she spoke without hope, knowing in her heart that Sandra would not back down, she put her hand over the barrel of the gun, curling her fingers around its deadly end.

Sandra paled, the hard edges Ruby had come to dislike so much flickering in and out of existence. "Why?" she whispered. "Why are you protecting a monster?"

That was what it came down to. It was exactly what it looked like, and Ruby had asked herself the very same question every day since Drayvex had come back into her life. Yes, Drayvex was monstrous in every possible way. But he was sometimes more than a monster. And sometimes, he was the only person in the world who was there for her. It wasn't that simple.

"I told you," Ruby said, looking straight into Sandra's anxious gaze. "I don't need protecting from Drayvex. I have bigger problems. If you would just listen to me, you'd already know this."

Sandra's face seemed to visibly harden all at once, and with it went any lingering remnants of the Sandra she knew. "I'll get to the point then."

Suddenly, Drayvex was right behind her. She knew he'd moved fast because Sandra's bravado was gone. Her finger twitched on the trigger, eyes wide and fixed behind her. Ruby braced herself on the other end of the barrel.

"If you have a point, I suggest you make it." Drayvex's voice was silky smooth and laced with a venom that poisoned her mind with fear of his intentions. "If I have to make my own, there won't be much of you left."

Alarm lanced through her. She angled her body to stare at him in horror, being careful to keep one hand on the gun. If he ever killed Sandra... Ruby sucked in a sharp breath. She would find a way to kill him herself.

"We wouldn't want to upset Ruby now, would we?" Drayvex looked every bit the demon he was: sharp teeth, claws like knives. Eyes that were black and soulless. She could feel him pacing in the depths of her mind, a hungry darkness just one wrong move from snapping wide open.

"Sandra," Ruby snapped, giving her a look that was both tangled frustration and fear.

Sandra's eyes darted back to her. For a moment more, they were wild and afraid, and then just like that, she became the hunter once again. "It doesn't matter that you've given up on yourself. I'm taking this straight to the top."

As she lowered the gun, Ruby let her fingers slide with caution off the end. It wasn't until she replayed the words back in her head that she really heard them.

"I'm going to do whatever it takes to make this right, Rube. To free you from that bastard's influence." Sandra's hard eyes glistened as she fixed on her.

Ruby scrabbled for words, a numb sort of panic throbbing through her. The top? "Sand, what does that mean?"

Sandra threw a disgusted look towards Drayvex, who seemed to have got bigger since Ruby last looked. "I won't stop," she said almost in a whisper, reaching out to place a hand on Ruby's shoulder, "until I get my best friend back."

Ruby couldn't breathe. She looked towards Drayvex and froze. It was in that moment she knew that his patience had expired—and that she would have seconds to stop him.

"Sand, run."

Sandra froze. "No."

The demon beside her unravelled in a violent flurry of seething darkness. *Yes, run, little hunter.* Drayvex's voice cracked through her mind as he rose like a malevolent tidal wave.

"Get out!" Ruby blasted, shouting in her face. "Just *go home*, Sand. And don't come back."

As Sandra stumbled out through the door, Ruby stepped between the swirling vortex and her best friend in the world, staring him down. Her own rage swirled inside her. "Enough!"

As she yelled at the malevolent being in her apartment, he rose even

Chapter 30

higher. *Says who?* mocked the monster in a familiar drawl. *You?*

He was trying to intimidate her. She wouldn't be swayed. "I won't let you hurt her." With a shaking hand, Ruby pulled out the luxlor from her jacket pocket and held it out before her. "If you value what we have in any way at all," she said, in a cool voice that didn't match how she felt, "you'll let her go."

The brief pause felt like a lifetime as she stood, waiting for Drayvex to respond.

And if I don't? His mental voice in her head was an angry force of nature unto itself. It was almost more than she could stand. *Are you going to wound me with my own weapon, Ruby Red? You think you can kill me because I made you?*

Ruby blinked back tears. No, she didn't think she could. Not even if she wanted to.

She let the luxlor drop to the ground with a crash. "I don't want to kill you. Just..." She sucked in a shaking breath. "Please, let her go." And then, when he didn't respond, she added, "I chose you, didn't I?"

The darkness fell still.

"Isn't that enough?"

Chapter 31

Drayvex considered Ruby from the other end of the flat, keeping about as much space between them as he could manage within the confines of her compact abode. She was one end; he was the other. She was slowly poisoning her liver in the kitchen; he was burning a hole in the back of her head. Neither of them spoke a word.

For the three hundred and fifty-seventh time in the space of Hell knew how long, she turned and glanced behind her. As she met his unblinking gaze, she held it for a moment, a dozen tangled emotions and accusations playing out across her face.

"If you value what we have in any way at all, you'll let her go."

Drayvex felt his teeth slip down inside his mouth as he glared at her, responding to his mood. She had no idea what she was asking of him. Or maybe she did, and he wasn't giving her enough credit. Maybe she was every bit the selfish, spiteful reprobate that he was.

He lingered on her as her green eyes probed him from afar. *If you valued anything outside of that ignorant human bubble you hide in*, he jabbed, his thoughts barbed, *we'd have been done with this shit long ago. But here we are.*

Ruby's face fell to a neutral blank. She turned away in a sharp movement, busying herself with the glasses on the counter behind with added

Chapter 31

aggression.

He sighed as frustration needled him, folding his arms to stop himself from breaking something. That was getting old fast. He didn't want her in his space, let alone his head. Not least of all, half of what he thought when he was angry was hot garbage.

Hot garbage he was entitled to.

Drayvex closed his eyes, willing into being what little composure she hadn't already destroyed. It didn't matter—

Something went *crash* in the kitchen. His lip twitched as the sound went straight through him. It didn't matter that they could barely stand to be in the same room. The fae and the *vânători* scourge put together weren't half the blinding headache that Saydor was. He was still their biggest threat. Still lost to the wind. Except now, they had the stone.

An unfamiliar stench tickled his senses. He reached forth out of habit with his mind, scanning for demon presence.

His eyes sprung open, fixing on Ruby. There was something nearby.

Drayvex crossed the room in a heartbeat, grabbing her from behind. As her fight response kicked in and her body reacted, he put his other hand over her mouth. "Time to go," he murmured with low urgency in her ear. "Now."

She stilled against him, her heart hammering. After a moment, she nodded.

He retracted his hand, his mind already five steps ahead. Ruby was the bane of his existence. The death of his sanity, the parasite that had melded with its host in the worst possible way. But she was the only creature in this multitude of worlds worth protecting. And anything that touched her would die.

The moment they stepped through into the magus nox, Drayvex could smell it again. The stench of demon was thick in the air, taking him from the edge straight to 'kill switch engaged'.

"Stay here," he growled to the knotted ball of angst and whiskey behind him, his attention fixed dead ahead. He heard her suck in a breath to argue and added with an irritable snap, "I mean it."

Drayvex followed the familiar odour down the long room, moving with slow, deliberate steps. There were only a small handful of demons that had access to this room, every one of them in his inner circle. It was a trove of lost knowledge and ancient dark magic that most demons would sell their soul for.

"Make yourself scarce, Malefic," he ordered the presence in a dangerous tone, "before I make you extinct."

A pair of glistening mandibles appeared from behind the immediate row of books, followed by the long, insectoid face they were attached to. It stared for a moment, indecision rendering it motionless.

"I see we're choosing violence today." Drayvex flexed in casual warning, studying the curved hooks at his fingertips as he waited for the penny to drop. "You're spoiling me." The skin that contained his true form could hardly be considered a disguise. Not to those demons with true magical prowess.

"My Lord," rasped a panicked voice. Malefic tumbled out from behind the shelving in a tangle of limbs. It fell straight into a bow, bending as low as its exoskeleton would allow. "As you wish. I live to serve."

The demon's wandering gaze suddenly snapped into focus, fixing behind his form.

Drayvex felt an edge of tension dig in with sharp claws. He knew what it was looking at.

"Oh, My Lord. You brought a snack." Malefic's pincer-like jaws twitched in anticipation as it gave the girl behind him a once over. "The meat doesn't get much fresher than that—"

The demon's head hit the floor and bounced. His temper surging white-hot, he slammed the far door shut with his mind and excessive force. The headless body collapsed in a heap.

As a pool of black expanded around his feet, Drayvex cursed himself. Malefic would be hard to replace.

He spun on the spot, turning to glare at her. It wasn't Ruby's fault that he had just killed his best seer; and yet, when she was involved, he was pure

Chapter 31

impulse and reaction.

Drayvex stalked back towards her, leaving the oozing body lying where it fell.

Ruby folded her arms and stared him down as he approached. "If there's something you want to say to me, then just say it." There was an air of quiet determination about her that contradicted the demand of her words.

He stopped in front of her, eyeing her with as much disdain as he could muster. Mercy, how he wished he could hate her the way he needed to. How such a small human could have such a devastating effect on his life, he would never know. "Fine. I will."

"Good." She chewed on her lower lip, tearing the skin.

"Great." He watched her blood ooze around the tear. His focus took a nosedive. Waste not…

"I know you're mad about Sandra."

Drayvex pulled his gaze from her lip and narrowed his eyes. Well done, Red. Astute as ever. "You mean the shit that you've brought in all over my doorstep?" His voice was unintentionally rough as she dug under his skin. He snapped his fingers, bringing the torches surrounding the vast room to life with a simultaneous *whomph*. "Do you know how long I've had those meddlers chasing their tails looking for me?"

Ruby pulled a face. "I didn't know she was going to involve her hunter friends. I had nothing to do with that."

"Over five centuries. *Five*." Drayvex inched in closer, baring his teeth. "You're more effective than a flame-thrower. I should aim you at my enemies."

"God, will you just listen to me? Sandra doesn't hear what I'm saying." She leant in with unflinching resolve, her voice rising. "She hears what she wants to hear, just like *you*!"

He sneered. *Him*, like that basic parasite? Drayvex felt something inside him snap. "Is that so?" he snarled, temper spilling out uncontained. "Then why don't you go fuck her life up instead of mine. You'd be doing us both a favour."

The moment he said the words, he wanted to squash them like the diseased things they were. His temper vanished as quickly as it had flared, leaving a restless tug in its place. *Vµiår nhfrèto,* she was his own personal Hell.

Ruby stared at him, some nameless emotion passing across her face. "Maybe I should," she murmured. "At least she actually seems to want me."

As she turned away from him, Drayvex reached out and grabbed her by the arm. She couldn't leave without him—she was physically incapable of using the portal. But the impulse to keep her from walking away was stronger than the logic that reminded him she was human. "Screaming Hell, wait." He held himself in place, working through the nagging itch that made him want to squeeze. "It's been a day of revelations and bullshit." He looked up from where his hand gripped her arm to the crimson cascade of hair. "Trust me. If I didn't want you here, you wouldn't be standing there debating it. You'd *know*."

Ruby stood for a moment with her back to him before turning back to face him. She looked conflicted. "How many times do I have to prove myself to you?" She stopped and ran a brisk hand through her hair. "I risked everything to bring you this stone, to warn you that your enemies were building a damned army behind your back. I faced down my best friend because she had a gun to your head." She paused before continuing with slow precision. "Every time I stick my neck out for you, it costs *me*."

Drayvex held those green eyes, searching. He'd known for a long time that indulging in the girl with the demon stone necklace was slowly unpicking his life at the seams. But for the first time, he saw their twisted unity from a god's eye view, saw the full extent of the beast that was chaos incarnate. It was killing them both.

"I've more than played my part, so get off my case."

He stared at her, letting his hand drop from her arm. He was a selfish bastard, yes, but he *had* let her go. And Ruby had come right back. His teeth inched down behind his lips. Was that because she'd wanted to, or because the piece of him inside her pulled her close?

"Is something wrong?" she asked.

Drayvex gave her a conceited smile, a distraction. "Was anything ever right?" he replied. No one in their right mind would choose him over themselves. It would be the bond. Well, there was nothing he could do about that. Without it, she was dead.

"Hilarious." Her gaze slipped past him, down to the headless body of Malefic on the floor behind. Her nose wrinkled. "Was that necessary?"

Drayvex smothered an exasperated sigh. No, it was not. He narrowed his eyes at her, silent and accusing. Is it necessary for you to smell like a walking buffet all the damn time? The biting remark hovered on his tongue, but instead, he said in a deadpan, "I ordered the steak and got the salad. Can't get the help these days."

As though they were taking turns, Ruby narrowed her eyes, suspicion practically rolling off her as she stared at him. "Not a big tipper. Got it."

He felt the twitch of a reluctant smile and then let it drop.

"Would that gun really have hurt you?"

Drayvex stared at her, incredulous as he was reminded once again of how little she knew of his world. It was a world embracing her in a death grip. He sighed. "It's called *srek*."

He watched the suspicion slip from her narrowed gaze, replaced by a curiosity that was always hungry. Always wanting.

Fighting not to roll his eyes to the ceiling, Drayvex tilted his head, watching her. "Molten *srek* runs through the core of Vekrodus, spews out of cracks in the land as a gaseous smog, both of which are harmless to the demons that inhabit its surface."

Ruby wrinkled her nose. "Then why—?"

"But in Earth's atmosphere, its properties change drastically. And yes," he said, almost deadpan. "It can and *has* destroyed lesser demons than I." He felt his teeth point as her choice of topic threatened to chip away at what little patience he had left. "I've never allowed myself to be shot in the damn head, but it stings like a bitch. *You* would know."

Ruby hung on his words for a moment. Then her eyes widened, and the penny dropped. "Sandra's bracelet. But, how did you …?" She trailed off as he gave her an exasperated look. The girl was one big distraction.

Drayvex held out his hand in silent expectation, gesturing palm-up. "Give me the stone." Business.

Ruby hesitated for a moment, eyeing him with a conflicted expression, before reaching into the folds of her jacket and pulling out the object within. It nestled in the palm of her hand like it was made for something her size, glowing a dull green. Circular threads swirled within the orb's depths, turning in infinite loops. It was dormant in her hand. He followed the stone with a pinpoint gaze as she offered it out towards him. It would light up like nobody's business in his.

She dropped the stone into his waiting hand. It didn't even flicker.

Or not. Drayvex raised the stone to eye level, boring into its depths, a useless rock on his palm. It should have reacted to his power. His power should have reached for *it*.

"What?" Ruby shuffled her feet on the stone floor, a nervous laugh escaping her lips. "Don't tell me it's a fake."

His black gaze lifted from the Lapis Temporis to the girl behind. Her feeble jokes would not save them. Mercy, could this piss poor day get any worse? "Oh, it's quite real," he said, a growl of frustration rising up from his chest. "It's just utterly fucking useless."

Ruby's face fell. She shuffled backwards. "I don't understand." Her eyes rose to the ceiling in what looked like a prayer for the dregs of her own precious sanity. "It doesn't work?"

Drayvex lowered the stone. Once again, that *shcrenta* was screwing them over from her comfy hole. He breathed out in a hard stream. "The stone has already been activated. But as your light-fingered friend is incompetent at best, she doesn't have the skill to follow through with her objective."

She stared at him, chewing on her lip. "Meaning...?"

He glared back, unmoving. "Meaning the stone's power is hanging in limbo." He heard the hard edge to his voice as it matched his plummeting disposition. "And that puts it far beyond our reach."

Ruby shook her head, her hair falling about her face. "Brilliant. Of course, it is. Because why would it be that simple?" The laugh that escaped her lips as she stole his sardonic line made him wonder just how many of those tumblers she had got through before he'd intervened.

Chapter 31

Drayvex studied her. "Hate to break it to you, Red. *Everything* was simple before you happened." He felt the twitch of a smile pull through his black mood. "I'm beginning to think the universe has a sense of humour."

The look that earned him would have sent the smallest of his minions running for cover. "Oh yeah?" She wrinkled her nose in disgust. "Well, you and the universe can both kiss my arse." And with that, she folded her arms and turned her back on him.

He watched her in fascination, her kittenish anger distracting him from his own comparative inferno. Her petulance was almost endearing, and against his will, he felt himself smirk. How the Hell did they both get here again?

Ruby turned to peek at him through a curtain of hair. "You're laughing at me now? Am I a joke to you?" She let her hair fall back into place, looking down at the floor. "You know what? Don't answer that. I guess that's it then. We're done for." She looked up, and without another word, paced off into the depths of the large room.

He shook his head. And he'd thought his underlings were hard work.

Drayvex could track her by smell alone. But Ruby was not quiet, and if she was trying to be, then darkness help her, she truly was a lost cause. He pulled up beside the shelf she was lurking behind and spoke to her through the books. "When you're done being dead-weight," he jabbed, letting the subtle weight of authority seep into his tone, "we still have things to do."

As the silence stretched between them and she made him wait, he flicked his tongue out in an impatient snap.

"Did you just call me dead-weight?"

Drayvex gave a sly smile at the indignation in her voice. He looked down at the stone that still sat in his grip.

He heard her sigh. "Things like what?"

He ran his tongue over his sizeable teeth, his mind spinning thread after scheming thread. "Oh, I don't know. Like dealing with the nature harpy and her brainless army?" He paused for effect, letting his words sink in. "Or maybe you'd like to leave it up to chance. I'm sure the humans of your city will be just fine hosting their violent guests."

Seconds later, Ruby appeared around the end of the bookcase. "No way. Tira wouldn't hurt innocent people." A soft frown formed above her eyes. "Would she?"

Drayvex held his face in an impassive mask. It was highly unlikely. "Hmm, let's see. A creature that thrives on bloodshed and chaos, loose in the city of the human that betrayed her." He rested a claw on his lip, making a show of thinking. "How long does a faerie hold a grudge?"

The face she pulled was one of pure disgust. "Fine," she muttered. "What do you want?"

Something inside him twisted. He ignored it. Playing Ruby was all too simple. That heavy, heavy burden that was her morality was the target on her back that said 'extort me'. He didn't enjoy it, but one of them had to watch their backs. And the creature was now a threat to them both.

Drayvex slipped towards her, stone in hand. As he held the swirling orb between them, she looked down. "We destroy the stone and the armies within," he murmured, losing himself in a potential future. "We destroy the fae who crossed us. And then we make that flaccid worm come to us. We break him, mind, body and spirit, before ending him and wiping him from history."

Ruby didn't respond, and he didn't bother to look up. He didn't know when *he* had become *we*. She didn't have a violent bone in her fragile body. What he did know, though, was that his enemies were also her enemies. Maybe that was reason enough.

"Or," she said in a small voice, "we don't destroy the stone."

Drayvex looked up from the stone's depths, raising his eyebrows in stony scepticism. "Oh?"

She shifted under his gaze. "What if we keep the stone intact and look for a way to undo the spell? We keep the fae trapped in their world so that we don't kill each other."

He stared at her, unmoving, as her restless fiddling escalated under his scrutiny. Ever the shining beacon. "You're confusing me with a demon that gives a damn," he said, standing up straight and looking down on her. "Oh, wait. They don't *actually* exist." There was no way he was sparing that creature and her rats' nest.

Ruby's expression wavered for a moment as she processed his words. Then out of nowhere, she became pure resolve, her entire attitude shifting. "Look, you were right, okay? If I hadn't intervened at the temple with Tira, we probably wouldn't be here."

He narrowed his eyes at her change in tone. But …?

"But I found the stone. I risked everything to bring it back, and I want the fae to live." She looked him dead in the eyes and held him. "You have options because of me."

Drayvex smiled as she turned the tables on him, giving her a show of fang. So they were extorting each other. So much for that blazing beacon of light. "Is that so?"

He watched Ruby as she held her nerve. It was true, she had been the one to claim the stone. But the sheer gall of this small human, to make her demands of a being such as he. There was more power in his breath than she had in her entire body, and yet she demandeth like a goddess. And he couldn't look away.

Making up his mind on the spot, he unravelled into a twisting cloud of darkness before her widening eyes. The stone fell to the ground at her feet with a thud. *I'll make you a deal*, he voiced in her head.

Ruby sucked in a breath as he slipped past her, coiling around behind her like a smoky snake. "I'm listening."

Good. He felt her shiver beneath his vaporous form, her soft heat against his cool darkness. *You can decide the fate of the stone and its parasites on one condition.*

She hesitated. "Which is?"

If Drayvex could smile in his gaseous form, then he would. He moved across the skin of her neck, his dark form shaping into a hand that encircled her throat in an easy caress. *The thief dies.*

A gasp escaped her lips. "No."

Yes, he thundered in her mind. *You do not get in my way. You do not speak of it again. Those are my terms.*

Ruby barely moved a muscle as she processed his proposal. He could feel the pulse in her throat, could almost hear her mind turning over. She may have the balls of something three times her size, but she did not get to leverage him and walk away with her precious soul unscathed.

If he had to take a hit, then so would she.

Drayvex felt her twitch in his mind, felt the flash of bile and resentment that came tumbling in with it, and knew what she would say next before she'd said it. *Darling,* he purred in response. *I can assure you, the feeling is mutual. Now, do we have a deal?*

Ruby didn't respond.

Chapter 32

The wind combed through the lone tree in the colour-splashed meadow, brushing its branches in a soothing rustle. Ruby leant into the cool breeze, embracing the moment with her eyes closed. She'd known this would happen. She'd told herself that choosing one side was condemning the other, that choosing Drayvex was sentencing the fae to their death—and she'd gone to him anyway.

She opened her eyes. The spread of colour that dotted the landscape was like something from a beautiful canvas. It wasn't enough to distract her.

Ruby breathed in the fresh air, doing her best to ignore the dark force of nature behind her. She supposed if she was honest, this was the best-case scenario. Drayvex had conceded to her about as much as any calculating killer could. But he was making her swing the sword, possibly for kicks. And it made her blood boil.

Her exhale was significantly less steady than the last. By choosing the many over the few, she was saving a ridiculous number of lives. Still, could she really be expected to stand by and do nothing as he tore Tira to pieces? She fixed a firm gaze on the far horizon, her stomach lurching. Of course, if she rescinded on their deal, then so would he.

He would kill them all with a smile.

"Your optimism truly knows no bounds." A smooth voice interrupted her peace, its devious undercurrent almost a taunt. "By all means, nullify that thread between us with my power."

Ruby looked down at the bracelet on her wrist, its dark, gleaming twists standing out against her pale skin. She didn't want Drayvex in her head. Right now, she could barely bring herself to look at his stupid, smug face.

"We both know that I'm in your head, with or without it."

Annoyance flared up within as he needled her. "Drop dead," she muttered, and then immediately regretted giving him the rise he wanted. He was right though. The part of him that seemed to now live inside her had been silenced, and yet here she was, giving him free reign inside her thoughts. She hated that.

"And then where would you be? Wanted three ways with no one to watch over that fragile neck. Are you going to save *yourself*?"

Ruby glowered out at the sea of flowers before her. She didn't need to be connected to Drayvex to know what this was about. She was getting in the way of an ancient feud he was desperate to finish. Maybe it was asking a lot. Maybe she would one day push her luck so far, he would turn around and kill her himself. But she didn't have the time or the patience to deal with his passive-aggressive mind games today.

"Didn't think so."

Ruby clenched her fist. "Teach me how to summon darkness."

The silence from the demon behind her was golden and delicious.

She smiled, reaching into her jacket and pulling out the luxlor. What, no snappy comeback? Turning to face him, she looked up and held the smooth orb out before her. "I've done it before. Just not on purpose."

Drayvex was lurking a few feet away, leaning against the tree they had emerged from just prior. His face was impassive as he studied her, the god-like cat that humoured the mouse.

Ruby stared at him, mirroring his cold-blooded calm. This mouse was fighting back. Light, dark; she wanted it all.

Out of nowhere, she watched a skewed smile spread on his face. "I thought you'd never ask," he purred, and his voice sent little tingles running down her spine.

Chapter 32

Here we go, she thought. What have I got myself into now?

The luxlor sat in a neutral state in her palm, waiting for her command. Clearing her mind for the umpteenth time, Ruby focused on its glassy depths, feeling the wind tickle her face and tug at her hair. The light came so easily. It poured out when she wasn't even thinking about it, blazing at her touch. The darkness was elusive and fought her like a wild thing.

"In your own time, human," came a scathing voice. "It's not as though we're being hunted three ways from Sunday."

She glared into the globe, her skin prickling. He was getting under her skin, stoking the storm inside her. Deep down beyond her surface reaction, she knew this. It didn't stop her from wanting to break his nose.

Ruby dug deep. The luxlor became ice in her palm. Darkness sprang forth.

It was always small at first, a twisting strand that flickered in the depths of the orb. But the more she coaxed it, the more it filled the space within. The light and the dark didn't just look different; they *were* different. Summoning light was weightless and warm, and it filled her like sunshine in a bottle. Bringing forth darkness was like jumping into an ice bath. It was heavy and cold, and satisfying to hold in ways that the light had never been.

She wondered if she was standing at the top of a slippery slope. Was darkness inherently bad? Was the light automatically good and pure, just because it was the light?

"I hope you have more than that," Drayvex growled from directly behind her. "I could have killed you twenty times over in the time it took you to call that pathetic cloud."

Ruby stiffened as he breathed down her neck. "Give me a break," she snapped, spinning to face the devil in her midst. "This isn't easy for me." How long had they been at this now, an hour?

Drayvex embodied the darkness she held, right down to the black pits of his eyes. "You want a break? How about a permanent slumber?"

She was unprepared as he launched himself at her, dissolving into a wall of black smoke as he rushed straight through her. Or it felt like he'd gone through her. A flash of heat and wrath, and then nothing.

"More."

He was behind her again. Ruby gritted her teeth. One word, a command that rang through her and triggered her until her own fire burnt her. That jerk was going to get it. Spinning to face him once again, she held the luxlor out before her. Darkness swam inside the globe. "And if I don't?"

Drayvex smiled, his teeth pointing right before her eyes. It wasn't a nice smile. "Dead girls don't get to complain. Now give. Me. *More.*"

Ruby felt his callous words grate inside her, sandpaper on her flesh. He wanted more. She would drown him in more.

The darkness in her palm responded to her, feeding off her. It was getting fat before her eyes. "I'll show you more, you sadistic prick."

The sly look in his eyes was the last thing she saw as the twisting strands of darkness poured out from the luxlor in a sluggish tornado, blocking him almost entirely from view as it filled her senses and bathed her in an icy embrace.

It was heavy. So heavy in her veins that she almost dropped to the floor, and yet she felt nothing as it gripped her. No fear, no pain, no anger. Blissful nothing.

Ruby didn't want to let go. The tornado she held in her palm was ludicrous, hypnotic. And then, she saw his feet. They were all that was visible of the demon before her, and they were tapping an impatient rhythm.

She let him have it. The funnel of darkness crashed down over Drayvex as she let it go, swallowing him whole. It swirled around him, faster now. Chaotic for one unhinged moment.

It broke apart as one, skittering away like a plague of insects from the figure before her, dissolving into the air. The demon that remained was untouched.

Ruby slumped to the floor, exhaustion hitting her hard out of nowhere. The luxlor rolled through the flowers. She ... did it.

"So the light-born has spine after all. Consider me impressed."

She looked up towards Drayvex, who all of a sudden seemed far less threatening as he stood, watching her with those piercing blue eyes. There

Chapter 32

was a softness to his voice that made her stomach flutter. Of course, he'd been baiting her. She'd walked right into his trap.

"Regardless," he said, the businesslike snap back in his voice. "You were slow. Think *faster*."

Stifling a groan, she slumped back, falling among the flowers. "You're relentless." Her heart hammered in her chest. Did she really want to play with these forces? She was no longer sure.

She heard his footsteps crush the grass as he moved towards her. "You think I was handed the throne of Vekrodus on a silver platter?" His voice had changed again, and suddenly, if they were at opposite ends of the meadow, it would have been insufficient. "That that psychotic bastard simply rolled over and gave me everything that was his in a gesture of fatherly love?"

Ruby tensed as his low voice reached her from the ground, a cold shiver running through her. If Drayvex was using the words 'psychotic bastard', his father really must have been something. Reluctant, she looked up at him and met his gaze.

Drayvex stopped and crouched over her, too close now, looking down at her in calculating thought. "No. I killed that fucker with my own two hands." His eyes were dark, his soft voice darker still. "I took what was his, and I made it mine. I've been fighting the infinite worlds to keep it ever since."

She stared at his beautiful, sinister face. Killed him. "I ..." She licked her lips. What could you say to that? Condolences?

"Complacency gets you killed, Ruby," he said, his breath tickling her face. "So when I say think faster, you think supersonic. When I say jump, you fly. Do you understand?"

Ruby sat up, almost head-butting the demon before her. He didn't flinch. She could feel his warmth enveloping her, count the individual sleek strands of hair falling into his eyes. She understood all too well.

"Earth to Ruby?"

Drayvex was looking out for her, in his own twisted way, and it hurt to look at that beautiful face. "Yes," she whispered, sucking on her lip. "I hear you." He was soaked in the blood of innocents, and yet it scared her how much she still wanted him. She felt something tug in her chest as she took him in, and then a dull, pulsing panic. He would always be tempting her, the forbidden fruit. And she would forever have to say no to him.

Drayvex scoffed. The sound brought her back. "I'm sorry, am I boring you?"

Ruby squinted at him. "Pardon me?"

"You're here, and then you're not." He narrowed his eyes at her, always watching. Always picking her apart. "It's like herding a horde of drunken imps through a narrow doorway."

She stared at him, her face slack as a laugh bubbled up her throat. It was more disbelief than actual humour. "Wow, okay. Rude much."

Drayvex rose to his feet, the corner of his mouth lifting. "They say the truth hurts." He turned away to glance across the meadow. "Now get your act together. We're wasting time."

Ruby pulled a face at his back as he left her sitting by herself and then looked down at her wrist. The little red gems were almost glowing. Damn that d-bag demon. Sighing, she took it off and slipped it into her pocket.

When she caught up to him and pulled up beside him, he didn't react. The Lapis Temporis was hovering a few inches from his palm, slowly spinning on its axis like a little green planet.

She looked away towards the little rundown shack that had appeared on the far horizon. This had to work. She had no plan B through to G like Drayvex would. The temple would hide the stone and keep the fae safe. The fae themselves couldn't exist outside of the stone, not without completing the magic, and that was the way they were going to stay. It was all she could do to keep them alive.

Ruby chewed on her lip, her stomach churning with nerves. So far, Tira was lost to the wind. If she stayed that way, Drayvex wouldn't be able to kill her. But if she was tracking them…

She glanced back at him, needing a distraction. She didn't want to be in her own head right now. "So, we're hiding the stone in the temple…" She trailed off. The creepy Hell temple that made Drayvex deranged. Was this really their best idea? "I assume we'll be able to get it back, should we need

Chapter 32

to?"

Drayvex never took his eyes off the stone, but as his lip curled in an impatient gesture, she almost expected him to roll them. "We cloak the stone in that wreckage of a *house*," he corrected her, the dull, flickering green surface reflecting in his eyes, "so that no power-craving junkie that enters the temple will find it. That glamour may be an illusion, but it's also a physical object. A house no human can survive in, and no magic-user would see reason to bother with."

Ruby tried to process as the house drew ever closer and the ground beneath her ever steeper. It was smart, she had to give him that. And no one had to die to make it work. Almost no one.

"As for getting it back." The ominous pause made way for the soft rustling of the grass in the wind. "The only being in existence that will have both the knowledge of its location and the power to uncloak it is myself."

She laughed. "Of course. How convenient for you." It was out of her mouth before her brain had even processed the words. Well, it was true.

For the first time, his gaze left the stone and slid sideways. "This is your arrangement," he said in a voice that was almost a purr. "Not mine. I'm merely, how you people say, going with the flow."

Ruby didn't respond. Yes, it was her arrangement. And everything that happened next was on her.

It took them less than five minutes to reach the stone's final destination, and as they crested the hill and the little battered bungalow came up before them in all its lowly glory, Ruby slowed to a standstill.

She felt Drayvex stop beside her, his silent scrutiny as she stared at the building with fresh doubt. Her mind was racing. If no human could survive inside that house, should she really go in?

"Are we getting cold feet?"

Ruby wrinkled her nose as he taunted her. "You wish." And she started forward towards the little bungalow. It was far too late for cold feet.

Drayvex was right. It could be any neglected old house in the middle of nowhere; abandoned, falling apart. Solid to the touch. She brushed her fingers over the wooden door frame, her eyes wide. It was real, but it *wasn't*.

The handle yielded to his touch as he pushed the door open. And as it swung away from them with a creak, the musty darkness inside yawned wide.

Ruby's skin prickled. She lifted her gaze to the demon beside her and wondered if he'd felt it too.

Drayvex lifted the stone to eye level between two clawed fingers. His tongue flicked out, and suddenly it was black and forked. "Stay close. This won't take long."

She chewed on her lip, her heart pounding in her throat. Her nerves were unravelling. "You go. I'll wait here." They were in the middle of nowhere. Nothing would find them out here.

Drayvex's gaze didn't move from the dark space before them. But she could almost feel the heat behind that withering look as he fixed on the dark space inside the house. "One day, you'll do as you're fucking told."

Ruby breathed out, irritated by his tone. "Not today." Or maybe ever.

"Fine," he said in a dispassionate voice. "I don't have time to carry you. Stay *put*."

Ignoring the jab, she ran a hand through her loose hair and watched as he slipped into the house. Everything was going to be fine. Sinking down into the swaying grass, she pulled out the luxlor and settled down to wait.

The wind died down. She changed the luxlor from light to dark, to light again. She lay on her back, counted the birds overhead. Wondered if Drayvex had screwed her over. Swam in guilt as she changed her mind.

Stay put, he said. This won't take long, he said.

"Well, well, well. If it isn't the little human wonder with nine lives."

Ruby's blood ran cold. Fear oozed through her, ice in her veins as the familiar voice pervaded her mind, her very soul. Saydor had found her.

Chapter 33

The familiar stench hit him out of nowhere, polluting the musty shack in a noxious cloud. It was a match to the sandpaper fury festering in the darkness of his mind.

Drayvex felt his fangs extend in response as he fixed on the empty cabinet, the place where he'd cloaked the stone. The skin of his hands darkened, hardened, his form slipping. This would end right now.

The sound of Ruby's voice reached him through the walls. It sliced through his anger with a keen edge, dread leaking into his mind like poison. Saydor had found her.

He lashed out, launching a seething shot of power into the cabinet before him. Shards of wood flew in all directions, the simulated reality of a glamour. The pieces all froze in mid-air, hanging in the balance for a moment before rewinding the damage. He'd known leaving her unattended was a terrible idea.

A cold calm descended over him. If that lowlife laid one finger on her, Drayvex would show him the meaning of the word pain.

In a heartbeat, he was outside. Saydor saw him coming. It didn't save him.

Drayvex smashed into the demon at speed, claws piercing straight through his bloated form and into his chest. The force of it sent him flying backwards through the air, and Drayvex was vaguely aware of Ruby tumbling off to the side as his fist followed through.

The demon hissed as Drayvex punched a hand-sized hole straight into his empty chest cavity and out the other side. Blood sprayed out from the hole, arching as they fell. Of course, the scum stain had severed his heart. Locked that pulsing lump far away from twitching claws. Drayvex had expected nothing less.

By the time they hit the ground, Drayvex was clinging to the final shreds of his human form. Black tendrils burst from him, aiming for the demon pinned beneath him. "You're mine," he growled, his voice carrying the duality of his forms. He pulled back his fist.

Saydor threw up a hasty barrier.

His tendrils hit it like rain. His fist slammed down onto the membrane, causing it to spark. "Smear my name to your sad little rejects all you like. You will never have what's mine."

Saydor's sneer turned to a sick grin. "Are we talking about the throne of Vekrodus, My Lord?" he taunted, panting under the weight of holding Drayvex back. "Or that delicious little firecracker you keep as a pet?"

Drayvex felt something inside him snap. An almighty crack rang through the air as the ground beneath them split, cleaved open with prying fingers of power. "Mention her again." He drew on his power, digging deep. "I *dare* you."

He unleashed it, a wave of pure, undiluted power, aiming for the barrier between them.

The dripping green tendrils that shot past him narrowly missed his shoulder as Drayvex dodged the attack. His own blast shot wide.

The demon slammed into him full force. The smell of singed grass hit the back of his throat. And as they hit the grassy earth in a speeding snarl of teeth and claws, he felt his wings tear through his back and snap wide.

Saydor had a ball of emerald flame ready and waiting as Drayvex rose in a blur. "You've got her well trained, I must say," the demon taunted. "When it comes to pissing off fae, she's almost as good as you." With a speed that your average high-class demon would struggle to match, Saydor swung it

Chapter 33

towards him.

Drayvex was not your average high-class demon. He grabbed Saydor and swung him around, using their momentum to build power. The emerald flames shot off Hell knew where. "Weak," he sneered, and sent Saydor flying. So that was how Saydor had found them.

Saydor crashed into the glamoured house, a demon-shaped wrecking ball that sent an explosion of debris flying in all directions. The house collapsed inwards, clouds of rubble rising in a plume.

Drayvex spat at the ground, disgust flaring as he fixed on the collapsed remains. That swine thought he could make a dirty deal with that shcrẹnta and lay claim to whatever took his fancy? Steal from a Demon Lord and live to tell the tale? He beat his wings, stirring the air around him as he fought to take control of the inferno raging inside him.

Drayvex paused as a rogue breeze placated him, carrying Ruby's scent towards him from across the space. He turned to face her.

She was scared. He could feel it as well as see it, that unsettling spark in his mind that was not his. Whether she was scared of him or of the threat to her life, he knew not. But she was clearly still with him, and as she watched him back, that didn't seem to change.

Drayvex was almost fully demon. But that didn't mean he couldn't be rational. He gazed at Ruby, his resolve darkening and settling. Saydor would not take her from him. That, he could guarantee.

* * *

Ruby stared across the open space at the creature that had taken Drayvex's place. He was looking right at her, an imposing figure with flesh that rivalled the darkness and wings that took up all the surrounding space. He had not one but two sets of wings, splaying out in a vicious leathery X.

Stay back. I'm going to deal with this.

Drayvex spoke in her head, his velvet voice as clear as if he was standing right behind her. She studied him, heart pounding. Working through the fear that was oozing through her, she took an unsteady breath and nodded at him. Go get him, Ruby thought towards the demon across the green expanse.

As Drayvex turned away from her and started forward, Ruby dragged her attention to the little house. It was worse for wear, reduced to heaps of rubble and debris. She suppressed a throb of fear. Saydor was somewhere inside, and she highly doubted he was dead. How had he known they were here?

Her eyes widened. Wait a second. Wasn't the Lapis Temporis in there too?

In that moment, a piece of rubble caught her eye. It was moving but not falling as gravity demanded. No, it was twitching. She squinted at it, unease creeping into her muscles.

Drayvex reached the house and stood before it, arms folded in expectation as the little destroyed shack did strange things before their eyes. All at once, as though possessed, the broken pieces of the house sprung to life. He didn't look surprised.

Ruby was not close by, but it still made her flinch. Pieces large and small were hovering in mid-air as though the house was haunted. They converged, meeting as one and forming a whole. And it was in that moment that she realised what was happening. The house was rebuilding itself.

Among all the commotion was Saydor. She caught him briefly, moving forward through the pieces of rubble like a seething cockroach before the house solidified around him.

As the door opened, Ruby held her breath. Saydor stepped out, his outline sending her into a cold sweat. The yellow devil and star of all her most recent nightmares. He didn't look hurt in any way, and as he stalked across the grassy clearing towards Drayvex, she could hear him.

It took her a moment to realise that he was laughing.

Just then, Saydor turned his head towards her, looking straight at her. A maniacal grin spread on his face, a sharp-toothed smile that would put a shark to shame. The sound of his laugh penetrated her mind like a blade and twisted inside her.

Ruby squeezed her nails into her palm. She would not let him take her

Chapter 33

alive. That she swore.

"Enjoy it while you can, low-born." Drayvex was burning. Covered in dark flames, his outline was very different from Saydor's. With the horns and the wings, he was something to behold. Ruby was glad they were on the same side.

The smile slipped from Saydor's face. He turned back towards Drayvex, stopping a few feet from him, and replaced it with a smile that looked as poisonous as the green gunk dripping down his fingers. "Enjoy what, high-born brat?"

Ruby dove her hand into her pocket. She grabbed the luxlor, gripping it as though her life depended on it. It was cold comfort, but comfort all the same.

"Your eyes," Drayvex drawled with lazy menace. He smiled back at the demon, and a different kind of fear shot through her. "While you still have them."

It was impossible to say which of the two moved first. Blink, and she'd missed it. But as the demons clashed a small distance away, it was impossible not to hear it.

Green clashed with black and exploded outwards in a ring, the sound of the impact hitting her eardrums and shaking the air around them. Saydor swiped out at Drayvex with dripping green tendrils, moving faster than she could follow.

Drayvex dodged the attack with relative ease, moving with an easy grace she wouldn't have associated with his bigger form. The flames that licked at his skin travelled down his arm and into his open claws, bursting into a dark inferno. "Predictable," she heard him jeer, baiting the demon with reckless abandon.

He launched the ball of ebony flames, and Saydor couldn't block it fast enough. It hit him square in the chest, sending him tumbling backwards.

Saydor was screaming in demonic chorus as he hit the ground in flames, but still, he bounced right back. With a savage snarl, he manifested his own crackling emerald ball and let it fly.

Except, it didn't fly straight.

Ruby's heart stopped. It wasn't heading for Drayvex. It was heading for her: a flaming green projectile the size of her head. And all she could do was brace herself for impact. Her eyes squeezed closed in reflex.

The sound of the attack meeting flesh made her flinch. Pain exploded, concentrated somewhere she couldn't fathom, and then disappeared.

An odd weightless sensation took over as she tried and failed to process this. She could smell burnt flesh. The force of it made her want to gag.

Tentative, Ruby opened her eyes. She felt them widen, sucking in a breath.

Drayvex was standing before her, facing her. The two wings that made up one half of a set covered her entirely, stretching out in a sort of leathery shield. It was immediately obvious why she could smell burning flesh.

Ruby couldn't take her eyes off the circular wound at the level of her chest. She swallowed a slick of saliva. The flames had burnt through his wing, leaving only the thinnest of membranes still intact that let in the light in a window of skin.

Horrified, her gaze slid to Drayvex. When she felt him thrash in her mind, she knew that the creature before her was far beyond her reach. He was staring at her with a remote consideration, his eyes a cold vortex of fury.

His wrath hit her like a mental storm, overwhelming her senses. Drowning her.

"How dare you?" Three words, barely uttered. A soft threat.

Ruby stared at Drayvex, equally mesmerised and horrified as he turned from her and stalked towards Saydor with slow, heavy steps.

Saydor narrowed his eyes and smiled as he approached, a wicked delight evident on his face. "My, Your Unholiness. Did I hit a nerve?" He was no longer on fire, and right before her eyes, his wounds had started to heal.

She squeezed the cool surface of the luxlor, frustration seeping into her thoughts. How did you kill something that could regenerate on the spot?

Drayvex stopped in front of Saydor, and the silence between them was deafening.

Saydor seemed to feel it too. She watched him struggle not to twitch as Drayvex bore into him. "I'll admit, it was a little wasteful. Cursed blood is hard to come by, no?"

Chapter 33

Drayvex inched in closer. "You seem to have forgotten your place, worm," he uttered, slow and precise. "Let me remind you where you belong." He smiled, baring his fangs in a smile that was anything but nice. "It's beneath her feet."

He moved faster than she could follow. She heard Saydor's screams before her eyes caught up with her ears, a primal sound that was outrage and agony.

Ruby's hand flew to her mouth. Drayvex's fangs were deep in the writhing demon's neck, and for a fleeting moment, with double vision, she felt what it was to be the apex predator.

It was happening so fast. He pulled out, tearing flesh. Saydor slumped to the floor, the perfect target as Drayvex followed him down and pounded him into the grass.

She stared at Saydor, watching the dark trails spreading over his yellowed flesh, his expression turning black. Please let this be done, she prayed in desperation. Stay down.

The explosion of green almost blinded her. Saydor was not done.

Ruby's heart hammered in her chest. She spun on the spot, looking hopelessly around her at the expanse of green surrounding them. At least it was remote. No one would get caught in the crossfire but her—

She stopped. They were not alone.

The gold-clad figure moving over the green made her blood turn to ice in her veins. Her ears rang, a clammy numbness spreading over her as she watched it move towards them.

It was Tira, and she was closing in fast.

Chapter 34

Before she had time to think, she was moving fast.

As the world stopped spinning and her back hit something solid, Ruby cried out against the sharp jolt of pain. They were behind the house. She struggled and realised she was being pinned against it by a strong hand.

Tira's golden eyes blazed as she stared down, the hatred on her face that had previously been reserved for Drayvex now directed at her. "I'm disappointed."

Her voice was cold. Ruby stared back, frozen, as her mind reeled and her heart ran away with itself. How could she make her understand? "Tira, I—"

"Don't use my name."

Are you okay?

Ruby flinched at the sound of Drayvex's voice. The golden goddess pinning her to the side of the house was breathing hard. *Define okay*, she thought back.

Ruby, he warned her.

"Where is it?" Tira's sharp demand split her attention. The hand that was heavy on Ruby's chest pushed down.

Her bones screamed. She bit down on her lip, stifling the cry that wanted to tear out of her. "I don't have it!" she hissed through her teeth.

Chapter 34

If you're waiting for me to intervene, you'll be waiting until you die, spat an equally unfriendly voice. *So pull yourself out of whatever miserable fucking hole you've crawled into and fight her.*

The pressure eased. Ruby tried to catch her breath. His words were hard, but the edge they carried made her restless.

Don't tell me you want to live. Show me.

Drayvex couldn't help her. And it was clear they both knew she was screwed.

Ruby pushed off the house, dislodging the hand on her chest. It pushed her back, slamming her against the house.

Tira's hand shot to her throat. "You gave it to that deplorable creature?"

She froze as the hand at her throat twitched. Reluctant, she looked up into the eyes of the wrathful sun goddess who controlled her fate and took a calming breath. "I'm sorry, Tira." She was. Truly sorry.

The fae before her shuddered, the hand at Ruby's throat tightening.

Ruby's hands flew to the hand constricting her throat. A darkness seemed to descend over Tira's features, almost like cloud cover on a sunny day.

"'Sorry' won't bring my people back."

She could hear Drayvex and Saydor going at it somewhere nearby. Every now and again, the ground shook. "You—" she choked. "You still—"

Pain shot through Ruby as she was slammed against the house for a third time.

You're so good at dying it makes me sick. The voice in her head was disgusted at her performance.

Stop it, she blasted back to him, digging her nails into the somewhat soft flesh of the hand crushing her. I'm not you.

"You still what, human?" Tira roared in her face.

You'll never be anything again. Goodbye, Ruby.

Ruby lost her strength. She couldn't breathe.

"You're not the World Destroyer's pet," Tira sneered, pushing herself into Ruby's face. "You're a monster, just like him. You have two faces. I only saw one."

Her hand dropped from her throat to her pocket, curling around the luxlor. *Wait*, she thought to him, panicked. *Don't leave me.* Her heart pounded in her ears. Her vision tunnelled. *Jerk.*

His silence spoke volumes. But the part of him she could still feel said something else entirely. His agitation was a gaping wound, bleeding all over her. And it fuelled her with the will to fight.

Half-blind, Ruby whipped out the luxlor, pouring all of her will into its glassy depths. She submitted to the darkness, and it claimed her as its own.

A wall of darkness hit Tira head-on. As the fae dropped like a weight to the ground, Ruby gasped in precious lungfuls of air.

Finally. Took your bloody time. Now do it again.

Ruby bent over, coughing and rubbing her bruised neck. *Again?*

She could feel the urgency behind Drayvex's snappy impatience. *Yes, Ruby. Finish her.*

Pulse frantic, she looked around her for the fae. An ear-splitting crack reverberated through the air from the distance, making her jump. She hoped it was Drayvex doing the damage. His telepathic mouth was certainly working well.

Tira was turning grey. The golden glow had been sucked from her skin, leaving her looking sallow and ill.

I'm not going to kill her, Ruby thought back to him, sick at the thought. *That wasn't part of the deal.* She watched the fae, horrified as she pushed herself to her feet and shook off the attack like a bar brawl punch.

Fuck your precious morals, Drayvex growled, too loud in her skull. *Are we too good and pure to fight our own battles now? You will die if you do not kill her first.*

Ruby contemplated running, but then dismissed the thought. She couldn't think with the devil on her shoulder shouting in her ear. Didn't she get an angel too? *I'm not a killer*, she argued back, fear-induced adrenaline pumping through her veins. *How did you outrun a mythical warrior? Where would she even go?*

There was a pause before he spoke again. *I see.* His voice was no longer rough, but soft and sly. *You're not a survivor either. I suppose that makes you the baggage.*

Chapter 34

She blinked, staring mindlessly as his words pierced her. Ruby Peyton—always the protected, never the protector.

As the fae started towards her, Ruby raised the luxlor out in front of her like a gun. "Stay back," she begged, trying to hold on to the wisps of darkness that still swirled inside the orb. "It doesn't have to be this way."

Tira stilled. Her eyes were an anaemic yellow and fixed on her as though she couldn't believe her eyes. "What are you?" It was a whisper, but Ruby heard her clearly.

She didn't answer. She was human to her very core. But something inside her was wrong. *Cursed*. Was that what Drayvex had meant when he'd told her she and the luxlor were the same?

The colour was returning to Tira's skin. Those golden eyes narrowed as they took her in, judging her. "You're a human, but you wield demonic power like you're one of them." Her face contorted in a look of pure hatred.

Anger burnt inside her, hot and fresh, as the beautiful savage before her judged her. "And you're a being of light," she bit back, "yet you're just as bloodthirsty and war-hungry as the monsters you hunt." She stepped forward, and the darkness inside the luxlor twisted and writhed in response. "At least Drayvex agreed to spare your people. You were going to lead them to war just because you could."

"My people are *dead*!"

The words Tira roared froze Ruby to her core. It didn't make any sense. She forced herself to speak. "What ... what do you mean?"

Tira sucked in a shuddering breath through her teeth. Her eyes blazed with the power of two small suns. "When you took the stone, you severed my people's connection to Moraea. Their potential lies with the stone, and therefore they cannot *exist* without the stone."

Ruby struggled to process what she was hearing. They were all gone?

"Thousands of fae died the day one human stole the Lapis Temporis," she sneered. "The day you murdered my entire family in one fell swoop. Well, guess what? Two of us can side with a demon for our own selfish gain. And Saydor was only too happy to oblige."

No. She shook her head, wordless. Her stomach squeezed. Tira had sold them out. "That's not—"

"I should have killed you long ago, demon child." Tira's muscles flexed.

Ruby flinched as the words 'murdered' and 'demon child' dug at her. Here she had been, arguing that she wasn't a killer. She'd been trying to save a race from being slaughtered by Drayvex's hand when they were already long gone. Had she really ended all their lives?

She sucked in a breath, trying to steady her racing pulse. No, that wasn't fair. Even if she had severed their connection to the world, those fae were already dead. They were ghosts of Tira's past, and Tira had never succeeded in bringing them back.

Suddenly, Tira moved forward, faster than she could follow. She lunged across the space between them in a blurred movement, fury on her lips.

Ruby's reaction was pure reflex. Whipping the luxlor up, she held it out before her and forced it to respond.

It didn't. As Tira kicked out her own overwhelming blast, Ruby felt it hit her with all the fury of the light.

A scream ripped through her as she dropped to the floor. Her every nerve ending was on fire. She'd never known pain like it. It intensified and blinded her, and she felt the luxlor roll from her limp hand.

A stream of growling curses erupted in her mind, a mix of tongues she didn't understand. *Did that knock some sense into that delirious mind of yours? You know that* Shcręnta *is the reason we can't use the stone to kill Saydor.*

Drayvex's voice was as sharp as a blade. Ruby shrank from his voice. She couldn't think. *Let me think.*

That creature stole your future to fix her past, just to make the same fucking mistakes all over again. Are you really going to take that on your back? Get. Up.

As the blinding light around her dimmed, the fire in her veins dulled to a full-body ache. Ruby fought back a hysterical laugh from the grassy floor. *Look at her,* she projected back. *Even if I wanted to fight for my life, do you really think I stand a chance against* that*? She's practically supernova.*

Tira started to walk towards her, her boots swicking against the grass.

Drayvex took a moment to respond. It occurred to her then just how much he must be splitting his attention. *And you're making her job even easier.*

Chapter 34

Tears swam in Ruby's eyes as she stared at the boots strolling towards her. Had she come this far just to roll over and die? She clenched her fist around the grass beneath her. No. No, she had not.

Okay, she thought at the demon fighting her corner. Okay, you win.

She dived for the luxlor with everything she had, moving fast. Tira reacted with superhuman reflexes, seeing Ruby's intentions just a fraction too late.

The moment her hand closed around the cool glass, Ruby threw it up before her. She poured everything she had into its depths: her fear of dying at Saydor's hands, of being cursed, of dying alone. Her anger and hurt at her best friend's dismissal and her refusal to listen. Every cruel word Drayvex had ever spat at her, the needless slaughter of her people at his hands. The way he'd burnt when she'd kissed him and the way her body had responded to his. The guilt after the pleasure.

The solid beam of darkness hit Tira square in the chest. It knocked her backwards with its sheer force, and as she fought to remain standing, Ruby pushed harder.

The rushing in her ears drowned everything else out, even Tira's cry that had carried on the wind. Her whole body was numb, weighted down by the cold darkness that threaded itself through her like lead and took all the pain away.

The fae before her was turning grey. The darkness was under Tira's skin, in her veins, and it did not agree with her. It leaked through her like poison, spreading in inky lines over her skin.

Ruby watched her, detached, as she poured all of herself into the luxlor, pushing every last drop out. Through sheer force of will, Tira slowly pulled out a dagger.

What is it you humans say about small packages? Something about dynamite.

She could feel something close to pride through her connection to Drayvex, and she had to check twice. It was the only thing she felt in that moment, a small point of warmth inside a full-body numbness.

Ruby clung to it.

Chapter 35

The glare of darkness radiated out from behind the shack. The aura was a blooming miasma in the vision of his mind, the part of him that saw power like a third eye, tracing back to its wilful wielder. Ruby.

She was a wildcard cloaked in shadow and vengeance, magnificent in a multitude of ways that a human had no business being. But she wasn't enough.

The burst of pent up power shooting towards him registered in the back of his mind as Drayvex focused on her. He felt it graze his shoulder as he evaded far too late, burning a trail in his flesh. It was one of numerous hits he should never have taken.

An unhealthy, wet chuckle floated across the charred, pitted space. "Don't worry. Her blood will still be effective for a short window after the faerie crushes her."

Drayvex dragged his attention back to the oozing lump that stood before him, baring his fangs as a hot flash of loathing consumed him. Saydor's wheezing voice was gasoline to his inferno of a temperament.

"I intend to utilise every drop."

Moving in a burst of speed, he Drayvex surged towards the bloodied figure, slicing at his stomach with blade-like claws.

Chapter 35

Saydor brought up a barrier, taking a partial hit as his slowing reflexes failed to fully block the attack.

Drayvex sliced at the defences again and again, shooting past in a spate of attacks. Poisoned and torn to shreds, beaten to Hell and back, the demon wore a secret smile that Drayvex would have loved to take extra time peeling off his face.

Saydor struggled to maintain a barrier. The king of the rejects was on the edge of death. Drayvex's venom was slow and deadly; if he didn't bleed it out soon, the damage would be irreversible. And yet, Saydor had never been more dangerous.

I can't. Ruby whispered through his mind, dealing her own invisible blow.

Drayvex stopped in a sudden still, his claws splayed and splattering onto the ruined grass. He put out subtle feelers and sensed Ruby's dark power fading. He didn't need to see her to know that she'd hit the wall.

He threw up a barrier as Saydor came back swinging, engulfing him in a wall of green flames. She was a natural. She'd taken to power faster than he'd thought possible for a human. But it had never been a fair fight. Not by a long shot.

Drayvex reached out to Ruby mentally, the cracks in his fractured composure widening. *If you want something doing*, he thought at her, goading her. He left it hanging. Mercy, what was the point?

The fae bitch would suffer for this. He would wring out every ounce of agony from her husk before he tore her apart, make her relive her worst moments until her mind bled and wept. Drayvex would destroy her.

"It's a shame such a rare creature should be slaughtered by your own enemy."

He stilled on the spot as the demon's words pierced and lodged in his mind like a spike. The flames around them simmered and died, leaving them face to face in the clearing. "*What* did you just say to me, low-born worm?" Drayvex heard power spilling into his voice, his fury, and knew that he was close to the edge. Control.

Saydor's sick smile widened. "Your precious human blood bank is fighting for her life. If only you'd finished the job all those years ago, *World Killer*."

His little remaining control shattered.

The shockwave of pure destructive power that exploded from him hit the demon he wrestled and kept going, spreading out from the epicentre that was himself. He heard Saydor scream. He heard the glamour house shatter into thousands of tiny pieces, and then realized, with a hard helping of reality, that he was going to kill Ruby himself.

Well done, jabbed his sarcastic inner voice. I suppose if anything was going to rip her apart, it was always going to be you.

The thought lanced through him. No. Not like this.

Drayvex dug deep as he burnt, precious seconds slipping through his fingers. Ruby's heart exploded from her chest as he relived her clone's death. And as he grasped at as much power as he could muster, he reached out to her, not knowing if he could stop it. *You're the calamity I would suffer every single time,* he pushed. *You know that?*

The darkness behind the house fizzled out. *Calamity,* came her soft voice. *Look in the mirror sometime. Oh wait, you can't.*

He smirked. With an unholy surge of strength, he threw up the mother of all barriers in a circular radius, cutting her off.

Everything that wasn't Saydor or the shack disappeared behind an all-encompassing wall of crackling power as it shot out and hit the confines of the dome-shaped barrier around them. It was an unrelenting wave of red death, and it was as hard and unmalleable as his own stubborn pride. But it bent to his will.

The burst of power lit up the dome in a flash before dissipating, plunging the Earth below back into shades of grey. The silence that followed lasted for three whole, golden seconds.

"Well." Saydor pushed himself to his feet, panting with the effort of fighting the poison that consumed him. His jaundiced flesh was a mess of weeping black clusters. "Temper, temper," he breathed, taunting through his pain. "You really are a fascinating atrocity."

Drayvex flexed on the spot, working through the sudden fatigue that smothered him as he kept his gaze fixed on the demon before him. He laughed out loud, sharp and humourless. "I can't say the same," he drawled.

Chapter 35

"You're just an atrocity. Bland. Tedious." A sharp echo of pain hit him for a moment and then vanished. Her pain.

I'm not strong. I'm sorry.

Another lance of pain thrummed down their connection. Drayvex bared his teeth, frustration digging at him like splinters lodged in his mind, nails in his blood. He couldn't stop this.

It's okay. I have no regrets. I would still fight beside you, even knowing where it ends.

He glared at the demon facing him down, remembering his previous warning to Ruby. That he would never choose her over securing the throne. It was business, after all. Nothing personal.

Saydor spread his arms out to either side of him in a gesture that told Drayvex he was far from done. "I see you for what you really are." His claws oozed green poison on either side. "All that arrogant command of your powerhouse father, watered down by the weakness of your whore of a mother."

Drayvex reached inside for power, the echo of Ruby's pain running cold in tandem with the fresh wave of loathing sparked by the mention of his malignant father. Enough. "Keep talking," he said, his voice containing a dangerous edge. "I'll show you the language of a true Demon Lord."

As Saydor punched out at him with poisonous tendrils, Drayvex made his move. He came undone with not a second to spare, his form unravelling into a pillar of liquid darkness that parted around the tendrils punching at his form.

Rising up as a tide of oblivion, he welcomed the darkness, stilling for a single moment as his every turbulent emotion plunged into blissful nothing. Then, when the echoes of her fear and pain were all that remained, he crashed down over Saydor and swallowed him whole.

Saydor thrashed, his movement limited as he was smothered within the cold, black embrace.

Drayvex felt the sting of poison as it flecked him from within and ignored it, squeezing himself tight. His form constricted and crushed, coils of viscous muscle, as the degenerate traitor struggled in his grip. *What was that?* he pushed roughly, forcing himself into Saydor's mind. *Speak up. I can't hear you.*

The tendrils that remained outside the struggle coiled around him, the toxic droplets seeping into his fluid flesh. He kept crushing, feeling bones crack under the strain. This form had a measure of resilience. It would buy him time.

They won't follow you for much longer, Saydor hissed in his mind. *They crave your death. Fresh blood on the throne.*

Drayvex twisted around the demon's throat, securing his hold. *They?* he mocked, resentment leaking through his mental paralysis like Saydor's poison. *Your vague threats are as pathetic as your game. Those ingrates will crawl on their bellies for the rest of their days if I so wish it. There isn't one single fucking demon with both the balls and the power to bring me down. And you, my deluded has-been, are no exception.*

A flash of burning light tore through him and ceased. Ruby was dying.

Saydor fought back, lashing out against him in true bestial desperation. It was a drop in the ocean he was drowning in. It wasn't enough that he was going to be forced to watch Ruby's lifeforce blink out of existence. No, he was going to be made to *feel* it.

Drayvex squeezed the cretin in his grip, feeling bones break. This was the way it had to be. He knew it; she knew it. But gods, they were so tangled. The pain, the fear, the anguish. He no longer knew where he started or ended.

Do me a favour?

Ruby's voice pierced through his mental defences, destroying what little distance he had managed to maintain. The chaos inside him swirled in a storm that was only picking up momentum. He sent it all surging through him in an all-encompassing pulse of power. Distance.

Saydor spasmed under him, slowing as though stunned.

Drayvex? she pushed.

He hesitated, fighting to twist the head he gripped with a vicious snap as the demon resisted. Name it, he thought.

The tendrils around him squeezed, moist and slick as Saydor ramped up

Chapter 35

the poison in a last-ditch attempt to get free. He welcomed the sting. The mindless distraction of pain. He was about to regain everything for the price of her life. Or was it the other way around?

Don't bring me back with the stone. Pl—

The blast hit Ruby and then echoed to him, the sentence she never finished rebounding in his mind.

Fatigue lapped at him. The sting of Saydor's poison burnt in his veins, going straight to his brain. He had a bad idea.

Are you bleeding? Drayvex pushed towards her, putting some force behind it. He wrestled with Saydor, forcing another pulse of power through himself to the unyielding lump of demon within.

The silence he received was unnerving. He stilled, trying to pinpoint her aura from the distance between them. *Dammit, Red, he blasted down their connection. I'm not finished with you. Wake up.*

Yes, breathed a familiar voice. *I'm bleeding. And so is my brain. You're so loud.*

Drayvex's relief was palpable. She was weak but alive. *Good,* he said. *Grab the bitch. Make sure you bleed on her well.*

No, snarled the voice of his saner self. *Leave her and finish him.*

Are you out of your mind?

He ignored them both. It was needlessly risky. He would need to relinquish his hold on Saydor and switch to a form that bled. But it was far easier than doing nothing as she slipped away.

Moving fast, Drayvex withdrew from Saydor all at once.

Saydor gasped as air rushed back into his crushed lungs, coming to life in a ridiculous show of resilience.

The moment he had solid form again, Drayvex sent him flying. The house exploded into chunks as the demon-shaped cannonball destroyed it yet again.

Carpe fucking diem, he thought, more to himself than to her, dragging a claw down his arm and tearing it open.

What are you—argh!

Drayvex drew on as much power as he could grasp in the second he had, sending it to his blood. Barbeque, he replied with vindictive edge, and then sent it down their link to her.

He felt it connect. Felt her blood light up like rocket fuel as she too lit up, giving the fae a taste of real power. He smirked, basking in what he knew would be that *shcrẹnta's* death throes. She'd thought the little human would be an easy slaughter. She hadn't accounted for him.

Drayvex sensed Saydor right behind him as he came at him from behind. And as the demon punched out and filled him full of nasty holes, the vicious glow of satisfaction he took from the fae's death stayed with him. If you want something doing, he thought with dark humour, do it yourself.

Chapter 36

Ruby stood motionless, locked face to face with a murderous fae in what a moment ago had been a one-sided struggle. Tira's eyes were wide and dead, her face frozen into a horrific expression of anguish. She wasn't moving.

Ruby gripped the fae's arms, her entire body tingling in the aftermath of what felt like dark lightning. The only thing she was sure of was that Drayvex had happened.

The echo of agony that ripped through her out of nowhere stole her voice. Her mind split down the middle, plunging her into an unstable double vision.

Ruby felt Tira slip through her bloody fingers as her spine arched, stiffening in a contorted plea. There were bursts of concentrated pain all over her body.

As fast as it had come, it left her. She collapsed onto her hands and knees on the splattered grass, her body long past the limit of punishment it could take. A slow dread oozed through her. What was that?

The slash on her arm was bleeding profusely. Hands shaking, she tore a piece of material from her top and tried to stem the flow. Every aching part of her was on fire.

Ruby reached out to Drayvex. Ouch, she thought towards him. Was that you? She snatched a glance at the motionless form lying a couple of feet away and then looked away fast as her stomach threatened to spill.

Oh god, they'd killed her. She was a murderer.

The crunches and creaks of the little house carried towards her as it rebuilt itself all over again. Feeling sick and oddly calm, Ruby pushed herself to her feet, keeping pressure on her arm. She closed her eyes and breathed out in a stream, trying to shake the heavy feeling settling in her veins. Drayvex had taken a hit, and now he wasn't responding.

She couldn't hear a lot, couldn't see beyond the house. Her head started to spin. It's fine, she reasoned. He can take care of himself. He would expect her to run, to look after number one. To keep moving in one direction until she found civilization.

Her heart pounded in her ears, unease dragging at her. Drayvex would come for her eventually. He always did.

Without thinking, Ruby started in the direction of the house. Just one glimpse, and she would go.

When she peeked around the side of the building, all of her calm came crashing down around her. It was like something out of a nightmare. Not like the many she'd had where Drayvex was the monster that devoured everything, but the few where she lost him.

Saydor looked as though he shouldn't even be standing. But it was Drayvex that was in trouble. The dripping tentacles Saydor controlled had punched straight through his body in multiple places like some kind of hellish tube system, the toxic gunk that secreted from them making a mess of whatever it touched. Grass, flesh.

Ruby's hands flew to her mouth as she almost lost her stomach. One had wrapped around his throat in a poisonous bind. But most of all, it was the way Saydor was gripping Drayvex's head—as though he was about to tear it right off.

She pulled away, putting her hands on her knees as the world span around her. The timing of it all was too much.

She breathed in slowly, breathing out through her mouth. They were exchanging words, but it was just noise. Her brain had stopped working.

Chapter 36

He looked both demon and human now, his forms fluctuating, warring for control as the poison wreaked havoc.

Ruby had fought alone. She had thought she would die alone. But Drayvex had come for her, broken his own rules. Protected her at the cost of his own upper hand. He'd sounded so sure of himself, so... well, so Drayvex.

The cost was immense.

If you think you're hiding back there, you really have learnt nothing.

Ruby rose up straight at the sound of his voice, no longer feeling the way her body screamed at her when she moved or the slash on her arm. You said you'd never choose me over the throne, she accused, directing her thoughts his way. Why would you do that? Huh? Her chest constricted. Breathe.

When he didn't respond, she crept back towards the edge of the house. She stood with her back against the dilapidated wall, her heart going crazy.

In case you haven't noticed, he eventually voiced, *I do what I want, when I want.* He sounded way too calm for her liking.

Ruby heard the awful sounds of a struggle from behind, the maniacal gurgle of Saydor's gleeful laugh. How can I help? she begged Drayvex. In her heart, she knew what the answer was.

You can't. Now go and live your fucking life, Ruby. And don't you dare look back.

In that moment, the only thing she heard was the ringing in her ears as she thought about what her life could be. The places she would go. To simply live her life, demon-free; the way she had been before she *knew* what she had. That would be a dream.

No, not demon-free, she corrected herself. Drayvex-free. He would never find her ever again.

Dazed, she peeked around the house once again and found him. Drayvex was fighting Saydor with everything he had. He was the dangerous predator you risked your life trying to catch. Maybe he would take Saydor down with him; maybe he wouldn't.

Despite this, it was clear he was weakening fast. Saydor would get at least one of his wishes today.

"Do you have any idea how long I've waited for this moment, brat?"

Drayvex stilled, his black tendrils wrapped around Saydor's throat as that gleeful voice taunted him through the clearing. The laugh that erupted from Drayvex sent chills running through her. It was spiteful and manic and devil-may-care.

It seemed to take Saydor off guard too, by his expression, the demon that held all the power as he poised, ready to tear off Drayvex's head. She could tell from Saydor's expression that this was not the way he'd pictured it going.

"You think they will listen to a spineless hack like you?" Drayvex jeered with a cruel smile, turning the tables even as he hung on the edge of oblivion. "That a pale imitation like you can be a Demon Lord? You're both the joke and the punchline. Do it. You won't last a week in my place."

Ruby swallowed, flinching as he met her gaze. She stared at the creature before her, hypnotised by the dead look of calm in his eyes. It was jarring, as though he couldn't see the enormous blade hanging over his head. There was no anger or betrayal, no fear or desperation. Nothing. And it was in that moment, she realised: Drayvex knew he was done for, and he'd accepted it. He didn't care.

"It's a shame you won't be around to witness my rise to power," Saydor snarled, wincing as the black tendrils around his throat squeezed. "Because it *will* be glorious."

Drayvex shuddered, falling alarmingly limp.

Ruby stared at him, suspended under the waters of her own tangled emotions as the horror show before her played out. A world without Drayvex. He was getting off lightly. Sandra would have him pay for every single human life he'd taken before they killed him. They'd be there a long time.

"Oh, *My Lord*, how I wish to break you," oozed Saydor. "It's almost a shame I have to kill you so quickly."

What kind of monster was replacing Drayvex at the top? Something worse? Ruby could have told herself that was why her heart was in a vice along with him. But she'd have been lying.

Saydor's claws pierced Drayvex's throat. "But I will not make the mistake

Chapter 36

of letting you live."

The truth was, a world without Drayvex scared her for all the wrong reasons. And she would not let him die for her today.

Ruby stepped out from behind the house. Throwing caution to the wind, she shouted out, making a desperate bid for their attention. "Wait!"

Both demons froze as her voice carried across the open space. Their eyes flicked to her, black and vicious and hungry. Oh, she had their attention alright.

Taking a deep breath, she pushed through her pain and started to trudge towards them.

What the Hell do you think you're doing?

Ruby couldn't bring herself to look at Drayvex as his sharp demand cracked through her mind. Instead, she looked up at Saydor. A malformed monstrosity, he was a pulverized mess. And yet, the physical reaction she had as she met this creature's abyssal gaze almost made her abandon Drayvex on the spot.

She stopped a few feet away from the two demons, her eyes fixed on Saydor. What happened next would hinge entirely on his reaction.

Don't ignore me, Drayvex snapped, his voice making her wince. *Whatever screwed up plan you think you have is about to crash and burn. Abort it. Now.*

Ruby resisted looking towards him. She could feel the fear that laced his aggression like a barbed-wire embrace. For a demon that looked on the brink of death, he sounded pretty far from it.

Saydor's eyes had narrowed to suspicious slits. "Oh, my dear," he purred, his pointed teeth on full display. "You really are full of surprises. Have you come to watch the show?"

Finally, she allowed her gaze to slip to Drayvex, and she almost recoiled. He was giving her a murderous look. She quickly looked away. "No," she said, forcing herself to look back up at Saydor. "No, I want to make a deal. Let him go, and …" She dug her nails into her skin. "I'll go with you willingly."

The moment the words were out of her mouth, Ruby felt the darkness in her mind batter her. "I beg your fucking pardon?" Drayvex snarled out loud. His seething outrage bled into her mind, mingling with her terrified determination in a confusing tangle of emotions.

He sounded strong, but Ruby could feel him weakening through their connection. It was an unnerving sensation, a separate state from her physical body but very much a part of her. He was a phantom limb.

Saydor almost lost an eye as Drayvex lashed out, and as the purulent demon doubled down on his death grip hold, Ruby could see the cogs going round in his skewed mind.

Drayvex laughed once. It was a hard sound. " You carry my mark. You belong to *me*."

Ruby forced herself to breathe. "No."

Her body was going numb. Was she still bleeding? Her eyes slicked with moisture. She had Saydor hooked, she knew she did. But it wasn't too late to back out.

Drayvex spat blood at the ground in disgust. "You really expect me to let you make a deal over my head with this parasite?"

She looked towards him and met blood-red eyes that were mingled with pale blue. No, she thought morosely. But you can't stop me.

The hiss that erupted from between his teeth made both her and Saydor flinch. He wasn't done. "Okay. You want to piss your life up the wall once I'm gone, then fine. Knock yourself out. *Literally*, for all I care."

All of a sudden, the anger was gone. The contrast left her stunned. And in that fleeting moment of vulnerability, there was something raw left behind. His pale eyes were almost pleading.

"But please, for the love of fucking Satan, Red. Just walk away."

Ruby felt a single tear spill over. She was inside out. And so was he.

Saydor had been watching them both, his narrowed eyes widening the longer they went back and forth. But Ruby had seen something blooming in the pits of those soulless orbs. It was something nasty and gleeful. And she knew exactly what it was.

Please.

Saydor wanted Drayvex dead. But he also wanted him to suffer. He was suffering now.

Chapter 36

Vμiår nhfrèto, *look what you've reduced me to.*

The swollen band of silence that extended over the entire clearing suffocated her as she watched the sadistic creature before her mull over her words. Or maybe it was Drayvex, she thought, as she drowned in nothing. They were so mentally entwined, she no longer knew.

Just then, a sick smile grew on Saydor's face.

Ruby's stomach dropped.

"I accept."

It happened so fast. One moment everything was suspended on the edge of a knife, the next she was plunged into a nightmare.

Saydor sank his teeth into Drayvex's flesh, stopping him in his tracks.

Ruby dropped to the floor as pain erupted in her neck. She felt the blistering fury of the demon she was connected to. The crushing weight of being disgraced by the enemy as his feral hiss hit her. Her own horror and dual feeling of utter powerlessness.

One single thought throbbed through her mind as she was whisked away by a monster. A memory. An oath. One that she would never let Saydor take her alive. How wrong she had been.

Chapter 37

The steady sound of blood splattering the stone floor echoed in his mind. The hungry vortex of fury yawned wide. For a fleeting moment, it immobilized him.

Drayvex clenched his fist and loosened it, the savage whispers that vied for his attention bouncing around his skull. He had purged himself of Saydor's poison, bleeding out until the floor in the halls of Vekrodus ran black. And then he'd kept going.

He raked his claws down the underside of his arm, tearing the hard flesh and ripping himself open. Blood as black as his soul oozed out, dripping down freely for a fleeting moment before his body closed the wound. Not a drop of poison remained in his system. But the mark on his neck was a burning brand, the mark of his failure. It was all he felt.

The godforsaken halls were a pity party for one. The demons that had lingered when he arrived couldn't get out of his way fast enough. Wrecked as he was, Drayvex would have gone through them all. Now, some time later, even Myna had not yet dared to disturb him.

Drayvex moved across the hall in a sudden burst, sending the black lake at his feet up in a pestilent spray of contamination and filth. As he burst through the far exit of the hall, he felt the tsunami inside him twist.

The memory was still fresh, a barely cooled corpse that had not even

Chapter 37

began to putrefy. He pushed it back, losing his grip for a brief moment as Ruby offered herself up once again, a sacrificial lamb to a monstrosity of a wolf.

When the elastic of his mind snapped back into place, he breathed out in a hard stream and moved down the unlit passageway with fresh purpose. As Saydor had pumped him full of toxic junk, Drayvex had felt nothing. As he'd stared that hag of a creature, Death, in the eyes, poised to lose everything he had ever built on a ludicrous whim, he'd laughed knowing that it was on his terms. She wasn't supposed to save him *back*. And then, the final domino had fallen in a giant 'fuck you'.

Heat rolled off his flesh as he paced through the bowels of his fortress, fluctuating between unquenchable rage and watching the cracks spreading in his mind with a detached mania. The gall of that miserable specimen, the lowly worm that couldn't fight its own battles. To be marked by such a creature was enough to make him want to carve it out of his flesh again and again until the magic died and it would surely stop growing back.

But the inescapable truth was that this was karma at its finest. He had sworn to protect Ruby and then failed. And that failure could not be undone with a blade.

His claws twitched at his sides, weapons ready and yearning for bloody retribution. If Saydor wanted a war, he would get one. Drayvex would be the war that would never end, the ravaging plague that killed everything it touched. He would take her back at any cost.

The sharp shock of pain hit him out of nowhere. He stiffened as it filled his mind. It echoed through him in a full-body jolt, his body trying to convince him he was under attack.

As fast as it had landed, it was gone. Drayvex stood motionless in the passage, the realisation of what was happening briefly crushing him before everything fell away. Everything but one frenetic, single-minded purpose.

Nothing ended until *he* willed it so. He flinched as he was hit by another crippling wave. Not even her.

The network of passageways twisted around him at breakneck speed as he moved for the magus nox. Ruby was dying. He could feel her weakening presence from across the worlds, the magic that bound her to him going into spasm, in its death throes. He felt everything she felt in real-time.

The door where Drayvex screeched to a halt had a demon in front of it. Its face barely registered the force of nature that was barrelling towards it as its head hit the floor. And as her fear and agony poisoned his mind, he decided then and there that nothing could be worth this. That he would rather be cold and dead than even remotely human.

It didn't take him long to reach the south wing. He turned into the final passage and slowed, his mind moving faster than his newly purged body. There wasn't much that he could do for Ruby from here, but he was far from defenceless. He would give her everything he had.

The small demon lingering in the passageway stared wide-eyed as Drayvex approached. He was an insect at best. One of many bottom feeders that nourished the elite of the fortress.

Drayvex resisted the urge to squash him flat as he slipped past, unwanted memories spilling forth unbidden. This one had protected Ruby and fed her, had earned her trust.

He felt the demon following behind. "M-my Lord?"

Drayvex cleared the length of passage in sweeping strides, moving towards the guarded door of the room that held an arsenal of power just for him. He stopped in front of the large guard and glared at it, hostility rolling off him in waves. "Remove yourself from my presence," he uttered as violence screamed in his blood, "or I will remove your spine from your body and beat you with it."

The guard at the door did not need to be told twice.

Drayvex could barely feel the girl with the piece of his soul as he entered the grand room. His window was fast closing. "I'm losing her," he said to the demon at his heels. The globe in the room flickered red, beckoning him.

"Oh, Your Greatness. N-no."

Ruby's face was seared into the vision of his mind; the chaos in her eyes in sync with his own as she'd thrown away her life for his. The horror as Saydor had got in one final twist of the knife. He approached the globe and stroked it with a finger, waking the power that swirled within its depths.

Chapter 37

"Ruby is Krick's friend."

The power of his ancestors swirled inside, sluggish strands twisting and tangling together. She was always doing the opposite of what she was told. Why the Hell would she sacrifice everything for a demon? For him, who was the worst to her of them all?

Drayvex breathed out, digging deep for control he no longer possessed. It no longer mattered. Bracing himself, he drew on as much of his power as he could grasp, gathering and holding it in a tight ball. He glanced down at the demon named Krick and felt a wild smile spreading. He was losing purchase. "I'm going to level the playing field."

Krick's small face wrinkled, confusion flitting across it before comprehension dawned. "Oh," he squeaked in panic. "Good gravy, My Lord, is that—?"

The explosion of power colliding with power sent a wall of pure darkness ripping out from the globe. A crack shot through the air, resounding, as the globe split wide open. And as raw power oozed to the surface, bleeding down the sides of the gash in trails of colour, Drayvex brought his fist down on top. Saydor was a cancer, eating through his and Ruby's lives. And they both needed a cure.

The moment he connected, the detonation in his blood almost knocked him off his feet. It was lightning and ungodly fire, and it lit him up like the molten core of Vekrodus.

Demon Lord after Demon Lord, reigns of terror going back thousands of years. Every hateful, lawless bastard that had come before him had pumped power into one trove. Drayvex drank it in, bloating with power as it seeped into his every cell, pouring forth in an unrelenting flood.

"Stop!" The cowering speck before him had fallen to its knees. "P-please, you can't."

The room flashed crimson, bathing everything around it the hue of ancient blood and wrath. The euphoria was brief. His demon form shuddered. Stabs of pain like a thousand daggers pierced every part of him as he pushed beyond his limits.

"My Lord, no one demon can handle this much power. You—"

The demon blinked out of existence as Drayvex flexed, his will becoming reality as fast as he thought it. Before he'd even finished the thought. Be gone.

Ruby's presence was a speck in the corner of his mind. This would either kill them both or set them both free.

Drayvex convulsed as something inside him shattered, the impact devastating. His mind broke off, separating from his physical self.

With his last remaining sense of self, he sent the power screaming down their connection towards her. Maybe you still have that luck of the devil, he thought, no longer able to feel her. No longer knowing if she was alive or dead. And as whatever remained of the power began to stitch him back together into something else entirely, something that resembled a dark, malevolent god, Drayvex smiled.

Nothing would ever get close to him again.

* * *

The steady sound of her blood trickling into bottles had become almost monotonous. She was on the verge of becoming desensitised to it, her mind growing as numb as her body. How many had that bastard taken from her now? She'd lost count.

Ruby squeezed her eyes closed as a wave of dizziness threatened her. Her breaths came in shallow pants as she fought to stay awake. Blood loss isn't the worst of ways to die, she thought. Maybe she would just fall asleep and never wake up.

Please, don't wake up.

The room she was being held in was dark and dingy. There were no windows, just a strange glow that she couldn't place, turning the entire room into shadows and silhouettes.

At first, the lack of light had made it all worse. Her imagination ran wild, panic escalating into a full blown attack that had made her wonder if she was dying. And as Saydor had flung her into a dark corner and opened his own veins up all over the hard stone floor, she had gasped for precious air,

Chapter 37

too scared to even twitch.

But the lack of light was not a curse. It was a blessing.

Ruby opened her eyes and let her gaze swivel around the room. Her battered body had been frozen into the same crouched position for too long, but she barely felt her legs as she hugged them against her chest. The tube in her arm, though. *That* she felt.

She watched the dark outline of Saydor prowl around the room as he busied himself with god only knew what, sluggish pulses of panic oozing through her. The stench of his blood had been like nothing she'd ever smelt. It had hit the back of her throat and twisted her stomach. If she'd eaten anything previous, she'd have lost it long before the blood reached her on the floor and started to soak into her clothes.

From across the room, Ruby saw his hulking outline turn towards her, and her fear came crashing back.

Saydor was crossing towards her. She couldn't see him fully, but he was no longer dragging himself like a wounded animal. In fact, he didn't look like he was in any pain at all.

Instinctively, she pressed herself against the wall as he approached, scrabbling in the gungy muck for purchase. Whatever this monster was made of, she hoped Drayvex was made of the same obnoxious stuff. Drayvex …

"He put on a good show, I'll give him that."

Saydor's voice slid through the darkness, making her want to curl in on herself. She resisted the urge to fold. He had taken so much from her already. She would not give him her pride.

All of a sudden, an invisible hand grabbed her by the throat. Ruby choked, her head hitting the wall behind her as something squeezed with a firm grip. Her head scrambled.

The figure before her was smiling. She could just make it out in the gloom, that shark-like grin. "Would you like to hear a story?"

Her stomach twisted. Now what?

He didn't wait for her response. "Once upon a time, when our Infernal Lord was just a suckling parasite squirming at my feet, there was a true

Demon King and his Queen. He was everything a Demon Lord could ever hope to be: formidable. *Diabolical.*"

Ruby stared at the creature, struggling to remain focused as he pinned her by her throat. The urge to fight back rose to the surface. She didn't like this one bit.

"But his Queen was rotten to the core. She had a nasty little affair with a human, and fell in love with her prey. It was not only the ultimate betrayal, but forbidden by demon law. "

Her jaw dropped, the will to fight leaving her all at once. Was ... was he talking about Drayvex's parents?

She could practically feel the smug radiating off the demon. "Oh yes," Saydor purred, dragging the latest bottle of her blood away from the tube with his mind. Her blood trickled to the floor through the abandoned tube, mingling with the gruesome black pool she sat in.

"I-I don't understand," she gasped. She had no regrets. Drayvex was alive because of her. She had no regrets. She had no—

The tube was ripped unceremoniously from her arm. Ruby screamed.

Saydor sighed, dramatising. "Oh, my dear. You're many, many things, but stupid is not one of them."

Suddenly, Ruby was dragged to her feet. She cried out as her neck jarred, and for a moment, she thought she was going to black out. She had no such luck.

The demon was in her face. She could smell the tang of his breath. The stench made her want to gag. "She was executed, of course," Saydor continued, acting as though he hadn't stopped. "Publicly."

Ruby could count his teeth, even in the gloom. She held her breath, her mind spinning. Drayvex had never spoken about his mother. The few times he'd opened up to her, it had been about his father. His exact words had been 'psychotic bastard'.

"The reason for her death became a family secret, buried by His Unholiness." He breathed in her face as he spoke, testing her gag reflex. "Mostly." His mouth pulled into a sick grin. "I was as good as family to him."

As Saydor let her go, Ruby gasped and slumped. *What* was forbidden

Chapter 37

by demon law? She rubbed her hand over her throat, a slow realisation creeping over her. Fraternizing with a human?

The demon had scooped up the bottle of her blood and disappeared into the gloom. But he was back before she had time to truly spiral. "He had me fooled," he said, the teasing tone gone from his voice. "But I could see it in his eyes the moment you stepped forward. So hostile, so utterly opposed, it reminded me of *her*."

She stared at the shadowed figure before her, a different kind of horror overtaking her previous fear. He never told her. All this time, Drayvex had been going against his own laws, and he'd never said a word.

"I think our World Killer is more like his mother than he'd had us believe. Isn't that right, Ruby?"

Ruby watched, her heart breaking as Saydor slipped across the room towards a stack of shelves. "No," she whispered. "You're wrong." It sounded weak, even to her. She'd fallen so deeply for the devil. She'd tried so hard to fight it—and he hadn't tried at all.

She tried again to deny it. "Drayvex took everything from me, every*one*. He abused me for his own ends." Ruby felt a tear trickle down her face. "We hate each other."

The laugh that floated towards her in the gloom went right through her. "Bravo," he purred. "I almost believe you."

Suddenly, she was ripped from the wall in a blur of movement. Ruby cried out in pain as she was slammed into a high-backed chair.

"Here's how it's going to go." Saydor snarled the words into her face like a demon possessed, slamming an object down onto the surface next to her and destroying her nerves. "I'm going to kill that arrogant fuck if it's the last thing I do. But first, I'm going to destroy him. And you're going to help me bring him crashing down."

Ruby shook her head, wordless terror seizing her as her heart threatened to explode. She would never.

The object beside her clanged as Saydor smacked it. As she watched the glistening black liquid slosh around inside, she realised what she was looking at. It was a tank.

Without another word, he pounced.

Ruby fought with everything she had left as Saydor pinned her to the back of the chair, but she may as well have not bothered. Biting down on her tongue, she screwed her eyes shut and willed the tears not to spill as a sharp pain jabbed into her arm—the same arm.

Breathing hard, she sat frozen against the chair as she felt him pull away, her eyes still closed. She didn't want to open them. She knew what she would find.

"A Demon Lord caught adopting a human as his own. The scandal would be enough in itself to topple any hellion from the throne. But to be caught attempting to turn his human lover …" The sly voice trailed off, finishing with a soft laugh that sounded a lot like a growl.

Ruby's eyes flew open. Saydor didn't need to finish. Her gaze flicked down to her arm, and her heart stopped when her fears were confirmed. She was hooked up to the tank.

"Well, that, my dear, would utterly destroy him if it got out."

She dived for the tube, grabbing for it in desperation.

Saydor was faster. Pinning her with easy strength, the demon tutted in a patronising way. "When I offered you the easy way, you should have taken it. I'm afraid you won't survive this."

Ruby could barely breathe. She didn't know it was possible to be this terrified of one person. One monster. "What … what are you—?" Her eyes flicked to the tank. "What is th-that?"

His answering smile was utterly wicked. "I'll bet he's *furious*. Oh, how I wish I could watch His Lordship writhe in his own skin. Mad for revenge."

The smile slipped as his eyes glazed, replaced by something far colder. "To be bitten by another demon is the worst kind of shame." He reached out and trailed a claw over the surface of the tank, sounding almost reminiscent. "And that high-born prick took great pleasure in each and every one."

She watched his fingers dance over the tank's surface, towards the small lever at the top. *Please, no. Please don't be what I think it is.*

"The marks faded, but I still feel each and every one. Burning with shame. But as I bled myself of his poison, time after time, I preserved each drop.

Chapter 37

Collecting them over the years for a rainy day." He stopped, fingers stilling as they wrapped around the lever. The metal creaked as Saydor twisted with glee. "You see, I want him to know that, in the end, it was he that killed you. *His* temper. *His* careless cruelty."

As the venom travelled down the tube towards her, her eyes widened.

"I'm afraid this is going to hurt."

Ruby shot her free hand out towards him. "Wait—"

The moment the venom reached her, she knew it. She felt herself convulse against the chair as pain travelled down her arm and quickly consumed her. Ruby screamed, destroying her throat. Her vision flickered, heart fit to burst.

It was pain like no other. Even Tira's blasts of pure light paled in comparison to the Hellfire flowing through her veins.

Saydor's maniacal laugh was disjointed, floating to her from everywhere at once. Make it stop, she begged, tears flowing freely down her face. Let me die.

She raked her nails across her skin. Ruby couldn't move, couldn't think. She couldn't breathe. And it hit her then with relief that she *was* dying. There was a god, after all.

"I'll send Drayvex your regards," came Saydor's cold voice. "And your corpse."

Maybe you still have that luck of the devil.

Ruby's disjointed mind stirred at the sound of Drayvex's voice. She ... couldn't form ... words. The pain dulled.

I've left you all alone, Mum. I'm sorry.

Her mind exploded back to life as something hit her like lightning. It descended straight from the heavens, or more likely, rose straight from the pits of Hell itself.

Ruby could see nothing, hear nothing. The sheer, crackling force burnt her from the inside out, pain and euphoria scorching her in tandem. It was fusing her back together with a power that terrified her more than Saydor ever had.

And then, nothing.

Ruby sat motionless, basking in blissful, full-body numbness. Emptiness. And then, giving herself entirely to instinct, she opened her eyes—and seethed.

The creature before her stared with widening eyes, the stain that was Saydor.

Pain burst in her mouth from every one of her teeth. She felt them prick her tongue and struggled to make sense of it.

The stain named Saydor twitched, and she forgot all about it. Instinct gave way to fury.

Her hand shot out for his throat, her marbled flesh both black and gleaming, but also pure white.

Ruby wasn't in Hell anymore. She *was* Hell.

EPILOGUE

Sandra's pulse danced in her throat as she stood outside the large, ornate slab of a door. It was a ridiculous thing, like being a schoolgirl all over again, standing outside the headmaster's office. Waiting to hear her fate.

Her mouth pulled down, the skin on one side of her face tight. Except, the Summum Venandi was no frickin' headmaster. And the *vânătorí* was no school.

A heavy clunk of metal came from within. Sandra squared her shoulders as the door creaked inward, readying herself for a battle. She would walk away with something today, no matter what.

"Come."

The deep voice of authority sent a little trill of ingrained fear shooting through her. She looked down at her worn combat boots, thinking of her best friend. Her breaths became heavy.

Sandra stepped into the dimly lit space, noting the attendant who had opened the door for her with a glance. Thinking of Ruby used to make her happy. These days, it just made her angry and sick to her stomach.

She slipped through the room, trudging towards the large figure looming behind the desk. This archaic space had always given her the creeps. It was more like a tomb than an academic office. Even the air had an oppressive quality to it that made it harder to breathe.

The door scraped closed behind her, taking with it the one chink of proper light in the room. It was time to face the music. Steeling herself, she glared straight ahead. Her hand rested on the gun at her hip, the habit forming the day she had been cleared to carry a weapon. The cold metal was a comfort.

Sandra came to a stop at the foot of the desk, standing to attention in the gloom. The large chair was facing away from her, its high back a solid wall between her and the permission she needed. Ruby had never needed her more. Sandra would be strong for the both of them now.

After a long stretch of silence, Sandra's agitation got the better of her. Every wall was climbable. "Sir."

The chair creaked, leather squeaking. "Sandra. What did we say about the necessity of patience?"

Sandra cringed in the gloom. Tightening her composure, she trailed a finger over the lump at her hip. "I'm sorry, sir. I wouldn't be here if it wasn't so urgent. But things have escalated."

A lone candle flickered on the desk. Shadows danced on the wall, making monsters of the mundane. There was only one monster she was interested in.

Guilt and hatred twisted in her heart as his face burnt in her mind. That bastard. She sucked in a shaking breath, feeling her training slip away as her feelings ate at her. "Dad ... she's my best friend." Sandra heard her voice break and knew she'd already failed. Her father didn't reward weakness.

The chair creaked. She straightened in alarm as he spun to face her in one sweeping motion, his large outline growing as he rose to fill the surrounding space. "Ruby?"

Sandra fixed on the figure before her in the gloom, her fists squeezing. "Yes. Please help me free her."

For a long moment, he said nothing, did nothing. She fought not to twitch, her gaze boring into his motionless shape—the man she'd come to both love and fear as a daughter of the hunt.

From the corner of her eye, she saw his arm reach out towards the desk. "Take what you need," his outline granted in a low rumble.

EPILOGUE

Sandra's heart hammered in her chest as she watched her commander reach out towards the flickering candle. He'd actually said yes.

"The full force of the *vânători* is at your disposal, my daughter." The flame spluttered and died as he pinched it between two fingers. The shadows became one with the darkness.

I'm coming, Ruby.

About the Author

Rachel Hobbs lives in South West Wales, where she hibernates with with her bearded dragon and her husband. By day she is a dental nurse at a small local practice. By night, she writes.

Her debut novel SHADOW-STAINED is the first in a dark fantasy series for adults, inspired by her dark and peculiar experiences with narcolepsy and parasomnia. She's since subjugated her demons, and writes under the tenuous guise that they work for *her*.

Fuelled by an unhealthy amount of coffee, she writes about hard-boiled monsters with soft centres and things that go bump in the night. The Stones of Power series continues with SOUL-STRUNG, the second in this monstrous series of four.

You can connect with me on:
- http://www.authorrachelhobbs.co.uk
- http://www.twitter.com/rhobbsauthor
- http://www.facebook.com/authorrachelhobbs
- http://www.instagram.com/authorrachelhobbs
- https://www.etsy.com/uk/shop/RHobbsAuthor

Also by Rachel Hobbs

Shadow-Stained (Stones of Power #1)
For her, it's her late grandma's legacy. For him, the mother of all black arts spoils, granting one demon the power of a God. *Immortality.*

When occult-magnet Ruby falls victim to Demon Lord Drayvex's viperous allure, she loses a sentient dark relic to his light fingers and appetite for power. Like calls to like. But when Drayvex himself loses the relic to a traitor to the throne, Ruby coerces him – the tyrant king with a soft spot for humanity – into helping her save her pokey old world village from becoming a ground zero of mass demonic carnage.

Both invested in reclaiming the relic, the one thing Ruby and Drayvex agree on is that it's in the wrong hands. Co-existing in a precarious arrangement between predator and prey, to save the planet they both love for different reasons, they must become a formidable double-team in the face of an apocalyptic takeover. Now, the fate of both human and demon alike rests with a killer that walks between worlds, and a woman with a curse in her bloodline.

Bite-Sized Fiction for Busy People - Ten Flash Fiction Stories

Ten sumptuous slices of short fiction. Bite-Sized Fiction For Busy People is perfect for those who love the escape a good story provides, but are too busy to sit down and read a full-length book. With each story being somewhere between one hundred and four hundred words, time is no longer a valid excuse not to read.

Serving as an introduction to the wonderful world of flash fiction, this short ebook will open your mind to the endless opportunities they provide. Running out of steam? Take a moment to immerse yourself in a story. Twiddling your thumbs on the bus? Indulge your imagination with a bite-sized treat.

CPSIA information can be obtained
at www.ICGtesting.com
Printed in the USA
LVHW021748121021
700249LV00004B/145